M000189204

HIS
OTHER
WOMAN

BOOKS BY LOUISE VOSS

The Last Stage
The Old You
The Venus Trap
Games People Play
Lifesaver
Are You My Mother?
To Be Someone

With Mark Edwards
Forward Slash
Killing Cupid

DETECTIVE LENNON THRILLER SERIES
From the Cradle
The Blissfully Dead
One Shot

KATE MADDOX SERIES
Catch Your Death
All Fall Down

HIS
OTHER
WOMAN

Louise Voss

bookouture

Published by Bookouture in 2021

An imprint of Storyfire Ltd.
Carmelite House
50 Victoria Embankment
London EC4Y 0DZ

www.bookouture.com

ISBN: 978-1-80019-619-3
eBook ISBN: 978-1-80019-618-6

CHAPTER ONE

Alanda

April

Despite the early flight, the kids had all stayed over so they could come and see their dad off at Gatwick. They were bleary-eyed and hungover in the back of the people carrier, after way too much wine at the leaving dinner Alanda had cooked the night before. Now they clustered around him, yawning, as Liam transferred a few travel toiletries into a clear plastic bag ready for the security inspections.

Alanda was rooting through the smaller of Liam's two backpacks, the light foldable one he was using as hand luggage: 'Oh Liam! You can't take that through.' She pulled out a bottle of Diet Coke and handed it to Becky.

'Brilliant. Thanks!' she said, guffawing, as she screwed off the cap. It fizzed loudly and spewed brown liquid for a moment before she got her mouth around the top.

'Oops,' said Liam. 'Forgot you have to buy your drinks on the other side. That's how long it's been since I last flew. Amateur mistake.'

'Anything else in there you can't take through? Happy to relieve you of any expensive aftershave,' Jake asked hopefully, as Alanda continued to search.

'Nice try, son. Even if I had brought expensive aftershave, you wouldn't get to keep it. I'm only going for three weeks, not three years.'

'Did you see that YouTube video of the man farting in the x-ray machine? You know, the one you have to stand like this in?'

Becky assumed a stance, legs apart and arms held up at right angles. 'It's so funny, it comes out in this little white cloud on the video.'

Liam laughed. Since childhood, Becky had always found anything fart-related utterly hilarious, particularly on the occasions when it concerned her twin brother. Alanda and Liam privately found it endearingly amusing.

'I'll make sure I don't embarrass myself,' he said, hugging her, as Heather rolled her eyes.

'Gosh, I'm going to miss you all,' he added, gazing at his family. Heather started twisting her engagement ring round her finger and looking anxious.

'Dad,' she began, but Liam already knew what she was going to say.

'Of course I'll be back in time! Wild horses wouldn't keep me away from walking you up the aisle.'

Still holding Becky with one arm, Liam put his other one around his youngest daughter's plump shoulder. She didn't look mollified though.

To be honest, Alanda thought, she didn't blame Heather for being worried. She would never admit it to the kids but she had butterflies flapping blindly in her belly at the thought of Liam being away for this long. It wasn't panic – she was a grown, independent woman. Worrying about surviving for a few weeks without her other half; how pathetic would that be? But she did feel concerned.

Whilst they'd never been apart for anything like as long as this, it wasn't herself she was concerned for; it was Liam. The fact that they had both acknowledged the need for him to get away and have some time on his own was a worrying indication of his current state of mind.

She knew she would miss him horribly, but it was more than just that. The 'what-ifs' were already waking her up at night, her eyes flying open in a midnight panic. When she could make out Liam's hump of a silhouette next to her, the pounding of her heart would settle a little and she would stretch out a foot to connect her toe with his shin, or a hand to lightly touch his back. The thought of him not being there *at all*, being thousands of miles away, made her want to hyperventilate with anxiety for his safety. Their catchphrase, even when one of them popped out to Tesco Metro for a pint of milk, was 'Don't get lost or killed!'

As if reading Alanda's mind, Heather chimed in with a what-if of her own: 'Yeah, but, Dad, what if you decided to extend your trip and come back, like, the week before the wedding, and then there was an airline strike or something, and you couldn't get back?'

Heather had always been the worrier of the three of them. Jake and Becky had each other to confide in, and poor Heather had seemed to spend her life anxiously fretting over problems that the twins blithely discarded. Liam and Alanda hoped that getting married to stable, calm Kevin would give her the security she had somehow never felt within the family.

Becky was a little put out that her younger sister would be the first of the three of them up the aisle, but Heather had always been far more mature than the flighty Becky.

'The wedding's almost three months away. Anyway, I promise I won't extend my trip.'

'What if you fall off the path on the Camino and break your back and nobody finds you?'

'Heather, I'm not going mountain climbing! It's mostly pretty flat, and there will be tons of other people walking too. And the Madrid route is the easiest. There's no way I wouldn't be found if anything did happen. I'll have my phone.'

'Dad, make sure you WhatsApp us when you land?' Jake's face had turned serious.

'Of course! Guys, will you please stop fussing? I'll be fine.'

Alanda sidled over to him and wrapped her arms around his waist, exaggeratedly pushing away their two daughters. 'Have an amazing adventure, my angel,' she said into his ear. 'I'll miss you too.'

'Come with me,' he said, only half-jokingly. 'I've changed my mind, I don't need to "find myself", not when I've got you lot.'

'Oh Dad, don't be daft, everyone knows you can only have a midlife crisis on your own.' Jake grinned, but Alanda spotted the sneaky punch on the bicep that Becky gave her twin. Still too raw for them to joke about, then.

'Me, walk three hundred kilometres? You must be kidding. We're just not used to being without you, that's all.'

Alanda kissed his cheek, and he put his hand up to cup the back of her head. As happened more and more frequently, she felt faintly self-conscious. Her hair used to be so soft and silky but since she hit fifty it was so much coarser; decades of hair dye taking their toll. Not that Liam would probably notice the change – thankfully he wasn't the most observant of men – but she missed her bright gold natural colour. These days it was streaked with grey, her hands freckled with liver spots like her grandmother's. Age had sneaked up on them both.

'Nor I you. But hopefully it'll do the trick and I'll come back a new man. Right, Madrid is calling. I love you all. Stay safe. Keep in touch and I will too.' He hugged the three kids one by one. 'Jake, let me know what's happening with the job hunt. Bex, good luck with the internet dating, don't do anything I wouldn't do. Heather, keep me posted with wedding arrangements, won't you?'

Then he kissed Alanda, long and hard, invoking puking noises from Becky and 'get a room' from Jake. Heather looked like she was trying not to cry, and when he broke off from the kiss, he spotted tears in Alanda's eyes.

'For God's sake, everyone, it's only a few weeks!' But Alanda could see how touched he was, at how much they all loved him.

'Don't get lost or killed!' she called after his retreating back. He turned, and her last image of him was his wide, loving smile before he vanished, waving, through the door to Departures.

CHAPTER TWO

Liam

Once through the security scanners, Liam gathered his possessions from their various trays and followed the crowd into Duty Free, wandering aimlessly through racks of astronomically expensive perfumes with no intention of buying anything. He caught a glimpse of his reflection in a mirror behind a display of aftershave and thought, *blimey, is this baggy-eyed man really me?*

He was neither particularly vain nor insecure about his appearance – never had to be, he thought, eyeing the six-packed, chisel-jawed model on a box of aftershave. He had always had Alanda complimenting him on his body, his looks, long after compliments were objectively warranted. It had been many years since anything like a six-pack rippled the front of his torso, and yet somehow Alanda still seemed to fancy him. Maybe she just had the memory of him when they first met permanently imprinted on her psyche, the way he had of her.

A sense remained of the imprint of her lips on his, the texture of her soft hair on his fingers, her scent. She still looked incredible, he thought with pride, and a residual sense of astonishment that she had stuck with him all these years. Other women in their early fifties had thickening waists and thinning hair, jowly smiles and yellowing teeth – not Alanda. She still turned heads, whether in a bikini on the beach or matching him pint for pint in the pub.

How fortunate he was, he thought. The luckiest, to have such a supportive wife. It was all very well, being lovey-dovey when life was easy, but she had been by his side through thick and thin, and things had been very thin indeed in the past few months. He saw his mother's confused face as he left her in the residential home; heard her reedy voice plaintively calling, 'Wait, Richard, I don't like it here, I want to go home!'

Had it been mean of him not to correct her, to let her think that it was his twin brother who had been the one to wrench her from her home and move her to that strange place?

It hadn't been mean. Richard had only been dead two weeks at that point, and the more he could spare their mother the sort of grief he was feeling himself, the better. He shuddered, briefly imagined trying to explain to her that he had found Richard's body hanging from a beam in his attic apartment, his lifeless eyes seeming to stare accusingly at him. No, it had been the one time when her dementia was a blessing rather than a curse.

Perhaps it was the immediate aftermath of being separated from his family, or the maudlin turn of his thoughts, but suddenly Liam no longer felt so lucky. As he emerged into the main Departures area, he made his way to the nearest free moulded-plastic seat and collapsed onto it. He missed Richard with a pain visceral in its intensity, even though they hadn't seen eye to eye for some years – a stupid falling out when Richard had accused Liam of dragging him over from America with their mother a decade ago, after their dad died, and then not helping him integrate, whilst allegedly 'bending over backwards to take care of Mom'. This had rankled with Liam and Alanda. They hadn't 'dragged' him; they'd encouraged him, after his life in the States had been so derailed by alcohol and drugs. At the time it had seemed like such a neat solution – to bring him and Violet over while Vi was still fit enough to live independently. She had been the one they'd worried about most, but in the event, it was Rich who was the problem.

Vi had adapted immediately, loving the proximity to her teenage grandkids, embracing the Women's Institute and the University of the Third Age, theatre-going groups and community choirs, even the odd date here and there... She adored her tiny house in the over-sixties sheltered accommodation complex, a honey-stone converted mews – but Rich had been furious that Liam hadn't found her somewhere where he could have moved in too.

Liam and Alanda felt they'd done all they could for him, finding and part-funding a flat for him in Basingstoke – near, but not too near, at his request – helping him get a job in a local supermarket, encouraging him to go to local AA or NA meetings, but Rich had obviously thought the only acceptable solution was for him to move in with them, and at the time it had been impossible. All the kids still lived at home then and they only had four bedrooms.

Relations thawed considerably over the years, and Rich seemed to have settled a bit more. He spent every Christmas with them all, and he and Liam went out for the occasional pint (when Rich wasn't in AA – which he dipped in and out of, as though it was a private members' club that he occasionally graced with his presence). Yet the twins never regained the easy closeness they'd had as children and teenagers, up to the point when Liam had first departed for England on his travels. But whereas Liam had built a life, a lovely life, Rich seemed consumed with bitterness and a sense of failure that he didn't have what Liam did. Rich had never married or had a successful relationship – except with coke and booze – and eventually decided that there was no point to life anymore.

His suicide last year left Liam racked with guilt, on top of the terrible shock of loss. He should never have encouraged those pints when he knew Rich had a problem, or let pass the obvious lies and fantasies about how well his twin's life was going. Since Rich's death, Liam had not been able to shake a conviction that he could have saved him, no matter how many times Alanda had tried to persuade him otherwise.

'Oh Rich,' he muttered. 'Wish we were going walking together, mate.'

The woman in the seat next to him looked up from her magazine and hastily moved to another area, the rumble of her suitcase's wheels sounding as alarmed as she looked.

Liam sighed. He felt thoroughly depressed that his chief emotions still seemed to be grief and exhaustion, not the energising excitement he thought he'd feel at the prospect of all the walking ahead of him.

How could he be tired already? He'd not even started yet! He wondered if it was the thought of the same trudge every day, meeting strangers – not something he relished at the best of times, now that he thought about it – miles and miles of one foot in front of the other, topped off by sleeping in a different bed every night, sometimes even on a bunk in a huge dormitory with more strangers...

He'd rather be back at work, losing himself in a complex garden design or up a ladder with a hedge-trimmer.

He'd only agreed because Alanda had been so enthusiastic and he wanted to please her, wanted her to think that he was OK, that this would help. And Alanda, always with everyone else's best interests at heart, had a way about her that swept everyone up in her wake before they even realised. How had he not noticed what was happening here? She'd chivvied and encouraged, jollied along and cajoled until even he thought it was a good idea.

'Didn't you say you'd always fancied doing it? Well, now you can!' Alanda had said triumphantly, as if that settled the matter.

Perhaps it was a good idea. He *had* thought it was a good idea, once, when he was younger and fitter; in fact, it was the original reason why he had come to Europe in the first place all those years ago. He'd flown over from Wisconsin straight after graduating high school, to spend a week staying in YMCAs and connecting with his British roots (both his parents were English and had settled in the States when he was a baby), and then the intention had been to make the same journey he was about to undertake now, thirty-four years later, to walk the Camino de Santiago.

But on a visit to Stonehenge and Salisbury cathedral, on the third day of his travels, he'd met Alanda and never left. She had been his waitress in the tea shop he'd stopped in for lunch, in a tiny tight black skirt and short, frilly white apron, a biro stuck in her blonde ponytail, and the biggest grey eyes and longest legs he'd ever seen.

It was love at first sight and all thoughts of the pilgrimage were chucked into the long grass of courtship and raging testosterone, followed swiftly by getting a job as a landscape gardener's apprentice, finding a flat together, marriage, kids, building his business, relocating Vi and Rich after his dad died ten years ago… He'd never thought about it before, but suddenly it seemed to him as though he had been frantically scampering around a gigantic hamster wheel for the last three decades.

So, it *did* make sense to do it now. It was meant to be a pilgrimage; a walk to help him come to terms with the grief and guilt of not being able to help Rich. Fresh air, big skies, home-cooking in little tavernas along the way. A proper chance to clear his head.

Yet somehow the thought of it made his heart sink. He sat back in the hard plastic chair and sighed heavily.

Movement, a flash of white in his peripheral vision, made him turn his head. It was one of those digital advertising screens next to a kiosk selling sunglasses, showing a video of someone skiing down a diamond-bright mountain against a vivid blue sky. The skier swooped fast and accurately, skis cutting through the powder, churning it up behind him in a shower of glittering snow.

Liam watched, transfixed. His heart began to beat faster as adrenaline shot through his veins at the thought of doing that. He hadn't skied since he was at school, but it was like riding a bike, surely? A day on nursery slopes and it would all come back to him. He could almost feel the biting cold air in his lungs and hear the clean slice of the skis' edges in the snow.

But he wasn't going skiing. Instead, he was going to plod along footpaths for the best part of three hundred kilometres and twenty-three days, with little to distract him but his grief. He'd had one big chance to do whatever he wanted, go wherever he fancied, and now he was doing something he felt reluctant about, just because his wife had told him he wanted to, swept along on a tide of second-hand enthusiasm. What kind of a wimp was he?

The skiing video was on a loop, advertising a resort called Les Portes du Soleil, and Liam sat for at least fifteen minutes, watching it over and over again. Les Portes du Soleil – the doors to the sun? The doors of the sun? Either way, it sounded wonderful. He googled it and discovered that it wasn't one resort, but a large mountainous area near Geneva with at least twelve ski resorts, partly in France and partly Switzerland.

Then he got up and headed for Gate 49 where, the departures board informed him, his flight to Madrid was now boarding. As he walked along the travelator, his feet bouncing on the rubber surface, he imagined he was whizzing down a cold, sunny slope instead. Was early April too late in the season to ski?

CHAPTER THREE

Once on the plane, his forearms making unwanted contact with the people on either side of him, Liam found he still couldn't shake the image of that digital skier flying down the mountain. *That* was an escape, an adventure, something to blow away the misery! Why hadn't that idea occurred to him first, darn it? The more he thought about it, the more he felt that all walking would achieve would be to imprint his losses further with every step; the opposite effect to the intended one.

Yet he couldn't *not* walk the Camino de Santiago. It was all arranged. What would Alanda say? He felt a stab of frustration. If she'd only come with him, it would be a different story. He wouldn't be setting off for his very own forty – well, twenty-three – days and nights in the wilderness, but instead a simple walking holiday with his beloved. It sounded a lot more appealing – but of course Alanda couldn't come with him. She had the wedding prep to help Heather with, the shop to run, and someone had to visit his mother now that neither he nor Richard could. He closed his eyes, trying to block out an interminable announcement over the tannoy listing the entire contents of the duty-free trolley, with prices.

What do you think, Rich? Walking or skiing?

Alanda and the kids were always teasing him for being so safe and predictable. What if he did something totally spontaneous, something he really wanted to do?

In his head, his brother was egging him on, as he always used to. *Do it, bro! You know you want to.*

He really did want to.

By the time they were instructed to stow their tray tables and make sure their seatbelts were fastened for the descent into Madrid airport, Liam had come to a decision, fidgeting with glee at the thought of it.

He was going to pick up his rucksack, and instead of heading off on the first 100km leg of the walk into the hills of Sierra de Guadarrama, he was going to buy the first available return flight to Geneva, or Zurich, whichever was nearer; preferably a ski holiday package of some sort. Three, maybe five days' skiing, to scratch this particular itch, and then he'd get back on track, literally, and do the walk too. He'd built in a lot of a wiggle room with the timings at the planning stage, intending to really take his time and have lots of days off to rest and explore the towns and villages he walked through, so he could just trim those out and use them all at the start for his skiing days instead. It would make for a more challenging walk later, but it would be worth it, and he was pretty sure he could still cover the distance.

Money wasn't an issue – he was about to inherit most of Richard's estate once probate was done. It wouldn't be a huge amount, just the proceeds of the sale of his one-bed flat in Basingstoke, but it would cover this extra outlay, plus the cost of Heather's wedding, and a good few months of Mum's care home fees.

This could be Richard's gift to him; the gift of spontaneity, freedom, the excitement that the Camino de Santiago wasn't offering.

And what was more, he wasn't going to tell Alanda, not until he had arrived in Geneva. She would only try and talk him out of it and he couldn't risk that, not now that he was feeling such a rush.

It felt like the most thrilling, reckless thing he had ever done.

*

As soon as he had picked up his rucksack – which already felt as though it was full of rocks – and got through Customs at Madrid, Liam switched on his phone and WhatsApp'd the family group chat Jake had set up. *Landed! Flight was fine. Thanks again for getting up early to see me off. Will send pics as soon as there's something interesting to show you… Love you all, and snogs to Mum (that's just to embarrass you, Bex) xxx*

He found a spare high stool at a Formica counter in a coffee concession near the various airline kiosks and started googling, a large espresso in hand and a still-rising sense of excitement as the results scrolled up.

After ten minutes he had favourited a beautiful Airbnb apartment right near the nursery slopes in a resort called Les Gets and found an intermediate ski package including lift passes, airport transfers and all the gear for a week, starting either today, or tomorrow if it was too tight to get everything sorted. But it felt imperative to his plan to be standing at the top of a ski run by the end of today if at all possible, partly because otherwise he wouldn't have enough time to get the walk done too.

Fortunately, he hadn't had to pre-book accommodation along the Camino route, apparently you just turned up and there would be a bed for you somewhere, even if it ended up being in a municipal *albergue*, a dormitory full of other walkers, so there was nothing to rearrange there.

That left the flight. The whole plan would come to nothing if there were no available flights – and it had to be the place he'd seen on the billboard and no other. With his pulse pounding in his throat, he approached the airline kiosks, brand new credit card (acquired for his travel expenses) in hand.

In the event it could not have been simpler, as if it was all meant to be. The first desk he enquired at not only had a return flight direct to Geneva, but it was leaving in just enough time for him to comfortably get back through check-in and Security. He'd be there by early afternoon and, providing he could get kitted out without too much hassle, could conceivably do a quick introductory run before it got dark.

He couldn't wait to send Alanda and the kids a WhatsApp of him on the slopes, gleefully thinking that never again would there be any accusations of 'boring' or 'predictable' levelled in his direction. It would blow their minds.

CHAPTER FOUR

Alanda

On Friday morning, the first full day of Liam's trip, Alanda woke up at five. Before even opening her eyes, she automatically rolled over to embrace him, as had been their ritual for over three decades. The shock of his absence on the other side of the bed hit her, in the cool sheets and silence of the still-dark bedroom, just as she'd always known it would. Before, though, it had never been anything to worry about – Liam's insomnia meant she often awoke in an empty bed, and she would know he'd either be downstairs watching guitar technique videos on YouTube, or up in the attic trying to practice the techniques through headphones.

But this was the real thing. Now he wasn't in either of those places. Now it finally, properly, sank in in that she would not see him, other than as pixels on a phone screen, for three long weeks. *This is not a drill*, she thought, rolling over and clutching her knees to her chest to stretch her lower back. It was always stiff first thing in the morning. She usually performed these stretches while Liam was making their first cup of tea. She'd laughed about it with him the night before he left, when he'd said he was going to have to buy her a Teasmade, because how on earth would she cope without a cup of tea in bed first thing?

'Do they even still make Teasmades?' she'd asked while thinking, actually, he had a point. One of the many things she loved about her husband was the fact that he automatically brought her up a cuppa in bed.

They had never been apart for this long before. She had been so focussed on trying to keep him out of the frightening mental abyss into which he seemed to be sliding, ever since his twin's death and his mother's Alzheimer's diagnosis, that she had not stopped to consider her own feelings. Now all she could think was that this was a mistake. They should have gone somewhere together. A safari, or snorkelling in the Maldives, or driving round New Zealand in a camper van… How could she have thought that sending him off into an enforced exile was a good idea? It might well make him worse.

But she couldn't have left Heather, not when the wedding date was fast approaching and there was still so much to be done.

She sat up in bed, reaching automatically for her mobile, but there were no further messages from him, neither on the family WhatsApp nor their private text conversation. She had texted him goodnight before she went to sleep, and he had not replied. Perhaps he was upset with her for sending him away?

Surely not. He had seemed up for it, grateful for her organisation – not excited, exactly, but more intrigued. Liam rarely showed actual excitement; all his emotions tended to be muted, soft-focus and understated, which often made it difficult to discern what he was really feeling. Although there had been no mistaking the slump he had been in for the past few months.

Morning darling, she texted. *Dying to hear how it's all going – did you get to the start of the trail OK? We need photos! Hope your phone's not playing up again, that would be terrible timing – I knew I should've made you take the iPad as back-up… Nothing much on for me today. Julie's in the shop all day so I don't need to worry about that. Going for a swim, planning to make a bit more bunting for H, then might see if Sadie's free for lunch. I'll pop in to your mum later too. Love you loads Xxx*

Liam's phone had recently gone through a phase of randomly switching itself off and then being difficult to re-boot, but the issue had apparently been resolved by a software update – perhaps he was having problems with it again. It was weird that he hadn't texted her to say good night.

Alanda switched on the bedside lamp, climbed out of bed and shrugged herself into her dressing gown, feeling flat and low, but not yet properly worried. Worry was still a shadow in the background that she could sense lurking behind her. Liam was a resourceful, intelligent, personable man, not a feckless teenager off on a gap year. If he had a problem with his phone, he would let her know some other way.

From what she had learned about the Camino de Santiago journey, part of the pleasure of it was how friendly all the pilgrims were, how willing to help lone travellers, and Liam, whilst fairly introverted, wouldn't rebuff overtures of friendship if he felt he needed the company. Or the use of someone's mobile to text her.

The house felt very empty now that the kids had all gone back to their respective flats – it had been so lovely having them stay over so they could all come to see Liam off. They hadn't all been together in the house since Christmas, almost four months before, and then Heather and Jake's other halves had been here too. It must be years since it had just been the five of them under the same roof.

And now she had to endure three weeks of her own company. This would be practice for if she ever became a widow, God forbid.

Oh, pull yourself together Alanda, she thought. It wouldn't kill her, as long as she made sure to keep busy during the days. She'd be in the shop all week. The kids would pop round for dinner when they could. She was so lucky they had all stayed local – although perhaps Jake's current search for a new job and a new man would take him to a different area. Hopefully not, though. Anyway, she would be fine. It was only three weeks. She had friends, a social life. She wasn't going to sit around moping and waiting for him to get back.

She sat down at the dining table with her mug of tea and a muddy burble of depressing news in the background. She and Liam had been halfway through a complicated jigsaw depicting Santorini, and she heard his voice in her ear, laughing that she would have to do all the blue sea and sky bits without him. Picking up a piece of turquoise, which could be either, she stared listlessly at it before putting it back in the box again.

It was exactly twenty-four hours since they had waved him off. Apart from the brief WhatsApp saying he'd landed safely, why had he not been in touch?

She sent him another text: *Getting worried now. Please contact us ASAP. X*

CHAPTER FIVE

By the following day, the family had all sent dozens of increasingly concerned pleas to Liam's WhatsApp and, no matter how frequently Alanda checked, none of the ticks next to the messages turned from grey to blue to indicate any of them had been read. Calls went straight to voicemail. Texts were unanswered.

There was either something wrong with his phone, or with him, but the latter thought seemed too catastrophic to contemplate.

'Not yet, anyway. I'm not going to panic yet,' Alanda said to her friend Sadie, who had persuaded her out of the house and into the local arts centre.

There was a free lunchtime concert taking place, in which someone Sadie knew was performing. If Alanda had been told in advance it was a ukulele band, she probably would have stayed at home, but she grudgingly supposed that it was better to be fretting in company rather than on her own.

Despite what she'd told Sadie, she *was* already panicking. Worst-case scenarios of fatal heart attacks, muggings and shootings were already rotating through her brain and clicking past her mind's eye in technicolour, like the images on one of the old View-Masters she'd always yearned for when she was a kid; a red plastic toy like binoculars, with a removable circle of pictures that you slotted in and viewed in 3D.

She and Sadie were waiting in the queue for coffees, to the accompaniment of thirty elderly gentlemen in stripy waistcoats and straw hats performing a barbershop quartet number. One old boy at the back was playing a small drum in a rhythm that implied he was listening to a completely different song in his head. 'Rapper's Delight', perhaps, Alanda suggested.

Sadie grinned, then saw how miserable Alanda's face was, despite her attempts at levity, and rubbed her arm.

'You're right not to panic just yet – but you must be in bits. Did you get any sleep last night?'

Alanda shook her head. 'Not a lot. Dozed off about three, woke up at five. Checking my phone every five minutes.'

They got their coffees and took them over to a table at the back of the old converted church, far enough back that they could still talk. The band struck up a new number and it took Alanda a minute or so to register that it was 'Mr. Sandman', a song that Liam used to sing the kids when they were little and he was on bedtime duty.

'Oh no, not this song…' she said, as her eyes filled.

Sadie squeezed her hand. 'Like you said, don't fear the worst. It's too soon. I reckon you're right, it's probably just a phone malfunction and he hasn't found anyone on the trail he can ask to use theirs. He can't just march up to someone and demand to use their phone. Or perhaps his messages aren't getting through when he thinks they are. Also – what if he can't remember your number? I mean, I don't know anybody's mobile numbers these days, and you got rid of your landline, didn't you?'

Alanda wiped her eyes. 'Yeah. It's true that he only remembers mine half the time. I kept testing him on it before he left, and he hardly ever got it right.'

'There you are then. There are loads of possible explanations,' Sadie said triumphantly. A little too triumphantly, Alanda thought, in that way people acted when they were so desperate for a resolution that they would act as if there had been one, when there was none. But it came from a place of kindness, not arrogance.

Sadie had always been someone who wanted everything to be right for everyone, and whilst sometimes Alanda and Liam found her a bit needy – she had been divorced for about ten years, no kids, and made no bones about being lonely – Alanda was very fond of her, as well as feeling sorry for her. Out of all her friends, Sadie was by far the most loyal and reliable. It was almost as if her own lack of a partner made her try that much harder to be a rock for everyone else. Alanda wondered idly if there was even a small part of Sadie that *hoped* Liam had left her, so they could both be single women together, and then doubly chided herself for being so mean-spirited towards her lovely friend, and at the thought that Liam would have left her.

Of *course* he hadn't left her!

'It gets harder not to catastrophise with every hour that goes by,' she conceded. 'I know it's not helpful and he'll probably ring me any second with some story about having to buy a new battery from a mobile phone shop on the Camino de Santiago…'

'Will there be any out there? I thought it was all villages he'll be walking through.'

Alanda sighed. 'I'm trying to be positive. I don't know. He started off in Madrid and was then getting a bus and a train to somewhere called Leon to start the walk, so I suppose it depends on when his phone packed up. I think Leon is a good-sized town so there'd be a phone shop there, I'm sure.'

'Perhaps he lost it altogether, or it was stolen?' Sadie suggested.

The ukulele band moved on to 'Meet Me on the Corner', which was a relief. 'Yes… actually that's more likely, because we know he had it when he arrived at Madrid airport.'

Maybe Sadie's blind optimism was beginning to rub off on her – suddenly Alanda genuinely thought it didn't seem too far-fetched a scenario at all.

Although if it had been stolen, why had he not gone to the aforementioned phone shop and bought another one? Or emailed to tell them?

'You don't see internet cafes anymore, do you?' she asked, hopefully. 'I was just thinking that he could have gone into one to email us to say he'd lost his phone – then I thought that I haven't seen one for years.'

'No need for them anymore, not since everybody started having smartphones,' Sadie agreed, licking cappuccino froth surreptitiously from inside the rim of her mug. 'Just goes to show how lost we are without our phones, doesn't it?'

'I knew I should have made him take the iPad as well. But Becky's had it for the last month, after her laptop died, and Liam didn't want to deprive her of it.'

'Hmm. Wretched technology, and our dependence on it,' Sadie said.

She had a small brown smear of chocolate powder on her chin, and Alanda stuck out her thumb and wiped it off.

'Thanks. Can't take me anywhere. No wonder I can't find a man.'

Alanda managed a laugh. 'You just haven't found one good enough for you. I mean, look at you, you're gorgeous.'

Words she had said to Sadie so frequently they felt like a mantra.

'I'm *striking*,' Sadie said glumly, her standard reply to compliments about her appearance. 'I scare off all the ones I like. Men don't generally go for striking; they want someone girly.'

Privately, Alanda thought she might be right. Sadie was tall and slim, but well-built with a strong jaw, a mop of dark-brown curly hair and statement glasses with black and white patterned frames. Really attractive, but not very feminine. Her job as a firefighter (or 'firemanwoman', as they joked) added to her air of masculinity – she was always bemoaning that not being able to find a partner in such a male-oriented environment was the equivalent of not being able to organise a piss-up in a brewery.

Feeling a wash of affection, Alanda leaned across and pecked her on the cheek.

'Thank you. I'm glad you dragged me out. Much better than sitting by the phone at home. One more question and then let's change the subject and pretend everything's normal…'

'What?'

The words suddenly dried up and wedged in her throat and she had to cough them out:

'How long should I leave it before I report him missing? It's been more than forty-eight hours now.'

Sadie squeezed her hand again. 'Oh, honey. I don't know. Tonight? Tomorrow? Listen, why don't you come back to mine for dinner? We could watch something trashy on Netflix and drink wine; try and take your mind off it. Then you could call in the morning if there's still no news?'

Alanda gave her a watery smile. 'Thanks – that's so nice of you but Heather's coming over later.' She didn't say that it was for a quick late-afternoon cuppa rather than an extended evening meal, but she wanted to be at home.

'Good. I don't think you should be on your own,' Sadie said. 'If you are, call me and I'll pop round.'

'Thank you. I'll be fine,' replied Alanda automatically.

Sadie put her hands on her hips. 'Boy, you are *rubbish* at accepting that sometimes you might need a bit of help or support.'

Alanda was surprised. 'Am I? I didn't think I was.'

Sadie snorted.

'OK. I'll ring you if I need to, honest,' Alanda promised.

CHAPTER SIX

Heather did come over later that afternoon. She sat motionless in the kitchen, her chin in her hand, tracing the pattern on the oilcloth kitchen tablecloth with her fingernail.

It was she who worried Alanda most. The quieter she got, the more cause for concern Alanda knew there was, and she had barely said a word for the half hour since she arrived.

'Darling, if Dad has to walk you down the aisle with his arm or leg in plaster, or his neck in a brace, or whatever, it's not the end of the world.'

Heather looked up then, her pleading eyes reminding Alanda exactly of Cindy, the Labrador her parents had owned when she was a kid.

'How would breaking his arm stop him contacting us?'

'I know, sweetie, it shouldn't. But there's no point in speculating when anything could have happened.'

'*You* just did,' Heather replied grumpily, pushing her hair out of her eyes. She had been growing out her fringe for the wedding and it wasn't quite long enough yet to stay back without flopping in her face. 'Anyway, I need to go. I've got a spin class at five.'

'Oh! That was a quick visit... Don't overdo it,' Alanda said, hugging her youngest daughter and wishing she wasn't leaving so soon.

She thought of her words later; what a spurious piece of advice to give a young woman who wanted to lose weight. Do it, but don't overdo it...

Had Liam overdone it? She pictured him climbing a steep hill, bowed down by the heavy rucksack, clutching his chest, ploughing on because she wasn't there to tell him to stop. He was a fit man, but fit men got heart disease all the time…

By six o'clock and with no sign Liam had seen or read any of their messages, Alanda decided it was time to call the police.

Well, she thought, immediately quaking at the thought, *I'll give it two more hours* then *I'll call*.

She wished she wasn't alone. She could have taken Sadie up on her offer – still could, so why didn't she? Being at home on her own was really horrible, staring at her phone every two minutes, waiting for what she imagined would be an imminent death-knock at the front door, two sombre policemen standing there with their hats in their hands… Yet somehow she just couldn't bring herself to pick up the phone to Sadie, or any of the kids.

She tried to find little jobs to occupy her for the next couple of hours but even spending forty minutes applying a paste of bicarbonate of soda to the black spots of mould on the grout between the bathroom tiles, then scrubbing it off with one of Liam's old toothbrushes – something she had been meaning to do for months – did not make her feel any better. The sound of her frenzied scratching of bristle on grout just seemed to magnify her own agitation.

Then she decided she'd try something more soothing: a crochet square for the blanket she was secretly making for Heather's as yet un-conceived baby (or, if she was honest, the baby of whichever one of her kids became the first to make her a granny, Heather being the front-runner), but it had been a while since she'd crocheted and she kept forgetting how to do it, eventually ripping the wool out in frustration and throwing it on the carpet.

It was at that point she realised that she really wasn't used to being on her own. Even since Becky, the last of the kids to move out, had rented her own flat, Alanda rarely had the place to herself. Liam always tried to time his garden jobs to coincide with her days in the shop, so it was fairly unusual for her to be home without him. She did not like it at all.

A cold fist of terror balled itself in her belly at the thought that she might have to get used to it. She saw her future self, rattling around in the house trying to kick away the loneliness constantly nipping at her heels, until she would eventually give in to it and it would transform into a toxic cloud which would rise up and asphyxiate her.

Eight o'clock loomed and she couldn't put it off any longer. A pint of Brewdog in her left hand for Dutch courage, she dialled 101 on her mobile with her right thumb, the beer glass chilling the skin of her palm. As she feared, making the call made it official: Liam was AWOL. She shivered with fear and the sudden cold from the beer.

The call was immediately answered by a machine informing her that 'call demand was unusually high, please hold for the next available operator', and tinny classical music assaulted her ear. She turned down the volume and stared out into the almost-dark garden, her eye caught by the shape of a fox slinking across the lawn.

Their garden was Liam's pride and joy, and the first full design he had ever implemented, right back when they were newly married. It had given him the confidence to set himself up as a garden designer, not just a regular gardener and, three decades later, the small back garden was still picture-perfect, better than ever as the shrubs and trees kept growing and maturing. He had planned it so there was always as much colour in it as possible and now, in early April, even though Alanda couldn't see them, she smiled at the return of the perennial frilly daffodils and tulips, irises and hollyhocks with which the borders were stuffed.

There was no way he'd walk away from all of this. However down he had been lately, he loved them. He loved his kids, his garden, his car, his life.

Didn't he? The View-Master circle of disaster pictures in her mind now had a few fanciful new additions: the long-standing mistress he'd somehow managed to keep quiet for years; the young, beautiful woman he'd met on the plane…

She took a swig of the beer, and its sharp fizz burned her throat and made her hiccup loudly. 'Pardon,' she said automatically to nobody.

The tinny music continued. *Please hold. You are number eight in the queue.*

Number eight, to speak to the police? She might be there for hours. Perhaps she should dial 999 instead? But that was for emergencies, and she still wasn't a hundred per cent sure whether this was yet an emergency or not.

She hadn't told the kids that she was ringing the police, still resolutely batting away their fears that something was wrong with repeated reassurances that it was bound to be a technical hitch, no news was good news, et cetera, and any other platitude she could muster.

Jake had agreed with her – although she had heard the doubt in his voice – whereas Becky had been almost hysterical on the phone earlier, screeching that he might be lying in a hospital somewhere, or worse, and wondering why his family weren't with him. Alanda had had to tell her to calm down.

On hold still – up to number four in the queue – her spiral of terror returned to the base camp of rationality: he had ID on him. If he'd had an accident, someone would have informed her.

And yet – yet – if he *hadn't* had an accident, maybe he had done something worse.

Finally, the tinny music ceased and an actual human voice came on the line: 'Wiltshire Police, how may I direct your call?'

'I'd like to report a missing person,' Alanda said, more firmly than she felt, immediately qualifying it: 'Well, he might be missing. I'm not sure. Liam Lodge. He's my husband.'

'I see. Please hold while I transfer you to the appropriate extension.'

The operator was gone, leaving Alanda with gritted teeth and the tinny hold music again. Thankfully, another voice came on the line shortly, and Alanda repeated her request, only this time minus the doubt in her voice.

Liam *was* missing.

'Right, OK, let me just take a few details to start with...'

Alanda spent the next few minutes wearily dictating her own name, address, mobile number and date of birth, and then the same for Liam, explaining the situation and her concerns, given that it was totally out of character for him not to be in touch apart from that one brief WhatsApp when he'd arrived in Spain.

The call handler was a very young-sounding woman called Chloe, who asked, in a strong Wiltshire accent, if she had a pen. 'I'm going to create an incident number which you'll need to keep and arrange to have an officer call you back.'

'Yes,' Alanda said obediently. She uncapped the biro Liam had been using for the Sudoku in the local paper and wrote down the number next to the half-completed puzzle.

None of it felt real, as if at any minute Liam would come downstairs from a lengthy session playing his guitar in the attic and ask her what she was doing. She imagined his brow, creased with surprise, and the concern in his eyes. God, she'd give anything to see that right now.

Chloe asked her something else.

'Pardon? Sorry, I...' It seemed inappropriate to say *I was miles away*, as if she didn't care. 'I missed that,' she said instead.

'What was he wearing when you last saw him on Thursday morning?'

'Standard sort of hiking gear. Rust-coloured cargo pants, a red North Face jacket, black walking boots. Big blue rucksack with a sleeping bag in the top, and a smaller backpack that was his carry-on.'

'And can you describe his appearance for me please?'

Not that she needed reminding of Liam's appearance, but Alanda still found her eyes drifting over to their wedding photo, an arty black and white canvas hanging over the fireplace. For the first time she thought that he did look different to how he had on that day. She'd always congratulated him on how well he was ageing compared to his peers, but the contrast between him then and now suddenly struck her hard. Then, he had been fresh-faced and smooth-skinned, with a full – if somewhat bouffant, since it was the nineties – head of hair and a whippet-thin body, laughing like he didn't have a care in the world. Well, he hadn't, not back then. His recent grief had bowed his shoulders, changed the laughter lines into hard-carved furrows, muddied his complexion. He looked all of his fifty-three years.

'He's six foot one, about thirteen stone I think and quite broad shoulders. Bit of a belly but not much. Salt and pepper hair, thinning a bit on top. Blue eyes, a dimple in his chin…'

'Salt and pepper hair?' Chloe sounded puzzled and Alanda sighed. How young did you have to be to have not heard that expression?

'You know. Black, but going grey.'

She obviously didn't know. 'Oh, OK.'

Alanda heard the sound of typing at the other end of the line. 'Should I send you a photograph?'

'Yes, that would be helpful, I'll give you an email address shortly. And he hasn't been on social media at all since he left?'

The assumption that everyone in the world was on social media bemused her. 'He's not on Facebook, or Twitter or anything else. We agreed he'd keep in touch via text and WhatsApp.'

More typing sounds.

'And where was he planning to stay?'

'As I mentioned,' – *don't be mean*, Alanda chided herself, *she's trying to help* – 'he's not staying in one place. He's gone on a long hike in Spain called the Camino de Santiago; some people do it as a pilgrimage but some just do it because it's a long walk with lovely scenery. There are various routes and he's doing the one from Leon, which is a three-hour train journey from Madrid, and you stay in hostels along the way. It's known as the French Way even though it's in Spain, don't ask me why.'

'Would he have bookings for these hostels?'

'No, I'm afraid not… you don't usually pre-book because you can't be sure how long it's going to take you to do each leg. But there are lots of hostels and it's early in the season, so we were assured that he wouldn't have a problem getting a bed. I've already rung the hostels near Leon, where he might have stopped on the first and second nights, and no luck – but I wasn't expecting it, really, because if he'd got to a hostel safely, even if his phone was lost or broken, he'd have been able to contact me from there to let me know he was safe.'

Chloe hesitated. 'The police officer assigned to this case will ask you more about this, but just briefly – what was Liam's state of mind like when he left home?'

'He… ah… he…'

Alanda found she couldn't speak. She took a gulp of her drink. 'Sorry.'

'That's OK, take your time,' said Chloe.

'What I mean is – he's had a hard time of it recently, so he wasn't on top form, but this trip was meant to clear his head, help him get over a recent bereavement – his twin brother committed suicide a few months ago – and before that he'd been finding it difficult to cope with his mum being diagnosed with dementia. They are very close.'

Chloe made a noise that managed to sound both sympathetic and alarmed.

Alanda found that she was gritting her teeth so hard that her jaw ached. 'Our daughter's getting married this summer and he was so proud to be giving her away. He would never… you know… leave us.'

CHAPTER SEVEN

Liam

It was the only time he really panicked; when he came round after the operation and there were people, nurses, all round his bed talking to him and to each other, and he could not understand anything they were saying. Once the anaesthetic wore off a little, he realised that one of them, a severe-looking nurse – thin face, thin dark hair scraped back, thin lips – was actually speaking English, but with such a strong French accent that it had taken him this long to figure it out. She kept asking a question: 'Do you remember anything yet?'

Did he?

Remember what?

He thought hard, or at least, he tried to, but woolly nebulous candy-floss strands of thought drifted untethered around his head without snagging on anything.

'Why you are 'ere?' she prompted.

He looked down to see his leg in plaster, raised at a forty-five degree angle and attached to a metal contraption, like a horse tied up to an iron gate.

'Snow,' he said eventually, his voice sucking and cracking through dry lips.

'*Oui*!' She sounded so enthusiastic, he hated to disappoint her by telling her that this was literally all he remembered.

'Your name?' she asked hopefully. He shook his head.

'Not a Scooby,' he said, without having the first idea what it meant. He somehow knew it wasn't a normal way to say *I don't know*, but that was all.

'Your name is not Ascooby? Your last name? Is this the name of someone else you know?'

He closed his eyes. It was all too difficult; his thigh was aching horribly and he just wanted to sleep. 'No. I meant, I don't know.'

Suddenly he didn't just want to sleep, he wanted to cry.

'Do you remember the name of your 'otel, or chalet?'

'No.'

She patted his hand, the one without a tube coming out the back of it. Cannula, he thought. Or maybe canola, cannelloni, cannelotti…? Who knew? It wasn't the only tube, either.

It was all very odd.

'Don't worry,' said the nurse. 'We will find. If you do not 'ave family or friends with you to report you missing, the 'ospital office, they will ask. They can call the 'otels, ask if somebody does not check in when he should, or does not sleep in his room for some days. The police will register you as a – euh – *une personne disparue*. Missing. But someone will be looking for you, I am sure.'

He yearned for someone to walk through the door then, calling his name – whatever that was – and holding out their arms, crying with relief that he was alive, and sorrow that he was injured. In his mind's eye he saw blonde hair and a wide smile, but that was as far as any detail went. It must be his mother, he thought, because suddenly he felt like a little boy who had fallen off a swing. Tears threatened again.

'My mother has blonde hair,' he mumbled.

'*Bon!*' said the nurse. 'You will soon remember everything else, *mon cher*. Now try and sleep.'

'My leg hurts.'

The nurse leaned across him and showed him something he had not noticed, clutched in his fist, the one with the tube sticking out of it. It was a small white cylindrical object with a button on the end. 'When the pain gets too, er, big, then you push this. It will give you more pain relief.'

He pressed it immediately. Her face seemed so much less severe than it had a few minutes ago, and in a few more minutes the throbbing in his thigh was already starting to ease. Relieved, he stopped worrying – his newest worry was not even knowing which country he was in. The nurse was speaking French, but he was sure he recalled someone speaking German to him in the snow? But it had ceased to matter, and he slid into sleep as easily as the pain medication slid through his veins.

No point in worrying about things he had no control over.

Darn it.

CHAPTER EIGHT

Katya

By nature of the fact that he was the only man under eighty on the orthopaedic ward, and the National Police had been in to talk to him, the man they called Jack was already a bit interesting to Katya. After a few days she gleaned that he had lost his memory – she had been wondering why he never had any visitors. Who could help being fascinated and intrigued? And he had absolutely gorgeous eyes.

She could see how long and thick his eyelashes were, from across the other side of the room, from her uncomfortable vinyl seat next to Uncle Otto's bed. Glancing covertly across at him on her daily visits to Uncle Otto had become a bit of a pastime.

It literally did pass the time – there was only so much conversation you could make with a confused geriatric who was recovering from a hip replacement *and* sepsis. Poor Otto, Katya thought. He was only meant to be in hospital for a few days. She read to him, but it always sent him to sleep within minutes.

Jack appeared to like it when she read, though. Quite a few times she sneaked a peek at him and caught him studying her as she turned the pages, even though she had gleaned that he didn't speak French. He would give a tiny grin of what seemed like secret complicity and look away. Although perhaps she was just imagining that. After all, she was in his eyeline, and she usually wore really bright primary colours which, in such a beige ward full of sick old men, made her stand out somewhat.

She didn't actually get into conversation with him for about a week, not until a hospital dietician – some sort of nutritionist person, anyway – came to visit him to check he was eating properly, and the woman could barely speak any English. All the other nursing staff were busy, so nobody came to their aid. Katya noticed them attempting and failing to communicate, despite the elaborate charades the dietician was performing. She heard her say the word 'selle' (bowel movement) and thought that would be a pretty tricky one to act out, so she called across in French, and then English, to ask if they needed any help.

The man's face lit up with relief and pleasure when he heard Katya speak. If she had known it would be that helpful to him, she'd have offered sooner, but most of the nurses managed pretty well with their broken English. Katya spoke German or French with Uncle Otto, so Jack wouldn't have known she was trilingual.

Such an expressive face he had, she thought, even though he must have been in quite a bit of pain and on some heavy-duty drugs. His right leg was in traction, and she wondered what had happened. Skiing or snowboarding, doubtless. She'd never seen the appeal of it herself, despite visiting Otto – and Auntie Monique, when she was still alive – most years. Katya's friends were always nonplussed that despite her uncle living so close to a resort, she'd never learned to ski, but it just wasn't for her. She did try it, twice, when she was about ten and twelve, but both times found it cold, wet, terrifying and unnecessary. She had never been a sporty child, and certainly did not fancy it now.

'Thanks,' he said, in a surprisingly clear voice. 'We're struggling a bit over here.'

He had a faint American accent and Katya wondered where he was from. Otto had been asleep since she arrived that day and she had just been reading her book anyway, so she was glad of something to do.

She walked over to Jack's bed and stood, slightly awkwardly, at the foot of it. When she surreptitiously glanced down at his chart, it just said *Nom: inconnu. Prénom: inconnu* (JACK) – real name not known. She was dying to ask questions, and he seemed so open and friendly, grateful to have someone to talk to.

The dietician, an efficient-looking, pencil-thin Swiss woman with stiffly lacquered wavy blonde hair, appeared utterly put out that Jack couldn't speak French or German – or perhaps she was embarrassed by her own failure to speak English. In fairness, it was very unusual for a Swiss woman not even to have conversational English. She also seemed a bit smitten with Jack, despite the fact that he was a tired-looking middle-aged man, probably a good ten or fifteen years older than both women, and of course not looking his best – who did, in hospital?

There was just something about him though, Katya thought. She had already noticed how charming and funny he was to all the nurses, language barrier notwithstanding. And he had such lovely eyes, even if they were a bit bloodshot. She thought it must be pretty hard to be charming and funny when you had no idea who you were or what you were doing there, but he managed it.

'I'm happy to translate,' she said shyly, 'if it's appropriate…'

She hoped the dietician wasn't going to dwell on his bowels too much, or it would be excruciating for them both, but Jack just looked grateful again. The dietician explained what she needed to know.

'She's trying to find out your food preferences to do you a meal plan for the next two weeks,' Katya duly passed on. 'It's routine.'

He grinned at her. 'Well, I don't think I'll be much help. I have no clue what I eat or don't eat.'

He seemed to be assuming that she was already aware of his amnesia. She contemplated pretending that she wasn't and asking him what he meant, before deciding not to be so disingenuous. Instead, she smiled back uncertainly and then spent the next five minutes listening to and transmitting questions the dietician read out from a sheet on a clipboard.

As he had predicted, many of them he just couldn't answer even after she'd translated, so Katya spent a lot of the time going '*il ne sait pas*' – he doesn't know. He had no idea if he was vegetarian, or had had previous surgeries, or any intolerances and allergies. He sounded increasingly apologetic, and Katya could see that the dietician was trying to remain sympathetic whilst feeling more frustrated by the minute. Eventually, she scribbled a few final notes and told Jack, through Katya, that she would be back with the plan tomorrow. Then she thanked them, and clip-clopped out of the ward on her blocky heels.

Jack and Katya exchanged smiles again.

'I'm Katya,' she said.

Something about his incapacity, both mental and physical, emboldened her. She was never normally able to introduce herself to men, but this was not a normal situation.

'I'm… Jack?' he said, and for a moment his face drooped, giving him a slightly jowly appearance. 'Temporarily, at least. I don't know why they picked that name. Or why they sent in a nutritionist to ask me about my food preferences when I don't even know what my real name is. Hey, as your dad is still asleep, would you mind staying here for a chat? It's so nice to be able to speak to someone and have them understand me properly.'

'He's my uncle, not my dad.'

Katya sat down in the chair next to Jack's bed. One of the nurses came back onto the ward, glancing in slight surprise at her sitting there instead of in her usual spot next to Otto, and her cheeks flamed as if she'd been caught doing something inappropriate. They looked across at Uncle Otto, who groaned and farted loudly in his sleep. She blushed deeper, but Jack giggled suddenly, an infectious sound that made her join in, guiltily clapping her hand over her mouth.

'You get a lot of that in here,' he said. 'So, Katya, I can't tell you what I'm doing here, but you can. Where are you from that you speak such good English?'

'I'm visiting from London – I've lived in the UK all my life,' she explained, 'although my mum was French. My dad was from Trinidad.'

She wondered if that meant anything to him. If he couldn't remember his name, how would he know where or what Trinidad was? But he just nodded.

'My mum was Otto's wife's younger sister, but she – Mum – died ten years ago and now Auntie Monique's died too, two years ago, so when Otto said he was having a hip replacement I offered to come over from London to stay for a couple of weeks to help him out around his apartment. He doesn't have any other family, and I'm self-employed so I can take time off whenever I want – with a bit of notice.'

'What do you do for work?'

'I'm a French tutor, mostly, and I do some translation work too.'

'Yes, you do.'

They both laughed, even though it wasn't particularly funny. Katya had the weirdest feeling that she had known this man for years; that it was she who had lost her memory and didn't know why or where they had met.

'So may I ask – what did you do to your leg?'

He looked at it ruefully, winched up and attached to a metal scaffold that reminded Katya of a gallows, only for legs. 'I broke my thighbone, apparently, but I don't remember the accident, just a brief memory of someone talking in German. I'm told I had been skiing – they found me half-conscious on a slope and called for help – but I don't know what happened or even what I'm doing here in France.'

'Did you hit your head?' she asked. He must surely have a head injury, but there were no outward signs of it: no bandages or lumps.

'Apparently not, even though they think I must have hit a tree – it takes quite a bit of force and speed to break a femur. I've had all the scans and so on. The doctors tell me I have a massive bruise on my backside – I won't offer to show you – but no sign of damage to my skull, thankfully, so they think what might have happened is that I crashed into the tree, broke my leg, fell over backwards, landed hard on my spine and it caused some kind of shockwave up into my brain, affecting the part that controls my memories.'

He paused and reached for a plastic cup of water next to his bed. Katya noticed that his hand shook slightly and he looked upset. Perhaps articulating his predicament was making it sink in more? He had really nice hands, slim and smooth, with good nails.

She marvelled at what a strange and complex instrument the brain was, that he seemed completely normal, and yet had such a void where his memory should be.

'Where was your ID? You really can't remember anything? You don't seem confused. Sorry… I didn't mean to bombard you with questions.'

He shook his head. 'It's fine. I had no ID on me, no wallet, nothing, which seems weird. The police said that nobody has reported me missing; they checked the place I hired my skis from to see if there were any unclaimed belongings from the lockers, but no. It's a mystery. I'm feeling a bit unloved, to be honest.'

He pulled an exaggeratedly sad face, but the look in his eyes belied the jokiness.

'You must have been here on your own, otherwise someone in your party would definitely have contacted the police,' Katya said. 'I'm sure your family will raise the alarm when you don't come home.'

'Maybe I don't have a family? I mean, why else would I come on holiday on my own?'

'Maybe,' she agreed, finding it difficult to know what to say. Was it better if he had no family at all, or a family who hadn't noticed he was missing? Perhaps he was recently divorced, she thought, but she didn't like to suggest that in case it upset him.

'I only know I'm in France because I've been told,' he continued, 'but even that's taken a few days to sink in. Apparently, Celine – do you know her? She's the nurse who speaks the best English – had to write me a note when I first got in here, because I kept asking over and over where I was and what I was doing, on a loop. Look.'

He pointed at a folded sheet torn from a notebook on the bedside cabinet and Katya picked it up. Written in biro, the note said,

You are in the hospital in Thonon-les-Bains after an accident on the ski slope in Les Gets. You have lost your ~~mind~~ memory but you are safe and will be OK in time we think. You have broken one leg.

The 'lost your mind' and 'one leg' made her smile, but she rearranged her face immediately, not wanting him to think she found the situation in any way funny.

'I'm sorry,' she said awkwardly. 'It must be a very upsetting feeling.'

He shrugged. 'Actually it isn't, not really. It's a bit frustrating, but there's nothing I can do about it until my memory comes back. It's kind of interesting, too, and strange, but not upsetting. I think I will be upset later if I discover that I'm actually a criminal or a…' He petered out. 'Oh, I don't know, something not nice. But for now, I don't know, so I'm not worried about anything except maybe what I'm going to do when my leg gets better, if my memory doesn't come back.'

He blushed then, as if he felt bad about complaining. 'Sorry. You don't know me and I'm keeping you from your visit.'

Katya opened her mouth to say it was no problem, Uncle Otto was asleep – but at that moment she looked over and saw that he had woken up. He was licking his lips and raising a shaky liver-spotted hand to his chin.

'Oh, it's no problem, honestly, I've enjoyed our chat. I'd better go now though. Please, if you need any more translating done, I come in every day to see Otto, and I'd be happy to help.'

'I have noticed you coming in every day,' he said, and something about his tone made her heart give a tiny skip of pleasure.

CHAPTER NINE

A week later when Katya walked onto the ward for the afternoon visit, she gasped out loud. Uncle Otto's bed was empty. Jack was sitting up in his own bed with an anxious look on his face, which made her heart plummet further. She was about to go over to him when Sister Celine rushed up and touched her elbow.

'We were just going to call you,' she said. Katya glanced at Jack and could see he knew what she was about to tell her – even though of course Celine was speaking French. 'Please come into my office a moment.'

'He's dead, isn't he? But how? He was fine yesterday!'

Her eyes had already filled with tears and she turned abruptly so Jack couldn't see the distress on her face.

Once they were squeezed into the cubbyhole of an office, Celine explained what had happened, just an hour earlier. It had been Jack who had raised the alarm as the nurses had all been off the ward dealing with another patient at the time, but even so it had been too late.

'It was a massive heart attack,' she said sombrely. 'I'm so sorry, Katya.'

Of course, Katya had been expecting it. Otto had clearly been living on borrowed time for months, even before the hip replacement and sepsis. But it seemed so cruel that he could survive all that pain and discomfort and not ever get back to his home, his armchair with the view of the lake, just once more.

Celine handed her a tissue. 'He would not have suffered,' she said. 'It all got too much for his heart.'

Katya couldn't help a sob escaping. 'Poor Otto.'

'Yes. He was really the most charming man.'

All the memories of Katya's childhood holidays here with him and Auntie Monique came flooding back, walks in the spring-flowered Alpine foothills, the delicious hot chocolate he used to make, the wooden toys he made her with which they played together – spinning tops and a rocking horse and a tricycle she loved for years after she outgrew it.

Katya's favourite childhood book was *Heidi*, and she secretly modelled herself on the eponymous heroine, even though in her edition of the book Heidi had blonde hair in two plaits, something Katya could never in a million years have got her own short black hair to do. Auntie Monique once made her a Swiss-style dress with a lace-up bodice and a red stripy apron just like Heidi's, and she wore it constantly until a growth spurt at around the age of eight made her actually burst its seams.

'You will need to sign some documents,' Celine said. 'You are his next of kin, aren't you? Someone will ring you with an appointment to do the paperwork and collect his belongings, and the death certificate, probably in a day or two.'

Katya nodded, a tear rolling off her chin into her lap.

'And you should contact a funeral director too, and a solicitor regarding his will,' Celine said gently.

She nodded again.

It was only as she was leaving, her head spinning with the grief of losing someone who had been a constant to her for her whole life, that Katya remembered Jack.

She had no excuse to ever see him again.

They had talked every day over the past week, some days for just a few minutes if Otto had been alert enough for Katya to read and chat to him, but other days, when Otto was out for the count, for the whole of visiting time. And Jack's face, whenever she walked into the ward! It lit up.

Although of course the man had no other visitors, she told herself, so naturally he would be more happy to see her than might be expected of two people who had met under these unusual circumstances.

Katya ducked into the Ladies' to make sure she did not have mascara running down her face – it had been about four days ago when she first realised she was putting on make-up before leaving Otto's apartment for the hospital every day, something she rarely did at home unless she was going to a party – and decided to go and have a last chat with Jack.

His face did not light up this time when she approached his bedside; instead, he held out his hand to her. She tentatively took it, tears springing back to her eyes. It was the first time they had touched and perhaps it was just the emotion of the occasion, but Katya really thought she felt a jolt of electricity up through her arm at the feel of his warm skin on hers.

'I am so very sorry for your loss,' he said formally, looking genuinely upset. 'It must be a huge shock for you. Please, sit down?' Then he hesitated. 'Unless of course I'm keeping you? You probably have a lot to do.'

Katya smiled at him and swiped a tear off her cheek. 'No, it's fine, I came in to see you, to say thanks for calling for help. Celine told me that you were the one who spotted he was in trouble.'

Jack's own eyes filled with tears and she was astonished at how emotional he was. 'I feel terrible that I didn't notice sooner. I'd been asleep, and I woke up, and… anyway. It's awful for you.'

'But at least he's not suffering anymore.'

They were silent for a few moments against the backdrop of the hospital soundtrack, the squeak of a trolley, the beeps of a monitor, coughing, the occasional moan.

Katya's mind was racing, but to her slight shame, it wasn't her late uncle who occupied her thoughts. She risked a glance at Jack, the man who was as much of a mystery to himself as to everyone else.

'So,' she said eventually, 'have there been any updates from the police? You said they were going to check the Interpol missing persons database?'

He shook his head. 'No. They did check the American and Canadian lists, but there was no-one on there answering my description. Anyway, more importantly – what are you going to do now? Will you go back to London?'

It wasn't more important, of course, but it was sweet of him to be concerned.

'I will, eventually, but there's so much to do first,' she said. 'I'm his next of kin – his only family now – so I'll have to organise the funeral, clear his apartment, decide what to do with it. It could take months.'

'And you can do that? I mean, you don't have a family waiting at home for you?' Jack's expression was slightly coy. Their daily chats until now had not veered into very personal territory. She hesitated, not sure how much she wanted to tell him.

'No family. And work has been really slow over the last year anyway, so it's not like I'll be losing out. Besides, if a job did come in, I can do it from here. I'm as happy here – in fact, I'd been thinking that I might even move over here permanently. Otto said he was leaving me everything in his will, and it's a lovely apartment. So much nicer than a tiny rented flat in zone three where I live.'

Katya felt a bit overcome again and had to stare at a few squares on Jack's waffle-weave hospital blanket to regain her composure.

'Zone three?'

'Oh sorry, that just means it's in London.'

'It sounds very sci-fi.'

Not for the first time, she found the technicalities of Jack's memory loss so strange. The London Underground zones were a blank to him, yet he knew what science fiction was. Very weird.

'Could I ask you a favour?' he said abruptly. 'I mean, it's a bit of an imposition, and probably the last thing you want to do, but...'

'Of course, what?'

'Seeing as you're not going back to England just yet, would you consider coming to visit me again, even though you don't have to be here anymore? I would miss you a lot, if I didn't see you again.'

They were both blushing furiously. Strange how so many of their encounters seemed to end this way.

'I'd be happy to,' Katya said. 'I was actually going to ask you if I could.'

'Good,' he said, sounding slightly strangled. His words had come out on an awkward cough. 'That means a great deal to me. Thank you.'

CHAPTER TEN

Alanda

'Mum, you look terrible,' said Jake, giving Alanda a hello kiss on the cheek. She held him tightly, inhaling the cold air of a late spring evening that clung to his jacket, mingling with the lemony scent of his aftershave and, underneath that, the comforting and unmistakeable Jake smell. She would know it anywhere, could pick him out of a line-up if she was blindfolded. Plus, right now, he was the closest thing she had to Liam.

She held him tightly and wordlessly until he wrapped his arms around her and reciprocated the hug.

'Oh Mum. It's so grim,' he muttered into her neck, and she could only nod. 'The girls here yet?' he asked eventually, disentangling himself.

'They're in the kitchen,' Alanda said, noticing that her son did not look so great himself. His skin looked sallow, highlighting the brown shadows under his eyes. 'Are you sleeping OK, darling? How's the asthma?'

It had always been a source of distress to her that her son had inherited her asthma. Her own flared up infrequently these days, but he still got the occasional bad attack, particularly when he was as stressed as this.

He snorted. 'Sleeping like a baby. Not. Asthma's fine though.'

'I'm not sleeping either,' she confessed. 'Come on. Kettle's on.'

'Did you make flapjacks?'

'Sorry. Heather's doing Slimming World and they're too many "syns", apparently.'

'Oh, come *on*, seriously?'

Jake said it jokily, but neither of them was smiling as he followed Alanda into the kitchen. He slung his jacket over the back of a chair next to Becky, slumping down into it and then straightening up to give her a kiss.

'Don't I get one?' Heather asked, giving him the puppy-eyes treatment.

'Come and get it – I can't be bothered to get up again. I'm too knackered.'

'Don't be such a pain,' Becky said, only half-affectionately.

Usually this sort of exchange would have ended up with them mock-punching and insulting each other, but Alanda could tell they were just going through the motions. They all fell silent again while she busied herself spooning coffee into the cafetière and getting four mugs out of the cupboard.

When she turned back around, the three of them were wordlessly holding hands around the table, as if about to conduct a seance. Something inside her broke to see her children so worried and frightened. Each time they met up, it got worse.

She put her hand to her mouth to try and stifle the sob rising in her throat, but it didn't work, and then it was as if she had been unstoppered. Unable to help herself, she started crying all the tears she had been suppressing since their last family meeting the previous week. All three of them jumped up and surrounded her, holding her, nuzzling into her like they had when they were small, only now they were trying to protect her instead of the other way around…

Within moments all four of them were crying, even Jake, whom Alanda hadn't seen shed a tear since he was twelve. He hadn't even cried at his Uncle Richard's funeral last year.

'What if he doesn't come back?' Becky hiccupped, clutching Alanda around the waist.

'I can't bear it,' said Heather, in between sobs. 'We're going to cancel the wedding.'

'What? No! You can't do that!' Alanda pushed her away so that she could look into her face to see if she meant it. Heather's face was blotchy and resolute.

'Right, let's all sit down and have a proper chat.'

Alanda steered them back to the table, placing a box of tissues in between them all. She wiped her own eyes with a sheet of kitchen roll and made the coffee, the fresh, earthy smell as she poured boiling water into the jug helping ground and calm her. Leaving it to brew, she unearthed a hidden packet of Hobnobs from the back of the cupboard. 'Sorry, Heather, but this calls for biscuits.'

Heather was the first to stretch out her hand to open the packet. 'What does it matter now anyway?'

Becky blew her nose and stared at her little sister. 'You're not serious, about the wedding?'

Alanda put the milk carton onto the table, and the sugar bowl and a spoon for Jake.

'Get a plate for the biscuits, please, Jake, and Bex, could you pour the coffee?'

She sat next to Heather and squeezed her hand. 'Darling, don't postpone the wedding, not yet, anyway? It's weeks away. There's loads of time for Dad to come back. We mustn't be hasty.'

Heather started to cry again. 'But how can I carry on planning while he's missing? It seems wrong! And it's no fun anyway, because I can't enjoy it, I just feel too worried and guilty.'

At that moment, Alanda felt a shot of rage zip through her like adrenaline. Sodding Liam! How could he put them all through this?

She put her palms flat on the table, the rage already dissolving into a toxic puddle of her own guilt. It was her fault. She had encouraged him to go.

Jake tipped biscuits onto the plate and took three, stacking them up on the tablecloth next to his coffee mug. 'When did you last talk to PC Laptop?' he asked.

'PC *Harding*,' Alanda corrected, although she did manage a smile. Jake had been there when the policeman had come round to the house to take a statement, the morning after she reported Liam missing. PC Harding was a short, compact man in his forties who had a surprisingly posh voice, but with such a mumbled delivery that it was hard to understand what he was saying half the time, more like an army colonel than a regular copper. As soon as the front door had closed again behind him, Jake had given him the nickname Laptop, 'Because he's a small PC.'

'Two days ago. We agreed to touch base in another week, unless of course there was any news from either of us.'

'I don't think I can take another week of this,' Becky said miserably. 'I'm going to take a few days' leave from Monday – I can't concentrate at work at all. I posted replacement bubble baths by mistake to all the people who'd complained about leaky body lotions, and then had to send the body lotions later, Marilyn was furious. I thought she was going to dock my wages.'

Marilyn was Becky's boss in Customer Services at Natural Worlds, the small skincare company where she had been working for the past two years. Becky mostly got on well with her, despite calling her a dragon and a slave-driver behind her back.

'Maybe you should take a week off, darling. Come and stay here and keep me company.'

Alanda was privately terrified that Becky would lose that job, fall out with Marilyn and get fired, or be made redundant. It was so hard to find anything paying decent money at the moment, and Becky was on a surprisingly good salary.

'Might do,' said Becky, wiping her eyes again. She looked too thin, thought Alanda. The twins had always had ridiculously fast metabolisms and could eat whatever they wanted and not put on an ounce, whereas poor Heather, now miserably staring at the crumbs of the Hobnob she had just practically inhaled, was the opposite.

'I think we need to be realistic,' Jake said, straightening his spine. 'Or at least look at the realistic options.'

He held out his hands – such thin, delicate fingers, thought Alanda with a pang of love – ready to count them off. 'One: he's dead.'

Even though they all knew this was the most probable one, all three women inhaled sharply and fearfully, as if saying it out loud would somehow make it true.

'Two: he's had an accident and hasn't been found yet—'

'That was a possibility for the first couple of days, but it's been almost three weeks now,' Becky interrupted. 'If he's that injured and hasn't been found after all this time, then surely we have to assume that's now number one on the list too.'

Alanda nodded slowly.

'Three: he's OK but has been kidnapped and isn't allowed to contact us.'

Heather rolled her eyes. 'For God's sake, Jake, this isn't some Liam Neeson movie. Why on earth would anyone kidnap him? And if they had, why haven't they demanded a ransom?'

'I don't know,' Jake said snappily. 'Mistaken identity? I'm just trying to think about any option, however unlikely. It's unlikely enough that he's missing and we don't know why, after all this time.'

'You know what I think?' Alanda looked at them all. 'And PC Harding agrees it's the most likely scenario. I think he's been mugged and was left unconscious. Someone found him, he's been taken to hospital, but he's in a coma and for some reason didn't have any ID on him – or they haven't found his backpack. Yes – what if he was mugged on the trail, they knocked him out, took his stuff to go through later, got the valuables and ditched the backpack? So as soon as he wakes up, we'll hear!'

The kids' faces were sceptical. 'But I thought you said the police had contacted all the hospitals near where Dad had been that first day, Madrid, Leon, the start of the trail…?'

'Yes,' admitted Alanda. 'But I was thinking, how do we know if they really did? We only have their word. There might be other hospitals they missed. I think we need to ring around ourselves, see if there are any unidentified patients who came in wearing hiking gear and who are in a coma.'

'What if Dad's got brain damage?' Becky moaned.

'Shhh, Becky, not helping,' Jake said, but he put his hand over hers. 'Yeah. It's worth a try. What about Interpol, are they involved?'

Alanda nodded. 'Interpol are about to issue a Yellow Notice. It's what they do for missing persons, or to identify people who can't identify themselves. So if he is in a coma with no ID, someone in the hospital should be able to look him up that way. Although perhaps they just haven't thought of doing it yet. I'm sure they will soon, if that's where he is – if for no other reason than that they're going to want to know if he can pay his medical bills, or if he has insurance.'

'How could he not have had ID on him, though?' Heather reached her hand towards the Hobnobs, then pulled it away, looking agonised.

'If he was mugged, then it's entirely possible,' Jake replied, taking a fourth Hobnob.

'Jake! Could you stop stuffing your face, just for a minute?'

Alanda was pleased to hear Heather having a go at her brother. It meant that she was feeling more in control of things again.

'So those are the options, I guess,' she said, but Jake held up his hand like a traffic cop.

'There are two more,' he said, and she could hear the pain in his voice. She knew what was coming.

'Number four: he's left us. He's been seeing another woman and he's gone off to start a new life with her. He'll get in touch eventually when he's settled, but right now he doesn't want to, because he knows it would be too painful for him.'

The girls gave a roar of outrage at this, Becky actually slapping Jake hard on the arm. 'How could you say that? Of *course* he wouldn't!'

Heather was crying again. 'Before the wedding?'

Alanda got up and hugged her. 'No, of course he wouldn't. Dad loves us. And even if, in the ridiculously unlikely event that he's got a bit on the side that he wants to leave me for – he would *never* ruin your wedding day for it. Never.'

She glared at Jake. 'Honestly, Jake, I think we can discount that one.'

Jake looked sheepish. 'I don't believe it either, I'm just trying to cover literally all the bases here.' He hesitated. 'Which leaves one final option – also highly unlikely but…'

Alanda sighed, wishing he'd just say it and then it would be out in the open, out from under the rocks in all their brains where it had been lurking. Perhaps then they could stop worrying about it.

Jake paused for such a long time that Alanda felt like shouting, *just get on with it*, like she did for TV talent shows where the presenter took forever to announce the name of the winner.

When he finally said it, Alanda could smell his sweet biscuity breath, belying the awful words; words that she had not even been able to properly articulate, not even when the police had asked her about Liam's mental state at the time he left.

'We all know how depressed he's been,' Jake blurted. 'Losing Uncle Rich was like the worst thing that could happen, unless it had been one of us who got killed. And then not even being able to talk to Granny about it…'

'He could have talked to *us*!' sobbed Heather.

'Shhh, sweetie, let him finish,' Alanda soothed, pulling Heather even more tightly towards her. Although she didn't want him to finish.

'What if – what if – he went away and then just felt so depressed that he did something? I mean, of course he'd never have intentionally gone through with it, but what if he had some kind of complete breakdown, started to… you know, and then it was too late by the time he realised and he couldn't stop? And nobody has found him yet, or nobody found him in time?'

Jake looked wildly at them all, as if willing them to disagree, to say it was a ridiculous thought.

But none of them could.

CHAPTER ELEVEN

Katya

'Hey! How's the mountains looking, babe?'

Nicole's hand loomed into the laptop screen in a beige blur, obscuring her face as she fiddled with the volume at her end.

'It's dark outside. But they were fine earlier. So—'

Katya needed to get in first before Nicole launched into one of her lengthy stories about the kids, or the plot of the last season of *Homeland*, or her new candle-making venture, and it would be difficult to get a word in edgeways.

'—Uncle Otto died yesterday. Heart attack,' she blurted, pressing her lips together to stop them wobbling. She'd known it would happen sooner or later and, frankly, it was a miracle he'd survived even a couple of weeks after the sepsis ravaged his poor old body.

'Oh no! Oh sweetie, I'm so sorry. Are you OK?'

The hand vanished and Katya saw Nicole's face, tight with concern and distress for her. One of her kids – Laurie? Or was it Tom? – ran behind her, yelling and brandishing something that was probably a weapon. 'Laurie! Shh. Mummy's on FaceTime. Say "hi Katya"!'

'Hi Katya,' came a faint obedient echo before the roaring recommenced.

'Hold on, I'll just shut the door.'

Nicole vanished then returned, after a brief muffled conversation in the background.

It still sometimes felt inconceivable that Nicole, Katya's oldest and wildest friend, had two boys who she was managing to parent with admirable efficiency. This was the woman who used to go on four-day benders – not all that long ago either.

'That's better,' she said. 'I bribed the little buggers with a game on my iPhone. So, how are you doing?'

Katya took a swig of the wine she'd poured before logging on for their weekly FaceTime chat. 'I'm all right… I think. Bit more upset than I'd thought I would be, to be honest. Glad for him, that it was quick. I don't know why I feel so upset though. I mean, he was old and ill and he's been struggling ever since Auntie Monique popped her clogs. It's just… weird. I've known him all my life and now he's gone. He was the last family member I was in touch with so that's it now. I officially don't have any blood relatives.'

Katya said it with a laugh in an attempt not to sound too self-pitying, but kind of snorted at the same time and she realised she was crying at the same time Nicole did.

'Oh my God, Kat, darling, you poor thing. I so wish I was there to give you a hug. You've got me and Phil and the boys. We'll be your family!'

Her kindness made Katya cry harder. 'Sorry. Let me just get some kitchen roll.'

She walked away from the screen into Otto's kitchen, the old-fashioned dark-brown units and flowery yellow lino floor as familiar to her as the kitchen in her flat at home. It still smelled of him – a scent of camphor and pipe tobacco that she knew she would really miss. She blew her nose on a piece of kitchen roll that looked as if it had been manufactured in the 1970s to match the décor, printed with elaborate flowers and patterns, and returned to the laptop.

'Honestly, I'll be fine. It's just a bit of a shock because he seemed to be getting better.'

'Well, the good news I guess is that you can come home now, right? We've got Elaine and Marisa's wedding coming up, and

Jonas's fortieth. I was worried you were going to miss them but at least you won't now.'

'I'm not sure,' Katya said, thickly. 'I've still got so much to do here. I'm – I was – his next of kin, so I'll have to organise the funeral, organise selling this place. It could take weeks.'

'*Weeks?* Oh no. You have to do all that on your own? I wish it wasn't term-time, I'd come out and help you if I could.'

'That's really sweet of you.'

'I hate to think of you out there all on your own. To be honest, I was hoping you'd have earmarked a hot French doctor for yourself by now. Maybe it'll have to be a hot French undertaker instead… Too soon?'

She fluttered her eyelashes and Katya did manage a laugh, although the thought of organising Otto's funeral made her heart sink. He hadn't even left any instructions as to what he wanted, beyond a brief mention of which church the funeral should be held at, and a list of people to inform. She had felt too reticent to ask him for more details.

She decided not to worry about it for now. 'Funny you should mention that though, about meeting someone over here…'

'Ooh, what? Who?'

Katya paused. It didn't seem right to say that she had really 'met' Jack, although technically that was correct. And she found him occupying a great deal of her headspace – a welcome relief from death and the prospect of funereal and probate admin.

'Sort of. You probably wouldn't fancy him. But it's someone I've really hit it off with. It's been nice to have a mate over here, someone to talk to.'

'What's his name?'

Katya laughed. 'I don't know.'

'Eh?'

'That's the thing, Nic, it's not a normal situation. I met him because he was – still is – on Otto's ward. He broke his leg skiing but he also lost his memory. *He* doesn't know what his name is either.'

Nicole stared at her so long and so exaggeratedly that she thought the screen had frozen. 'No way,' she said, eventually.

'I know. It's so weird.'

She could almost see the questions falling over themselves to get out of Nicole's mouth, and she held up her hand to pre-empt them.

'I met him about three weeks ago when he appeared on the ward. He was in the bed opposite Otto and although he was mostly asleep for the first couple of days, I was kind of intrigued by him. Everyone was gossiping about him – nobody knew who he was, he couldn't remember anything, he didn't have any phone or ID on him when he had the accident. He doesn't speak French or German. Nobody visited him or reported him missing.'

'How old is he? Where's he from – I mean, does he have an accent?'

Katya gazed up at a cobweb strung from the light fitting, visualising Jack's face. 'It's hard to tell. Older than us. I guess he's probably late forties? Still got all his hair, so maybe he's not that old. People never look their best in hospital anyway, do they? He's got a slight American accent but I couldn't tell you what sort, you know, it's not obviously Brooklyn or Deep South. Could be Canadian maybe? He has amazing eyes... and he's funny too, Nic. He really makes me laugh, and I think, wow, that's quite something, that he can be in that sort of state and still have a sense of humour. I dunno. I mean, he's not amazing-looking or anything, pretty normal really. There's just something so lovely about him. All the nurses love him – he's one of those people in life who you can't help but warm to.'

'Wow,' Nicole said. 'That's... bizarre.'

'Tell me about it. You'd think by now someone would have reported him missing. He must have come on holiday on his own, unless his wife or whoever was actually trying to get shot of him... which seems unlikely. He's so nice.'

'But what do you talk about, if he really can't remember anything? And is it really nothing? He has no idea about his past at *all*?'

'He doesn't seem to,' Katya said. 'It's called retrograde amnesia, or a dissociative fugue – the person functions normally in every respect except remembering who he is, or anything about himself. I googled it.'

'Like Jason Bourne in *The Bourne Identity*?'

'Huh. Yeah, I suppose so. Hadn't thought of that.' She paused. 'Everyone calls him Jack.'

'Why?'

'No idea. I think that's just the name they gave him when he first woke up and couldn't remember his own. The police have been in a few times, and the hospital administrators are on the case with Interpol, trying to get him ID'd, but nothing's come up so far.'

'Gosh.' Nicole took out her vape and sucked enthusiastically on it, momentarily vanishing into a cloud. Katya imagined its sickly-sweet smell, and it made her briefly homesick. 'But wait—'

'I know what you're going to say. You're going to say it's impossible for someone to just be untraceable in this day and age. You're going to say, surely he's on Facebook, and surely someone will have reported him missing…'

Nicole laughed. 'Pretty much.'

'You'd think, right? But apparently not. I don't know how he's going to pay for his hospital stay, not if they don't know who he is. No access to bank accounts or insurance or any of that stuff. And where's he going to go when he gets out? He can hardly stay there indefinitely, waiting for his memory to come back. Poor guy. Can you imagine how he must be feeling?'

'Kat…' said Nicole warningly. 'You're not thinking about…?'

She hadn't discussed it with Jack but Katya couldn't stop thinking about it. The hospital bills he'd be running up must be colossal – unless perhaps they had some kind of a fund to cover the John Does of this world. But more pertinently, where did a man go, with no identity and no money? A hotel wouldn't take him without means of payment. Would he be shipped off to some grim hostel for the homeless in Paris or Zurich? He'd have to go *somewhere* once he was well enough.

She sighed. 'Look. I'm not going to offer to pay for anything for him, obviously. I don't have a bean until Uncle Otto's apartment sells, anyway – assuming I decide to sell and not keep it. This is not like one of those internet dating scams, where someone tells you they're the love of your life and by the way please could you lend them sixty grand so their kid can have an operation… But it did cross my mind that—'

'No!' spluttered Nicole. 'I knew it. You're going to invite him to stay with you when he gets out.'

'Why not? He was really good to Otto, and kind to me. Why shouldn't I return the favour?'

'It's too… risky. Surely you can see that? You've only known him a couple of weeks. He seems nice, I get that, but even if he is, he might have some kind of brain damage that makes him volatile! Or… or… I dunno, what if he's grooming you?'

Katya laughed. 'He can barely groom himself. The bloke's bedridden. And no, Otto only died yesterday so it wouldn't have occurred to him that it was ever an option to stay with me. I admit, I'd been thinking of discussing it with Otto, that I could maybe look after both of them when they got out, but it was just a thought. It's not like this is going to be some big romance, Nic, honestly. We just chat, like friends. We get on, I like him, and it's nice for both of us to have the company. I'd like to help him if I can.'

'What if he has some sort of a relapse and you end up being his *carer*?'

'Nic, stop. I'm not saying I'm definitely going to invite him. I'll carry on visiting him for now, and then we'll see where we are. His memory could come back at any minute.'

'What will Danny say?'

Katya looked out of the window, where the black hulks of mountains crouched underneath the star-patterned sky. 'Danny and I aren't in touch at the moment,' she said. 'We split up, remember?'

Perhaps it was just that the news of Otto's death was starting to properly sink in, but suddenly she felt a rush of emotion so strong that, for a moment, she couldn't breathe.

CHAPTER TWELVE

Katya

May

Katya had never spoken to a funeral director before. She'd seen them, when she was a kid, carrying her mother's coffin into the church, and she sort of assumed from that experience that they were all men who always wore top hats and black suits. Funny how that image had persisted into her thirties.

To her shame, when she pushed open the door of Fromentin Pompes Funebrès, a week after Otto's death, she thought that the attractive young red-haired woman at the desk was the secretary.

'*Bonjour. Je m'appelle Katya DeLorenzo. J'ai un rendezvous avec Monsieur Fromentin.*'

The woman stood up and smiled. '*C'est moi. Je suis Isabelle Fromentin. Appellez-moi Isabelle.*'

She held out her hand and shook Katya's. 'Would you prefer English or French?' she continued, in perfectly accented English. 'I saw from your email that you are British and visiting here. I am so sorry for the loss of your uncle.'

'Thank you… I don't mind,' Katya said, still completely flustered at her mistake. The woman's email signature had been *I. Fromentin* without specifying a gender, and Katya felt it was awful of her to have assumed Isabelle was a bloke.

'You don't look like a funeral director,' she blurted and Isabelle laughed.

'I hear this a lot. But it is an easy mistake. The company has been in my family for years – my father retired eight years ago and I have been running it since. Please, sit. Would you like some coffee?'

'Thank you,' Katya said, watching her walk across to a little kitchen area, slim and neat in a tight pencil skirt and the sort of pointy high heels that made her toes curl with anticipated pain.

As Isabelle fiddled around with filters, deftly slotting one into the holder and filling it with grounds, then pouring water into the reservoir, Katya wondered if she had already attended to Otto, pulling him out of a long drawer and carefully washing his wrinkled, emaciated body with those same delicate fingers. He would have appreciated that. Although never lecherous, Uncle Otto had always had a great appreciation for an attractive woman. She imagined Isabelle dressing him, in whatever it was that dead people wore in their coffins…

'What will he wear? Otto, I mean.'

Katya felt a dizzying sensation that she seemed to have mislaid her sense of propriety – on reflection, she thought, this was probably not the first question she ought to have asked. But Isabelle took it in her stride.

'It is up to you, as next of kin. If you want him to be cremated in a particular suit or outfit, you can bring it in.'

Katya shook her head, tears threatening. He wouldn't care, anyway. Otto hadn't been a religious man, although he wanted his funeral to be in the little church that he had occasionally allowed Auntie Monique to drag him along to. *Hedging his bets*, he had told Katya in hospital – beckoning her close to whisper the words in her ear – 'If there is a chance for me to be with Monique again I don't want to miss it. It would be awful if she was waiting for me and I never arrived because I hadn't followed correct procedure.'

He was joking – but not entirely. Fair enough, Katya thought.

'You have the death certificate from the doctor?' Isabelle asked, putting a cup and saucer in front of her, in the same tone she had just said, 'Milk and sugar?'

Katya pulled the envelope from her handbag and passed it across.

'I'm sorry,' she said, faintly, 'I don't actually know what a funeral director does, other than, you know, preparing the body. Even though he was really old and really ill, I thought he was getting better. I really didn't think I'd have to be doing… this.'

Isabelle smiled at her so sympathetically that she got a huge lump in her throat. 'It's OK,' she said. 'It is not something usual, or pleasant. I will explain.'

She settled herself into her big leather swivel chair, as if she was about to tell Katya a story with a far happier ending, and proceeded to talk her through the process and all the options.

Within forty-five minutes, everything was sorted. Katya had selected a coffin, they had booked the church, thrashed out a rough order of service, chosen a couple of poems and agreed that the vicar could do the eulogy. Katya felt a little guilty that she wasn't offering to deliver it, but she felt exhausted and too emotional. Having to attend the funeral of her last surviving relative with no friends there for moral support was bad enough.

She had a handwritten list of Otto's friends to ring up and break the news to, but she hadn't managed to do it yet, telling herself there was no point until she had details of the funeral to give them.

The thought of Otto painstakingly copying out names and numbers in his shaky, spidery handwriting, knowing that she'd need it one day, probably soon, to be able to contact them… her throat closed up at the mere thought of that list, lying where she had left it on the arm of his ancient saggy sofa. But she needed to get on with it. She hadn't even informed his best friend Karol yet, and Karol visited him in hospital once a week. An image of him sprang to her mind, a tiny, wizened old man swamped by a beige mackintosh. Otto's face had lit up every time he'd arrived on the ward – they had been friends for fifty years.

She would have to tell him, today or tomorrow. It would be awful if she forgot and he tottered onto the ward only to see someone else lying in Otto's bed.

Katya had a sudden pang of wishing that Jack would be well enough to come to the funeral with her, and then dismissed it immediately. Even if he was sufficiently recovered to be allowed out in a wheelchair, she would never in a million years have presumed to ask him unless he offered first. He had only known Otto for a few weeks anyway, and the poor man had enough problems of his own to want to make an awkward, painful taxi trip to mourn a man he'd only exchanged small talk with.

She decided she needed to stop obsessing about Jack. They had grown closer over the last week and she found herself thinking of him more and more. But then, the situation was heightened by both her own loneliness and the awareness that at any moment he could regain his memory and head back to wherever he came from. Then she would never know what might happen between them.

She turned her attention back to Isabelle, grateful for her kind manner and understanding, understated sympathy. She was someone Katya would be friends with if they'd met under different circumstances, she thought, and idly wondered what Isabelle would say if she asked her out for a drink. She'd probably think she was hitting on her, rather than just the truth; that Katya was a lonely Brit far from home, missing the companionship of friends her own age. She decided to ring Nicole again as soon as she got back, to stop her embarrassing herself in front of either Jack or Isabelle – or possibly both…

Their meeting concluded with the agreement that Katya would ask Karol and his wife Adalene to accompany her in the car which would collect them all half an hour before the service.

Katya went back to Otto's apartment, picked up the handwritten list of his friends' numbers to start ringing, but for a long time, found she couldn't. She sat in his shiny old armchair instead, looking out at the pink-tinged clouds reflected on the glassy surface of the lake, the taste of funereal coffee on her tongue and a deep heaviness in her heart. Otto would never look out at this view again. She had never felt so alone.

Eventually she sighed and dialled the number at the top of the list. 'Hello, Karol, it's Katya. I'm afraid I have some really bad news…'

CHAPTER THIRTEEN

Alanda

As they waited on the pavement to be buzzed into the bridal shop, Heather was talking manically, in a way that anyone listening would probably assume to be excitement.

Alanda, however, knew that it was more akin to desperation, and her heart expanded painfully. She so didn't want to spoil anything for her daughter, who had been planning this wedding for months, but, dear God, the sheer effort it was costing her to keep the corners of her mouth turned upwards… To sound engaged and encouraging felt like an overwhelmingly mammoth undertaking, when the truth was looking increasingly bleak – either the wedding would have to be postponed, or it would have to go ahead without the father of the bride.

Once we get inside, she thought, *it'll be easier. Maybe.*

'Nobody's answering.' Heather broke off from a monologue about the optimal heel height of a bridal shoe and peered inside, pressing her face to the window, the sides of her palms leaving faint smudges on the glass. 'Did we get the wrong time? Ring again!'

Alanda pressed the doorbell a second time, noticing the typo on the sign attached to the wall by the door. 'Bepoke Designs'. She tutted. 'There's even a mistake on the door sign. *Bepoke* Designs? That's a shocking mistake.'

'Oh Mum, as if it matters. Stop going on about it!'

'It absolutely matters,' said Alanda. What sort of impression did it give of the shop's owners if they couldn't be bothered to spellcheck their promotional material? She had already pointed out to an indifferent Heather that the text on the shop's website was positively littered with errors. She'd be mortified if her own shop had a spelling mistake anywhere, ever.

'Please don't say anything to the owner, Mum,' had been Heather's only response, in the same tone that she used to say 'Mu-um! Oh my God, you are SO embarrassing!' when she was much younger, and Alanda had told off a youth for cycling on the pavement, or read out an interesting sign about an historical site in an apparently over-loud voice.

'I love that dress in the window. Do you think it's nicer than mine? Is it too late to change my mind?'

'Heather! You've paid for it, of course it's too late.'

'Oh, chill out, Mum, I was joking! I love my dress.'

Heather hugged her quickly, then hastily wiped at the smears on the window, making them worse. 'Here she comes!'

The woman approaching on the other side of the glass door was youngish, early thirties perhaps, short, with long glossy dark hair but unfortunately squashed-looking features, as if something heavy had compressed her.

'Hi Heather. And you must be the mother of the beautiful bride. Sorry for the delay, I was in the little girls' room.'

This was one of Liam's least favourite euphemisms. Alanda shook the woman's proffered hand, unable to help imagining the discreet shudder that would cross his face, if he were there. *Don't think about him, not now. This is Heather's day. Don't spoil it.*

'Yes, hi!' Heather was beaming with anticipation as the woman unlocked the door and ushered them inside the cool, carpeted, lavender-scented shop. It was so good to see her smile, Alanda thought.

'Mum, this is Gaynor. Gaynor – Alanda.'

'Lovely to meet you,' Gaynor said, addressing Alanda with a friendly squint. 'Do you have your mother-of-the-bride outfit yet?'

'I think I'll let you both focus on getting Heather's dress just right first,' Alanda said, glancing dubiously at the rack of short taffeta dresses for ladies of a certain age, in unlikely hues of lobster pink and bright turquoise. How could she begin to contemplate what outfit to wear, when she didn't even know if Liam was dead or alive?

The 'not thinking about him' strategy clearly hadn't worked, she thought.

'Where's mine, is it here?'

Heather rushed straight over to the rails to separate the padded satin hangers and forensically examine each dress. Alanda had only seen photos of it so far – the sort of big, pouffy affair favoured by Disney princesses – as Heather had chosen it on a previous visit with her bridesmaid, her best friend Phoebe. Alanda had been invited too but had been in bed with a migraine that day. The dress had been too tight and Heather had wanted some sheer short sleeves added to it, 'to hide my bingo wings'.

Alanda wondered if, had she been present, she might have prevented Heather making a mistake? She was a big-boned girl, and Alanda wasn't sure that a full, low-cut dress would do her daughter any favours. She hoped she was wrong, though, seeing how thrilled Heather was to try it on again.

Since Liam's disappearance, poor Heather's moods had vacillated wildly between grief, despair, anger, excitement, hope and today's maniacal excitement. Alanda knew her daughter well enough to know that she had decided to temporarily sweep her father's disappearance under a metaphorical carpet.

Alanda thought back to her and Liam's wedding in 1992. She had worn a straight, beaded sleeveless shift in pale gold with matching headband, more like 1920s flapper girl than Cinderella at the ball. Liam had said she just needed a cigarette in a long gold holder to complete the outfit when her father walked her up the aisle, and they had laughed at the notion of a bride smoking a fag on the way to the altar. They'd both smoked back then, although gave up as soon as Alanda found herself pregnant with the twins.

If Liam did not come home in the next month, who would walk Heather up the aisle? It would have to be Jake, but it would be so bittersweet. Alanda looked over at her youngest, exclaiming with delight as Gaynor produced her dress from a separate rack at the back of the store, vanishing completely behind a vast balloon of net and tulle as she brought it over.

It would break Heather's heart not to have her dad there to see her get married.

CHAPTER FOURTEEN

'Is Liam at work, dear?' Violet asked, knotting her fingers together in her lap, twisting and weaving them in the way she had started to do when she moved into the home last year, and now did constantly. It always made Alanda want to put out her own hand to gently still them, but she knew from experience it made no difference. When she did, Violet would only pull hers out from underneath and slap her wrist away, before resuming the knotting.

'Yes,' Alanda answered, with a pang of guilt at the fib, but knowing it was easier than even beginning to try and explain the truth. Violet obviously did not remember that Liam hadn't been to visit her for almost a month now.

'How are you, Vi?' she asked, tucking the crocheted blanket around her mother-in-law's lap before it slipped off with the constant movement of the old lady's hands.

Violet rolled her eyes. 'Awful. It's horrible in here. Nobody speaks to me. The nurses hit me all the time.'

Alanda caught the stricken glance of the young carer passing behind Vi's armchair and shot him an apologetic smile.

Tayo was the most gorgeous, gentle soul Alanda had ever seen, who always kept a special eye out for Violet. On more than one occasion, Alanda had thought that if she ever had to end up in a home – God forbid – she wouldn't mind it so much if Tayo was put in charge of feeding her soup. She'd just gaze into his limpid brown eyes and nothing else would matter…

Then she felt guilty for having inappropriate thoughts about a man who was the same sort of age as her kids.

Everything made her feel guilty at the moment, even things which oughtn't. Like Liam being missing. Like trying to put a brave face on every new day without news of him.

'Oh Vi, really? Are you sure? Tayo brought you in some chocolate muffins last time I was here, just because he knows you like them so much!'

'That's because he felt bad about it. He's the worst of them all,' Violet said with a disdainful sniff.

Alanda felt a second's worth of doubt – could it be true? Even if just one carer, once, had given Violet a sly slap, it wasn't something to be glossed over and unreported, not taken seriously because she had Alzheimer's and nobody could separate a single cable of truth from the complicated skein of fantasies inside Vi's poor old head.

Then she felt guilty all over again. It was so tedious, feeling like this – when would it ever stop? Not till Liam came back, she suspected.

The manager, Jennie, walked up to them and perched on the footstool in front of Violet's wingback armchair.

'Hi, you two, how are we both today?'

Vi was staring at the TV, so Alanda made an anguished face at Jennie in reply. She really liked Jennie – she was the reason she and Liam had picked this particular care home for his mother a year ago when her dementia became too unmanageable for her to stay alone in her house any longer. Liam had been in tears looking around that first time, and Jennie had been the perfect combination of understanding, sympathetic and businesslike so as not to make Liam feel even more embarrassed than he already did. Alanda had felt like crying too – all those shells of people, slumped motionless around a blaring TV, nobody speaking, heads drooped and hands useless in laps, the lives they'd had all but forgotten; lives as lovers, parents, singers, teachers… Each resident's door had a small noticeboard next to it containing information about the occupant in their younger days, and Alanda always found the little descriptions of the residents' lost primes utterly heartbreaking.

Old age has nothing to recommend it, Violet used to say, back before she began to lose her mind. Wasn't that just the truth, thought Alanda.

'Violet says that people are hitting her,' she told Jennie reluctantly, trying to keep her voice upbeat.

Jennie took Violet's gnarled hand in her own, and Alanda noticed that Violet didn't bat it away.

'I was going to ring you today and tell you—' she began, and Alanda's heart plummeted. Tears sprang into her eyes. Liam would be devastated if Violet was being mistreated in any way.

'No, no, please don't be concerned, it's nothing too bad.'

Jennie smiled at Alanda. She had amazing eyes, huge and green, in an enviably unlined face. Her cheekbones were emphasised by a neat tight ponytail, the whole effect making her age impossible to guess. She could be anything between thirty-five and fifty, thought Alanda, although surely to have enough experience to manage this large residential home so well, it was more likely to be the top end of the age range.

'It *is*,' protested Violet, snapping to attention. 'I told you,' she added sulkily to Alanda.

'There was a small altercation between Vi and Doreen this morning in the games lounge,' Jennie continued. 'It seems that Doreen had picked up a jigsaw that Vi decided she wanted, and a tussle ensued. Tayo happened to pass by at the moment when Doreen gave Vi a little slap around the head, but you weren't hurt, were you, lovely?'

Jennie addressed Violet, who immediately disagreed. 'I *was* hurt! She hurt my hair.'

'It's all forgiven and forgotten now. Doreen's apologised, but we wrote it down in our incident book and had a phone call booked in to tell you.'

'Poor you, Vi, that must have been unpleasant.'

Alanda squeezed the old lady's thin shoulder, sagging with relief that this was all it had been. She felt wrung out with emotion.

'I'm going to get some water,' she said abruptly.

Jennie followed her out to the water cooler in the corridor. 'You OK? Tell me to get lost, but if you ever want a chat over a cup of tea and a slightly bendy Rich Tea biscuit, my office door is always open.'

The kindness almost unravelled Alanda. Jennie obviously knew the situation with Liam – everybody in Salisbury did, after *The Journal* ran the appeal to find him about two weeks back. She hated the range of glances she now attracted whenever she went anywhere locally, from sympathy to pity and, often, suspicion. *Bet he just had enough and left her*, she imagined the whispers behind her back. Unless that was her own paranoia…

When people offered a listening ear, Alanda usually gave them the brush-off, but something about Jennie gave her a sudden urge to throw herself into the woman's arms and howl. Instead, she busied herself by filling a plastic cup, the cooler gurgling loudly as it disgorged the water.

'That's so kind of you,' she said. 'Liam would be beside himself that his mum is saying all this stuff about people hitting her.'

'Of course,' Jennie replied briskly, 'who wouldn't? But I am a hundred per cent certain that she's only referring to the handbags at dawn with Doreen this morning. None of the staff would ever lift a finger to her, you know that, don't you?'

'Yes of course!' Alanda failed to prevent her voice going up an octave. 'Of course.'

'You have enough on your plate at the moment; you don't need to be worrying about Violet as well.' Jennie hesitated. 'Is there any news of Liam?'

Alanda bit her lip and took a swig of water so cold that she felt it travel the entire length of her oesophagus. She shook her head.

'No. It's so hard to believe that in this day and age someone could just vanish like this.'

'Do you want to talk about it?'

'I'd better get back to Vi.'

'Vi's fine, look.' Jennie gestured towards the day room, where Tayo had sat down next to Violet and was reading something to her out of a magazine. She loved being read to, even when she couldn't follow the content.

'OK. Just a couple of minutes. Thanks.' Alanda found she really did want to talk, to someone who wasn't in the police or a close friend, or a member of her own family, all three categories coming under the heading 'Already Dangerously Overburdened'.

She followed Jennie along the corridor to her office door, where Jennie punched in a code and gestured to her to sit down. 'Coffee?'

Alanda shook her head, mortified to realise that tears were already beginning to pour down her cheeks. Jennie mutely handed her a box of tissues.

'I had to go to a wedding dress fitting yesterday with Heather, my youngest. The wedding's in six weeks' time and she probably won't have her dad back to walk her down the aisle, but she's totally in denial. She keeps saying she knows she will, that he wouldn't miss it for anything, that he'll be back and it's some kind of midlife crisis – but I know something terrible's happened. Liam loves us! He adores Heather; adores all of us. He would never, ever be so cruel that he would take off and not be in touch. No way. It's obvious something is badly wrong.'

'But if – God forbid – he was dead, you would know. No news is good news, surely? And as you say, he would never just up sticks and not keep in contact.'

Alanda couldn't look at the sympathy in Jennie's eyes because she knew it would just make her sob even more. She blew her nose and tried to slow her voice.

'He could be lost somewhere. Kidnapped – maybe someone mistook him for someone else. Had an accident or a nervous breakdown. Be in a coma. There are millions of possibilities.'

'And I'm sure all of them have kept you awake at night,' said Jennie. 'You poor thing. It's appallingly stressful.'

'Accidents do happen on that walk. I mean, it's not unheard of. I looked it up.' Alanda glanced at Jennie to see if she knew what she was talking about. It had been in the newspaper articles.

'The Camino de Santiago,' Jennie confirmed. 'My dad did it in the '60s. Yes, there can be bad storms in the Pyrenees, I've heard that too.'

Alanda liked that Jennie wasn't sugar-coating the possibilities. After all, anything was better than the two worst options: Liam was dead, or Liam had voluntarily left her for a new life somewhere else.

'You get these stamps in a booklet, a sort of passport, on the way, and they make a note of your name at each stop, but nobody has any record of Liam having stopped anywhere on the route.'

'Could he have gone somewhere else instead?' Jennie perched on the edge of the desk. 'I mean, tell me to mind my own business if you like, and I'm sure you've gone over this with the police…'

'No, it's OK. Yes, they have asked, and I told them it was highly unlikely. Liam is not a man known for spontaneity. If he said he was going to walk the Camino de Santiago, that's what he'd do. He messaged us from Madrid airport to say he'd arrived safely, but his phone's been switched off since then…Unless he did that on purpose,' said Alanda, swallowing hard to dislodge the huge lump in her throat. 'To throw us off the scent, before he headed off to South America to start a new life with the secret lover he's been shagging for the last decade.'

'He wouldn't do that,' Jennie replied, briefly gripping Alanda's forearm. 'I've only known Liam for a year or so but he's such a kind, genuine man. He would never do something like this deliberately.'

'I don't think so either. Anyway.' Alanda stood up, feeling embarrassed. 'I'm so sorry for crying all over you. I'm sure you have plenty of dramas going on here to deal with, without me boring you with my personal problems as well.'

Jennie smiled. 'Dramas a-plenty,' she agreed. 'Usually involving missing false teeth and bickering over who wants to watch *Countdown* and who wants *Antiques Roadshow*. But please don't apologise, seriously, I'm used to emotional outbursts in here. I'm making light of it but relatives are often to be found in here crying their eyes out.'

Alanda nodded, remembering Liam's face, his jaw set with the effort of not breaking down as he saw the wingback-chair-and-pureed-vegetable fate he was sealing for his mother by incarcerating her – his words – in a strange place amongst dying people. 'That's hard too,' she said. 'So much guilt, even when you know they can't cope at home anymore.'

'Indeed. It's only natural. And I do think that Violet is mostly pretty happy here. We love having her.'

Jennie turned briskly to her computer, tapping the keyboard to wake it up, and scanning a list of emails.

'I'll let you get on, then.' Alanda headed for the door, wondering if Jennie was trying to get rid of her, just another hysterical relative in her office.

But as she reached the door, Jennie said, tentatively, 'Any time you need a chat, please don't hesitate, Alanda, I mean it. You've got my mobile number; call me, even if you're not in here visiting. I know we don't know each other well, but if you need a friend, just call.'

Alanda was taken aback, both touched and slightly mortified. It was true that she had long ago identified Jennie as someone *simpatico*, a like-minded person who could be a friend, but this all felt slightly heavy-handed. She didn't want a friendship built on pity.

'Thank you,' she said, and closed the door quietly behind her.

CHAPTER FIFTEEN

Katya

'I used to really like watching you read to Otto,' Jack said, on Katya's next visit. 'Couldn't hear what you were saying, and I wouldn't have been able to understand if I could, but I found it very soothing. I liked the shapes your lips made.'

He laughed, embarrassed at his frankness. Katya felt flattered – and, she realised, somewhat to her own surprise, slightly aroused. Jack's hair was tousled and he needed a shave, but it made him look stubbly and rugged, like a cowboy who'd lost his horse.

A cowboy in pyjamas with one leg hoisted in the air...

'Would you like me to read to *you*?'

'No, chatting's fine, thank you for the offer, though.'

Katya suspected he probably would have really liked it if she had whipped out a book and begun to read, but was too shy to impose on her that way.

She had visited Jack every other day since Otto died, and it was getting a tiny bit easier each time not to picture her lovely uncle in the bed opposite, greeting her with a smile and a tired wave of his brittle, bruised wrist every time she entered the ward. She supposed it was a bit like the old adage of getting straight back on the horse when you fell off. At least by visiting Jack she wouldn't have a phobia of hospitals triggered by Otto's demise.

They had fallen into easy conversation now – easy, albeit one-sided. He asked her loads about her childhood and past, whereas there was no point in her putting questions back. She did try, a few times, but his lack of knowledge seemed to distress him.

'Do you know, I can smell your perfume even with my eyes closed, whenever you come in here?'

He quite often blurted out things like this, slightly unfiltered. Katya wondered if it was his personality, or because of his brain injury.

'Oh dear, is it too strong?' Perhaps it was overpowering everyone, she thought. She blushed at the thought.

'No, no, it's gorgeous. It's sort of... flowery and light. Weirdly, it reminds me of bright colours – although that's probably just because you wear bright clothes.'

'Maybe your brain is overcompensating for the memory loss, by making your senses more heightened?' she suggested.

He shrugged. 'Who knows?'

'So how have you been?' Katya asked. 'Sorry, that's a dull question, isn't it?'

They seemed to spend an inordinate amount of time apologising to one another, she thought, wondering why. She was not by nature a particularly self-effacing person, and Jack didn't seem to be, either.

'I'm so bored,' he replied, rolling his eyes. 'The nurses found me a couple of English paperbacks – one romance that I couldn't get into at all, and one by Dick Francis about horse racing that was really hard going. Celine's going to lend me an old tablet of her son's, with a few movies downloaded onto it – apparently I'll be able to put subtitles on. But my attention span's still pretty short. It's difficult to concentrate on anything. I feel like I'm about a hundred.'

Katya smiled at him. 'You don't look it.'

'What age *do* I look?'

She bit her lip. 'Um... gosh, I've never been very good at guessing people's ages. Maybe late forties?'

'Yeah, that sounds like it could be right. I wish there was some way to tell.'

'Maybe they could tell by your teeth, like they do with horses?'

He laughed. 'Or cut my leg off and count the rings. How old are you, if you don't mind me asking?'

'I don't mind. I'm thirty-two.'

'Are you? You look so young! I thought you were about twenty-five.'

'I knew I liked you,' she joked.

They sat in companionable silence for a few minutes, watching the ward life unfold around them. A young nurse opened the curtains around the adjacent bed and hurried silently past bearing a bedpan in her outstretched hands, frowning fixedly at it as if she was almost at the finish line in an egg-and-spoon race. A machine began bleeping next to another bed, then stopped abruptly. In the quiet, Katya was aware of a wheezing sound, like bellows, which seemed very nearby.

'What's that noise?'

Jack looked slightly sheepish. 'It's my squeezy sock,' he said, pulling back the blanket and showing her the inflating plastic cuff around the calf of his horizontal leg, a clear tube running from it. 'Keeps the circulation going, apparently, and stops you getting blood clots. They're called IPC devices. Sexy, hey?'

'Ha. Dead sexy... Oh yes, of course. Otto had those, but I think there was so much other noise going on from the machines around him that I never really noticed them.'

Looking at the plastic tube made Katya suddenly aware of the other tubes snaking out from beneath Jack's blanket, attached to gruesome hanging bags containing unspeakable-looking liquids. Her earlier feeling of arousal was instantly quashed.

'How long will you have to be in traction for?' she asked, feeling sorry for him and simultaneously slightly mortified.

'Another week or so, I think,' he said vaguely. 'Or was it two? I can't remember. I don't even pay that much attention, to be honest. Time is all such a blur at the moment. I don't even know how long I've been in here.'

'You came in around the same time as Otto. Seventh of April. It's the fifth of May now.'

Jack groaned. 'Feels like I've been lying here for months.'

Katya reached across to pat his hand, then thought it would seem too forward and dropped it back by her side. 'Really good news that you'll be out of traction soon, though,' she said.

'I can't wait to get out of bed and move around,' he said. 'But enough about me. How are you doing?'

He looked sympathetic but not, Katya thought, with the cloying, head-to-one-side, simpering kind of concern that she was getting used to since her bereavement. She sighed.

'I'm fine. I knew it was coming. He was ninety-five, he had a really good innings and he's out of pain now... I'm dreading the funeral, though.'

'Poor you. Yes, I'm sure that won't be easy.' He paused. 'I wanted to ask, and should've done before – Otto didn't mind you coming over to talk to me, did he? I'd hate to think he felt short-changed from your visits.'

'Not at all,' Katya said. 'He felt sorry for you and said a few times he was glad that we became friends.'

Jack laughed. 'There is a certain irony to a ninety-five-year-old man who had sepsis, high blood pressure and a broken hip feeling sorry for me.' Then he looked mortified. 'Sorry, Katya, it's probably way too soon to joke about his condition... I'm so sorry.'

Katya laughed too, although there were tears in her eyes. 'No, honestly, it's fine. Like I said, he had a really good innings. And for what it's worth, he said he felt sorry for me too, so you don't need to feel too special. He was worried that I didn't have anybody my own age to talk to over here.'

'Don't you?'

She scrunched up her mouth small so her cheeks puffed into two rueful little circles.

'No, not in France. All my friends are back in London. But we FaceTime, and I keep in touch with them on Facebook too.'

'I've heard of Facebook. One of the nurses told me about it. I wonder if I'm on it? And what's the difference between Facebook and FaceTime?'

'FaceTime is like a video call you do on your phone.'

'Not if you don't have a phone. Or anyone to call.'

Jack was joking, but there was a flash of panic in his eyes.

'Otto had an old pay-as-you-go mobile,' Katya said. 'It's pretty ancient so it wouldn't do FaceTime – that's only on newer smartphones – but it works, and then at least you'd have one?'

'And I could call you!' Jack said, perking up.

'You could,' Katya agreed. 'I'll charge it up and bring it in tomorrow.'

CHAPTER SIXTEEN

Katya walked self-consciously out of Otto's apartment to the shiny black funeral car waiting by the pavement, the hearse parked up in front of it. Her black interview suit was too old and too tight and she hated not wearing anything colourful. It had felt ghoulish, packing the suit to bring with her just in case, but she was glad now that she'd had the foresight. None of her other clothes would have been remotely appropriate. Her breath was coming in short, stressed bursts and she already felt on the verge of tears. What if nobody else showed up? She couldn't bear it. She wished she had asked Nicole to fly over for a day to help her through this – but it was too big an ask.

Karol and his wife Adalene were already sitting in the back of the car, peering expectantly out, both of them dwarfed by the huge stately vehicle. There was a violin case on the parcel shelf – Karol had asked if he could play, which Katya had told him would be a lovely gesture.

The driver, a young, embarrassed-looking boy in an overlarge suit, held the door open for her and she slid in next to the couple, nodding gratefully at them and trying not to look through the windscreen at the coffin in the hearse. Even though she had never met Adalene before, the old woman immediately reached out and squeezed her hand, which choked her up before they had even pulled out into the traffic. She wasn't completely on her own.

They were such kind people. Katya visualised them in their younger days, in the 1960s: drinking cocktails, laughing and chain-smoking in a restaurant with Otto and Monique, never imagining they would one day be this old and tired, moving stiffly, attending funerals with grim regularity.

It was only a short journey to the chapel, under an oppressively grey sky. It was as if the mountains were bowing their heads from grief and respect for one of their own, and the lake seemed unusually still and silent as they drove slowly alongside it.

Isabelle the undertaker was waiting outside the chapel to greet them, her bright auburn hair a welcome beacon of colour amongst all the black clothes. There weren't many people in the little chapel, but more than Katya had feared there might be. The few friends of Otto's she had contacted had obviously spread the word.

She was deeply touched to see so many old people sitting in the pews on their own in dark overcoats, heads bowed. Were they alone because they had nobody else? Husbands and wives all long gone, perhaps funerals now the only social activities. It was so depressing. *I can't let that happen to me*, she thought, with something approaching panic. What if she was destined to be alone for the next fifty years?

She had to have a stern word with herself to try and nip the maudlin thoughts in the bud.

To her consternation, Karol and Adalene did not follow her into the front pew, painstakingly taking their seats across the aisle instead, fussing around with coats and hats and service sheets. Karol's trembling fingers fiddled with the clasps on the violin case and then, clutching the instrument by the neck, he got up again and moved up to the area above the altar, genuflecting as he passed Otto's coffin where the vicar was waiting.

The vicar, who also looked to be in his eighties, gave Karol a nod and Karol tucked the violin under his chin and lifted the bow, pausing dramatically for a moment. Then he began to play.

Katya was astonished at the sound that burst into the silence, soaring, sweeping, filling every corner and puffing out from between the wooden arches of the barrel-vaulted ceiling over their heads.

She had no idea he could play like that. Gone was every trace of his shakiness, and even his rheumy gaze was firm and clear as he looked into the middle distance, lost in his performance.

From that moment, she was gone. She sobbed, silently but uncontrollably, into her tissues until she'd reduced seven of them to tiny wads of compacted misery and she thought she was going to explode with the effort of trying to keep from disgracing herself by howling. Karol had told her the piece he was going to play in advance, but she hadn't heard of it. She didn't know enough about classical music.

As the final notes died out, quivering like dewdrops on grass, there was a bit of commotion from the back of the church as the door creaked open and some muttered conversation ensued. Katya was too busy blowing her nose on a remaining dry scrap of tissue to pay much attention, but as Karol sidled back to his pew and the vicar opened his prayer book to begin the service, she registered another sound, a sort of quiet squeak and footsteps from the side of the church, coming closer.

She glanced over her shoulder – and then did a double-take. She could not believe what she was seeing.

Jack was coming down the side aisle towards her in a wheelchair, pushed with difficulty by Sister Celine, who was so tiny that even though Jack was not a big man, it must have been like pushing a car up a hill.

Jack looked as incongruous in the church as a giraffe in a hardware store. He was dressed in a strange selection of evidently borrowed clothes; scrubs, a tweedy jacket and with one brown brogue-type shoe on his good foot – the one in plaster elevated in front of him by a protruding leg-rest. A thick woolly sock completed the picture. He was neatly shaved with his hair combed back, but with the sort of pallor in his cheeks that indicated this expedition was taking its toll. And yet he was smiling at Katya with such warmth and sympathy that she instantly started crying again.

Celine parked him at the far edge of the pew and retreated to sit at the back of the church, not seeing Katya's too-late wave to indicate she should join them too. Katya slid across the slippery wood pew until she was near enough to Jack that their shoulders touched. Too overcome to speak or even smile back at him, all she could do was to reach over and take the hand he was holding out to her.

He was here, for her. This man she hadn't known a month ago, who didn't even know himself, and yet it meant everything.

CHAPTER SEVENTEEN

For Katya, everything changed with Jack after that, like a light being switched on, transforming a dark space into somewhere warm and inviting. Perhaps it was as simple as him not being a bedridden patient, just for the hour of the funeral service. He had come for *her*; he was supporting her for a change, instead of the other way round, and she could tell it meant a lot to him to be able to do it. It must be so emasculating, to be a patient lying passively waiting for crumbs of kindness to be dropped. Let alone one who didn't even know who he was.

He'd gone straight back to hospital after the funeral, declining Katya's offer to join them for tea and cake in the vestry. Sister Celine had to get back to the ward to start her shift, and he gave this as the reason, although it was very clear that he was in pain and exhausted.

'Thank you so much for coming,' Katya said to them both, as Celine manoeuvred the heavy wheelchair in a 180-degree turn towards the door. 'I can't tell you both how much it means to me.'

'We were both very fond of Otto,' Celine said, hugging her. 'As we are of you,' she added, whispering it in Katya's ear. 'One of us, especially.'

She spoke so quietly and quickly that Katya couldn't even be sure she had heard her correctly.

'*Alors*, we must be off,' Celine said, at normal volume. 'Our taxi should be here, and Jack needs to rest now. This is the first time he has been out of the hospital. But now, hopefully, you'll be able to start doing it more. Not going to funerals, of course…

but there is a very nice rose garden in the hospital, did you know? Nice for visitors to sit with patients. I'll give you some driving lessons, Katya.'

She pointed at the wheelchair and winked, and Katya felt a warm glow of pleasure at this tacit approval, this encouragement to be back to visit again soon. She was glad – she still often felt a little self-conscious, visiting Jack, like she was ambulance-chasing or something.

'I'll come and see you tomorrow,' she said to Jack, mentally deciding that she would take Celine some flowers or a bottle of wine, to thank her for bringing him.

'Great,' he replied, holding her gaze. 'Good luck with the rest of the day. Do you have much else to do now? I have an idea that you have to take Otto somewhere else…?'

He looked momentarily stricken, and Katya realised he was referring to her going with Otto's body for it to be cremated. How did he remember that and not his own name? He must have lost people in the past, if he had that particular residual memory. For a brief, hideously guilty moment, she hoped it was a wife that he had lost.

'The vicar is taking care of that,' she said. 'He said it was OK.'

The truth was, she hadn't been able to cope with the idea of attending Otto's cremation immediately after the funeral. Undertaker Isabelle had been lovely about it and reassured her that it absolutely wasn't necessary or expected, but she still felt bad. At least the vicar would be there, so Otto wouldn't be alone…

'All I have to do now is to have a cup of coffee and a biscuit, then I'm going to go back to Otto's to put my feet up.'

'Good idea,' said Jack. 'I've half-joined you already.' He gestured at his raised leg and grinned. 'I'll text you later.' He pulled the small, elderly Nokia from his jacket pocket and waved it at her. Katya had given it him on her last visit, navigating to the Contacts menu to show him how she had added her name – her full name, for some reason – and number. 'Weirdly, I do remember how they work,' he'd said, and then, 'Thank you, Katya DeLorenzo. Cool name.'

He hadn't contacted her on it yet, though, and she had been too busy with the funeral arrangements to contact him. She watched as Celine wheeled him back off down the aisle, and then joined the rest of the congregation in the vestry, feeling as exhausted as Jack had looked. It must be the wild swing of different emotions she'd gone through in the past hour, she decided.

She arrived back in the apartment an hour later, even more exhausted after making polite conversation with every single one of Otto's aged but delightful friends. Ripping off the uncomfortable heels and suit the minute she was through the door, she put on grey sweatpants and her *Oi-Oi Oyster* sweatshirt, sat down in Otto's reclining armchair and pressed the lever until she was almost horizontal. Then she pulled out her phone, ostensibly to FaceTime Nicole, who she'd promised to ring to let her know how the funeral had gone.

There was a text on the screen: *Hello Katya ;)* Even though she knew who it was from, she got a faint shock when the name of the author showed as UNCLE OTTO.

Hello Jack, she texted back, smiling from ear to ear. *How are you feeling?*

Knackered! And my leg hurts.

Oh dear. I'm sorry.

No it's fine. I was so happy to be up and OUT. This hospital has an outside! Did you know?

She laughed. *I did know that, actually. Did your taxi take you past the lake? It's so pretty.*

Yes. Perhaps you can take me to see it more closely next time I'm allowed out?

I would love to do that X

She momentarily panicked about the X, especially as there was a pause of a few minutes before the next text arrived. Too much? Too soon? Then –

Can't wait! And in the meantime, I look forward to seeing you tomorrow – as long as it's not an imposition of course… Xx

Two kisses! Phew.

See you tomorrow, Jack. It's not at all an imposition. And thank you again for coming today, it means so much to me. Sleep well Xx

Then she edited the words UNCLE OTTO in her phone's directory to read JACK instead. It felt symbolic, somehow, although she was too tired to think about how.

CHAPTER EIGHTEEN

Alanda

Alanda was in a country pub waiting for her children. In an attempt to try to avoid the sob-fests of previous weeks' meetings, she had declared that she would take them all out for Sunday lunch, instead of one of their regular and increasingly emotional family meals at home. She was fed up with cooking joyless roasts, anyway. Nobody seemed to enjoy the food.

She'd not tried this pub before – an intentional choice. She didn't want to risk a place that she and Liam had previously frequented, with or without the kids. It came highly recommended: an old coaching inn in a village deep in the Wiltshire countryside, with a warm grey stone exterior and tasteful tones of khaki and dark green on the walls inside.

They were all late, and Alanda felt a stab of vulnerability as she sat alone at a huge old oak table, with other family groups all around her, chatting and laughing and all of them with a dad. She should have invited someone along as support for her – Sadie would probably have come. Although, she thought, it was hardly fair to expose Sadie or anyone else to the ripe emotions of the kids.

She looked around, at the arty Victorian framed prints of butterflies and flora hanging on the green walls, and the nets of fairy lights strung from the ceiling. Young black-and-white-clad waitresses almost ran back and forth from the kitchens, balancing trays piled with roast dinners, each plate topped precariously with a huge Yorkshire pudding. It all seemed so normal, and suddenly she was glad she'd come.

Jake was first to arrive, clutching a clipboard with a typed list on it. He took his *de facto* role as stand-in head of the family very seriously.

Alanda stood up to hug him and felt a rush of love for her only son as they embraced. He looked horribly tired, but his hair was freshly cut, and he had at least shaved. She wished he had someone at home to look after him, but he had been single since breaking up with his last partner, Carlo, who he'd caught cheating on him with his personal trainer, a few months back. Jake never spoke of it, but Alanda knew it had deeply hurt him – the pair had lived together for six years. Now Jake had no boyfriend and no job either, having been made redundant from his marketing post at the start of the year. Alanda feared so much for him.

'Hi Mum,' he said, releasing himself from her over-zealous embrace. 'This place is lovely! Good call. Am I first? I thought I was going to be late.'

'You *are* late,' said Alanda, scrutinising him with a smile. 'It's just that the girls are even later.'

On closer inspection and despite initial appearances, Jake looked even worse than he had last week, the huge shadows under his eyes having turned from brown to almost black, as if he'd applied Halloween make-up.

'Still not sleeping, sweetheart?' she enquired.

He completely ignored her and changed the subject. 'Is Kevin coming?'

Jake wasn't all that keen on Heather's fiancé. He thought Kevin was at best a bit of a wet blanket and at worst, homophobic. Alanda privately agreed with the wet blanket bit, but not the homophobia. She suspected that Kevin's reticence around her son was far more likely to be a fear of receiving the sharp edge of Jake's tongue than disapproval of his lifestyle.

'Yes, as far as I know. I included him in the booking, so I assume so. Be nice. He's almost literally part of the family.'

Jake rolled his eyes and sat down next to his mother. 'Of course I will. You know I'm happy with him as long as Heather is. Have you ordered any wine yet?' He picked up the menu and scanned it with a long finger. 'Shall we get a bottle of Merlot?'

'Everyone's driving, except Heather, who's still on her diet.'

'One bottle between five of us – no, four, if Heather doesn't crack? No harm in that.'

Alanda was about to ask how his job hunt was going, but the door opened again and the other three came in together, Becky first, followed by Heather, and Kevin, who looked as if he was entering the lions' den. There was a flurry of greetings, coat-removing and seat-taking. Becky had had her hair cut and dyed even whiter blonde, and Alanda commented how good it looked.

'Doesn't it?' agreed Becky, rubbing the short hairs at the nape of her neck.

Alanda smiled, wondering where she got her self-confidence from. It wasn't from her; that was for sure. Liam was more confident than she was, but still possessed nowhere near Becky's industrial quantities of self-belief. She just wished that it could have been shared out a bit between Becky and Heather, who could have done with a far more generous slice of that particular pie.

'Ha ha, Jake's got an actual *clipboard*,' Becky commented. More of a jeer than a comment, Alanda thought despairingly, but Jake didn't take the bait, merely standing up to hug his twin and admire her hair. He did slide the clipboard off the table and prop it on the wall behind his chair, though.

Jake had WhatsApp'd them all beforehand announcing that they would put together a social media campaign which he would spearhead. Alanda was glad to hear it, both because it would give him something concrete to focus on, and because she was secretly worried that neither the police in the UK or Spain seemed to be taking it very seriously at all.

'So, how is everyone doing?' asked Heather, her eyes immediately filling with tears as if this was the question she had been waiting for someone to ask her, so that she could tell them that in fact she wasn't doing well at all…

'Oh darling,' Alanda said, hoping that this wouldn't happen at the wedding. Poor Heather just looked so completely beaten when her face crumpled like that. Alanda automatically hugged her, as she always did, but she wondered if she should try and do something more to stop this happening every time they met up, some or all of them dissolving into tears when they were together? Then she dismissed the thought – after all, she felt the same. She would just have to be strong for them all. And surely it was cathartic, a release that they could all only experience in each other's company.

At least her idea of convening in public seemed to be working – Heather did not completely break down, as she might have done at home, but instead blew her nose and concentrated on reading her menu. Crisis averted.

'Right. Let's order,' Alanda said, releasing Heather, who immediately snuggled into Kevin's side. He looked ridiculously pleased as he put his arm around her. Poor lad, she thought. He was like a dog, desperate for attention and approval. Probably couldn't believe his luck, getting Heather to agree to marry him.

They were each other's first serious relationship – weedy little Kevin apparently hadn't ever had a girlfriend before which was a fact that Alanda had fretted over when the couple first got together, until Liam had reminded her that the same had been true for them too. And Kevin was a decent lad who worshipped Heather. He had a steady job earning good money as a mechanic, and he was kind. What more could you want from your child's life partner? Not bad-looking either, if you overlooked the sticky-out ears.

'Then we can hear your publicity ideas, Jake, while we wait,' Alanda continued. 'Everyone want a glass of red?'

Roasts and drinks ordered – Diet Coke for Heather – Jake picked up the derided clipboard and started reading out the listed items, his voice slightly strained like it used to be when he was a little boy wanting to be taken seriously:

'One, Twitter appeal; two, Facebook post; three, Instagram post; four, call BBC Wiltshire and ask them to broadcast the appeal – which we'll write today, and one of us could record, or offer to go into the studio and be interviewed; five, contact *The Salisbury Journal*, contact all the expat British publications in Spain, especially in the area Dad's in, and get someone to print the appeal. Six – chase the police and see if anyone's actively pursuing the investigation via Interpol. Who wants to do what?'

'I don't think even local radio would have us on to talk about it,' said Heather doubtfully. 'It's not exactly the sort of thing they do, I mean, it's hardly of local interest.'

'Don't be so negative,' Jake chided. 'We can always try. Mum, do you have a decent photo of Dad we can use? That's the first thing we need. But let's make it different to the one you gave the police, not a work one.'

Alanda gulped. The thought of Liam's smile, the special one he reserved for her whenever she took his picture, being broadcast all over the world… it made her feel a bit sick, even though of course it was a means to an end. She took her phone from her jeans pocket and started scrolling through the photo galleries. There were surprisingly few recent pictures of him, partly because they hadn't gone on holiday for ages and partly because, these days, if she bothered to take a photo it was usually a close-up of a beautiful bloom or a sea view at sunset.

'There's this,' she said, showing around a shot of Liam standing on a Welsh mountain from a couple of years back. 'But he's looking a bit windswept.'

'Not that.' Jake dismissed it with a wave. 'There must be a better one. Anyone else got one?'

The girls looked at each other and shook their heads guiltily. Both their phones were full of pouty selfies of themselves and their friends and, in Heather's case, numerous soppy shots of her and Kevin with their heads together, looking loved-up.

'Oh, I like this one,' Alanda said, scrolling back to some pictures taken on a weekend away in Cambridge. 'Will this do?'

In it, Liam was sitting at a table outside a half-timbered pub, a full pint of Guinness in front of him, and a satisfied expression on his face as he contemplated it. She could cope with this one being out there, just about, because it wasn't personal; it wasn't their shared look of intimacy.

She felt a sudden deep stab of missing him, an actual twist of pain under her ribs, so strong that she could imagine the cold steel blade plunging in. She wanted to see that look again; their entire history held in the tender gaze between them. Endless mornings waking up together, endless embraces and condolences and shared hilarity. She swallowed hard.

'That's way better,' said Jake. 'Text it to me?'

'And us, please,' Becky said. 'If you WhatsApp it, then we'll all have it.'

'God,' said Heather, 'imagine if Dad reads the WhatsApp posts and sees his photo, he'll wonder what the hell we're up to.'

Becky stared at her, eyebrows knitted, with a look that managed to be both impatient and tolerant. 'Seriously?'

'Oh yeah. I guess if he reads the group posts and still doesn't get in touch then that's a whole other problem...' Heather tailed off.

'Anyway!' Jake interrupted. 'We need to decide who's going to do what. I've done a draft of the tweet and the Insta post, they can be exactly the same. The Facebook post can be longer. Mum, could you write that? You're good with words. Just make it, like, really emotional, a real tear-jerker...'

Jake sounded so detached, Alanda thought. 'Yes, sweetie,' she said. 'I'm sure I can manage that.'

It was all she could do not to burst into tears then and there.

'Bex,' he continued, 'would you be up for ringing Radio Wiltshire and *The Journal*? I know it's all village fetes and thefts from sheds usually, but they're always looking for juicy stuff to fill the pages with. They ran the police appeal a few weeks back, but there's no reason they wouldn't do another article.'

'This is *Dad* you're talking about,' Becky said, frowning at him. 'Not "juicy stuff".'

Jake sighed. 'You know what I mean. So, will you?'

'I suppose so.'

'Heather, could you google what newspapers Brits in Spain might read?'

'Could do,' she said hesitantly. 'Although it was mostly *The Sun* and *The Express* last time we were in Ronda, remember? Wouldn't Facebook pages be easier? I bet they're all in expat Facebook groups.'

'That's a really good idea, darling,' Alanda said.

Jake nodded approvingly and Kevin beamed, as if the compliment had been directed at him.

'Great. OK, so why don't you join as many Facebook groups for expats in Spain as you can find, particularly around Madrid? Then post the photo and the words. Hashtags too. Hashtag missing person, hashtag Camino de Santiago, et cetera.'

Heather took out her phone and tapped out a few notes. 'On it,' she said.

Their food arrived, great boats of Yorkshire pudding floating in lakes of steaming gravy, with meat and roast potatoes sticking up like islands. Everyone made noises of appreciation, except Heather, who wailed, 'Oh my gosh, there must be a thousand calories in this!' but tucked in with as much enthusiasm as they all did.

By the end of the lunch, they all looked far more relaxed and agreed they felt energised. It was so much better to feel that at least you were being proactive, rather than having to sit back passively waiting for someone else to do something. They concurred with Jake's wording for the Twitter and Instagram posts. Alanda had promised to do the Facebook one when she got home – which Jake would put up from his own account, since he had over a thousand Facebook friends ('But surely you don't *know* them all?' Alanda had enquired, flabbergasted, when Jake had announced this fact). Heather would share it with the Spanish expat groups and any other missing persons resources she could find. Becky would ring around the local press and radio stations and update them as soon as she had any news.

'This *has* to work,' Heather said, as they said their goodbyes in the car park. Alanda didn't know whether it was an expression of confidence that it would, or of desperation that it had to, but since she felt the same either way she merely nodded and kissed her daughter on the cheek.

'Someone will have information,' she agreed. 'Someone will come forward.'

She just hoped it would be soon, because the wedding was only three weeks away and, she thought, her poor heart simply could not take this for much longer.

She drove home in a fug of depression and negativity to find a beautiful potted magnolia on the doorstep, with a note from Sadie attached to the pot: *Hoped you'd be home for a movie and wine afternoon. I'd have called but I wanted to surprise you. Text me when you get back and I'll come over?*

Alanda was touched. She took her mobile out of her pocket to text Sadie back – but was overcome with a miserable exhaustion so strong that all she could do was to dump the plant in the hall and head straight up to her bedroom, where she crawled into bed and pulled the covers over her head. She'd reply to Sadie later.

CHAPTER NINETEEN

Alanda had been keeping away from her shop, as much as she could. It was starting to feel to her as if some sort of a memo had gone around to every Salisbury resident, suggesting it was their mission to 'pop in' and 'see how she was doing' and ask if there was 'any news'. It made her want to scream, even whilst being simultaneously touched by their concern.

Since the social media campaign launch, it had got ten times worse. She had been interviewed on the local news, and her photo had appeared in both local and national newspapers – they had asked for a picture of her and Liam together, as well as the one of him on his own. Now even people who hadn't already known where she worked would be paying for their tea lights or birthday cards and, when she handed over their change, they would look at first puzzled, then a ghoulish light would appear in their eyes.

'Oh, it's *you*.'

The faces would immediately be rearranged into the standard expression of sympathy; head cocked to one side, mournful smile from beneath knitted eyebrows. 'I saw you on the news. You poor thing! It must be torture. Is there any news?'

The Thoughts-and-Prayers brigade, as Becky called them, would often reach across the counter and place a hand over hers, and murmur that they were praying for her and Liam, for him to 'come home soon' – as if he'd gone out for a pint of milk and got lost! Alanda gritted her teeth so hard and so often that she was worried they would be worn to stumps.

It was mostly because her clientele tended to be elderly women with too much time on their hands. After a couple of weeks of wishing she owned the vape shop next door instead, where the customers were far less likely to care about anything apart from whether she had the grapefruit and kiwi juice in a nicotine strength of 0.3, she had asked her Saturday assistant Julie if she would like to work four days a week instead of one. Julie had been delighted.

The kids had been a bit dubious about Alanda being at home so much more, wrongly taking it as a sign that she was giving up on life. They probably imagined her as a Miss Haversham figure sitting alone in the front room gathering dust, Alanda thought, reassuring them that if she had more time off, she could better take care of herself. Swim, meet up with Sadie, check the social media channels, have lots of long baths…

They took a lot of convincing though. Becky in particular had been worried about business long before this – poor old Salisbury had really suffered since the Novichok attack. Half the shops in the town centre were empty and forlorn, junk mail piling up inside the doors, windows dirty; 'To Let' signs were commonplace.

'You can't afford not to be there every day!' Becky fretted. 'Julie's OK but she doesn't engage with the customers like you do. Do you want to lose your business as well as Dad?'

But Alanda shook her head. 'It's fine. Business is down, but I'm not about to go bust. And currently it's the customers engaging with me that's the problem.'

Privately, she reflected on how Becky channelled her emotions. She seemed more worried about the shop than about her father, but Alanda knew this was because the shop was something that was, just about, under their control, whereas they had done all they could to find Liam, and now they were just treading water and feeling helpless.

Becky had always been like that. Where Heather wore her heart on her sleeve, Becky had to have any emotions practically crowbarred out of her.

'Isn't it better to keep busy?' Becky had persisted.

In the end Alanda had to explain that it was really the constant stream of well-wishers in and out of the shop all day that was upsetting her, and then finally they understood.

It was a Saturday morning, a few weeks after the first flurry of publicity. Alanda was blearily dusting the glass display shelves – as she always had to do first thing after a few days of Julie at the helm – standing on the small folding steps, half-hidden by a selection of macrame pot holders suspended from the ceiling, when the bell over the door jangled loudly and a woman sidled in, clutching a newspaper. Alanda climbed down the steps, batting away fronds of the spider plants in the hanging baskets.

'Good morning!' she called, far more cheerfully than she felt after a night of completely broken sleep featuring several nightmares about Liam. He had appeared as, respectively, a headless dragon, one of the zombies in the *Thriller* video and finally, a corpse in a shroud, being lowered into a grave in an open coffin. Alanda had woken up sobbing, 'Why has nobody shut the lid?' It was one of those days when she was glad she had the shop to go to, otherwise she would have become that person her children were worried about, the one who stayed in bed crying all day.

'Can I help you with anything in particular, or are you just browsing?'

The woman approached her. She was in her sixties, perhaps early seventies, but looked older at a glance, with the sort of hair that Alanda's granny used to get 'done' at the hairdressers every week, a rigid shampoo and set. The picture was completed by the shopping trolley she pulled behind her, which narrowly missed sweeping a pair of wooden bookends off a low shelf.

'It's about your husband,' the woman blurted.

Alanda swallowed hard, adrenaline spiking and clearing out all the residual sleepiness. This did not seem like a routine sympathy call.

'Something specific about him?' she asked cautiously. Perhaps the woman had just worded it badly and had merely come to offer the bog-standard 'thoughts and prayers'.

The woman placed the newspaper carefully on the counter. It was a copy of the issue of *The Salisbury Journal* that had run an article on Liam a few weeks back, and it was folded open at that page.

'This is him, isn't it?'

Alanda gazed at the photograph of her husband, smiling out at her in black and white, looking like he didn't have a care in the world. Well, he hadn't had, not back then as they sat outside that pub in Cambridge, drinking creamy Guinness and soaking up the spring sunshine…

'Yes,' she said. 'That's Liam.'

The woman had a strange expression on her face, almost but not quite gleeful, the way that people sometimes did when there was bad news to gossip about; news that didn't personally affect them, of course.

'I didn't know whether to go to the police, or talk to you. My friend from bridge club said that you owned this place, so I thought I'd talk to you.'

Alanda was getting a worryingly unpleasant vibe about all this. 'There is a helpline number on the article,' she said. 'But of course, if you have any information then please do tell me.'

She went to sit behind the counter, suddenly feeling that she wanted something solid between her and this woman, to whom she had taken an intense and immediate dislike.

'I saw him, last month. In Salisbury. In fact, I've seen him quite a lot. He goes to visit my neighbour across the road. A *lot*,' she reiterated, with an almost lascivious glint in her eyes.

Alanda stared at her. 'Ri-ight. Who's your neighbour?'

The woman pursed her lips as Alanda waited. This was the first 'concrete' report of a sighting, but Alanda found she was completely unmoved. As if Liam would have flown to Madrid to throw them all off the scent, just to sneak back to Salisbury to visit this lady's next-door neighbour on the down-low! Preposterous. She felt relief that it was such obvious nonsense.

'She's a divorcee called Melody. I'm sorry to break it to you, love, but he's obviously having an affair and that's why you haven't seen him. He always turns up in disguise, like, a hat or something.'

Alanda's lips twitched. It wasn't funny, of course, but yet – it totally was. It was the way the woman pronounced it 'dee-vorsay'. She had a mental image of Liam skulking on Melody's doorstep in a variety of stick-on moustaches and silly hats.

'I'm not lying!' said the woman hotly, seeing Alanda's suppressed grin.

'I'm sure you aren't,' Alanda replied. 'And he probably does look like Liam, but I'm certain it's not him.'

The woman tapped Liam's photograph in the newspaper. 'It *is* him.'

'Well,' Alanda said, hysteria rising in her gullet. 'I do really appreciate you coming to tell me – any information can be helpful – and I'll pass it on to the police, but I think I'll beg to differ. It can't be Liam.'

'I don't think you're taking this seriously enough.' The woman looked actually cross, and Alanda could not prevent a small snort escaping her throat, which she tried to change into a cough. 'I'm giving you a *lead* here! The least you can do is follow it up.'

Alanda wondered if the woman wanted her to accompany her then and there, round to the house to confront Melody in person. She imagined them barging in to find Liam with his feet up on a reclining leather sofa watching *Coronation Street* in his Y-fronts (he didn't wear Y-fronts, but for the purposes of this flight of fantasy, it seemed to work).

'Oh, hiya love,' he'd say. 'This is Melody. She's a *dee-vorsay*.'

'I will,' she promised, gritting her teeth. It had been a long, long time since she had wanted to laugh as badly as she did at that moment, perhaps not even since her schooldays, because she and

Liam had always laughed whenever they wanted, without ever needing to suppress it.

Liam would have found this hilarious. She imagined him there, hiding behind the racks of birthday cards, shoulders quaking, and it made it even harder to hold it together.

'Well, again, thank you for coming in. I must be getting on,' she said, wondering if the woman was ever going to go.

The woman stared at her again. If it hadn't been so funny, Alanda would have found it faintly terrifying. Suddenly and involuntarily, a proper laugh escaped her. 'Sorry,' she said. 'I think it's the stress.' She laughed again, picturing Liam's face behind the birthday cards. Was she losing the plot?

'You're not right in the head, you,' the woman proclaimed, grabbing the newspaper and stuffing it back into her shopping trolley. 'You try and help someone, and get it thrown back in your face. Well, I'll tell you what, you mad cow; I can see why he left you now. You're one sandwich short of a picnic, you are.'

'Takes one to know one,' Alanda retorted, openly laughing now. She got up and went to hold the door open for the woman. Up to that moment, she had intended to ask for her name and number, so that at least the police had her details on record – to file under 'Nutter' – but now she just wanted her out of the shop as fast as possible. 'Thanks again.'

The woman pushed her way past without another word, her face red with rage.

Still chuckling uncontrollably, Alanda went back behind the counter. She felt so full of this weird hysterical emotion that it was almost uncomfortable, like eating a second helping of pudding when you were already stuffed, but not being able to resist. It really wasn't funny, but she found she couldn't stop. She picked up her phone and called Heather, taking great gulps of air to try and control herself.

'It's Mum, you'll never guess what just happened!'

Heather mistook the heaving breaths for sobs and instantly panicked. 'Oh my God, have they found him? Where is he? Is he *dead*?' Her voice rose and rose until she was almost screeching the word 'dead'.

Alanda immediately regretted calling her. The laughter died in her throat. 'No, no, sweetie, nothing like that. Don't worry, please. It's something funny that happened in the shop just now, that's all. It really made me laugh – even though it probably shouldn't have done.'

'What?'

Suddenly it no longer seemed remotely funny.

'Oh... er... Nothing. You know what, thinking about it, it's not worth mentioning.'

'Mum, you're being weird. What was it?'

Alanda knew then that there was absolutely no chance of Heather finding any of it amusing. In fact, probably the opposite. Heather would take it seriously and be outraged that she hadn't bothered to get the woman's details. She'd probably demand to go round to the woman's neighbour's house and hammer on the door to see if her dad was in there.

'Nothing,' she repeated firmly. 'Tell me what you're up to. Did you finish writing the place names yet?'

Heather spent the next five minutes filling her mother in on her calligraphy exploits – she and Kevin were doing as many of the reception decorations themselves as they could – during which time Alanda's hysterics had well and truly subsided, leaving her feeling drained and exhausted.

When Heather's monologue finally ran out of steam and she hung up, promising to 'pop over later', Alanda locked the shop door and flipped the sign to 'Closed'. Then she went out of the back, into the tiny staff bathroom, sat down on the toilet with her elbows propped on her thighs and her head in her hands and sobbed until her eyes puffed up like bath pillows.

Talking to Heather had reminded her that not only was Liam, in all probability, not sneaking around Salisbury with a divorcee called Melody, it was also looking very unlikely that he would be back in time for the wedding.

Just as she had finally stopped crying, she wondered if Heather had written out a place card for her father, imagining her youngest daughter painstakingly inscribing 'Dad' in curly letters on the small tent of lacy white cardboard, and it set her off again. The desperate hope that would have been contained in each of the letters… and yet, how much worse if she hadn't done one at all?

Either way, it was heartbreaking.

CHAPTER TWENTY

Katya

Next time she visited, Katya tentatively broached the subject of Jack's plans after his discharge, but without indicating what she was hoping might happen. She was too paranoid that she might have misread the situation, that he would furrow his brow and look confused and say, 'You're inviting me to do *what*? But I barely know you! Thanks, but, um, I'll be fine,' and she'd want to die of the awkwardness. Although where else he would go, she had no idea. A local hotel or Airbnb, perhaps, if some kind beneficiary at the hospital offered to front the cash for the bill? It seemed unlikely.

When she arrived at the ward, Jack's bed was empty and, as with Otto last month, the sight of the flat sheets and smooth, blank pillow made Katya's heart stall in her chest. Then she saw him, through the open door of the little visitors' room at the end of the ward. He was watching TV and flipping through a magazine in a desultory fashion. He was still in a hospital robe, but in a proper chair rather than the wheelchair, his cast propped on a coffee table and the empty wheelchair next to him.

'Good afternoon,' she said, shyly sticking her head round the door. 'I thought you'd been discharged for a minute there, when I saw you weren't in bed.'

This was not true. For a moment, she thought he'd died too, and even the recollection of that brief instant felt unbearable.

'Hi Katya!' His face lit up. 'No, still here… they don't know what to do with me, it seems. In the meantime I'm being encouraged to move around as much as I can. My physiotherapist's going to try to get me on crutches in a few days, and he said that once I'm confident on them, they're booting me out.'

This could be her opportunity to find out what he was planning to do next, she thought.

'What about the memory loss? Aren't they concerned about that?'

He shrugged, smiling ruefully. 'Well, they are – they said retrograde amnesia doesn't usually last this long – but there's absolutely nothing anyone can do about it. My brain scans are all clear. I don't have any other symptoms. The consultant said we just have to wait and see. My memory might come back suddenly, or gradually, over the next few months – or the worst-case scenario is that it won't come back at all. Which would be a bit grim. But they think it probably will.'

A bit grim. No kidding, thought Katya.

She took off her denim jacket and threw it over the arm of his wheelchair. 'Hot in here today,' she said, sitting down in an orange vinyl armchair opposite him.

'Woah, you clash with that chair,' he said, grinning. This was true. She was wearing a salmon-pink satin shirt tucked into vintage purple cords.

'Sorry. I'll bring you some sunglasses next time.' She giggled, looking down at herself. 'I'm channelling my inner kids' TV presenter.'

'I like that you wear bright colours,' he said. 'Specially in here. You're a tonic. Have you always done?'

'Um… I've always liked them, but I'm noticing I'm less bothered about matching stuff, the older I get. It's quite liberating. It felt so weird, wearing a black suit at the funeral. I didn't like it at all.'

'It did look strange. Glad you're back being colourful.'

'Thanks,' she said, giving him a thumbs-up and immediately feeling even more like a children's TV presenter. 'So… where will you go, once you're discharged from here? Will you need to stay nearby for physio appointments and so on?'

He closed the magazine, looking pensive, and carefully placed it on the seat of the wheelchair, which was fast becoming a repository of their discarded items.

'They've said I can continue the physio for a few weeks. It's very good of them, seeing as I don't know how, or if, I'm going to be able to pay for any of it. The staff here have been amazing. I mean, unless I turn out to be an EU resident, or to have travel insurance, I'm going to have the most colossal bill waiting when my memory comes back – assuming it does – but they aren't putting me under any pressure to pay anything.'

'How can you, anyway, when nobody knows you're here?'

'Exactly. It's a dilemma. The administrator who's in charge of my case has hinted that I might be able to live in a room on site for a while, in accommodation that's meant for families with sick kids – but obviously it depends on whether they need it for any parents. If not, I might be able to stay in nurses' digs nearby.'

'That's really decent of them, isn't it? Even if it goes on for months?'

Jack's eyes were troubled. 'We just have to assume that someone is looking for me, somewhere, and hope that they find me before I outstay my welcome too much here. Or that my memory comes back. As I said, it's unusual that it hasn't yet.'

'I'm sure your family must be beside themselves with worry,' said Katya.

'If I have one.'

'There'll be someone, I'm sure. There's no way that nobody knows you're missing.'

He frowned and lowered his eyes. 'I've been in here for weeks and weeks. It's looking less likely by the day.' Then he looked into her face. 'But you know what? It's OK. Either way it's OK. If nobody comes forward, it's not like I know what I'm missing. All I can do is just start my life from this point and try to be positive. And if they *do* come forward, then I'll have the pleasure of knowing that there are people out there who love me and have missed me.'

'Good attitude,' Katya said, impressed, whilst simultaneously feeling deeply sorry for him.

She was so relieved to hear that, even if he turned down her offer to stay, he would still be around in Thonon-les-Bains, at least until his memory returned. She felt so... invested. Invested in him, and his recovery – but, she realised, not remotely invested in helping him find out who he was. Perhaps it was because she had subconsciously turned him into a replacement for Otto, and before him, Danny, as someone in her life to care about?

There was something else; something Katya felt quite guilty about. As she had said to Nicole on their last FaceTime chat, she didn't want him to discover his real identity. Not yet, anyway. Well, of course, it would be great for him to know, but Katya was sure that he must have someone who cared for him out there, maybe a wife or girlfriend. She didn't think he had a male partner, as he had very definitely not shown any signs of being gay. But then, she said to Nic, that could be another curveball, couldn't it? Imagine if he was actually gay, but the memory loss had confused him enough that he'd forgotten?

It would be very ironic, if she was falling for someone who turned out to be gay.

Nicole told her – in no uncertain terms and with some added swearing for emphasis – to stop putting more obstacles in the way and focus on what she was going to do. If she was really certain that it was a good idea, to offer Jack a home and her support. Nicole still thought it was mad, but Katya could tell she was trying her best to be supportive.

'Would you like me to wheel you outside for some fresh air?' Katya suggested now. 'We could try and find that rose garden Celine mentioned.'

She'd intended to invite him to move into Otto's once they got outside, figuring that pastel rose petals and the cushion of soft blue sky would somehow make it easier for him to think about his immediate future than the bland, beige, pain-filled ward – but even though it was indeed very pleasant in the garden, she still chickened out. It was another two visits before she felt brave enough to risk it.

That day, she merely studied his face, his long lashes resting on his cheeks as he tipped his head up to feel the warm sunshine, and all she knew then was that she didn't want to lose him.

CHAPTER TWENTY-ONE

Katya

June

'I am *so happy*.'

Jack said this almost every day, usually about five minutes after they had woken up and Katya made the tea. It was always in a tone of incredulity, as if he couldn't believe their good fortune, or as if he really had never known happiness before.

Secretly, Katya hoped the latter was true. She was increasingly feeling that she wanted to be the only one who made him happy.

When he first came to stay, straight out of hospital, Katya had given him Otto's room. It made sense, as she had always stayed in the small spare room, and she had no desire to move straight into her dead uncle's bedroom.

It had been a good excuse to get it properly cleared of Otto's string vests, big trousers and other old-man paraphernalia including braces, pipe-cleaners, rancid combs and a collection of half-used aftershaves which looked like they belonged in a design museum for Products from a Bygone Age.

Katya chucked out all the awful nylon bedsheets and bought brand new linen and bedding, had the carpets and curtains professionally cleaned, and got a new mattress delivered. The whole endeavour had taken several days and many trips to the charity shop, but she'd wanted to do it before Jack moved in.

'Why, because you get a cup of tea in bed every morning?' she teased.

'As soon as this is off' – he gestured down to his cast – 'I promise you that I'll be the one bringing you tea, every morning without fail.'

'Can't wait,' she said, grinning at him and putting her empty cup on the bedside table so that she could hug him. He looked and felt so gorgeous in the mornings, his warm body wrapped around hers, his big hands cupping her bottom… He never had sour morning breath or sleep in his eyes like Danny had.

Danny definitely had lots of positive attributes but, even though he'd been a sweetheart, and impeccably well-behaved in public, some of his more private habits had not been as appealing. So it was a daily revelation to her that Jack always smelled so good.

She told Jack about her ex's enthusiastic farting skills one day, and he'd laughed like a drain.

'Don't you ever fart?'

'Of course. Just not in front of other people, when I can possibly avoid it. Don't you?'

They were clearly still at that new stage of the relationship where you didn't break wind in front of the other one (not that this had ever stopped Danny, she thought).

Jack first kissed her just two days after he moved in. When it finally happened, it had been so natural that it was as if they'd been together for years. He had been hopping around the kitchen at the time, trying to make tea, and dropped the lid of the milk carton onto the lino floor.

'Darn it,' he said, forgetting that there was no way he could reach down on one crutch to pick it up but trying to, regardless. At the same moment she had lunged for it herself, and their heads collided painfully. They both recoiled, laughing and grimacing, and

Jack's free hand shot out and caressed the side of her skull on the spot where his had connected with it.

She stood, stock still, and their eyes met. It was happening, already.

His hand didn't drop; he just continued tenderly stroking her hair. Not breaking eye contact, he let his fingers slip across her ear until he was cupping her cheek with his palm. It was the most sensuous gesture – she felt soppy thinking it, but it was as if his eyes held her whole future in their clear blue gaze. She couldn't breathe, and her heart seemed to be trying to break out through the bars of her ribcage.

Later she thought it was her who moved first, drawn towards his lips, not a scrap of embarrassment or hesitation. Just the utter conviction that this was right; that this was the start of a whole new amazing chapter in her life.

She moved into Otto's bedroom with Jack just a week or so after that first kiss, and now she no longer even thought of it as Otto's room. It was their room. They stripped off the ancient flowery wallpaper and painted the walls white – Jack had done the bottom half, as high as his arm-span reached from the wheelchair, and Katya had done everything above that.

Jack still needed to rest quite a bit because his leg really started to hurt after he had done his physio, or gone out on crutches for their daily walk/hop along the lakeside, so they would both get into bed most afternoons and lie there for hours, chatting and kissing and making love. Katya felt as if she was in some sort of blissful bubble. It was their haven now, their nest, and she found she never wanted to leave.

They had their own little routine – tea in bed, make love (challenging at first, when one quarter of the total number of legs involved was encased from ankle to hip in plaster, but they got used to it), Katya would go for a run along the lake, come back, shower, and they would read the *Guardian* and the *New York Times* online together. She kept waiting for something to trigger a memory in Jack – a place name, a politician, an event – but nothing beyond his early childhood seemed to be coming forward.

He remembered how to write, text, type, cook and, he thought, drive – although of course even if Katya had had a car, the cast on his leg would have ruled that out – so it seemed that his skills remained unaltered. It was just facts about his personal identity that he'd lost.

He was having regular appointments with the neurologist at the Thonon-les-Bains hospital, and regular physio (Katya hoped beyond hope that he had good travel insurance because he wasn't half going to need it at some point), who said that this sort of skill-retention was typical of retrograde amnesia.

He did have occasional flashes of memory but was never sure if they were from his own life, or a film he'd seen. Once he told Katya that he was sure he had been to a carnival as a kid and put a coin in a fortune-telling machine called Zoltar. That night they watched the movie *Big* on Netflix, which Katya looked up because she remembered that scene too, and he sheepishly conceded that this could well have been where he got the idea from.

Another time he dreamed he'd had a twin brother who died in a shootout between rival narcotic gangs. Katya had her doubts about that one, too. A more practical dream was one in which he said he was playing the guitar on stage in front of a huge audience, and the most notable element about it was that when he woke up, he remembered each of the chords of the song he'd been playing.

'E, A minor, F, D, G, E, D,' he said, making different shapes with the fingers of his left hand to demonstrate, with an air of surprise on his face.

'Wow,' said Katya. 'I reckon you really do play guitar.'

She didn't say anything more, but next time she went out, she made a point of visiting Thonon's *brocante*, an Aladdin's cave of a flea market in which she was certain she'd seen second-hand guitars hanging on the wall in the past. Sure enough, she found one that she was assured was in decent condition and bought it for Jack.

Katya had never given anyone a gift which elicited as much delight as that guitar did. After he'd hugged and kissed her, Jack tuned it up as if to the manner born, and began to play something delicate and complex, with a look of astonished ecstasy on his face.

'So now we know something definite about you,' Katya laughed, slightly overcome by the joy on his face. 'You *are* a musician! Maybe you really are a rock star?'

But she never pushed him to try and get him to remember more. 'What's the point?' she said. 'Your memory's not going to come back by me nagging you about it.'

The truth was, though, that as delighted as she was at each layer of unpeeled memory, she was also secretly terrified of him remembering it all.

If he had been happy with her already, the guitar definitely made him more so. Each time he picked it up, she saw the tension drain from him. He spent hours playing, and Katya never tired of listening.

She had a few short translation jobs to do, on and off, from a few of her regular clients back in London, so she would sit at her laptop at Otto's kitchen table and Jack would serenade her in the background while she worked.

He never seemed to play the same thing twice, which made her think he must have been serious about it before. And he had a good ear, too – if a song came on the radio, he would pause, listen intently, and then, after just a minute or two, take up the guitar and gently strum along, almost note perfect, even if he didn't know the song.

Then, one day, he looked out of the kitchen window and down into the apartment block's gardens – each of the six flats had one small square of garden directly outside their private garage. Otto and Monique, for all their many talents, had very definitely not been green-fingered. Their square of garden was planted solely with regimented diagonal rows of red geraniums – Otto had done it a couple of months after Monique's death when he'd been crazed with grief and couldn't concentrate on the usual stuff he would do to keep himself occupied. The geraniums, Katya always thought, looked very sad and slightly deranged, although perhaps she was merely projecting.

Jack now gazed down at the garden contemplatively. 'I think I could fix that.'

She thought he'd spotted a hole in the garage roof or something. 'Fix what?'

'Your bit of garden. I could make it look really nice. We could go to a garden centre and I could tell you which plants to buy, and where to put them. I can't help you plant them, obviously' – he gestured at his leg – 'but I'm sure I know how to tell *you* to do that. If you'd like to.'

She stared at him. 'So you can do garden design as well as play guitar? Cool.'

It was cool. She liked the snippets she was gleaning about him. It was like a collage that you built up with scraps of tissue paper stuck one on top of the next until it formed something textured and abstract up close, but with an image from a distance. Because what was not to like about someone who was brilliant at guitar, loved cooking and knew how to plant a garden? It wasn't as if he'd announced he knew how to prepare and eat a human limb, or illegally hack into a bank's computer system. Katya was sure he was her type. And it reassured them both to know that he was really just a decent, down-to-earth man.

More importantly, it confirmed that they would have fallen for one another under whatever circumstances they'd met, not just these.

CHAPTER TWENTY-TWO

'In a *normal* new relationship, right, when you strip down the layers,' Katya commented contemplatively, squeezing shower gel into her hands and rubbing it in big, sensual circles over Jack's back, 'so many of those outer layers are stories, aren't they? Oh, sorry, no point asking you that, you won't remember. But they are. You fill your new partner in on a lifetime of missed events and anecdotes – there's always so much to catch up on. We don't have any of that. Well, apart from the things I tell you. But it's interesting how little I need to tell you. I just feel like I'd be droning on down a one-way street if I did, and it wouldn't be fair on you because you can't contribute.'

She had to speak loudly to be heard over the hum of the elderly electric shower motor, and Jack laughed. 'I love how philosophical you always get when we're in the shower,' he said. 'It's like the running water kind of unstoppers you.'

He didn't really need help in and out of the shower any more; he had got used to duct-taping the bin liner over his plaster cast, and there was already a fold-down plastic chair and a handrail installed in the cubicle from Otto's days, but somehow it had become a bit of a ritual for them. One which usually ended up with Katya straddling him on the chair, with her weight balanced to the right to avoid putting pressure on his injured leg… they had got it down to a fine art.

'I don't mind, I want to hear all about your life. I really do,' he said, reaching back and sliding his hand up her inner thigh.

But she found it was true; she didn't actually want to tell him. All the pain of past failed relationships, the crushing disappointments when things hadn't turned out the way she had hoped – none of it even seemed to matter anymore. They were truly living in the moment, and neither of them could possibly imagine that filling in missing histories could in any way improve on what had been developing over the last month.

The sort of closeness that made them both beam and sigh with delight every time they hugged. The electric chemistry, where mere touch provoked an immediate physical response and, more often than not, meant that it would be a matter of moments before their clothes were torn off in a frenzy and they would be on the floor, or the bed, or the sofa, greedily devouring each other's naked bodies as if it had been weeks instead of hours since the last time. Or, as now, in the shower.

'Is this normal?' he asked. It was the third time they'd made love that day.

Katya laughed. 'No! Not in my experience anyway. I've never had a relationship like this, where I literally cannot keep my hands off you.'

'What, you never have, really?' Jack put both his hands around her waist, and then lower, stroking her as she moved on top of him. 'But then, of course, I have now remembered that for three years on the trot, 2005–2008, I was voted Sexiest Man on the Planet by an international panel of carefully selected high-profile individuals of all ages and genders, so who could blame you?'

She giggled again. 'Oh yes, I think I read about that. There was an article in the *Guardian* about the huge and very public meltdown you had in 2009 when you only came second. You stormed the podium, snatched the trophy away from the winner, punched him and then burst into tears.'

'I did not burst into tears. Honestly, those hacks will say anything for a story. All I did was demand a recount. There's no way that footballer would have got more votes than me!'

They did this a lot. One of them would drop in some utterly ridiculous 'fact' about his past that the other would enthusiastically corroborate. In this alternate reality, Jack's real name was Lord Lancelot Lloyd Looming, and he owned half of Scotland and most of Wisconsin. A British peer, rock god from an '80s band and renowned Lothario who'd fallen on hard times – he was down to his last eighty million. He had taken himself skiing to 'recharge the old batteries' and 'take stock' before embarking on a new humanitarian venture to end world poverty (they hadn't worked out quite how he was intending to do this, but the finer details were not important). Lance Looming was single, of course, but had been unlucky in his three previous choices of wife, each one a bigger gold-digger than the last, and he had never known true love – until now.

The moments of levity helped. But yet Katya knew that Jack worried about everything, if he allowed himself. He had let slip the other day that he only had her word to go on about what was normal or unusual in a new relationship, for example. They had sex an unusually high number of times a day, so he worried that maybe he had a sex addiction, and this was the reason why he'd been on a ski slope by himself, with nobody looking for him – because it had wrecked every romantic partnership he'd ever had before. Poor Jack, she thought. It must be horrible. She was concerned about her earlier comment, that he might have taken it as criticism that he was unable to participate in the bonding exercise of telling each other their stories. She hadn't meant it like that; she just didn't feel like banging on and on about her past when it was all so one-sided.

So many worries for them both. If she allowed herself, Katya was also paranoid that Jack's passion for her wasn't real, that he had latched onto her because she was his life-raft in the choppy endless sea of the world. He had nothing to compare it to, so of course it was going to be great.

Yet at other times Katya was convinced that what they had was truly remarkable in its intensity, and unique, at least for her. She'd had quite a bit of experience of being in relationships, she told Jack – one long term and four of a few months each – and as with all human interactions an element of trust was involved. She just had to trust her instincts that Jack wasn't a psychopath or a narcissist – although perhaps the fact that he had no stories to contextualise him as a person did make it a tad more tricky than usual.

Later, once they were out of the shower and cuddled up, wet-haired and warm with a glass of wine on the sofa, Katya mentioned this. Jack's response was one of immediate consternation.

'Oh Kat – what if I *am* a psychopath? How would I even know?'

She wished she hadn't said anything. 'Sweetheart, you're definitely not. Psychopaths can't form meaningful relationships, or show vulnerability or empathy or affection. I mean, look at you! Look at us. You're the most affectionate and least psychopathic person I've ever met! You say exactly what you're feeling.'

'Is that why you like me so much?' Jack asked. Katya could tell he was only half-teasing. 'Because I'm not hiding anything from you?'

Katya snuggled into his armpit, not meeting his eyes. There was so much she could have told him, but was choosing not to. Was that the same as hiding things? Not if he didn't ask, she decided. The inevitable pain it would cause her to tell him about those losses felt too much, as if it would mar their happiness. There was just no need. She didn't want anything in their relationship to cause either of them the slightest smidgeon of pain; not ever.

'Not hiding anything, Lord Lance? You're hiding *everything*. It's just that you're hiding it from yourself too.'

CHAPTER TWENTY-THREE

'Come on, please don't feel bad, please. We're celebrating!'

'What are we celebrating?'

'Us! Your cast coming off soon! Life!'

And perhaps even more than that, Katya thought, if I'm really lucky…

Jack had clearly felt torn, allowing Katya to hire a car and pay for a night away in a nice hotel for them – on top of all the other expenses she continued to incur on his behalf. He'd tried to talk her out of it several times, but she maintained it was far more for her own benefit than his and he'd eventually given in.

'But you know I'm keeping a tally of what I owe you. I want to pay you back, one day. I feel awful letting you do this.'

That had been a few days ago. Now, as the little rental car sped up along a narrow pass under the brightest of blue skies, snow-capped mountains studding the vast horizon, Katya turned to him.

'Glad we came?'

'So glad… I feel a bit overwhelmed, to be honest. It's incredible.'

'Epic, isn't it?' Katya grinned.

'Especially when all I've got in my memory bank is the hospital, our apartment, the park and the lake. The lake's lovely, of course, but it's not… *this*.'

He gestured expansively out of the passenger window. Katya opened both their windows and the crisp, sweet scent of Alpine flowers filled the car. She smiled to herself, noting the way he had said 'our' apartment.

'So, assuming you were last in this area when you had your accident, everything would have been totally white then, not just the peaks. It looks so different in winter, but I prefer it in the sun. Spring is best, though, because there are so many more flowers everywhere, and the air smells even better than this. It's so beautiful, isn't it? And wait till you see the hotel, it'll blow your mind. Mum and I came here once before when Otto and Monique had their wedding anniversary there. Hopefully it hasn't changed.'

The hotel hadn't changed. Jack, who had no recollection of ever being in a hotel before in his life, couldn't stop marvelling at everything, which made it even more magical for Katya. He kept pointing out the wonders of it all: the thickness and softness of the bed linen; the towelling bathrobes and matching slippers; the home-made shortbread wrapped in a napkin in a little wicker basket next to the coffee machine, like a baby in a manger. The absolute charm of all the uniformed waitresses and bar staff, fussing round them in a way that managed not to be at all intrusive or irritating, just delightful. The wine, the incredible food, the crystal glasses and heavy silver cutlery… it was all a revelation to both of them, not just Jack.

'Can we live here for ever?' he asked Katya as they sat on a terrace drinking Irish coffees from tall glasses, fresh whipped cream swirled on top, watching the sun slide down in a peach blaze behind the mountains.

She giggled. 'We'd better buy a lot of Euromillions lottery tickets. Uncle Otto didn't leave me quite enough money for more than a couple of nights. I'm so glad you like it, though.'

'This *view*!'

'I know, right? Isn't it stunning?' It really was, Katya thought with utter contentment. Miles and miles of Alpine peaks reaching into the distance as far as the eye could see, green and fresh-looking. 'Let's do a selfie,' she said, pulling out her phone and chivvying him to move his chair round so that the setting sun would be in the background. 'Say cheese!'

The sunset light cast a soft golden glow on both their faces as they put their heads close together and grinned goofily on cue.

'Cheese? Why?' Jack asked, and she laughed again.

'I'm so lucky,' she said, ruffling his hair.

'It's me who's the lucky one,' Jack said, pulling her face gently down so he could kiss her. He tasted of cream and chocolate and brandy.

Their dinner that night was so rich – scallops, followed by venison and dauphinoise potatoes, followed by salted caramel tarts with ice-cream, none of which Jack said he ever remembered tasting before – that they were both happy to go to bed at nine thirty, groaning with pleasure at how full they were. All they wanted to do was to cuddle up together in that vast white bed and fall asleep like a pair of puppies.

Katya woke up the next morning, a shaft of sunlight splitting through the gap in the room's heavy damask curtains. Her stomach was churning unpleasantly. Dashing into the bathroom, she made it just in time to vomit into the toilet.

It was rare to puke with such a sensation of joy, she thought, her excitement rising as she rinsed out her mouth. Could it really be…?

She cleaned her teeth, waiting for her belly to stop roiling. *It might just be because of the rich dinner*, she thought. *Don't get ahead of yourself.* She hadn't dared hope, not when there had been so many previous disappointments.

But it wasn't the first time she'd been sick in the morning recently.

She reached into her washbag for the test that she had brought with her.

A minute later she flushed the toilet again and walked slowly back into the bedroom, her heart racing. Jack was standing up next to the bed, slotting his arms into his crutches, looking concerned.

'Sweetie, are you all right? Was it the scallops? I feel fine, so unless you had a bad one…'

She slid back into bed and beckoned for him to join her. 'I'll tell you in a minute,' she whispered, burying her face into his neck.

Jack laughed and cuddled her. 'What – you don't know already?'

'Not yet,' she said enigmatically.

'Are you feeling terrible?'

She shook her head. 'Not terrible. Queasy,' she conceded.

'I hope it passes soon.' He stroked her hair away from her sweaty forehead. 'Do you still want to drive up the mountain to that fondue restaurant later?'

'*Blehhh*, fondue,' she said, making a face. 'Maybe. Not right now.'

'Sorry. I need a pee.' Jack began the laborious operation of getting out of bed again – the hotel bed was higher than he was used to, so it involved more care than usual – but Katya put her hand on his arm.

'Hang on a moment,' she said, jumping back out of bed and almost running to the bathroom again, leaving the door slightly ajar behind her.

'Kat, are you OK?' he called. 'Are you being sick again?'

She didn't reply.

'Katya?'

She leaned her forearms on either side of the wide shell-shaped basin, looking at him in the mirror as he hobbled towards her.

He came across and tentatively rubbed her back through her thin nightdress, caressing the soft bumps of her spine. She could feel the callouses on his hands, left by the crutches, snagging slightly on the slippery silk.

'Hey,' he said. 'What's that?'

She turned to face him, slowly, the beam on her face widening as she straightened up and thrust at him the narrow white stick she'd been holding.

Suddenly, a look of recognition flashed across his features. 'Wait – is it…?'

She nodded, tears running down her face.

'And those two blue lines mean…?'

'Yes. Jack… I'm pregnant.'

How many times she had yearned to say those words. The times she had done, only for it all to end in blood and tears and sorrow.

This time it would be different; she could feel it. This time she would have her happy ending; she and Jack and their child. It felt so simple.

'Oh my goodness,' Jack said with wonder, as they stared at one another. 'I thought you were on the pill?'

'I was. I am. I must have missed one or two. Or it didn't work properly. I've been sick a couple of times recently, so I was wondering… I brought a test with me, just in case… Are you OK with it?'

Katya gave a sob, wrapping her arms round his waist.

He wiped the tears off her face, shaking his head slightly, then dashed the tears off his own cheeks, laughing incredulously.

'We're going to be a family? Yes, Katya, yes. I am very OK with that. There is nothing I would rather do. Be. Do.'

'Doo-bee-doo,' sang Katya, laughing and crying simultaneously, her heart swelling with love and delight. It would definitely be different this time.

CHAPTER TWENTY-FOUR

Alanda

Jake clinked a knife decisively against his wineglass and the chatter subsided as Alanda pushed back her white gauze-wrapped chair and stood up, her speech in bullet points on the index cards in her hand, all eyes upon her.

For a moment, the hush was absolute, such a startlingly reverential contrast to the hubbub of a few seconds' earlier. The chatter had, up to that moment, been deafening, bouncing off the low vaulted ceilings of the venue.

Alanda had several thoughts simultaneously: if they'd known it would be this noisy in here, Heather and Kevin might have chosen a different wedding venue; and a realisation that the agog expressions on everyone's faces as she looked out at them was because they all wondered what was coming. She could sense the tension in them, as though they'd adopted a collective brace position in readiness for a potential crash of emotion. Her emerald-green satin shoes were pinching her toes and she focussed on the pain to try and steady her nerves. She'd definitely be taking advantage of a pair of the flip-flops Heather had sourced for the disco part of the day later.

The guests may have been bracing themselves at that moment, but Alanda felt like she had been braced for it all day, all week, all month – in fact, probably since the moment she'd reported Liam missing. She'd only had a sip or two of wine with the meal, determined to keep completely in control. She didn't mind public speaking, generally, finding it only moderately stressful – the last time she'd done it was at her now long-deceased mother's seventieth birthday – but to have to give the father-of-the-bride speech in Liam's place was a triple pressure.

She and the kids had huddled together before the cars arrived to take them to the church for the ceremony, arms around each other's shoulders, a moment of acknowledgement that this wasn't what any of them wanted, but that they would make the best of it.

None of them smelled like themselves, Alanda thought as their heads were together. A cacophony of hairspray, too much aftershave (Jake) and clashing perfumes. It all felt wrong, but she couldn't let herself give even the smallest indication that she felt this way.

'You know Dad would want us all to be happy today,' Becky said, in a choked voice, which set the rest of them off. She was so rarely emotional.

'Don't make me cry, Bex, my make-up will run,' said Heather, already crying. Alanda dabbed under Heather's eyes with a clean tissue.

'Oh, my darling, you look so beautiful,' she said. 'Cry now, if you need to, so you don't cry later.'

It was true, Heather looked stunning. Her hair was in long, shiny chestnut ringlets, and the flower crown she wore had cornflowers dotted through it which brought out the azure of her eyes. Her ivory dress hugged and enhanced her curves down to the hips, where the tulle skirt spread in a glorious cloud to the floor. Alanda had had her doubts about this dress, but she had to admit she'd been wrong. It was perfect for Heather, and Heather looked perfect in it.

Her baby, the smiley, squidgy, placid baby who'd been the image of her father when she was little, was now setting out on her own adventure into married life – without Liam to cheer her on.

'Dad would be so proud of you,' she added in a whisper, which almost set them all off again. 'We'll show him the photos when he gets back. It's a terrible shame he's not here, but like Becky said, we *know* he wouldn't want us to be sad, not today. We have to be so brave, all of us.'

She'd sounded far stronger than she felt. But it had worked, and they had walked into the church in their finery, heads held high and smiles plastered on their faces.

Alanda had taken her seat in the front pew and then, to the strains of the 'Wedding March' played almost hilariously badly on the organ – something else that would have made Liam snigger if he'd been there – Jake walked his little sister up the aisle, followed by Becky and then Heather's three best friends as bridesmaids. Becky was lean and tall in a turquoise satin sheath dress that looked incredible on her, although not quite so good on the podgier bridesmaids following bashfully behind.

When Kevin turned around to see his bride, his face had broken out into a beam so wide that every single other smile, however forced initially, had instantly become genuine and joyful too.

Now the ceremony was over, with only a few more tears than were to be expected, this was the next big ordeal to survive, thought Alanda. She cleared her throat, trying to stop her hands trembling as she put on her reading glasses and held up the index cards. *Once this is over, I can relax.* She glanced down at the empty chair next to her at the top table, imagining Liam there, cheering her on.

Except he wouldn't be cheering her on, because if he'd been there, she wouldn't have needed to be standing, about to give his speech.

Don't think about that, she urged herself as Jake passed her a microphone. *Don't screw it up.*

'Hi everyone,' she said, a little too loudly, making several of the elderly relatives jump and adjust their hearing aids.

'Sorry. Hello. *Unaccustomed as I am…* ha ha…'

She could see Heather give a tiny frown of incomprehension in the direction of her bridesmaids, who were on a table with several of Heather and Kevin's friends, a gaggle of identikit young men and women, the men self-conscious in suits and the girls all with long, ironed hair, fierce eyebrows, too much cleavage and pouty lips.

Alanda felt a moment's distress at Heather's brief disloyalty, then gathered herself. It was probably born more of discomfort on Heather's part, because her mother was having to do this instead of her beloved dad.

'So, you see, I'm not the bride's father. I'm the bride's mother, as I'm sure you all know. And as I'm sure you also all know, we are missing Heather's dad Liam terribly today. He will be so sad to have missed this wonderful celebration too, although we are looking forward to him coming back so we can tell him all about it. We don't know where he is or what he's doing, but we know in our hearts he will be back with us soon. So, before I say anything else, I'd like the first toast to be to him. Please be upstanding for, in spirit, the father of the bride.'

Chair legs screeched on the flagstone floors as everyone got to their feet and raised their glasses. 'The father of the bride! To Liam!'

Alanda saw Liam's mother Violet look around for him in confusion but raise her glass anyway with a hand as shaky as Alanda's own, and it almost undid her, but she managed to grit her teeth.

Several of the guests were dabbing at their eyes, and Heather gave a small sob that she managed to convert into a self-conscious laugh, leaning into her new husband's shoulder as he hugged her.

Hold it together, you have one job, Alanda reminded herself.

The rest of the speech went smoothly and she felt herself relax into it, her voice becoming firmer and her punchlines delivered – and received – with more enthusiasm. She talked about Heather as a child, how proud the family were of their youngest, how beautiful she looked today, how happy they were that she had found love with Kevin; all the things Liam would have said himself if he'd been there, and suddenly, with the toast to the newlyweds as her closing words of the speech, the spell was broken.

From that moment it was as if all the guests collectively decided that the spectre of Liam's absence had gone, at least temporarily, and the delight on everyone's faces was natural and unforced. Everybody clapped and cheered as Alanda sat down, draining her almost-full wineglass and sliding off her uncomfortable shoes.

'Thank God that's over,' she whispered to Becky, seated to her left.

'You did great, Mum,' Becky replied, chinking her glass against Alanda's.

Kevin stood up to give his speech next, nervously running a finger around the inside of his collar. The poor boy looked green with nerves, thought Alanda. But he did OK, stumbling his way through a list of thank-yous and a rather embarrassing story of his and Heather's first meeting, which had been in a nightclub, and Heather had been so drunk that she had had to excuse herself to go and vomit in the alley outside, right after their first kiss. Heather looked mortified and Becky rolled her eyes, but after that small hiccup, Kevin managed to get to the end of the speech, only interrupted by Violet standing up and shouting, 'Young man! *Will* you stop talking, it's market day!' much to the bemusement of those present who weren't aware of her condition. Her carer managed to get her to sit down again with some soothing words and one of the heart-shaped shortbread biscuits which had been served with the coffee.

The best man's speech followed, delivered by a skinny bloke called Morton who Alanda hadn't met before (apparently he'd been conceived after an A-ha concert, she was later to learn). As well as being saddled with a name like Morton, the poor bloke had unfortunate buck teeth and when he took off his jacket and rolled up his shirt sleeves, sweating profusely, his arms were covered in tattoos as thick and indistinct as his diction.

Alanda wondered if he'd wanted the tattoos to give him a sort of confidence, as he seemed to lack much of it. She felt for him as he stumbled through his speech, but she could see the genuine affection he had for Kevin and eventually he got through it. His adoring girlfriend was gazing up at him, hanging onto his every word, so he must be doing OK, Alanda thought. Each to his own. He definitely wouldn't find her, Alanda, anything to write home about either.

Jake had loosened his tie and was sinking glasses of wine at an alarming rate, his face very pink, but he looked relaxed and happier than Alanda had seen him since Liam went missing. He laughed over-heartily at one of Morton's limp anecdotes about the groom – another tale of too much alcohol consumed – and she thought how handsome their son was.

She tried to take mental snapshots of everything, to tell Liam about it later, not wanting to miss a single detail.

Extraordinary, she thought, watching Heather and Kevin's bashful first dance, how adaptable we all are. Two months ago, it was unthinkable that this day would go ahead without Liam, and yet now everyone looked as though they were thoroughly enjoying themselves. At a glance, nobody would have known that anything was amiss.

It made her feel a bit sad, if she was honest. Could Liam's absence be so easily glossed over? He wouldn't be in any of the wedding photographs.

The bride and groom had had dance lessons and were now making a decent fist of a simply choreographed routine to a cover version of 'Can't Take My Eyes Off You', a song whose lyrics had always deeply offended Alanda in the same way that typos in promotional material did. The extraneous and erroneous 'of' in the line 'can't take my eyes off *of* you' made her feel extremely stabby. She actually turned to Liam to comment on it, before she remembered that he wasn't there and for a moment thought she would have to flee to the Ladies' to compose herself. But Jake rescued her, plucking her champagne glass out of her hand and leading her onto the dance floor to join the other couples, now that Heather and Kevin's big solo moment was over.

Being whirled around with Jake brought her back from the edge of her funk and within minutes they were both laughing. She decided to think positively: this wedding was proof that life went on, and that they would all survive if, God forbid, the worst happened and Liam never came back.

CHAPTER TWENTY-FIVE

Alanda

July

'We must stop meeting like this.'

The voice from behind her made Alanda jump and slop water from the small watering can she had found next to a standpipe. She was on her knees by the gravestone, filling up a small lidded grave vase, having unsuccessfully tried to break off dahlia stems to arrange them in the holes of the vase. But the stems were proving very unwieldy and she had just been cursing herself for forgetting to bring scissors to trim them.

She turned to see Jennie, the care home manager, standing behind her, her expression a mixture of amusement, pleasure and embarrassment. She had a small hairy dog on a lead with her, which contemplated her grumpily from the safety of Jennie's legs.

'Sorry,' Jennie said. 'I didn't mean to sneak up on you. We'll bugger straight off if you want to be on your own.'

'No, no, it's fine,' said Alanda, straightening and trying to stand up. As she transferred her weight from knee to foot, in curtsy position, she staggered and almost fell sideways.

Jennie's hand flashed out and caught her arm to steady her.

Alanda laughed. 'Must stop drinking in the daytime,' she joked, regaining her balance.

'Wouldn't blame you if you were, frankly,' Jennie replied, smiling at her. 'Again, apologies. It's really not on to creep up on someone in a graveyard. This is Alfie, by the way. I've just taken him for his early evening constitutional and we always cut through here to and from the park.'

'Hi, Alfie. He's cute. Don't suppose you've got any scissors, have you? I forgot to bring some for these.'

Alanda gestured at the long-stemmed dahlias in her hand, flopping at a ninety-degree angle from where she had unsuccessfully tried to shorten them.

'Actually, I do,' Jennie said. 'I've still got some in my handbag, I think, from when I had to trim a resident's hangnail the other week. Keep forgetting to give them back to the occupational therapist.'

She pulled a small pair of nail scissors out of a side pocket of her cavernous bag and handed them over. 'I don't usually carry a handbag on a dog walk,' she added, 'but I need to get milk at the OneStop.'

'I'm not one to judge,' Alanda said, snipping at all the broken stems. 'Never go anywhere without mine… Brilliant, thanks.' She hesitated, then pointed down at Rich's gravestone. 'Liam's twin brother. He committed suicide last year. I try and put flowers on the grave once a month – for Violet and Liam, really. Personally, I don't see the point of leaving flowers. It's not like he's in there to appreciate them.'

She remembered a story Liam had once told her, that when he was a kid, he'd thought the holes in the top of grave vases were airholes, to let the buried bodies breathe. At the time she'd thought it was the sweetest, saddest thing she had ever heard. Now she wondered if she would ever be sticking flower stems into those holes on *his* grave.

If she would ever have a chance to say goodbye to him.

'Maybe he can somehow see you do it,' suggested Jennie.

Alanda sighed. 'I'd like to think so.'

'I'm so sorry though – what a terrible thing to happen. You've had a hell of a year, haven't you?'

'Yeah. First Vi going into the home, then Rich, now Liam, all within the space of a year... Talk about an *annus horribilus*. Anyway – do you live round here, if this is your dog walk route?'

Alanda didn't want to dwell on her moans. It felt as if she did nothing but vent to poor Jennie as it was; a woman she barely knew.

'Over there,' Jennie said, gesturing towards the new estate across the main road from the cemetery. 'Nothing fancy, a little three-bed semi I bought when I split up with my ex, but it suits me. Close to town and work. Quiet neighbours. Are you in town, or out in a village? I can see you in a rambling country cottage in Chilmark or somewhere.'

She paused, blushing slightly, and Alanda thought how different she seemed outside of work. Less sure of herself; more approachable. Jennie looked different too, in sturdy walking boots and jeans instead of the neat tweedy suit she usually wore at the care home, her dark hair in loose waves on her shoulders instead of in a tight ponytail. Her cheeks were pink from the wind – or the blush – and she wasn't wearing any make-up. Alanda warmed to her even more. She was definitely her kind of gal. She thought that Sadie would like her too. Perhaps the three of them could all go out for a drink some time.

'Ha. I wish. I'd love a rose-covered thatched cottage. No, we're in town too. Near Elizabeth Gardens.'

'Oh, lovely,' Jennie said. 'Listen – do you fancy a cuppa, or a glass of wine? Sun's over the yardarm, almost. My house is clean, for a change. It's my day off and I always clean first thing, get it over and done with.'

'Aha. A good time to visit then.'

'Exactly. Well, say no if you need to get on, but the offer's there.'

'Thanks – no, I mean, yes, that would be lovely. I don't have anywhere else to be.'

Alanda poked the flowers hastily into the vase, replaced the watering can next to the tap, and dumped the cut stems into the bin, saying a brief mental goodbye to Rich – even though she didn't believe he could hear her. 'Ready when you are.'

Jennie's house was nothing special from the outside, one of many identical boxes in the little Close, but as soon as they were through the front door, Alanda could immediately see what a good eye for design she had. Huge abstract oil paintings in bold primary colours decorated the walls and one corner was full of instruments; a saxophone on a stand next to an old upright piano, next to a ukulele resting against an acoustic guitar.

The room smelled of lavender and lilies, the latter scent coming from an oversized vase on the driftwood mantelpiece. There was no evidence of a new partner, no photos or men's shoes by the door.

'One-woman band?' Alanda asked, gesturing towards the musical instruments. The music in the book open on the piano looked impressively complicated, dozens of teeny-tiny black notes packed tightly together like frogspawn, all jostling for position, veering high above and below the stave.

'Yeah. I've got those little cymbals you strap to your knees somewhere too. Tea, or glass of wine?'

'Tea please, I've had way too much wine recently. Your place is really lovely, Jennie. It's got such a great feel to it.'

'Thank you,' Jennie said, grinning. 'I like it too.'

'I didn't know you were musical.'

'Why would you?'

'I suppose I wouldn't… I'm impressed, though. That music looks impossible!'

'Do you play?'

Alanda snorted. 'No. Well, I think I can do "Chopsticks" but that's about it. Liam's really good at guitar but otherwise we aren't a musical family. Although I did join the community choir for a while, until I realised that I was the one everyone was giving funny looks to on the high notes. Then I was too embarrassed to go back.'

'That's a shame. Perhaps you were just in the wrong section – you should have been with the altos or tenors if you were struggling with the high notes.'

'Ah no,' Alanda said. 'To be honest I didn't really enjoy it much anyway. The woman running it was like a schoolmistress, kept saying things like "Now, ladies, let's warm up our lovely tonsils, shall we?"'

'Sounds like my Pilates teacher,' Jennie said, laughing. She pulled a selection of boxes of tea from a cupboard and indicated for Alanda to choose one. Alanda pointed at the camomile as she dumped her bag on the floor and put her coat over the back of one of the kitchen stools. Jennie gestured for her to sit as she continued to chat:

'You know those people who smile the whole time when they're talking? She does that, and sort of screws up her eyes. I think someone must have said she's pretty when she smiles, so now she thinks she has to smile incessantly. It's creepy, and so… winsome. But fascinating, though. The psychology of it.'

'Does she teach down at All-Sports? Blonde, pretty, a bit chunky? I think I know her too! Becky – my daughter – and I call her Lovely-Nice, like Truly Scrumptious, you know, because she says "lovely" constantly.'

Jennie laughed again, the delighted guffaw of recognition. 'Yes! That's her. Ooh, I'm glad you're as much of a critical bitch as I am. Perhaps we should start a campaign to outlaw the overuse of "lovely".'

'And people who say "guys" all the time,' Alanda agreed, watching Jennie pour boiling water in two mugs. 'I tried to count the number of times she said it last time we went, but I gave up after about seventy-eight, because she literally said it every single time she opened her mouth.'

'*OK guys, downward-facing dog… right, guys, lie on your backs… Great, guys!*' mimicked Jennie, stirring the teas and fishing out the bags. 'Yes, she does, doesn't she? I'll never be able to not count again.'

She turned to hand Alanda a mug, but the smile faded when she saw Alanda's suddenly devastated expression.

'Are you all right?'

Alanda sighed, tears springing into her eyes. 'Yeah, sorry, I'm fine. I was just thinking how lovely this is, to feel normal again for a minute, complaining about nothing and not thinking about Liam… which of course made me think of Liam.'

Jennie sat down on the stool next to Alanda's, gazing sympathetically at her. 'I was going to ask how you're doing. It's to be expected, you know, that you're very up and down. How long has it been now?'

'Three and a half months,' Alanda said, gritting her teeth to try and prevent her lip wobbling. 'No news, no sightings, nothing. It's like he just vanished into thin air. And the wedding – the wedding…'

'How was it?' Jennie reached across and gave Alanda's hand a squeeze. 'I was thinking about you all that day, hoping it was going well. Seeing Vi all dressed up and looking forward to going out, even though she didn't know where she was going – it was kind of amazing and heartbreaking at the same time. Tayo said she had a really nice time, although she thought that the bride was her sister. Was it your daughter Becky who got married?'

'No, her younger sister, Heather. Yes, Violet did seem to have a nice time,' confirmed Alanda, managing a smile. 'I'm so glad she was able to be there.' Her face fell again. 'And I'm glad she didn't seem to realise that Liam wasn't there. I really didn't think Heather would want to go ahead without him, but in the end they decided that if they didn't do it now, and worst comes to worst, it turns out he's dead – then they'd feel even less like celebrating. It was the right decision. They want to start a family; they need to get on with their lives.'

'Must have been a day of very conflicting emotions… *Alfie!*' she called suddenly, making Alanda jump. 'Sorry, Alanda. Alfie – get down, right now!'

The dog had sneaked up onto the sofa while they were talking, and he slid off again, looking both guilty and resentful. 'Good boy,' Jennie said, turning her attention back to Alanda.

'It was,' Alanda said. 'Everybody cried buckets but, you know what? Once the ceremony was over and everyone had cried, it was like we were all cried out, and it became a proper party. Kind of surprising really, how resilient we all are when it comes to the crunch.'

'A bit like a funeral, then, I suppose,' Jennie said contemplatively. 'All the emotion comes out at the service and then everyone gets pissed and has a great time at the wake.'

'Yes. Definitely the same vibe,' said Alanda. 'Although I had to keep stopping myself from feeling devastated at how upset Liam would be to miss it… if he's still alive.' Her lip wobbled again. 'Dammit,' she said. 'I hate it when I can feel my chin wobble. It reminds me of Carrie in *Homeland*. Liam and I used to count the number of times her lip or chin wobbled and laugh at how intensely irritating it got.'

Jennie smiled. 'Yup. You're definitely a woman after my own heart. I thought that too – although please don't think it's irritating when *you* do it. You have every right to be emotional. Carrie, however, not so much. She gave CIA agents a bad name, with all that huffing and crying.'

'Oh, the incessant huffing!' said Alanda, accepting the sheet of kitchen roll Jennie handed her. 'Drove us crazy.' She blew her nose. 'That's the sort of thing I miss most. Liam and I were such good companions, and watching TV together was one of those little rituals we really loved. We'd sit cuddled up together on the sofa and take the piss out of everyone in whatever we were watching. I can't even watch TV anymore unless I watch it on my laptop in the office, or in bed. I can't bear to sit on the sofa without him.'

'Sounds like you had a wonderful relationship.'

'We did – we do. I mean, I don't have a lot to compare it to – he was my first and only proper boyfriend before we got married, and neither of us has ever strayed, to my knowledge – but yeah, it always felt pretty good. I always listened to my friends moaning about their husbands and thought, wow, I'm glad Liam's not like that. He was – is – just… easy, you know? Affectionate and loyal and funny and we still fancy each other. I guess you can't ask for much more than that, really.'

'No,' said Jennie, in such a heartfelt way that Alanda couldn't help but wonder what had gone on in her past. 'You really can't.'

She slid off her stool to pick up Alfie, who had been hovering around her feet, and he lolled in her arms like an ecstatic hairy baby.

'Did you really never have a boyfriend before you met Liam? How old were you?'

'Seventeen, almost eighteen. I mean, I'd had a couple of encounters before that. A few dates and snogs and a bit of light petting, you know, but nothing serious… I used to get asked out a lot, I suppose, but I thought boys were mostly stupid and smelly, and then I got a reputation for being frigid. The first boy I kissed had train-track braces and they ripped my lip open when we were snogging. We didn't notice until both our mouths were full of blood. It was gross.'

'Ha, yes, that is pretty gross. Funny, though. I'm not surprised you were put off boys till you met a decent one.'

'I keep thinking,' Alanda said, contemplatively gazing out of the kitchen window into Jennie's neat little courtyard garden, 'that we had hardly any of the dramas that most couples get in life, at least not until Vi got dementia and Rich killed himself. It's like fate decided I'd had it too easy up till now and piled it all on me at once. Pretty much nothing since the torn lip, and now all this. Sometimes, when I'm on my own, I feel it all pressing me down like an actual weight, till I can't breathe. The thought of never seeing Liam again is just… impossible.'

Jennie didn't speak for a moment, busying herself with rubbing Alfie's belly.

'Does it feel different, as time goes on? I mean, the first few weeks you must have been on tenterhooks waiting for news every minute of the day. Did that change, now you're three months in? It must be so exhausting for you to be waiting and waiting endlessly.'

Alanda was grateful for her directness. There wasn't really anybody else who asked her questions like this – the kids never asked her how she felt about it at all, and even Sadie seemed very uncomfortable about broaching the subject.

'It does feel different,' she said, gazing at the dog, who was now settling down in his mistress's arms, closing his eyes and allowing himself to be rocked. She envied that feeling of being cradled and safe, and felt, rather than remembered, the imprint of Liam's arms around her in bed, his light kisses peppering her bare shoulder to make her giggle, that feeling of utter contentment. 'No less hideous, and I'm still on tenterhooks, but the big thing I've found is that I am functional again, on a day-to-day basis, if I'm not on my own. Work helps, although I went through a few weeks when it didn't, when people kept asking me if there was any news—'

'Where do you work? I've never asked you before.'

'I have an arty sort of gift shop on the High Street. Mugs and tea-towels and silkscreen-printed scarves. It's called Hector's House – I named it after a kids' TV programme I used to love when I was tiny.'

'I know it, it's lovely. Don't remember the programme though. Go on…'

'Yeah – no, that's it really. For the first couple of months I just wanted to lock myself up on my own so I'd be there in case he came back, but now it's the opposite. I hate being home alone now, because that's when I miss him most, and with the kids I have to be OK otherwise they freak out. At work I can keep busy and put on a brave face. Friends make me feel close to normal, unless I'm feeling really bad, for short bursts of time at least.'

'Well, I'm more than happy to help you avoid solitude whenever you feel like a drink or a bit of company.'

Jennie sounded shy, and Alanda remembered that she had made a similar offer before. She wondered if the woman was lonely.

'I guess you work pretty long hours at the home? You always seem busy, when we cross paths there.'

The dog had begun to squirm so Jennie put him back down, and he trotted over to his water bowl, his nails clicking on the granite floor, proceeding to drink so noisily that Jennie had to raise her voice slightly.

'I do work very long hours. The paperwork is crazy – forty residents, and all of them with huge files of medical needs, financial statements, funding applications, blah blah blah. I find that side of it all very dull, but I have to keep on top of it, so I tend to stay late in the evenings. I prefer the face-to-face element, chatting to the residents and staff, sorting out all the various personnel issues and so on.'

'You're a people person,' said Alanda, smiling at her. She picked up her handbag, which was by her feet, in search of a lip balm – the stiff breeze in the churchyard had made her lips feel dry and tingly. Or perhaps it was the ghost of a memory of that first metallic bloody kiss, she thought. She found the lip balm in the side pocket next to her phone, which was lit up with a text from Jake, plus notifications of several missed calls. Hopefully he'd got an interview for that PR job he'd applied for. She hadn't heard the phone ring at all.

It couldn't be anything to do with Liam, otherwise the police would have got in touch with her first.

'I suppose so,' Jennie was saying. 'Definitely only after I've had my first cup of coffee, though.'

But Alanda didn't reply. She had opened the text, gasped and dropped the phone to the floor, making the dog yelp at the sudden crash.

'What is it?' Jennie jumped off her stool and retrieved the phone, whose screen was now peppered with hairline fractures. The words of the text beneath were now distorted but still legible:

Call me!!!! There's been a sighting of Dad – in a SKI RESORT in France, wtf?! Sounds convincing though.

CHAPTER TWENTY-SIX

With a pounding heart, Alanda practically ran out of Jennie's house and drove straight back home, considerably over the speed limit all the way around the ring road. Joan Armatrading had come on the radio just as she got in the car, and Alanda whacked the volume up full and permitted the lush sounds of 'Down to Zero' to accompany her, letting it reverberate around the interior until the bass rattled, soaking up the confusing emotions threatening to engulf her: joy, that Liam might definitely be alive; terror, that this might turn out to be a false sighting; fear, that he might have lied to her about going to Spain…

Jake was waiting outside the front door for her.

'I didn't have my key because I didn't know I'd be coming over,' he said, hugging her impatiently the second she pulled onto the driveway and jumped out of the car.

'Tell me everything,' Alanda said breathlessly, letting them both in and dropping her bag and coat in the hallway. 'Have you spoken to this person?'

'No – I literally texted you as soon as I saw her tweet,' he said. 'Oh Christ, Mum, what if it's really him? Wouldn't it be amazing?'

'Of course – although what the hell would your father have been doing at a ski resort? Surely it couldn't really have been him.'

'Midlife crisis?' Jake suggested, going into the kitchen and flicking on the kettle before immediately turning it off again. 'No, not tea. This calls for something stronger.'

He opened the fridge, found half a bottle of wine in the door and poured both of them a glass before Alanda had time to object. She opened her mouth to, but instead grabbed the glass and took a large swig. Jake was right. This was no time for tea.

'Show me the tweet,' she said, holding out a trembling hand for his phone.

He pulled up the Twitter app and passed it over. 'The original tweet just said she'd direct messaged me and to check my DMs. This is the DM.'

Alanda put on her glasses and read it out loud:

'*Hi – I'm pretty sure I saw this man on April seventh….* Oh Jake, that was the day he flew to Madrid! So he can't have been in' – she read on, her heart sinking – 'Les Gets.'

She pronounced it Les Gets, with a hard 's' in Les and a hard 't' in Gets. Jake automatically corrected her: 'It's pronounced *Lay Jay*. It's in the Haute-Savoie, in France.'

'Whatever. It can't have been him. He wasn't in France.'

'You haven't finished reading! It could be.'

She read it again, more slowly. '*I'm pretty sure I saw this man on April seventh in a cable car. I recall the date because it was the last day of our snowboarding holiday in Les Gets and my husband and I were going up for one final run in the afternoon. We chatted to him, briefly. He had a slight American accent, and he said he was a bit nervous about skiing because he hadn't done any at all since he was seventeen. Does that sound right?*'

'Since he was seventeen!' Jake said excitedly. 'A slight American accent! Didn't Dad always say he wanted to go skiing again one day, because he'd only done it once, in Colorado when he was on a high school skiing trip?'

'Yes,' Alanda said slowly, her heart still racing so painfully she wondered if she might be having a heart attack. 'And we never did, because I didn't want to. I was too worried about having an accident and not being able to look after you lot for weeks after, if my arm was in plaster or whatever... but...'

Jake looked sober again. 'Yeah. But... if it was him, why did he tell us he was going to Madrid to walk the Camino de Santiago?'

'He was going to Madrid,' Alanda said. 'He *did*. I saw his ticket. The airline has confirmed he was on the flight. So it must just be coincidence.'

She handed the phone back to Jake and knocked back her wine. 'My heart,' she said. 'I thought it was going to explode. But it can't be him.'

'Wait, Mum, we don't know that! It's worth looking into, surely?'

Alanda shrugged, noticing that the orchid on the kitchen windowsill was looking particularly droopy. She filled her empty wineglass with tap water and dripped a steady dribble into the flowerpot, trying to avoid the roots. Her heart wasn't exploding like a firework anymore, it felt more like a damp squib, writhing weakly on wet grass before fizzling out.

'He'd definitely have told us if he had some mad change of plan and decided to go skiing instead,' she insisted, her back to Jake so he couldn't see her expression.

'Would he, though? You know Dad, maybe he felt so guilty about not doing the walk, after all the arrangements you'd made for him, that he decided he'd just do it on the quiet? Or maybe he was going to tell us when he got there, and something was wrong with his phone? We know it was playing up. And then he crashed into a tree or whatever, and is in a coma... It's worth ringing round the local hospitals. That could be why the police haven't found him, because he's not in Spain at all and we've been looking in the wrong place!'

This did sound more logical than any of the other explanations she'd heard so far.

Jake carried on, a wobble in his voice. 'Mum, this could be the best possible explanation. He had a midlife crisis, went skiing, had an accident and is in hospital. He was on his own, so you can rest assured that he didn't run off to start a new life with another woman… He's not dead, because otherwise we'd have heard.'

'I didn't think he'd run off with another woman,' Alanda said stiffly, although in her darker moments she absolutely had done, on many occasions since Liam vanished.

'Stop watering that poor orchid, you'll kill it!' Jake said, and Alanda abruptly withdrew the glass. She hadn't realised she was still trickling water into the pot. That would probably finish it off. *Oh, who cares about a sodding orchid*, she thought, suddenly and unaccountably angry at the confusion Liam's disappearing act was causing them all.

She went and sat back down at the kitchen table, pouring herself another half glass of wine. Her head was already spinning from the first.

'And go easy, you'll give yourself a headache,' Jake said, gently taking the bottle from her shaking hands.

At what point did the children start parenting the parent? Alanda wondered idly. Both Jake and Becky had been doing it for a while.

'I know, this is huge,' he continued. 'And it could just be a coincidence. But I'm going to follow it up. We'd be mad not to.'

He tapped out a message on his phone then looked back up at her. 'Right. I've sent her my number and asked if she'll ring me. I want to know if there was anything more to this conversation. Then I'm going to ring around all the local hospitals.'

'Maybe start with the French police,' Alanda suggested. 'If any of the hospitals had an unconscious man they couldn't identify, they'd notify the police – wait, maybe he was mugged? He can't have had any ID on him otherwise they would have been in touch.'

'Mugged, on a ski slope?'

'Well, I don't know, do I? If that woman on Twitter rings, you could maybe ask her if there was anyone else in the cable car. Or—'

She hesitated.

'What if he had a fatal accident, and they haven't been able to identify his body? Or his body's lying at the bottom of a ravine somewhere?'

Jake reached across the table and squeezed her hand. 'Well, all the more reason to contact the French police. Get PC Laptop to do it for us. But I'm sure that's not the case. Also – this is Dad, remember. In the highly unlikely event he did randomly decide to go skiing instead of hiking, he'd never venture off the nursery slopes. He's far too cautious and inexperienced to go off piste.'

'Yes, you're probably right.'

'But, something else doesn't really make sense,' Jake said, running his hand through his closely cropped hair, 'unless Twitter woman's wrong about the date: for her to have seen Dad in a cable car that day means that he must have lied about which flight he was getting, or he got to Madrid and boarded another one straight away. Then he'd have had to hire skis plus all the gear – all in time to be in a cable car by the afternoon?'

'I know. Seems unlikely. But he didn't lie, like I said, we *know* he was on that first flight, remember? We can try and work out the timings, to see if it would just about have been possible.'

'Perhaps he was only intending to stay one night, and then head back to the Camino? He'd have busted a gut to get on the slopes that same day, get as many runs in as possible.'

'Maybe,' Alanda said doubtfully. 'Worth trying to find out if he booked a hotel room in the resort?'

'Hmm. Worth a shot, perhaps. It would be very near the end of the season so not everywhere would be open. But I think the gendarmes and hospitals should be our first port of call.'

'Gendarmes are the armed police, I think,' Alanda said. 'Normal French police are called something else.'

'Whatever,' Jake said impatiently, checking his phone again. 'Oh – she's replied! She said she'll give me a ring at seven this evening. Oh Mum, seriously, I've got a good feeling about this. I think we're going to find him. Everybody's just been looking in the wrong place all this time.'

His eyes were shining with tears, which made Alanda well up too. All the weeks they had spent frantically tweeting, re-tweeting, sharing Facebook posts, badgering local and national newspapers to run articles. She had come to hate that photograph of Liam outside the pub in Cambridge. It seemed to taunt her with the futility of the whole exercise. The tweet hadn't gone viral or anything – who really cared about one lost man, however emotional their plea had been? There were so many others seen as more deserving; missing kids and teens, people with mental health issues, confused grandmas… Alanda suspected that most viewers of their campaign would likely assume that Liam had vanished of his own volition. It had been shared hundreds of times, though to no avail, once they'd weeded out the nutters, the mistaken and the deluded.

Until now.

'I hope you're right. But don't say anything to the girls yet. I don't want to get their hopes up.'

CHAPTER TWENTY-SEVEN

The appointed time ticked nearer, appallingly slowly. As they waited for the woman's call, Alanda and Jake tried not to hover around Jake's mobile. They were on the sofa in the front room, sitting as tensely as if they were in the waiting room of the local STD clinic. A car alarm was going off outside intermittently but persistently, and Louise next door had just started her daily saxophone practice, of which they could hear every squawk and bum note through the party wall. Neither of these noises was in any way tension-diffusing.

'I should've got her number,' Jake fretted. 'What if she changes her mind?'

'She wouldn't have responded to the appeal in the first place if she didn't want to help. She – what's her name? – doesn't come across as any sort of time-waster. And if I was her, I wouldn't give out my number to a random stranger, so it was much better for you to give her yours.'

'Liz Lewis,' Jake said. 'She's only got 320 followers on Twitter. And why did she DM me, instead of ringing the police tip line?'

Alanda snorted. 'Jake, just because she's got less than a thousand followers doesn't mean she's a troll or a time-waster! I only have about 150 and most of those are friends, people I know from Pilates or swimming or the shop. She may well have left a message on the official hotline too, and the police haven't got back to her, so she's showing initiative and getting in touch with you as well?'

'Could be,' Jake said huffily. 'But for the record, having all your mates as followers is *not* how you're supposed to use Twitter. God, why is the time going so slowly?'

'We've still got twenty minutes. Let's do something to take our minds off it.'

'What?'

Jake's tone was decidedly chippy. It reminded Alanda of when he was a young teenager, moaning about having to tidy his room or accompany the rest of them on bracing New Forest walks (which he always enjoyed, once he'd stopped grumbling about it).

She slid off the sofa onto the rug with her iPad on her lap. 'A quick yoga relaxation. Come on. Sit down.'

'Oh come off it, you're kidding, right?'

'Nope. Humour me. My back hurts and I'm stressed. This will really help.'

He sighed heavily but joined her sitting cross-legged on the rug in the living room. Alanda positioned the iPad on the footstool and put on the first yoga video that came up in the YouTube search results. A predictably bendy-looking young girl in Lycra talked them through some deep breathing and stretches and, miraculously, after a few minutes Alanda did start to feel a bit better, considering the tenterhooks. After a couple of stretches, Jake slipped off his trainers and made more of an effort to join in. There was a bit of colour returning to his cheeks, and he seemed calmer. She made a mental note to try and practice this every day, and to encourage Jake to do the same.

They were about halfway through the video, both in Downward Dog position, when Jake's mobile rang, a few minutes early. He almost fell forward in his haste to grab the phone, bumping into Alanda, who wobbled but managed to regain her balance, as if they were engaged in a game of Twister without the board. It would have been funny were it not so tense.

She shut down the yoga video as Jake picked up his phone, putting it on speaker.

'Hello, Jake Lodge speaking. Is that Liz?'

'Hi, Jake, yes it's me. Sorry, I'm a couple of minutes early.'

'No problem. Thanks so much for talking to us. I'm here with my mum, you're on speaker, I hope that's OK.'

'That's fine.'

Liz Lewis had a nice voice, warm, with the faintest trace of a Liverpool accent. Alanda wished she'd suggested FaceTiming instead, so that they could see her expression. Then she reminded herself that Liz Lewis had no agenda. She didn't *have* to ring them. She was trying to help. There was no need to try and catch her out or check her body language for signs of deception. The woman either had really seen Liam, or she had been mistaken.

Alanda wiped her sweaty palms on her leggings and leaned back against the sofa. They were both still sitting on the floor. She reached out and grabbed Jake's hand.

'Hi Liz,' she said, loudly, her eyes fixed in the middle distance in the way you always did when on speakerphone. 'We're so grateful to you, really. I can't tell you. There's been absolutely no news at all so far so obviously we were really hoping this Twitter campaign would help—'

She was going to continue, but Jake cut her off. 'Anyway, could you talk us through what happened when you saw him in the lift, and what made you think it could be my dad?'

Alanda liked the way he said 'my dad', with the possessiveness of a smitten small boy. It was so sweet that she forgave him for interrupting her; usually a cardinal sin in the Lodge household – or, 'Lodge Lodge', as Liam used to pretend he was going to re-christen their house. He was always threatening that he was going to get it etched onto a name plaque and nailed to the gatepost. The memory gave Alanda such a pang of missing him that she had to swallow hard to stop herself groaning.

'Sure. OK. So, like I said in the DM, my husband Jonathan and I were skiing in Les Gets. It was our last day, which I remember 'cos we weren't sure if we'd have time to get one more run in before the shuttle picked us up to take us back to Geneva to get our flight, which was about nine p.m. It was three-ish, I think. Jonathan and I were sort of arguing about it, actually, because I was worried we didn't have time and he kept convincing me we did, one more run and we'd be out of there in an hour – turned out he was right, although we only just got the bus in time… So, anyway, this bloke gets in the gondola behind us and drops one of his skis, and it almost hits Jonathan on the head and so he apologised and then we got talking…'

Jake and Alanda exchanged glances. Liam was notoriously clumsy. Dropping a ski was exactly the sort of thing he would do. Plus, he would definitely have immediately apologised. But then, so would any decent person, thought Alanda, trying to temper her rising excitement. And Liam had categorically *not* flown off to go skiing when they'd left him at the airport that morning.

'Can you remember exactly what he said?' Jake's voice sounded a bit strangled.

There was a pause on the line. 'Well, not exactly, like. I mean, there was the sorrys and the awkward laughs, and then Jonathan goes, "Meeting friends, are you?" because it's fairly unusual to see someone heading off to ski on their own – they don't recommend it, you know – and the guy said, "Nope, just here for a couple of days. On a whim, as it happens."'

Alanda made an involuntary noise in her throat. Jake squeezed her hand so tightly it hurt.

'On a whim!' They both said it at the same time. *On a whim.* Oh my God, thought Alanda, it really could have been Liam.

'Then I said something like, was he confident, skiing on his own, and that I'd never have the nerve to, and he said, "Well, I hope so. I've not done it since I was seventeen." That's what stuck in our minds. It seemed a bit, well, mad, to do that, on your own…'

'That could explain it all,' Jake said slowly. 'Did you say Geneva is the nearest airport?'

'We flew to Geneva, but you can also go via Grenoble and Lyons,' said Liz. 'Oh, and I almost forgot, there was one more thing he said that could be important…'

'What?' they chorused.

'So, we must've looked a bit concerned or something, 'cos after he said about not doing it since he was seventeen, he goes, "But it's fine, I've got my phone, in case I get lost or fall over." Then he pats his jacket pocket – then the other one – then his ski pants' pockets, and says, "Oh, I must've left it in the locker. Darn it!"'

Jake burst into tears, flapping his hand in front of his eyes, doubling over with emotion and the effort of suppressing the sounds threatening to explode out of him. Alanda felt completely different – a calm, of the sort she had not experienced since Liam went missing, settled on her, making her feel so light that her soul soared, a hot-air balloon of exhilaration and relief at the news, like those dreams where you could fly. It was the 'darn it' that convinced them. It was one of Liam's expressions, and he deemed it suitable for use in most occasions, from the post being late when he was expecting something important, to almost slicing off his finger with the mandolin in the kitchen.

She rubbed Jake's back in firm circles, an attempt to ground herself as much as him. Neither of them could speak.

'Hello?' said Liz Lewis. 'Are you still there?'

After they'd thanked Liz Lewis profusely and terminated the call, Alanda jumped to her feet and hugged Jake, who was still visibly overcome.

'Oh darling!' she said. 'What the hell was Dad doing, *skiing*?'

Jake wiped his eyes with his wrist and sniffed hard. 'It's like I said, I bet: he suddenly got it into his head that he wanted to do something spontaneous. So he could boast to us that he wasn't this stuffy old fart, set in his ways. I bet you anything he was planning to send us a photo of himself on the slopes to surprise us – but then he lost his phone and had a wipeout in the snow.'

Alanda pulled away. 'Let's have another drink,' she said. As they headed down the hall into the kitchen, she turned back to look at him. 'But if that's so, why hasn't he been in touch since? If he didn't have ID on him, he could be lying in a morgue somewhere with a tag on his toe. Or buried under an avalanche somewhere.'

She suddenly felt nauseous. Narrowing down the possibilities of where Liam was also narrowed down the possibilities of what had happened to him, and 'dead from a skiing accident' was suddenly a lot higher on the list now.

'He could've lost his memory,' Jake said, already frantically tapping away on his phone. 'Happens all the time. Liz Lewis would have said if there'd been an avalanche at that resort.'

'God, I hope so,' she said, swallowing. She opened the fridge. 'Wine or beer?'

'Actually, Mum, I'll pass… Look.' He held out the phone to her and she saw a list of French hospitals. 'These are the ones nearest Les Gets and they all have their hours listed as nine a.m to six p.m, so there'd be no point in ringing round tonight. I'm really sorry to do this to you now, but I'm going to head home. I feel a bit sick. I think I just need to take a sleeping pill and go to bed. I've got an interview with that marketing company first thing.'

'Oh… OK. Yes, I feel sick too. And sorry, darling, I'd forgotten about your interview in all the excitement. I'm not in the shop tomorrow so I'll ring round after my walk with Sadie and let you know.'

'*After* your walk?'

'Yes,' Alanda said firmly. 'It's an early walk, and then I'll spend the rest of the day on it, with a clear head. And I'll let PC Laptop know to update the system in the UK about Liz Lewis's sighting. Can you contact Interpol as well? I'm never sure how joined up things are with them.'

'OK, will do. Are you sure you don't mind doing all the ringing round on your own? I could come over after my interview.'

'Thanks, but don't worry. Get a good night's sleep and good luck for the interview – they'll snap you up if they've got any sense.'

'Speak to you tomorrow. But definitely keep me posted.' He had already slung his messenger bag across his back and was ramming on his bike helmet. With a slam of the front door, he was gone.

Alanda wondered if the speed of his departure was more about a subconscious unwillingness to process the potential implications of this news about his dad, a fear that it would turn out to be a dead end – or worse. Jake had always had a tendency to run away from difficult situations.

Then she realised, that by insisting on keeping her walk date with Sadie in the morning, she was doing exactly the same thing. It was terrifying.

CHAPTER TWENTY-EIGHT

The next morning, on an early muddy country walk through the Fonthill Estate with Sadie and her two overenthusiastic spaniels, Bumble and Bee, Alanda relayed the details of the momentous phone call. Her initial euphoria had worn off a bit – the hot-air balloon was still aloft but sinking slowly, and her eyes were gritty and puffy from an almost entirely sleepless night – although Sadie's reaction was gratifyingly positive.

'That's incredible! Why didn't you tell me? Oh my God, I'm so excited for you! This is wonderful news!'

They were walking past the lake, whose surface was ruffled by a brisk wind, causing the ducks to bob up and down comically. Alanda thought their faces looked panicked, although of course this was pure projection… and was she projecting too that the sighting of Liam, about a thousand kilometres from where he'd told them he would be, was a good thing?

Doubt was creeping in, blackening the edges of her vision like an encroaching faint, and even Sadie's excited squawks weren't helping assuage the fears.

'I'm telling you now. I wanted to wait till we were walking. It's a lot to take in. And, the more I think about it, the less I'm sure how wonderful it is…'

Sadie gave her a brief impulsive squeeze, and one of the dogs immediately tried to join in. 'Get down, Bumble! She can't stand being left out of any sort of display of affection. What makes you say that?'

Alanda tried to brush Bumble's muddy paw prints off, but only succeeded in smearing mud further on her leggings, coat and hand. The dog had bounded away and was now chasing her brother through a series of deep puddles.

'I think it boils down to two things. The fact that he didn't tell any of us he was going skiing, and the fact that he's not been in contact since. I think it's more and more likely that he was living some kind of double life, biding his time till he could leave.'

Sadie physically halted Alanda in her tracks, moving in front of her and holding up her hand as if about to push her away. 'No! Absolutely impossible. If it *was* him in that cable car, he was on his own.'

'Doesn't mean anything,' Alanda said briskly. 'Perhaps his girlfriend – or other wife – just didn't fancy skiing on the first day of their holiday.'

'And Heather's *wedding*,' wailed Sadie. 'You really think he'd have bailed on you all before that?'

She looked so distressed, running her hand through her curly hair, her eyes so full of pain, Alanda thought anyone would assume it was *Sadie's* husband who'd gone AWOL.

Sadie had a point, though. It would be unimaginably cruel and out of character for Liam to intentionally leave before the wedding.

'No,' she conceded slowly. 'It's hard to believe that. But what if there was some reason he had no choice? An ultimatum from his other woman? Maybe she's terminally ill or something. Or maybe he was actually intending to come back for the wedding and something stopped him? Not that we'd have let him, if he's doing this on purpose.'

She picked a stick up off the path and slashed angrily at the waist-high ferns, making Bumble and Bee leap around her feet, hoping she was going to throw it for them.

'Alanda,' said Sadie. 'I would bet my life that Liam's not doing any of this on purpose. He adores you. Have you ever had any indication that he's having an affair? Had he changed towards you?

Got more secretive, not as romantic? Not been where he's supposed to be? Sex life gone down the tubes?'

Alanda shook her head. Liam had been as romantic, warm and affectionate as ever, right up until their farewell at the departure gates. She recalled his face, the love in his eyes as he gazed at her enough to blur out everything else, the huge departure terminal shrunk down to the size of his dilating pupils and the hustle and bustle of chat and tannoy announcements fading into silence.

Don't get lost or killed.

And yet...

'He spends a lot of time in his music room up in the attic. Well, spare bedroom, but we call it the music room because he keeps his guitars in there – I can't hear the guitar at all when I'm down in the kitchen, so he could be doing anything. And he doesn't sleep well, so he's often up for hours at night too...'

'You're making mountains out of molehills. Why would you even torture yourself by thinking like this? Something really positive has happened and you're trying to find reasons to make it seem like a bad thing.'

Alanda sighed, and threw the stick as far as she could for the dogs, watching it arc up into the air and spin, almost in slow motion.

The dogs tore off after the stick, barking in ecstasy. 'Just preparing myself for the worst, I suppose. And trying to work out why he would lie to us. I mean, if he wanted to go skiing, he could just have gone skiing, I wouldn't have stopped him! Why did he feel he needed to lie about it?'

'I don't know why you think he did lie. He said to the woman in the cable car that he'd gone there "on a whim" – doesn't that tell you all you need to know?'

'It's just so out of character. What – between getting on a plane at Gatwick and arriving in Madrid, he changed his mind and decided that he'd really wanted to go skiing all along? It's ridiculously implausible.'

Bee had won possession of the stick and came trotting back with it, glancing triumphantly over his shoulder at his sister. He came up to Alanda, but wouldn't drop it.

'I can't throw it again if you don't let go!' she told him, trying to wrest it out of his jaws.

'But not impossible,' Sadie said, checking her phone the way she did every five minutes. Alanda always wondered what or who she was expecting. 'I think you should put aside the worries for now and focus on finally having some information to work with. What will you do next? Have you told the girls?'

'Not yet. We don't know for sure it's him and I don't want to get their hopes up unnecessarily. Jake's going to update Interpol and try and get them to check Liam's DNA against any local unidentified men. We gave them a sample from his hairbrush when he first went missing. I'm going to ring round the nearby hospitals in the meantime, just on the off-chance, and in case Interpol drags its heels.'

She shuddered involuntarily at the thought of having to ring around hospitals. Her worst-case scenario was being told that a man answering Liam's description was lying unclaimed in the hospital mortuary...

'I'm amazed you didn't get onto it straight away.' Sadie was always commenting on Alanda's behaviour in a tacitly critical manner. If she hadn't been such a good friend, it would have been extremely irritating.

'Jake looked it up last night and they all had office-type opening hours for general enquiries. And besides, I needed a while to absorb it. Prepare myself for potential bad news, I suppose. I'm going to do it as soon as I get home.'

Why was she being so defensive, she wondered?

'Want me to stick around?' Sadie smiled at her and Alanda returned it.

'Thanks, honey, but I'll be OK. I'll update you as soon as there's any news.'

*

The first place she called was a hospital near Mont Blanc that she immediately mentally rechristened 'Mont Blank' – the receptionist spoke terrible English, the dodgy phone reception did Alanda's schoolgirl French no favours at all, and after a frustrating five-minute conversation where she ended up almost yelling *'Avez-vous un homme inconnu?'* she eventually abandoned the call in frustration. She had hoped it meant 'unidentified man' but when she looked it up on Google Translate to check, she discovered it actually meant 'unknown man'. 'Unidentified man' was *'homme non identifié'*.

'Close enough, surely?' she demanded of the small felted llama in her eyeline, one of the more successful crafting attempts cluttering the shelves of her office. 'Maybe it's my accent.'

Perhaps she should ask the police to make all the enquiries. But she didn't trust them to get onto it straight away. It was clear that Liam, as a mentally unimpaired adult, was not a priority, and she strongly suspected that they thought he'd probably done a runner with another woman.

Alanda sighed and dialled the next number on the list. She could come back to Mont *Blank* later, if she had to. She wished she'd taken up Jake or Sadie on their offers to be with her – there was something utterly terrifying about the possibility of finding out, from an anonymous voice on the end of a phone line, that Liam was dead, and she did not want to be on her own when or if that happened.

It won't happen, she told herself. *It hasn't happened.*

The next hospital receptionist spoke good English, which made everything a lot more straightforward. No, they had not had any unidentified males admitted in April.

Next…

She tried three more with no luck, in and around Évian, before ringing one of two hospitals in a place called Thonon-les-Bains, which was about an hour and a half away from Les Gets. It seemed a bit far, she thought, for someone who'd had an accident – about the same as driving from Salisbury to London, and you would never be taken that far to a hospital in the UK unless you needed some sort of specialist attention. But then, that area of France was less populated, and this did seem like a big medical centre.

She was on hold for about eight minutes, listening to some tortuously distorted hold music which was starting to drive her to distraction. She was about to hang up when finally a woman answered, speaking so rapidly that Alanda couldn't identify the name of the establishment, even with its name written on the computer screen in front of her.

'*Bonjour. Parlez-vous anglais?*' she asked, when there was a pause.

'Yes,' said the woman, in a heavily accented voice. 'A leetle bit.'

Oh thank God, thought Alanda.

'Thank you – *merci* – I am calling from England. My husband disappeared in April, and we think he may possibly have decided to go skiing in Les Gets. We haven't heard from him since, so I am wondering if you happened to have an unidentified man admitted to your hospital?'

'*Mais oui,*' the woman said straight away, sounding so excited that Alanda's heart jumped into her throat. She wouldn't sound excited if he was dead, would she?

'Jack! We 'ad a man who we called Jack. E' lost his… brain. *Non.* His, 'ow you say it, mind?'

'Memory!' Alanda found that she was panting with anticipation. Oh, how she wished the kids were here to share this! 'His memory? He couldn't remember anything?'

'Yes. We was trying to learn who he was. We think he is American.'

'He is American! Well, he grew up there. He has a very slight American accent so I can see how you would think that.'

Alanda stood up and began to bounce lightly on the balls of her feet, her pulse thudding in her ears, trying so hard to suppress the swoosh of hope in her belly that it solidified into a solid lump that threatened to make her vomit.

'Can I send you a photograph of my husband, please? He is called Liam Lodge.'

'Of course! *Mon Dieu*, I 'ope that this is him.'

'Is he still in hospital?'

'*Non*. He was discharged some weeks ago. He had a broken leg and this is why he was here for so long.'

'Where did he go when he left hospital?'

Another pause. 'I don't know, I am sorry. But I will give you an email address now, and please send us your details so we can confirm if our Jack is your 'usband. We all knew about him, you see, and wanted to 'elp him find his family.'

Alanda was so touched that for a moment she couldn't speak. *Our Jack*. The thought that it could be him, he could still be alive, and people had cared for him in her absence… it was everything. Not to mention that he hadn't betrayed her, or left her.

'Thank you. Thank you so much for your kindness,' she managed eventually.

Our Jack, she repeated to herself. *My Liam.*

CHAPTER TWENTY-NINE

Katya

Katya was jogging along the Lac Léman promenade when her thigh started vibrating. Her heart, already pounding from the run she was currently halfway through, skipped several more beats when she fished her phone out of the side pocket of her running shorts and saw the name on the screen: 'Hospital'.

Nobody from the hospital had rung her for months, not since Otto died. More worryingly, Jack was out and about – or at least, he had been when she had left the apartment half an hour ago. He had gone out, with only one crutch, since the plaster cast finally came off yesterday, to get milk from the grocery shop round the corner. Katya imagined him falling down the steps and hitting his head or falling into traffic. His mobility was improving all the time, but he still needed crutches for anything more taxing than a few steps across the bedroom and was wobbly as a newborn baby giraffe.

'Katya DeLorenzo,' she panted into the phone, leaning against the curved white iron railings of the promenade to try and catch her breath. The railings were cool against her hot hand.

'Katya, hello, it's Sister Celine,' said the high-pitched voice, in French.

'Celine? What's happened, what's the matter?'

'Don't panic. It's not an emergency,' she continued. 'Not exactly…'

'You have Jack there?'

'No, no, please don't worry, nothing has happened to him. At least, not that I know.'

'Then what is it? Is it something about Otto? Sorry if I sound strange, I'm out running.'

Katya was puzzled, and slightly in shock at the thought that Jack might have had another accident. Sweat was rapidly cooling on her body and, even in the heat of July, she began to shiver. She walked across to a bench in full sun on the other side of the promenade and sat down, stretching out her legs in front of her and focussing on the logos on her running shoes.

'No, it's not Otto… Something has happened though, and I thought you should know. Perhaps I ought to have told Jack directly, but I think it would be better coming from you, so you can discuss together what you do.'

'What?'

Katya knew, though. She knew what Celine was going to say. She'd known it was only a matter of time before this happened. Of course he had a family who would track him down eventually; of course.

This was it, then, and so hot on the heels of her conviction that this was their happy ending. The cruelty of life, that just when she thought things were finally going right for her, instead it was probably the beginning of the end for her and Jack, the loveliest, kindest man she had ever met.

Worse, when their child was curled up inside her, safely anchored to the wall of her womb, gently undulated by her stride as she ran. At that moment, the pain felt so great that she wanted to run away with both of them, scoop them both up, the lame and the tiny. They were her whole world. It didn't make any difference that she had always known, deep down, that it probably wouldn't be like this for ever.

On the phone, Celine cleared her throat. 'Are you still there, Katya?'

Katya nodded stupidly, then realised Celine couldn't see her. '*Oui.*'

'OK. So, the switchboard had a phone call yesterday. A phone call from England.'

Her legs began to shake, even though she was already sitting down. She felt sick.

'Who was it?'

'It was a woman with a strange name, she had to spell it out to the receptionist. Alanda Lodge. She was asking if a man had been brought in to the hospital on April seventh, if there was anyone in a coma, or dead, because she believed that her husband might have been skiing at Les Gets that day and they had not heard from him since… The receptionist knew about Jack, of course, and she asked the woman to send her a photograph of her husband.'

Katya could not speak for a moment. A maelstrom of thoughts whirled through her mind. Was she ready for this? It might not be Jack… oh, who was she kidding; who else would it be? April seventh was the date he had arrived in hospital, she knew that without checking, because that was the same day as Otto's surgery. She had only arrived in Thonon the day before. Perhaps she and Jack had even been on the same flight.

'And was it?'

'Yes. It was.'

Katya did not know what to say. What could you say, when you knew you were about to lose the father of your child?

'What's her husband's name?' Her voice sounded small and subdued.

'It's Liam – short for William. Liam Lodge, he's known as.'

So. Liam Lodge. She tried to recalibrate and failed. He wasn't Liam, he was *Jack*. Her Jack. Her tears were falling, so hard that a man in cargo shorts walking a small sausage dog stopped uncertainly by the bench and looked nervously at her. He stretched out a tentative hand and raised his eyebrows in the universal gesture of *I see you are not OK, can I do anything to help?* Katya shook her head at him, and he walked away.

So, as she had suspected, 'Liam' had a wife.

Celine was talking again and Katya had to force herself to concentrate.

'She rang back just now and they put her through to me. I just got off the phone to her.'

'What did you tell her?'

Celine sighed. 'I did not know what to say. Of course, I told her about his accident and the memory loss and all the medical stuff. I told her that he was discharged a few weeks ago. Naturally she wanted to know where he went after that.'

'Did – you – give her – my – address?' Katya couldn't stop herself sobbing out loud, and the words emerged in staccato bursts.

'Shhh, Katya, don't cry,' soothed Celine. 'I'm so sorry, *chérie*. No, I have not. I wondered if I should, and then I thought it was not up to me. After all, we don't know why Jack went skiing on his own in the first place. I felt I could not ask her if they were divorced or still married, so I don't know what their situation is. For all we know, Jack did not want her to know where he was. She didn't know he'd gone skiing, or even that he was in France – she said he had planned to go hiking in Spain. I pretended I didn't know where he had gone, but she made me promise to try and find out, so I thought I would ring you straight away. She is going to ring back again tomorrow.'

'So she hasn't got his mobile number, his new one?'

'No,' said Celine. 'Not yet.'

'Oh, Celine,' Katya said. 'What should I do? I'm – we're – having a baby. I'm pregnant.' The words came out as an agonised wail.

'*Mon Dieu*, Katya, I don't know what to say. *Félicitations!* And yet… oh, this is so difficult. I wish I could help.'

'And you didn't tell her anything … about us?'

About how happy we are, she thought. *How happy we thought we might just get to be together.*

'It is not my place to tell her anything like that. But for what it's worth, I think this could be a good thing, in the end. He needs to know who he really is. It would be impossible for you two to move on while he still has no identity. This way you are not trapped in one situation any more. You can get on with your lives together. Start your family. Settle down without this hanging over you both. One thing I do know is that Jack – Liam – loves you so very much. It is obvious. It was obvious to me right from when you two first met.'

CHAPTER THIRTY

'Mademoiselle Katya DeLorenzo?' enquired a deep, resonant male French voice.

'*Oui?*' Katya asked, with a sinking heart, thinking *now what?*

She'd had to answer it. It was the fourth time that day the words 'Unknown Caller' had flashed up on her screen, and it seemed likely they were just going to keep trying until she picked up. But Jack had been with her every other time and, after Celine's bombshell, she was reluctant to answer any calls from people she didn't know, particularly not in his presence.

It had been two days since Celine broke the news of Jack's real identity, and she had thought of nothing else since. She'd promised Celine she would tell him, and she really had been meaning to but every time she opened her mouth, she found she just couldn't do it.

She knew that he had to know; it was probably downright cruel not to explain immediately – but she also knew it meant that their days of being in this little bubble of love and togetherness might be numbered, and she found she wanted to hang onto what they had, in its simplest, most pure version, for as long as she possibly could.

She decided to not even look online, for now that she knew his real name, she knew she would find appeals and photos and evidence of his other life; a life in which people – other people – loved him deeply and wanted him with them.

She was nowhere near ready to let go of him, even though she'd always known she might have to. She had never felt so jealous or confused – and guilty, that she was keeping those loved ones away from him for longer than necessary. Would he hate her for it?

Jack kept looking at her, with concern in his eyes, and asking if she felt OK. She would laugh it off as just 'feeling weird', and that it was no doubt pregnancy hormones making her feel all over the place – which, in fairness, it probably was. One time he took her hand and said, seriously, 'I'm sure that not knowing anything about who the father of your baby is must be truly horrible. I don't blame you for feeling emotional.'

But now she did know, and that was the problem! When he added, 'But I am one hundred per cent here for you, no matter what,' she burst into tears.

Jack hadn't seen her cry before, apart from at Otto's funeral, and he looked terrified as he took her in his arms and rocked her like a baby till she quietened down.

It would all come down to what his current relationship was with the woman calling herself his wife, Katya thought. That was what would determine her future, and the future of their new little family.

That day, they had come out shopping for presents for Jack's pretend birthday. Now, after an hour or so wandering around the men's department of FNAC, he had gone to the Gents' – which was not a quick trip, on his crutches.

Katya had promised to buy him some new clothes. Obviously they had no idea when his birthday really was, so a month or so ago they'd decided on a date pretty much at random, but not too far ahead because she knew he badly needed something other than the cobbled together mish-mash of Otto's shirts and pyjamas, some charity shop shorts and trousers, and a few T-shirts and underwear she'd bought him when he first moved in. It was the only way she could get him to accept anything new from her.

His complete lack of resources was beginning to get to him, Katya could tell. She absolutely did not mind paying for everything though; she was happy to, but it must have been pretty emasculating for him, she thought, to never even be able to get a round of drinks in, or take her out to dinner.

And now Katya felt guilty as well as sorry for him, because, since Celine's call, all she had to do was to say 'Your name is Liam Lodge, and you live in England. You have a wife – or ex-wife – called Alanda,' and then in a couple of phone calls or clicks of a mouse, his wealth would be restored. Katya imagined it like in a Disney film where a wizard would wave a wand and, in a puff of smoke, suddenly there would be bags and bags of gold sitting at Jack's feet.

She owed it to him, she knew she did, especially now after the gift he had given her, the grain-of-rice sized gift in her belly. And of course she *would* tell him.

Just not right now.

While he was in the toilet, Katya waited in the book department of FNAC, leafing through the titles of new releases with unseeing eyes, and that was when her phone rang for the fourth time.

'I'm Jean-Luc Portas, I'm an agent from the National Police, and I understand that you are friends with a man whose identity we are trying to establish, known just as Jack?'

'Friends with' seemed an almost insultingly shallow way to describe what Jack and she had together. But Katya supposed perhaps he was trying to spare her feelings. It would have been rude of him to say 'shacked up with', or maybe he thought anything else would be too presumptuous.

'Yes. I got to know him when he was in hospital. He was on the same ward as my uncle, who I was visiting every day... until he – my uncle, I mean – died. I offered Jack a place to stay when he came out of hospital.'

'That was so kind of you. I am sorry for the loss of your uncle.'

He sounded nice, this Jean-Luc Portas, but Katya was in full fight-or-flight mode, like a mother swan protecting a gaggle of cygnets. She waited, knowing what was coming next, glancing up through the bookshelves to see if Jack was swinging his way back towards her. (He had developed a very cheerful, ebullient sort of way of being on crutches, as if he was shouting 'wheeeeeee!' every time he swung forwards, even more so now the plaster was off.)

'I am calling you because we believe we now know his identity. A relative in England has come forward and is trying to find him.'

A relative. Not 'a wife'.

'I see,' Katya said, forcing her voice to stay calm and steady and not betray that she already knew. She leaned back against the fiction shelves – authors with surnames G-N – and took a deep breath. Thank God Celine had given her some advance warning. 'Well, that's great news for Jack.'

She'd thought they would have longer…

'Do you have a phone number for him?'

'Hmm? No – sorry, I don't. He'd been using an old mobile of mine when he was staying with me, but unfortunately it packed up a few days before he left.'

Her heart was hammering. It was astonishing how easily the story began to unspool out of her, as if she'd been rehearsing it for weeks.

Well, she supposed, in many ways she had been.

'He said he would be in touch when he got settled in his new place.'

The cop sounded both regretful and suspicious. 'He has moved out? When?'

Katya pretended to consider. 'Um… must be a couple of weeks ago now. I said he could stay as long as he liked, but he said he didn't want to be a burden on me any longer than necessary.'

'I see. And where has he gone?'

'I'm not sure.'

This was ridiculous, she thought. It would take him a matter of moments to check the veracity of her story. Where the hell *would* he have gone? It couldn't be 'to a friend's' or 'to a hotel' for obvious reasons.

She panicked. Then she remembered the conversation she and Jack had in the hospital, the day they visited the rose garden.

'It's something to do with the hospital, I think. Someone there was helping him with all the admin – really difficult to get anything done when you don't have any ID – and he said they had offered him a place to stay somewhere connected with the site; might have been nurses' accommodation, or maybe a room they have there, that's usually for the families of sick children to stay in? Yes, I think that was it. To be honest, I wasn't paying much attention. He promised to ring me when he was settled and we're meant to be meeting for coffee…'

'So you haven't seen or spoken to him at all in the last two weeks?'

Saliva flooded Katya's mouth and she felt dizzy. Vague misdirection was one thing, but telling an outright lie to a direct question felt like a step too far. A direct question asked by a policeman, no less. What had she got herself into? Of course, saying Jack had gone to stay somewhere organised by the hospital would only ever buy her a small amount of time, it was so easily checked, but she hadn't been able to think of a single other option on the spot. Would she be in trouble for obstructing an investigation?

Jack would be back in a minute. Katya slunk out of the book section and into the make-up hall adjacent to it, where she hid behind a Benefit concession and pretended to examine a display of sparkly eyeshadows. He could not overhear this conversation.

She decided to try a different tack. 'The thing is, Officer, I don't know where he went because, well, I'm not sure if you were aware – you probably are, because otherwise how would you have my phone number? – I expect someone at the hospital told you, but Jack and I had become very close. We started a relationship when he came to stay with me at my uncle's apartment.'

She waited, but Officer Portas made only a non-committal sound down the line. He must have known already.

'It's been quite difficult, with his memory issues, and in the end we decided that it wasn't going to work out. We had a bit of a row, actually…'

Should she have said this? What if the officer thought that she'd *killed* him! Her imagination was running riot. Sweat was now popping out all over her, sticking her shirt to her skin even in the cool air-conditioned department store. This was hideous. Why was she doing this? It was only prolonging the inevitable.

She cleared her throat. 'I asked him to leave, and he did. So we broke up. I'm planning to go home to England in the near future, once I've finished getting my uncle's apartment ready to sell. I think your best bet would be to contact the hospital, I'm sure they'll know.'

She felt such a pang at the thought of selling the apartment. She couldn't bear the idea of someone else living there. It would forever be hers and Jack's, and Otto's before that.

'I'm sorry to hear that,' said the officer cautiously. 'I will go back and ask at the hospital again.'

He didn't believe her, she could hear it in his voice. *Oh Katya, you idiot*, she thought. She had lied to the police, and for what? To buy a couple of days, if that?

But she had to be the one to tell Jack. She didn't know why it felt so important, but she supposed it was because it would still give her at least an illusion of control over the situation.

'I have to go,' she said, unable to prevent a faint choking sound leaving her throat. 'Please let me know if there is anything I can do to help.'

She could see Jack through the doorway into the book department, searching for her.

'Could I give your mobile number to Mr Lodge's family? I'm sure they will want to thank you for being so kind to him, and get more information as to his whereabouts, if necessary.'

'No, I would prefer you did not pass on my telephone number. And please do not tell them what I just told you, that we started a relationship. The man has lost his memory, he can't be held responsible for anything he did. It's over now, and I don't think there is any benefit in his family knowing about that part of it.'

'Very well,' said the officer. 'I suspect you're right.'

CHAPTER THIRTY-ONE

Alanda

August

It had been three days since the receptionist at the hospital in Thonon-les-Bains confirmed that the photograph Alanda emailed across – Liam raising his Cambridgeshire pint to the camera – was definitely the mystery patient they'd had with them since early April.

That blissful moment of 'yes', she thought. She would never, ever forget the moment the reply had arrived, pinging onto her iPad screen. The memory was up there with the look in Liam's eyes when he'd got down on one knee all those years ago and proffered a small black box containing the beautiful opal engagement ring she still wore; or the moment of calm at the birth of her children, after the pain and blood and effort, that first proper look into their perfect little faces.

Bless that sweet receptionist, whose excitement jumped out of the letters of her typed message. Days later, Alanda was still welling up every time she thought about her kindness: *Dear Mme. Lodge, Oui! Yes! This is our Jack! We are so happy for you. We will inform the police immediately. Someone will call you back with an address for him.*

Alanda decided not to tell any of the children, not even Jake, which she felt particularly mean about, because he'd just heard he had been pipped at the post for the job he interviewed for the other day. Not yet. The relief she felt at the news Liam was still alive was profound and overwhelming, and there were uncomfortable prickles of guilt that she was keeping this relief from the kids when they too could experience it but, more than that, she could not, would not, risk it being a dead end. To still not be able to find him, for whatever reason, having got so close would be even more devastating – and there was a nagging worry that after three days, surely someone in France would have tracked him down by now?

She did not tell a soul, apart from PC Harding. Not the kids, not Sadie, not even nice Jennie at Vi's home. It was her burden to shoulder, until it was completely safe to announce that they had Liam back again.

He had not been in touch. Every time the phone rang she thought it might be him, now that they knew her number; she yearned to hear his voice. But nobody called back, from the hospital or anywhere, not even the lovely receptionist.

Almost three days. Sixty-four hours.

Jake of course had asked, and she told him that she was still ringing round the local hospitals, and that PC Laptop was liaising with his French counterparts (which he had said he would, but there had been silence from that direction too).

Jake would kill her when he found out that she knew Liam was still alive and hadn't told him – but she was determined to deliver Liam back to them unequivocally, or not at all.

In the meantime, the worry kept growing. She'd rung the hospital every day, but not managed to speak to the same receptionist again and each subsequent time she had endured either a frustrating conversation where she couldn't make herself understood, or a generic recorded message instructing her to dial the extension number she needed if she knew it and which did not allow her to leave a voicemail.

PC Harding, when they'd spoken, had been fulsome in his congratulations at the family's successful investigative work, and also agreed that it was best to keep the news quiet until they had intelligence as to Liam's exact whereabouts – his words – which made Alanda even more convinced that the police all believed Liam had done a runner and didn't want to be found. Even now, when it had been confirmed he'd lost his memory, Alanda thought indignantly.

But then in that case... *why* had Liam not called? She couldn't shake a worry that even though he could still be suffering from memory loss, there might be an additional, more sinister, reason for him not being in touch. They must know where he'd gone, surely?

These thoughts went round and round her sleepless tortured mind until, at five a.m. on Day Four since Liam's identity had been confirmed by the hospital, Alanda went online and booked a flight to Geneva, departing at noon that day. If the mountain wouldn't come to Mohammed...

She arrived in Thonon late afternoon, stepping off the Léman Express train from Geneva feeling slightly travel-delirious, as though she'd been buffeted by a high wind; so many new experiences and emotions one after the other. There was something undeniably strange at the best of times about starting the day in one country and then being in an entirely different one by the afternoon, let alone when you hadn't even planned on going until dawn that morning.

It was much hotter than she'd expected, too – the forecast had said showers, so she was wearing her red spring raincoat, which had been fine on the air-conditioned train, but now instantly made her sweat so much that the waterproofed outside would have been better as a lining. She stripped it off and carried it in the crook of her elbow, marching more resolutely than she felt towards the station exit.

She had fibbed to Jake and the girls, telling them that she and Sadie were going to grab a couple of nights in a spa to try and de-stress a bit while waiting for news from France, and instructing them to text rather than call as reception was always iffy in the hotel. She said she'd make sure she rang straight away if there was any news, and they all seemed to buy it without question. If they tried to ring her, the international ringtone would give the game away immediately – but none of them were particularly fond of speaking on the phone anyway unless absolutely necessary. As with most of their generation, they preferred the brevity of a text, usually peppered with emojis and GIFs.

What GIF would they use if she found their dad? Alanda wondered idly.

She was in a minicab now, on her way to the police station in Thonon. If she got no joy there, then she would try the hospital again. But the police allegedly knew about Liam, so it was worth a try. If the hospital wouldn't give her an address, perhaps the police would.

It only took a few minutes to get there, a bland white frontage bearing the words 'Hotel de Police' underneath what looked like a block of flats. Alanda, still feeling delirious, had a brief mental image of a hotel staffed entirely by policemen, police chambermaids, police barmen and receptionists…

She paid the cab driver, extended the handle of her wheeled overnight bag, rumbling it across the tarmac and in through some sliding doors, for the first time wishing that she hadn't come on her own after all; wishing Sadie or the kids were with her.

'*Bonjour,*' she said to the officer behind the desk, trying to keep the tremor out of her voice. '*Parlez-vous anglais?*'

CHAPTER THIRTY-TWO

Katya

Perhaps Jack was synching with her own mood, Katya thought, because they were both on very poor form that afternoon. It was a bit of a shock, actually, to see him like that. She had never known him to be anything other than sunny, positive and – since he'd moved in – happy, unless he was in pain.

She knew exactly why *she* was in a funk of worry and confusion, but what was his excuse? Sympathetic pregnancy hormones, perhaps. That was a thing, wasn't it?

'What's the matter, sweetie?' she asked tentatively. It was a muggy, overcast day so they were inside on the sofa, trying to watch a documentary about the evils of sugar, but she could tell he was concentrating on it as little as she was.

He turned and smiled at her, reaching out and stroking her cheek, then nuzzling his head into her neck. Instantly, she felt soothed and a little bit better. His frequent spontaneous gestures of affection were one of the things she most adored about him. She knew it wasn't healthy to make comparisons, but Jack and Danny were so different in that regard. Danny had loved her, she knew, but he expressed it in his own way, through generous gifts and flowers. That had been lovely, of course, but she would have preferred twenty hugs and whispered endearments a day to any number of raffia-tied bouquets. She always came away with the uncomfortable impression that Danny spent money on her because he didn't know how, or didn't want, to express affection.

She would instantly then feel guilty because that was likely a consequence of being raised by cold and distant parents, and nothing that he could help, not without therapy.

Then why hadn't he gone and *got* therapy? She'd suggested it often enough.

Jack began to speak, so she pushed the memories of Danny's emotional stuntedness out of her head. That was another thing she loved about Jack; he was never afraid to say what he felt. Katya wondered if it would be the same once his memory returned.

'I'm sorry,' he began, and she felt a jolt of panic. Had he somehow found out that she was withholding his identity? 'I know I'm a bit subdued, and I'm sorry I keep banging on about it, but I just can't stop thinking that our poor baby will grow up with a dad whose life history – whose real name! – is a total void before the age of… well, whatever my age is.'

Katya's eyes instantly filled. The knowledge that she could enlighten him in a single sentence, but was choosing not to, gave her palpitations.

Jack hugged her, misunderstanding the tears as tears of acknowledgement, not of guilt.

'Your memory will come back,' she said, desperately, her voice muffled by his armpit. 'The doctors said it would be really unusual for it not to.' She forced herself to tip up her head and look him in the eye. But not to tell him the truth… 'Hang in there, my darling. And besides, our baby won't care what your past is. He or she will have you, us, and that's all they'll need.'

If you said something with enough passion, could that ever make it true?

Oh, this is crazy, she thought. *What am I doing?* Perhaps that was what pregnancy did to women. You'd do anything to protect your child; anything. At that moment she thought, fiercely, that she'd never tell him the truth. If it came down to a choice between his memory and their happiness, she would have to take the path of selfishness, not just for her sake, but for their burgeoning family's, too.

'Why hasn't it yet, though? I'm getting so worried. And not knowing anything about myself is starting to get me down, which is making me worried that this is the reason why *you're* upset, and that's the worst thing of all. I mean, how is it ever going to work between us when I have no identity? I adore you, Kat, unconditionally – but I can't stop thinking, is this just because I don't remember what the conditions even are?'

'Oh sweetheart,' she said, thinking, *OK, so I have to tell him.* It was so cruel not to. She took a deep breath, opened her mouth – but nothing more came out.

'And not being able to contribute financially, at all… that's getting me down too,' he admitted miserably.

She was going to tell him then, she really intended to – but he carried on speaking.

'Do you know what occurred to me this morning? It's silly, but…'

'What?'

The moment had passed.

'It occurred to me that my cast coming off the other day was when I really started worrying about this stuff. It sounds stupid, I know, but it was like this hard shell protecting my leg was also protecting my… *heart.*'

He glanced at her to check her reaction, and her own heart swelled at his admission of vulnerability (something else that Danny was notoriously terrible at).

'I was lying on that bed in Orthopaedics watching it being sawn off and looking at my poor scarred leg coming out, and I felt so… exposed. It looked terrible, all thin and the skin was a horrible grey-blue. I must've made a sound because the nurse who was sawing stopped. She thought she'd nicked my skin. I couldn't tell her that it wasn't a physical wound, more of an… an… existential uncovering… Oh sorry, Kat, this sounds so pretentious.'

'It doesn't. Honestly.'

Tell him.

I can't.

'You know what I think?' she asked briskly, making a monumental effort to sound upbeat. 'I think that two very major things have happened in your life, our lives, recently.'

Three things, actually. But I'm somehow completely unable to tell him about the most major one.

'One, we only found out that we're having a baby a few weeks ago. Two, your cast came off but you're still in pain, which must be depressing. These are both really big deals.'

It was true, she'd been thinking that Jack had been setting too much store by the removal of his cast, as if it would suddenly solve the issue of not only his mobility but also his memory. His leg was still stiff and sore in the thigh-length Velcroed splint that the hospital had given him to wear, and he still needed crutches, so it was no wonder he felt down.

'Especially the baby,' he agreed, tenderly reaching out to place his palm on her belly. 'And I'm worried about you. You've been really quiet recently and we should both still be over the moon. Are you still feeling sick?'

She shook her head. 'Just… worried about you, that's all.'

'Me? You don't need to worry about me!' He said it brightly, then slumped against the back of the sofa. 'Well, no, that's not entirely true. Oh Kat, I feel so concerned for *us*. For you. What are you letting yourself in for? This baby will tie us together for ever, and I'm a man who doesn't know anything about himself, not even his name. I'm so fed up with not knowing. I could be a murderer. A dictator, a despot, a paedophile, an escaped prisoner, a tyrant!'

This at least made her laugh. 'You're the least despotic and tyrannical person I've ever met.'

'I could be married,' he said, soberly.

She winced, a sudden frightened jerk, and she waited for him to ask her if there was something she knew that he didn't.

Gathering herself, she pulled his face close to hers until they were nose to nose. 'Yes, you could be married. And there's every chance that this won't last for ever. We have to accept that.'

He reared back, astonished that she could have said such a thing. It was the first time either of them had properly acknowledged it.

'It will if we both want it to, I want us to be together. Don't you? You sound like you don't care! Kat, we're having a baby.'

Katya closed her eyes. 'It's not that simple. I really, really love you, but we don't know what's gone before. What's expected of you. I'm everything to you now, but you don't know how you might feel if that turns out not to be the case.'

Jack glanced sharply at her again but she just bit her lip and looked away.

'I won't feel any different,' he said. 'I know I won't.'

She nodded. 'I won't either,' she said.

It was as close as she could get to telling him the truth.

CHAPTER THIRTY-THREE

It was a physical knuckle-rap, rather than someone buzzing in from outside the building. Nobody ever knocked at the apartment's front door.

Katya pushed away her chair and got up. 'Must be a neighbour.'

'Typical,' Jack said. 'Just as you've dished up. I bet it's that funny old lady down the hall, the one who's about three feet tall with the dowager's hump.' He glanced curiously at her from his plate of spaghetti bolognese. 'Are you OK? You look weird.'

She knew how she must look: terrified. She tried to rearrange her features back into something approximating normality, but felt like crumpling. It would be the police again, and this time she'd have to come clean; admit she knew.

It was too soon. Just hours after their heart-to-heart that afternoon! She couldn't bear it.

'I'm fine.'

Katya walked carefully up the mezzanine steps, across Otto's large brown rug, the one they were hoping to replace with something more modern and colourful as soon as they had the money, then stopped, turned and walked back to the kitchen table. She sat back down and reached for her glass of water.

'You know what?' she said, unable to stop her voice sounding, to her ears at least, a monotone of impending doom. 'Let's leave it. We're eating and it'll get cold.'

Jack frowned. 'What if someone's in trouble? I'm sure they wouldn't knock unless they needed something.'

Katya looked down at her plate, studying a mushroom with what appeared to be great interest. Her hand was shaking as she held the tumbler.

Jack reached out and clasped it in his own. 'Kat, what is it, my love?'

She shook her head. 'Nothing! I'm just tired, and not liking the thought of small talk with one of the neighbours. Hopefully they'll go away.'

They sat in silence for a few more seconds, listening out for retreating footsteps, but none came. Then another knock, this one louder. It made them both jump, even though they had been expecting it.

'I'll go,' said Jack, reaching for the crutches propped against the kitchen wall.

'Don't be daft! I'll go.'

In the end they both stood, Katya reluctantly and Jack slowly. Katya retraced her steps across the rug towards the door, her shoulders rigid with tension. Jack stuck his arms into the crutches and swung himself along behind her.

Later she remembered what was playing on Spotify through their little Bluetooth speaker: John Martyn's 'Don't Want To Know', the sound swelling around them, making it seem as if the music was offering them up to the fate waiting in the hallway.

Katya reached the front door and fiddled with the knob of the Yale lock, as if she was pretending she had forgotten how to operate it, taking so long that by the time she was inching the door open, Jack had caught up with her and was standing at her left shoulder. He was just reaching out to prop one crutch up so that he could give her shoulder a supportive squeeze, help share the potential load of a chatty neighbour, as he still then obviously assumed it would be, when he stopped, the movement of his arm frozen in mid-air as his mouth fell open.

It wasn't the police. There was a woman standing on the doormat: a tall, slim, beautiful blonde woman in a red mackintosh. She looked initially apprehensive and then, as soon as she saw Jack standing behind Katya, collapsed to her knees, clutching the doorframe and almost howling with emotion.

Oh, Katya thought miserably. *There goes our future. There goes our happiness.*

CHAPTER THIRTY-FOUR

Liam

He recognised the woman instantly, in the familiar red raincoat he remembered her buying in Venice, from their last romantic weekend together. He'd teased her about it because he said she looked like the red-coated figure from the movie *Don't Look Now* when she stood next to the canals, only taller… She wore the diamond earrings he'd given her for their twentieth wedding anniversary, and he could smell the perfume that in a flash he knew she loved, The One by Dolce & Gabbana.

When her hands flew to her mouth and she sank to her knees, he recognised the opal engagement ring he'd given her, next to a wedding ring whose chunkier twin he knew he owned, but wasn't wearing for some reason – oh yes, he'd taken it into the jewellers in Salisbury to be enlarged after it had got too tight, and it hadn't come back in time before he left for his trip.

He and Alanda had made those rings together in a goldsmith's workshop years ago, before their wedding; he even remembered the leather bib across the bench, the smell of the solder and the tap of the little hammer on the gold. The kids had teased him about middle-aged-spread sausage fingers. He'd been upset that he had to go off on his travels without his wedding ring…

The kids. The other wedding – Heather's wedding, his little girl! Had he missed it? The twins. Becky and Jake.

Their names were strange in his brain and yet utterly familiar, like tasting something he hadn't eaten for years and wondering why not, because it was so delicious. Memories flooded back over him, in a tsunami-like wave that filled his eyes and ears and nose and mouth and threatened to topple him with their strength and intensity.

Alanda.

'You're my *wife…*' he said, wonderingly. 'I remember. Alanda! I remember you!'

Alanda was kneeling there, crying openly as she stared at him in wonder. She staggered to her feet and pushed past Katya, seeming to not even see her, flinging her arms around him, a stream of words flowing out of her like an incantation, and as all the lost memories continued to pour over him in a deluge of history, he started to cry too.

'Liam, Liam, oh my God, Liam, darling, you're alive, oh thank God, I've found you! I found you, I can't believe it, my darling, we thought we'd lost you, my darling man…'

Both his crutches clattered down to the parquet floor as Liam put his free arm around his wife, the scent of her hair overwhelmingly beautiful, and so familiar that it was too overwhelming. His wife. Alanda. His beloved wife. He even remembered that her name meant 'little rock; harmony; peace'. His little rock, back with him again.

Neither of them even noticed Katya slip out of the apartment and quietly close the door behind her.

CHAPTER THIRTY-FIVE

Alanda

Alanda stood on the middle of the threadbare rug with Liam's arms around her, both of them crying and hugging each other so tightly that there would not have been enough space to slip a cigarette paper between their bodies. She felt as if his arms were all that was holding her up, as if the rug was a raft on the parquet sea, rocking as they clung to one another.

She had never, ever, experienced such a pure joy, not even when their children were born. To feel the familiar contours of his sturdy frame pressed up against her again, the rough feel of his chin against her cheek, the blue of his eyes deepened by his tears. He smelled the same yet different, a shower gel she didn't recognise but the same scent underlying it.

The love of her life. Her husband. Back.

She could not stop touching him, stroking his hair, his ears, the fuzzy bristle at the back of his neck, clutching his fingers in turn, each individual one so familiar.

He burrowed his nose further into her neck, inhaling her too, completely overcome. When they kissed, gently but with their old passion, it was as if nothing had changed, as if he had merely stepped out into the garden and had come in for a cup of tea.

After a few more minutes, he pulled away reluctantly. 'I need to sit down. My leg hurts if I stand still for more than a few minutes.'

'Of course, sorry,' Alanda said, feeling suddenly shy. She looked around her. 'Let's sit. Where has – whatshername – gone? Have we scared her off? I didn't mean to chase her out of her own flat!'

A shadow clouded Liam's eyes as he realised the girl had left. 'Oh dear,' he said. 'Yes. Poor Katya, she must have decided to give us a bit of space.'

He slotted his wrists into his crutches and swung across to the sofa, where he sank down gratefully, wiping his eyes.

Alanda sat next to him, cuddling into his side. 'It was so kind of her to put you up,' she said. 'I can't imagine what you'd have done without that sort of hospitality. I mean, presumably you couldn't have checked into a hotel or anything, with no money. Has your memory really literally only just come back, or were you starting to remember things before I showed up?'

Liam smiled at her. 'Literally just now, in one fell swoop. Before you knocked at that door I had no idea I was Liam Lodge, or that I had kids… The doctors said that something like this might happen, that one memory would trigger all the rest.'

'The kids!' Alanda leaped up and delved into her handbag, pulling out an iPad. 'We must FaceTime them. They don't even know I'm here. I didn't tell them, just in case something was wrong – I don't know, like, you had brain damage or something. But the hospital confirmed it was you from the photo I sent, and then I didn't hear anything else for three days, and I couldn't bear to wait around anymore so I booked the next flight. They think I've gone away for a couple of nights to a spa with Sadie.'

'Sadie?' Liam looked blank.

'Oh – right – memory not back one hundred per cent yet then – Sadie's my best friend. Tall, dark curly hair, two dogs?'

He shook his head. 'I remember the kids though. I want to talk to them. Can we?'

'Of course! Oh my God, they are going to flip out… hang on. Let's do Jake first because I think Becky might be round at his flat tonight. She said something about going over to help him repaint the spare room.'

She pressed a button on her iPad, beaming, so glad she'd kept it a secret so that she could give them this moment. They heard the beep of the FaceTime call alert, a rustle, a crackle, and then Jake's face filled the screen.

'Hi Mum!' he said. 'Are you feeling a bit more chilled? How's the spa?'

Alanda grinned. 'Hi darling. Is Bex with you?'

He paused, suddenly suspicious. 'Yes… in the other room. I'll get her. Why do you ask? Becky, Mum's on FaceTime! We're painting the bedroom,' he explained.

Becky appeared, cramming her face next to Jake's so they were both in the frame. Alanda thought how they looked almost identical at that moment, even though in real life they weren't alike, not really.

'Yes, I thought you said she was coming over. Hi, Becky darling. Glad I've caught you both. I have—'

Emotion overcame her and she started crying again. 'No, no, don't panic, I'm fine. Everything's fine,' she spluttered, noticing that Liam was weeping too.

She tried again. 'It's just that I have someone…'

'Mum? What's going on? Is it Sadie? Are you at the hotel? It looks like you're in someone's house!'

Liam was watching from his side of the sofa, sobbing quietly, too overcome to say anything. Alanda had wanted to break it to them gently but in the end, she just managed to say, 'It's wonderful. It's a miracle. Look!' and then turned the screen around so that they could see their father sitting there, wiping his eyes and greedily taking in their faces.

He broke into a beam and opened his arms as if he could really hug them. There was a stunned silence and then the twins started screaming, pushing each other out of the way to see their father, to make sure they weren't mistaken, that it really was him smiling at them.

'*Dad!* Daddy, oh God, is it really you?'

'Where are you? What happened? We missed you so much! I can't – I can't—'

'You look amazing! Just the same!'

'Where have you *been*?' This was Jake, although he was laughing with relief through his tears as he said it.

'Hi kids,' Liam managed. 'I love you. It is so good to see you…'

Alanda came and sat back down next to him, so that both of them could be on screen. 'I found him,' she said, hugging him with one arm, the other holding the iPad out in front of them. 'I found him!'

Squeals and more sobs followed. Finally, they all calmed down enough to speak properly.

'Have you told Heather?' Becky demanded. 'She's going to *freak*! You missed her wedding.'

Liam looked devastated. 'Did I really? Oh, that's terrible. No, we'll call her next. I lost my memory in a skiing accident. Seeing Mum is what just brought it back.'

'So it *was* you in Les Gets,' Jake said slowly, clearly trying to get his head around it. 'Someone saw you in a ski lift and recognised you from our social media campaign. Mum, are you in *France*?'

'Yes darling, in Thonon-les-Bains. I rang the hospital and they said they'd had someone who might be Dad, and then they confirmed it when I emailed them a photo so I decided to come here myself.'

She decided she didn't need to mention the four-day time lapse.

'I went straight to the police station this afternoon when I got here and managed to get them to give me the last address he was at. They didn't think he was here anymore so I wasn't expecting to see him when I knocked at the door – but here he was!'

'Dad, what in God's name were you doing skiing? You were supposed to be walking the Camino de Santiago.' Becky actually wagged her finger at him, which made him laugh.

'Really? I don't remember. I don't know what I'm doing here. I can't remember how the accident happened, or how I lost my phone and ID...'

'How bad were you hurt, Daddy?'

Becky hadn't called Liam 'Daddy' since she was about ten, thought Alanda tenderly, squeezing Liam's hand.

'I smashed my thighbone, sweetie.' He gestured down to the leg brace. 'The cast only came off last week. It's been months! But even though I lost my memory, I didn't have any other injuries.'

'And how didn't Interpol figure out it was you? The hospital must have reported you as a missing person, surely?'

'I have no idea,' Liam said, looking to Alanda for clarification.

'I think they were looking in the wrong place,' she said. 'Partly because of your accent, and partly because you were meant be in Spain, not France. But they definitely should have been able to see that you'd got another flight the day you left, from Madrid to Geneva. And then we'd have found you months ago.'

She made a mock-cross face at him. 'Why you couldn't have just gone skiing instead, and *told* us you were going...'

'Did I have insurance? Because it's going to be one hell of a bill.'

The twins laughed at the expression of relief on their father's face as Alanda confirmed he had, and she was pretty sure it included winter sports cover too.

'I'm going to call Heather,' said Becky, 'then we can all be together as a family. You ready for more screaming?'

She pulled out her phone and within a few seconds, Alanda heard her say, 'Heather, are you sitting down? We have something to show you. Sit down! Good. Right. OK, so Mum just FaceTimed us. She's still on the line. Are you ready?'

Alanda and Liam heard Heather's voice, tinny and irritated, through two screens: 'This better be good, Bex, I'm in the middle of doing my roots.'

Then Becky swung her phone around, in the same way that Alanda had just done, to reveal Liam. They all waited for the screams, but there was silence, so much so that Alanda thought the call had frozen on the screen.

Heather was there, in an off-white bathrobe, her hair wrapped in a towel and her face pink and unmade-up. Her mouth was hanging open in a shocked and stunned 'o' of amazement and delight. She reached out a hand and her finger was shaking uncontrollably.

'Dad?' she whispered, tears immediately pouring down her face. Then she yelled, 'Kev! Come quick! Mum's found Dad! He's alive!' She jumped up and they were all treated to the sweet sight of Kev rushing in and whirling her around, as she clung to the phone with one hand, and to him with the other. Kevin's face loomed into focus.

'Wow. Hi. Are we happy to see you! You missed a helluva party though.'

'So I just heard – hi, new *son*,' said Liam, smiling but looking simultaneously desolate. 'I'm so sorry, guys. I can't believe I missed your wedding.'

Heather plumped herself back down on her bed and stared into the phone. 'I don't care,' she said, her voice breaking. 'It doesn't matter. All that matters is that you're safe, and you're coming home. Where are you, anyway?'

'I'm in France, sweetie. I had a skiing accident – long story. Mum came to find me and I only got my memory back when I saw her just now. I'll fill you in on the rest of the details when I get back.'

'When are you coming home?' Heather repeated, laughing and crying at the same time. 'This is, like, the best thing that's ever happened to me. I'm so happy!'

The others laughed too, and Liam leaned his head on Alanda's shoulder. She noticed his skin had suddenly gone a bit grey-looking. It was a lot to take in, all at once, if his memory really had only just returned. He probably still got tired easily.

'Listen guys,' she said, 'we've got a lot of logistics to sort. Let's talk again later. I'm booked into a hotel near the hospital, can we call you when we get there?'

The kids nodded, Jake and Becky with their arms around each other, Heather and Kevin the same, and all of them beaming fit to bust.

'We'll come over to yours, Jake,' Heather announced. 'Let me get this bleach rinsed off and we'll be there in half an hour. Kev, let's book a cab so we can all have a drink; we can take a bottle of the leftover wedding fizz. Oh God, Dad, Mum, this is… even better than our wedding. It's the happiest day of my life!'

CHAPTER THIRTY-SIX

Katya

Katya blundered out of the apartment building onto the street, looking up as if she had just been set down there by a tornado. She'd had the presence of mind to grab her handbag, which had been on the radiator by the front door, but no cardigan or jacket, and it had been raining on and off all day. It wasn't raining now, but the road surface glistened pewter in the fading light of dusk as she blindly headed as far away from Jack's wife as she could. Taxis swished past, slowing down when they saw her but then speeding away when she didn't hail them.

Her phone was in her jeans pocket and she was tensed waiting for it to vibrate, waiting for Jack to text her to say 'Kat, don't panic, we're divorced. Come back, I want you to meet her' – but at the same time, she knew that wasn't going to happen. Not from the way they had embraced when they'd seen each other and he had recognised her. It had clearly been so much more than relief that he was still alive.

She had always known it was a risk, but now the stakes seemed so high, and the pain so deep, that in that moment she truly wished she'd never met him. If he'd only been on a different ward to Otto, their paths would not have crossed. She would have listened in on the nurses gossiping about the nice man on the next ward who'd lost his memory and speculated with them about what he was doing alone on a skiing holiday, but that would probably have been the extent of it.

She had never expected to fall in love like this. Her life had been entwined with Danny's for so many years that what she and Jack had would have been unthinkable back in March, when she'd told Danny that they should break up. They had agreed that she should go and spend a few weeks in Thonon looking after Otto, and then they'd see where they were. She would contact him when she was ready.

She hadn't contacted him, nor he her.

She should be positive: she had the baby. A baby who would probably grow up never knowing who its biological father was, but a biological father to whom Katya would always be unspeakably grateful.

Next time she looked up from the pavement, she was five blocks away from the apartment. It was seven o'clock, the shops were all shut and the restaurants and bars just stirring into life for their evening shifts. She suddenly badly wanted a drink – one glass of wine wouldn't hurt the baby, surely, and she'd not touched a drop since the positive pregnancy test in June.

Katya walked into the nearest bar, a sleepy, dark room that looked like it ought to be a cellar, which suited her mood and need for anonymity. It was almost empty apart from a drunk couple pawing at each other at a table near the window, so she dumped her bag on a chair as far away from them as possible and went up to the bar. Lucky them, having each other, she thought, turning her back on them. She wondered if Jack and Thingy were pawing over one another in her flat.

Would he even still be there when she got back?

'A small glass of Gavi please,' she asked the barman when he came over to take her order.

He was a young bloke, didn't look sixteen, let alone old enough to work on his own in a bar. He glanced at Katya, visibly blanching at how distraught she looked. When he opened his mouth to say something, perhaps ask if she was OK, she dumped a ten euro note on the bar and pretended to examine her phone before he could speak. She did not want pity from teenagers.

At that moment, she felt pure rage. Rage, and jealousy. She couldn't *stand* the thought of Jack sleeping with someone else, caressing them and belonging to them.

She felt so angry that she wanted to squeeze her wineglass between her palms till it shattered. She wanted to storm over and hit – yes, *hit*, she had never hit anyone or anything in her life – that smug slobbery couple in the window. Bang their heads together because they had what had just been robbed from her.

And she couldn't even get drunk.

She forced herself to sip the wine, but it wasn't in any way a pleasurable experience despite the number of weeks she'd been without it – she was so wound up that she found herself dying to just chug it, and the act of slowly sipping only wound her up even more.

Think of the baby, she told herself. *You have a baby.*

At that point, fortunately for her sanity, her phone rang. She snatched it out of her pocket with a rush of hope rising that it was Jack, but Nicole's name was on the screen instead.

Katya toyed with the idea of cutting her off – she was hardly in the mood for chit-chat – then sense prevailed and she answered.

'Nic. Help me, I'm in a state. I need talking down.'

There was a brief stunned pause, and then, 'Katya, what is it? Where are you?'

She looked around. 'Some bar, a few blocks from home. I had to get out of the apartment. It's all over with Jack.'

'*Is* it? I'm so sorry.'

Katya gulped, and studied the woodchip wallpaper on the wall beside her table. It had been painted over with a pale salmon-coloured gloss paint, which did nothing to improve its appearance.

She would not allow herself to cry, not then, not with the teenage barman looking nervously across at her every five seconds.

'His wife just showed up. They were all over each other. His memory came back the moment he saw her. I'm pretty sure they're still married.'

'Oh *no*.'

'Yeah.'

'Kat, I'm so, so sorry. What are you going to do?'

'I don't know. I want to get out-of-my-mind drunk, but I can't. I want to go and kick her out of my flat but I'm afraid he'll go too. What should I do?'

'Oh hell, what a dilemma. How did she get your address?'

'I don't know that either. Probably from someone at the hospital, they'd have had this address as the last known place he was seen. I don't think she was actually expecting to find him there when she knocked.' Katya laughed mirthlessly. 'Someone must have let her into the building, because she didn't even buzz from outside, she knocked, literally right on the doorstep. If she'd buzzed from downstairs, I might have had time to stall her.'

'That's such a shock, out of the blue like that. You probably *are* in shock right now.'

Nic's voice dripped sympathy and Katya felt a stab of guilt.

'Thing is,' she said reluctantly, 'I actually found out she was looking for him a couple of days ago. She rang the hospital, and reception told this nurse who I'd got to know really well, and she – Celine – tipped me off. So I knew, Nic. The police rang me about it and I lied to them. Told them we'd split up and I didn't know where he was. I thought it would buy me a bit of time… I was going to tell him tonight, ironically. I *was*!'

She was protesting, even though Nicole hadn't challenged her.

'Yeah. I imagine it's the sort of thing you'd have to work up to, for sure.'

Bless her, she wasn't at all judgemental. Katya loved her fiercely then, and wished herself transported to her house, drinking wine on her squishy lime-green sofa.

As if she had read Katya's mind, Nicole said, 'Come home, Kat. Even if it's just for a week or so, get your head together, let the dust settle and let him do all his joyful reunion stuff with his kids and what-have-you... Has he got kids?'

'I don't know. I couldn't bear to google him after Celine rang me.'

'What's his real name then?'

'It's Liam. Liam Lodge.'

Katya heard Nic's intake of breath. 'No way!'

'What?'

'*That* guy? Oh God, I knew about him! It's been all over Twitter and Facebook. His kids – yes, he has got kids, but they're all grown up – ran this massive appeal, but they thought he was in Spain so it was all focussed towards that. It literally never crossed my mind that it might be your bloke. I remember it because I assumed he was having some sort of blokey midlife crisis and had just done a runner to Spain with some bimbo twenty years younger. I remember feeling sorry for the wife, that she was so deluded... You even sent me a photo of him and I still didn't twig! I'm so sorry, Kat. If I'd looked more closely at his picture on Twitter—'

'If you had, I might never have had the best relationship of my life.'

Katya remembered the photo she had sent Nicole. It was a selfie of her and Jack lying in bed, about two weeks after she'd moved into Otto's bedroom, heads together, their hair ruffled and goofy smiles plastered on their faces. Nicole had texted back, *TMI, babes, post-coital or WHAT? xx ps He's hot, nice work!*

But then Jack would have known who he was much sooner, and perhaps nobody would have got hurt. Was she being horribly selfish? If it wasn't for the baby, she'd have concluded she was. But now – all bets were off. It was every woman for herself.

'Oh honey. Don't say that. He might be back at the flat breaking it off with her as we speak.'

Katya felt a flare of hope at this. She so, so wanted it to be true. But then she remembered the way they had greeted each other, and plunged back into the ice bucket of her despair.

'I can't come home, not until I know what he's going to do,' she said miserably, trying to anchor herself and avoid losing the plot altogether.

She planted her feet, still in the sparkly flip-flops she wore around the apartment, squarely on the tiled floor, feeling the chill of it through their flimsy soles. The tiles were sticky with old cocktails, and she made herself listen to the faint sucking noise as she lifted her left toes, then her right, then her left, then her right… *Hold it together, Kat.*

'Here's an idea,' Nic said, vaping heavily down the line.

'Yes?'

'Well, in the spirit of "better the devil you know" – how about you invite her to stay at the flat with the two of you? If she saw you on your own territory, as it were, she might realise that it's all over between them, and that you're his future now. Tell her about the baby. She might even understand. After all, we still don't know why he went away on his own in the first place. They might be in the process of splitting up. You don't know.'

This was true, but she knew she couldn't invite the woman to stay. 'She might expect to sleep in the same bed as him. *I* would, if I hadn't seen my husband for four months. Then what, I'm supposed to literally give up my place in his bed? There's no way.'

'As I said, they might be splitting up, and this is all just part of the process?' Nic didn't sound any more convinced than Katya was.

'And they might not be. He might not even have told her about us.'

Nic snorted. 'Well, if he hasn't, then I'm not so sure he's the right one for you. But I do think you need to give him a bit of time to get his head round it all. You've known for a few days, and he's just found out. Could you stay in a hotel tonight, do you think, give them a bit of time to talk?'

Katya felt herself getting upset again. 'Why should I? *They* can stay in a hotel if they want to talk.'

'Shhh, it's OK,' Nic soothed. 'You're right. You shouldn't be kicked out of your own place. I'm just brainstorming.'

'I know. Thank you. And thank God you rang – I might have ended up crying all over the barman, and he's already looking at me like he's a step away from pressing a panic button.'

'You're allowed to be upset. I'll stay on the phone as long as you need, and we'll figure something out.'

'OK. Thanks again, Nic.'

'It's fine, nutter. And – Kat?'

'Yes?'

'I am so, so sorry you're going through this.'

After terminating the call, Katya sat very still for a while, her empty wineglass in front of her. There was a lip gloss mark on the rim she hadn't noticed before. She wasn't wearing lip gloss, and it made her feel queasy to think she had drunk from a glass with a strange woman's leftover lip-marks on it.

If that wasn't a metaphor for her current situation, she thought, studying the striations miserably, then she didn't know what was… The print's grooves and furrows were so clear she could almost imagine that she would be able to identify their owner on the street. She focussed on them for a few minutes, trying to clear her head, but it was impossible.

As impossible as ever finding anyone she loved as much as she loved Jack.

She thought of her relationship with Danny; how frequently it had felt that they were on different wavelengths. So close, and yet so far. He'd been a decent bloke too, probably comparable with Jack in terms of humour, patience and generosity – yet there had always been something missing. Every time they had got back together over the years, they had started with the best of intentions. A break had helped them gloss over the small irritations and niggles until each reunion had really felt like a fresh start, and they'd launched back into it with an enthusiasm that waned with depressing alacrity. This last break-up had been the worst, especially coming after they had committed to staying together for good. Make or break. And yet it had still broken and they had separated once more. Permanently this time, it seemed.

Would a baby have made the difference to them, the difference they had always hoped it would? Would he take her back now, with another man's child in her belly?

Did she *want* to go back?

She and Jack had no irritations or niggles whatsoever – but then perhaps that was because of Jack's lack of known baggage, and the newness and novelty of their relationship. Perhaps if they stayed together, in three years' time they'd be snapping at each other like good 'uns about whose turn it was to empty the dishwasher.

Somehow Katya didn't think so. What she had with Jack was so different, so… right.

She was working her way up to leaving the bar, since her phone was down to seven percent battery, and she didn't want to ask the barman if he had a charger, when suddenly into the silence of the empty room – the snogging couple had gone, at some point, and she was now the only customer in there – a slow piano introduction began playing, so loudly and suddenly that it made her jump. There was no sign of the barman so presumably he'd gone out the back and put the music on.

Her breath caught in her throat as she recognised the song as soon as the vocals started: Ben Folds, 'The Luckiest'. She and Jack had listened to this just the other week when they were making dinner. He'd paused to listen, in the middle of chopping a tomato, and said, '*I'm* the luckiest, because I get to have this whole new start with you. The fact that I don't know what's gone on in my life before, whether it's been good or bad, it doesn't matter, does it? Because if it was good, then I'm lucky because it was good. If it was awful, then I'm lucky because it's all changed and we get to be together from now on.'

Katya remembered looking at the shiver of tomato seeds on the chopping board and his long, sensuous fingers around the knife, his dimples and the smile in his voice as he spoke, and thinking, *This is the happiest I have ever been. Ever.*

Now, in the bar, listening to that same song, she had very different emotions. Neither of them in that moment had stopped to consider that it was all very well for them, in their little bubble of love and infatuation – but what about the other people involved? If Jack's life had been good before he met her, it meant there would be people out there who loved him and missed him and would think that 'the luckiest' were the very last words they'd ever use to describe their own situation at that time.

And now one of those people was in Katya's apartment, probably feeling as lucky as Katya had done last week, whereas she was sitting in an empty bar on her own, musing on the capricious whims of fate and wishing she could get absolutely hammered.

Feeling about ninety years old, Katya stood up, replaced her empty glass on the bar and trudged back out into the darkening street. Where could she go? She couldn't go back to the apartment. She didn't want to hang around anywhere else. She considered going to the hospital and waiting in there; nobody would think anything of it. Maybe she could even catch Celine on a break and they could have a cup of coffee. She was so sensible, she might have some thoughts on what Katya could do.

But she dismissed that idea. She couldn't face speaking to anyone else. She only wanted Jack.

She decided to go and hang out in Otto's workshop. It was a warm night. She'd been meaning to go in there to sort it out anyway, but hadn't been able to face it before. And – although it was a bit stalkerish to admit – she'd get a view of the apartment's kitchen windows from it.

Each of the apartments in the block came with its own garage out the back, with an up-and-over door that made an unforgettable metallic clang when shut. Otto and Monique never had a car, so Otto had converted their garage into his carpentry workshop, and he was delighted when Katya took an interest in what all his tools were for. She loved the quiver of the saw, the heft of the mallets and the smooth mushroom-top of the brace, the bradawl with its deadly-sharp point and the negative space of the hacksaw. The compartmentalised boxes whose trays slid out to reveal screws and nails of all imaginable sizes.

She liked watching him work. It became their thing, and her mother encouraged it, mostly, Katya realised in retrospect, so that she and Monique could go and do 'girls' stuff' together, like drink lurid green cocktails and get their hair done.

As soon as she unlocked the garage door and went inside, Katya wished she had thought of going there earlier. It was a haven, a time capsule, a reminder that even though Otto had gone, the feeling of safety and security he engendered in her had not. It still had the same smell she always associated with him – it was the next best thing to having him there to comfort her.

She shook open a folding camping chair and sat down just inside the open garage door, imagining that Otto was sitting next to her. They would both look up at the lit window of his apartment and he'd come out with one of his wise, but often weird, German sayings. Probably *Alles hat ein Ende, nur die Wurst hat zwei'* – 'Everything has an end. Only the sausage has two.' Katya managed a smile thinking of it, but then she saw movement through the kitchen window and the smile dropped from her face.

Jack was leaning against the sink, filling a glass of water. He looked so emotional that Katya wouldn't have recognised him if she hadn't known it was him. She couldn't tell what sort of emotion, though. It could have been grief, confusion, exhaustion – or maybe a mixture of all three. He certainly did not look overjoyed, or anything close to that, though, and her heart gave a tiny hitch of optimism. In her mind they had been kissing and embracing from the moment she left, but this was not the face of a man reunited with the love of his life, surely?

He paused, the glass still in one hand, not turning around but letting his head droop slowly until he was staring fixedly into the sink, looking utterly browbeaten and defeated. Katya's heart went out to him so absolutely that it was all she could do not to leap up and wave her arms around to attract his attention. But she didn't want him to think she'd been spying on them, so she sat still and watched, hope blooming guiltily inside her chest.

Then, to her surprise and shock, she saw Alanda's arm, gesticulating behind him in an angry way. She listened as hard as she could and heard shouting. Alanda was yelling at him!

Oh my, Katya thought. *Oh my. They aren't together. Or he's told her he wants to be with me.*

Perhaps all was not lost. Perhaps it would be the best possible outcome for Jack and her – that he now knew his identity, and they could move on with their lives.

Katya sprang back up from the chair and slid out from underneath the garage door, slamming it joyfully closed.

She was going home.

CHAPTER THIRTY-SEVEN

Liam

Liam leaned against the back of the sofa feeling suddenly exhausted, as if the weight of replacing all this lost information in his brain was too great for him to even be able to support his head; a deluge of facts, emotions, truths, family...

It was utterly disorientating to him that not half an hour ago, he and Katya had pulled up chairs at the table, about to eat spaghetti bolognese, listening to John Martyn, safe in their little bubble of love.

The spag bol was still there, a congealed reminder on their plates, and the music had stopped when Katya left. How was it possible to feel so much joy and despair simultaneously?

What the hell was he going to do now?

He thought of Katya, in her quirky, colourful clothes, the most kind-hearted, tender, beautiful, generous girl who deserved nothing but happiness. They had been on the start of a journey together, even though they had both known that something like this might happen – but what else could they have done? You couldn't ignore feelings that strong.

It had been a gamble, of course, but wasn't everything in life, to one degree or another? Going skiing instead of walking the Camino had been a gamble, and one which had caused his family untold amounts of pain – but at the same time, those disastrous effects had led him to meet Katya, and now how was he supposed to live without her, and the baby?

Bile rose in his throat and he thought for a moment he would vomit. The baby. He couldn't possibly abandon her and their child; they didn't have anybody else. But yet, he imagined himself telling Alanda he was leaving her to be with Katya, and the image was absolute anathema. Impossible. How could he put her and the kids through any more pain?

He groaned out loud, passing his hand over his eyes.

'Oh sweetheart, is your leg hurting?' Alanda said, putting her iPad down on the sofa cushion between them and wrapping her arms back around him. 'Here, put your foot up. Has your hostess got any wine? I reckon we could both do with a drink.'

'I've got a glass, on the table,' Liam said in a strangled voice. 'There's a bottle open in the kitchen. Wineglasses are in the cupboard above the toaster.'

Alanda handed him his glass of red and disappeared into the little kitchen. 'Do you think it would be OK if I had a bit of this spag bol? There's loads left in the pan and I'm starving. All I've had all day is a sandwich on the plane.'

'I'm sure it's fine,' said Liam, faintly, wondering what Katya would think if she came back now and saw Alanda, with her feet literally under Katya's table, drinking her wine and eating the meal she had cooked for them both.

'Shall I heat yours up too?'

'No… it's OK. I'm not hungry. Must be all this emotion.'

Alanda laughed, misreading his tone. 'I'll just zap a bowl in the microwave and then I want to show you the wedding pics – I've got a load with me, not the official ones, just the ones people took on their phones. Heather and Kevin got them to upload them all to a website, such a great idea, isn't it, so everyone can see everyone else's. There's a gorgeous one of your mum. Oh, Liam, you should've seen her, she did so well, and the care home made her look so lovely in her flowery dress and that hat with the big purple rose on it, remember, I bought it in that shop in Tisbury…'

Alanda was chatting on and Liam heard her fumbling around, the way one does in an unfamiliar kitchen, opening and shutting drawers and cupboards, and then the *peep* of the microwave buttons followed by the roar of its engine, making her speak up to be heard above it, but he couldn't concentrate on anything.

It was easier just to close his eyes and pretend he didn't have to make the biggest decision of his life, very soon. He wondered where Katya had gone. Had she taken a coat? It was early August but it had been raining and muggy all day, and it could get chilly once the sun went down, even in summer. Perhaps he should call her mobile. It wasn't good for her to be wandering around in a state, which she was bound to be.

All their plans… His heart contracted with guilt and misery.

Then he looked across to see his wife standing in the kitchen doorway, holding a bowl of steaming food and a glass of red wine, smiling at him – the curve of her lips, when she smiled! He had missed it so much without even knowing what he'd been missing till now – and suddenly all he felt was a great wash of love for her, and excitement at remembering how lucky he was, to have what they had together.

'So much to ask you,' she exclaimed, her mouth full of spaghetti. 'I don't even know where to start. Let me get this down me, then I'll show you the pics. Wasn't it amazing to speak to the kids? I hope Jake's letting the police know you've been found, in the flesh. Honestly, everyone was so kind. Except this one woman who came to the shop and got really aggressive when I said I was pretty sure you weren't having an affair with her next-door neighbour…'

Liam did not want any talk of affairs. Instead, he agreed it had indeed been amazing to speak to the kids. He couldn't take his eyes off the front door, dreading the sound of Katya's key in the lock, his euphoria of just seconds ago having subsided back into anxiety.

'You all right, my darling? You look so worried!'

Alanda always had been extremely perceptive like that, he remembered.

'Feeling a bit overwhelmed, if I'm honest,' he muttered, mustering a smile to try and reassure her.

'In a good way, I hope.'

'Yes… of course,' he said, meaning it.

'How did you meet – Katya, is it?' Alanda enquired between mouthfuls of food and drink. 'Like I said, what a stroke of luck for you.'

He glanced sharply at her, but there did not seem to be any tone of censure in her voice.

'She translated for me when I first came into hospital – her uncle was on the same ward as me, with sepsis. They were very close, so she'd come over here from London for a few weeks to visit him. She was planning to stay and look after him here for a while once he got out, but sadly he died a couple of weeks after we met. By then we were friends – she'd started to visit me every day at the same time as him, because I didn't have any other visitors. She had to stay on to sort out his probate, and there's a spare room here, and she knew I didn't have anywhere else to go, so…'

He tailed off, feeling horribly disloyal.

'*So* kind of her,' Alanda said again. 'She seems lovely. We must keep in touch with her. I didn't realise she was English too.'

Liam waited for her to add something like, 'Very pretty, isn't she?' or 'And there's been nothing else going on?' as he might have expected, but she merely changed the subject and started telling him about how Violet had had a few ups and downs in her home recently, but Jennie the manager was so good with her, as were all the staff, and how she and Jennie were sort of becoming friends…

'Right, I must just have a wee, then let's look at these photos,' she announced, standing up. 'Where's the bathroom?'

Liam pointed down the hallway. 'At the end, you can't miss it,' he said.

When she had gone, the room felt filled with Katya's absence, more so than Alanda's. Perhaps, Liam thought, it was because he knew Alanda would be back any minute. And surely it had to be over between him and Katya.

Alanda was his future once more.

The thought hurt his heart again.

He hauled himself gracelessly to his feet and limped into the kitchen on one crutch, suddenly parched. Alanda had left two of the cupboard doors open in her search for crockery and he remembered, with a rush of affection, how she did the same thing at home too. He could visualise their own kitchen now, a lovely extended kitchen-diner with an Aga and a battle-scarred oak table. He couldn't wait to see it again, whilst simultaneously dreading leaving here.

He reached for a glass and filled it with cold tap water, leaning against the sink to steady himself.

At that moment he felt, rather than heard, something behind him, a vacuum of emotion, like the moment of stillness in the pressure drop before a tornado hits. Then the roar of touchdown.

Turning awkwardly to avoid jarring his hip, he saw Alanda standing there with an object in each hand. She was waving them both at him, furiously gesticulating, too angry to even speak yet.

With a mixture of resignation and sadness, he registered that the game was well and truly up.

The *game*? Whatever else it was, he thought, it had never been a game.

In her left hand, Alanda held the small framed photograph that Katya had given him for his fake birthday, a selfie of them kissing by the lake shore, two seagulls swooping above their heads like witnesses.

In her right hand was the positive pregnancy test that Katya had insisted on keeping, propped into the corner of the frame, its double blue line a reminder that they were soon to become a trio.

'*I. Don't. Believe. It!*' Alanda actually screamed out each word, in a way he had never heard her scream before.

He turned back, shut his eyes, lowered his head.

'I didn't want you to find out like this,' he said quietly. Why had he not thought to close their bedroom door as soon as she turned up?

Because she had turned up, and he'd been so happy to see her, and so happy to get his memory back. Of course, it hadn't occurred to him to close the bedroom door; subterfuge had been the last thing on his newly full mind.

She was ranting, properly ranting and raving, waving her arms around, then flinging first the test and then the photograph to the floor, the glass shattering at her feet. It was so unlike her that Liam wondered if he had misremembered her character; maybe she'd always been like this? *No, of course not*, he chided himself, *she's just had a massive shock*.

'You absolute bastard!' she yelled, crying unashamedly like a child, her fists balled by her sides now, tears almost spurting sideways from her eyes. 'After everything we've been through in the last four months, thinking you were dead, the sleepless nights, the stress, the police, the speculation, the worry – oh my God, the worry – the uncertainty and, poor Heather having to get married without you there, and you just get shacked up at the first *fucking* opportunity with another woman, a *younger* woman, and now she's pregnant? How could you, Liam? How could you do this to us?'

She collapsed onto the floor, shoulders heaving. Her breath was coming in strained gasps and Liam remembered she had asthma.

He limped across the floor but his strapped-up leg would not allow him to sit down with her, so he had to hover next to her, trying to stroke her hair but getting furiously and repeatedly batted away. 'Leave me alone,' she sobbed, her breath now raspy.

'Alanda, please listen to me, I didn't know,' he pleaded. 'I didn't know. I didn't remember anything. You know I would never do anything to hurt you intentionally; I love you. I thought because I'd been on holiday on my own, we thought, we assumed I must be single…'

Alanda snorted. 'Yeah right. Bet you thought about that for all of five minutes, the pair of you.'

It was awful seeing her like this. But worse, she was now having to pant, unable to catch her breath at all. 'Sweetie, where's your inhaler?' he demanded urgently. 'You need your inhaler.'

Alanda waved impatiently in the direction of her handbag and he limped over to it, but it did not yield anything apart from her purse, her phone and a lipstick. Searching through the side pockets, he felt increasingly worried. 'It's not here.'

She looked up from her prone position, tears smearing mascara across her face, her shoulders heaving and her lips turning blueish. She'd cut the palm of her left hand on a shard of glass and blood was dripping onto the parquet and onto her denim skirt.

I did that to her, Liam thought, and for a brief but savage moment he wished he'd been killed on that ski slope. He'd ended up hurting her as much as he had hurt Rich. He'd let them both down.

Perhaps this was some sort of hideous karmic punishment for not saving his brother when he'd had the chance.

But there was no time to be self-pitying. He grabbed the kitchen roll off the counter and unwound several sheets, which he wrapped around her hand and pressed to stem the flow. 'You did bring it, didn't you?'

'Must – have – left – in – suitcase – at – hotel,' she panted, her eyes huge and full of fear as well as rage.

CHAPTER THIRTY-EIGHT

Katya

Katya wasn't sure what she had expected when she turned her key in the apartment door, but it certainly wasn't the sight of Jack's wife, coughing and gasping for breath on her knees, blood smeared on her face and in her hair, broken glass around her.

'Oh thank God, Katya, help,' Jack said as soon as he saw her, his face chalky-white. 'She's having an asthma attack. Do you know anyone with an inhaler?'

The woman's skin matched his pallor. Katya rushed across and crouched down next to her as she writhed and lashed out, trying to hit her. Alanda's hair was hanging in rats' tails around her face and her heaving breaths sounded like snarls; a cornered wild animal. She couldn't have looked more different to the beautifully turned-out woman who'd stood apprehensively on the threshold less than two hours earlier.

'Don't touch me, you husband-stealing bitch,' she wheezed, vitriol vying with distress and humiliation in her eyes as Katya tried to help her off the floor and into a chair.

Katya's mind was racing – would it be quicker to call an ambulance or start knocking on neighbours' doors to ask if anyone had an inhaler? Then she suddenly remembered, there always used to be one in the side pocket of her washbag, left over from a nasty chest infection Danny had had had a few years ago. She wasn't even sure if it was still there. Worth a try, though.

'Hang on,' she said, leaving Alanda crumpled where she was and running into the bathroom. The washbag was stored in a cabinet under the basin, and Katya grabbed it and tipped it upside-down. All the items knocking around in it that she didn't use on a daily basis, and which she'd meant to clear out before she came over here but was now massively relieved that she hadn't done, scattered onto the bathroom tiles: nasal spray, nail-clippers, stray cotton buds whose tips had turned grey and burst, a now-redundant tampon, a blister pack of travel sickness pills, dried up lip-balms and, phew, the blue inhaler.

She snatched it up, with no idea if it was even still working, and tore back into the living room. Alanda looked as if she was in labour, still kneeling but gripping the ladder-back of one of the dining chairs as she tried unsuccessfully to catch her breath.

'Try this,' said Katya, pulling off the cap and shaking it vigorously, because Jack's wife didn't look like she would even have the strength to perform this small act. Alanda grabbed it and closed her lips around it, breathing in as deeply as she could. For a moment nothing seemed to change, and then she took two more puffs and gradually her breathing became less laboured.

Something Alanda had just said suddenly registered with Katya: *you husband-stealing bitch.* He must have told her. Then she worked out what the broken glass was – the photo of her and Jack – and realised that, unless he'd been cruel enough to show her the photograph, she must have found it by their bed. Either way, she knew.

But, Katya thought, *is she calling me a husband-stealer because I've successfully (albeit inadvertently) stolen him, or because she thought I wanted to?*

There was nothing she could do to find out yet, though. She waited for Alanda to calm down and get her breath back. The woman had crawled over to the sofa and was sitting on the floor with her back against it, looking utterly spent.

Blood had seeped through the kitchen roll wrapped around her hand, so Katya went back into the bathroom and found an old brown surgical bandage that must have belonged to Otto, and a tube of Savlon. She didn't want bloodstains on the sofa. And she definitely did not want any physical reminders of this horrendous evening.

When she returned, Jack was hovering about looking stricken, taking a step towards his wife and then a step towards Katya, like a knight on a chessboard trying to decide which direction was safest.

'Can you bandage her hand?' Katya asked, brusquely. 'I don't think she'll want me to do it. I'll clear this lot up.'

'I – am – here – you know,' Alanda wheezed, but the fight had gone out of her and she allowed Jack to limp over, sit down on the sofa and inspect her hand to make sure there was no glass stuck in it, before applying Savlon, winding the bandage around and tucking in the spare end.

Out of the corner of her eye Katya watched him do it, his movements so tender and delicate that her own breath caught in her throat. He loved his wife, it was clear.

But which of them did he love the most?

Katya fetched Alanda a glass of water and a box of tissues for her streaming eyes and nose, which she accepted without a word.

'Should we call a doctor?'

Katya directed the question at Jack, but Alanda answered, her voice clipped.

'No. I'll be all right in a minute. It was just the shock.'

Jack hadn't said a word since he'd asked Katya about inhalers. He was still on the sofa, and when his wife hauled herself up to sit next to him, he automatically put his arm around her shoulders. Alanda looked for a moment as though she was going to pull away, but then sagged exhaustedly into his side.

Seeing them together made Katya want to run away again, but this time she told herself he was only doing it because she'd had a fright, and it was traumatic having an asthma attack at the best of times, let alone in a strange apartment belonging to a woman you had just found out that your husband was expecting a baby with…

She imagined Otto was with her, sitting in his favourite chair by the window, counselling her with his brown eyes, stroking her hair with his liver-spotted hand. What random German expression would he trot out for this occasion?

She wished Otto *was* there, that he hadn't got ill – although then she'd never have met Jack, and she wouldn't be pregnant… oh, it was impossible. *If wishes were horses* – that was another of Otto's sayings, although Katya had never really understood the point of it, in English or German.

If wishes were horses, beggars would ride.

Well, I mean, she thought, *of course they would*. How was *that* helpful?

She could never have imagined that anything would ever be this difficult.

'Could you leave, please? Both of you. I want you to go now.'

The words cost her so dearly that, for a brief fanciful moment, she imagined the foetus inside her howling with the same pain that she was feeling, the smallest of shrill keens, the flutter of tiny fists pounding the wall of her uterus.

She held her breath, waiting for Jack to say no, that of course he wouldn't leave her. He belonged to her, Katya, and Alanda would just have to get used to it.

There was a long pause in which time seemed frozen. Nobody looked at anybody else.

Finally, Jack limped over to where she stood in the kitchen doorway. 'Kat… this is – I don't know. This is so awful.'

There was a faint snort from Alanda. Or it might have been the remnant of an asthmatic wheeze, Katya couldn't tell.

'We'll go,' he said decisively. 'Alanda and I need to talk; I owe her that, Kat. They've all been beside themselves with worry because of my stupidity… Are you OK with that?'

Katya shrugged, feeling like a sulky ten-year-old. 'I said I wanted you to go, so yes.'

'I'll ring you in the morning, I promise,' he said, tears in his eyes.

CHAPTER THIRTY-NINE

Alanda

Alanda and Liam were in the back of a taxi speeding towards the hotel through the rain-slicked streets of Thonon, both of them ashen and shell-shocked. They held hands but each was staring out of a different window, and they did not say a word to one another for the duration of the short journey. The taxi driver sucked his teeth and gave up trying to engage them in conversation after Alanda repeatedly muttered, '*Nous ne parlons pas français*,' in response to his questions about what Liam had done to his leg and if they were on holiday.

We don't speak French, she thought. *We don't speak anything.*

At that moment she wondered if this was it, if their connection had been severed like a ripped-off limb, too savagely to ever be repaired.

The short journey felt as if it took hours, but they eventually arrived back at the hotel, a quirky two-star place with shiny dark wallpaper, cobwebs in the corners and a smell of old fried food. It was the first one she'd found with reasonable reviews that cost less than eighty euros a night. When she'd checked in earlier and walked up to her second-floor room, it hadn't even occurred to her to make sure there was a lift, even though she'd already known Liam had a broken leg. Consequently, when they'd both practically crawled into the reception, dying to lie down and try to decompress, there had been an additional fifteen minutes' negotiation with the receptionist to switch them to a ground-floor room.

Now, at last, they were alone, and Liam was beside himself.

'You do understand, don't you?' he kept pleading, to the point that Alanda felt irritated with him – or she would have done, if the asthma attack on top of a day of travelling and several sleepless nights hadn't left her feeling utterly wiped out. She didn't have the energy to be irritated. 'Please say you understand.'

Irritated. Imagine that, she thought. In all those dark months when she thought she would never see him again, if someone had told her he'd be getting on her nerves within a couple of hours of their reunion, she'd have laughed.

But, lovely as it was to have him back with her, there did not seem much to laugh about. Alanda really couldn't tell if it was just because he felt so guilty, or because he actually wanted to be with the girl now. She was trying to forget the sight of Katya's closed-off expression when Liam had agreed to come back to the hotel with her.

'Liam's right. We need time to talk, alone,' Alanda had said, as firmly as her trembling post-attack ribcage permitted.

Katya had been watching Liam's face for his reaction, and hers had fallen when she saw his expression of guilty resignation. She had even packed an unfamiliar overnight bag for him – it must have been another gift from her, Alanda thought, with a pang of envious grief. Not one she herself would have chosen, the bag was made of some kind of rubber material, like a large black hot water bottle. She'd watched the girl as she took his clean pants and socks off a drying rack in the corner of the room, folding and packing them into the hot water bottle in such a proprietorial manner that Alanda wondered if it was only the extreme fatigue and weakness preventing her from hurling herself at Katya and scratching her eyes out.

What had she become? She did not recognise herself.

Then again, she supposed, she had never had a rival for her husband's affections before. Not once in all these years had Liam even flirted with another woman, to her knowledge. And this was one hell of a rival. Young, beautiful, kind, independent – and carrying his child.

'I didn't know,' Liam wailed, tearing at his hair until it was standing on end in all directions, like a madman. 'If I'd known, Al, of course I would never have started anything with her, or anyone. If I'd even had a hint of memory of you and the kids! I've wrecked it. I've ruined everything for everyone.'

In the end, she felt too sorry for him to be angry anymore. Who could say she wouldn't have done exactly the same if she'd been in that situation? You would feel so lost, to be injured and in pain in a world where you knew nobody and nothing about yourself, not even your real name. You would inevitably be drawn towards someone, anyone, showing you even a smidgeon of kindness, let alone someone as special as Katya seemed to be. Alanda groaned at the memory of the girl's flawless honey-coloured skin, huge clear brown eyes and long shiny black curls.

Even though she hadn't had the foresight to pre-book a ground-floor room, Alanda had managed to pick up a bottle of good brandy at the airport, suspecting that whatever happened she'd probably need a drink at some point. Now she and Liam sat awkwardly on the old-fashioned slippery eiderdown, sipping at the brandy from flimsy plastic tooth mugs.

She knew she shouldn't be drinking alcohol after the asthma attack, but the burn of the liquor going down inside her felt like essential fuel, keeping her alive more than the Ventolin had. On top of that, she was utterly mortified that her husband's lover had been the one to save her – not just that, but had seen her *in extremis*, helplessly rolling around the floor panting, covered in blood and snot, swearing at her and hitting out wildly like a total madwoman… Of all the emotions she had expected to experience when she and Liam were reunited, humiliation had not been one. If she'd wanted to scare Liam into the arms of another woman, that had probably done the trick nicely.

Hell yes, she needed a drink, she thought, visualising Katya's perfect figure.

'You haven't ruined everything. Not intentionally, anyway.'

That hadn't helped. When she looked at his face, he was crying again. 'Oh Al,' he entreated. 'That poor girl. Honestly. She lost her last relative a couple of months ago. I'm all she's got.'

Alanda bit back the urge to say both, 'Yeah, you mentioned that already,' and, 'Not any more. She doesn't have you anymore,' in the same breath. Instead, noticing that there was a bloodstain on the sleeve of her white shirt, she crawled off the bed and into the bathroom, stripped it off and put it in a basin of cold water.

It had taken all her energy to even stand up, but she needed to get away from Liam's tears, just for a moment. Was he crying for who he'd hurt when he'd been lost, or for who he was hurting now that he was found? How could she be angry with him when he was so clearly in as much pain as she was?

When she came back into the bedroom, still in just her bra, he had composed himself and was gazing at her with something like wonder. He managed a smile. 'You look beautiful,' he said, holding out his hand.

'Are you insane?' she replied, bashfully and exhaustedly. 'The state of me!'

'You look beautiful to me.'

He pulled her towards him and she allowed him to encircle her with his arms as she stood between his legs. He buried his face in her cleavage with a sigh, and she felt the tension begin to drain from his shoulders.

They stayed like that for a long time, until Alanda shivered. 'I'm getting cold.'

'Let's get into bed. Can we?' He sounded like a child, and Alanda smiled.

'Let's,' she said, sliding out of her skirt before helping him up so they could slip under the puffy covers. 'I'm so tired. I don't think I've ever felt this tired in my life.'

They lay still for some time, cuddled up together, slotting back into their old familiar positions; face to face with Liam on the right, Alanda to the left, her left leg draped across his – the leg brace feeling huge and intrusively rough against the soft skin of her inner thigh – his arms around her, rubbing her back gently. At some point he undid her bra so that he could stroke unhindered circles.

Alanda wanted to ask him if it felt weird, after his recent months with Katya, but then decided she didn't want to know, and didn't want to risk him stopping. At some point she said, 'You still have all your clothes on, and I'm practically naked,' and then immediately felt self-conscious about her almost-fifty-two-year-old body, still slim but not without its lumps and bumps, flabby bits and wrinkles.

She'd never worried about it before – but then, she thought again, she had never had a thirty-something rival before. She wondered how old Katya was. She looked young enough that she could even still be in her twenties, with her ripe, smooth skin.

That was a depressing thought.

Liam took off his shirt and pulled his shorts and pants off with difficulty over the leg brace.

'Do you have to wear that all the time?' she asked, wondering if she should offer to help. All the lust she had felt a moment ago had dissipated, at the unfavourable comparisons she imagined Liam was making. Not that he was showing signs of it.

'Well, no. Not anymore. I just feel more… protected with it on.'

Alanda was going to say, 'like a condom for your leg,' but decided against it. There must have been a dearth of condoms in his and Katya's world. How stupid were they, anyway? How could they have let this happen?

Briefly, she felt so angry she almost climbed out of bed but forced herself to stop thinking about it. Perhaps the asthma attack had been a blessing in disguise, because she really did feel too tired for the anger to last more than a flash.

Even though Liam was cuddled close to her and his caresses were becoming distinctly more sexual, she didn't seem to be able to prevent her eyelids closing and her body sinking into the soft mattress, her head spinning slightly from the brandy and emotion. She wanted to make love to him, stake her claim on him, remind him that she was his, but she was too tired… The last thing she remembered was Liam's voice in her ear and the feel of his hand stroking her forehead.

'Sleep, my darling girl, sleep. You need to. We can talk in the morning. I love you.'

She awoke several hours later, stumbling her way to the bathroom in the pitch dark. When she returned and slipped back into bed, Liam groaned and rolled over to her side, wrapping his arms around her. The simplicity of the movement, the pure sensation of being so close to him again, his warm breath on her, when she had feared she would never feel it again, ever…

Overwhelmed afresh, she began to sob. Somehow it was easier to let go in the darkness, and tears poured from her eyes onto the pillow, into Liam's hair, his mouth. He murmured endearments and held her more tightly, until she eventually stopped crying and fumbled her mouth towards his.

Gradually all her inhibitions and pain, rage and confusion subsided. Their bodies melded even closer together as they kissed and kissed, until it felt natural for him to slide inside her, as tenderly and naturally as he always had done.

That was finally when Alanda knew she had her husband back again and that maybe, just maybe, everything would be OK.

CHAPTER FORTY

Liam

'I don't want to see you, Jack,' Katya said bluntly when he rang her mobile the next morning. 'Sorry – "Liam", I mean. It's too painful. When will you be going home?'

She sounded so calm and down-to-earth that he was momentarily speechless. He flopped back on the hotel room bed, staring unseeingly at a zigzag crack in the cornicing on the ceiling. Alanda had gone to the embassy to begin the process of bringing him home, instructing him to 'say what he needed to say' to Katya in her absence.

'I assume you *are* going home.'

Why would Katya have assumed he was definitely going home? *Because you are, idiot*, he thought. There was no doubt about it.

He and Alanda had stayed awake after they'd made love, talking and hugging. With each passing hour his old life had come back with sharper clarity, until he'd found himself wholeheartedly embracing the idea of being back in England as soon as logistically possible, the entire past four months seeming like some sort of hallucinogenic dream. It was around six a.m. when they both finally drifted back into a warm, sated sleep for a couple more hours.

And yet now, with Katya's voice in his ear, he was pulled back to the dream life once more, and his old one retreated. The dusty old green velvet sofa in Otto's apartment. Lake Geneva sparkling in the sunlight. Katya's warm body, with their baby a little peanut in her still-flat belly, her soft voice whispering caresses in his ear.

This must be what it's like to be schizophrenic, he thought.

Her voice did not sound soft or caressing this morning, though. It didn't sound like her at all, in fact.

'Yes. In a couple of days,' he said reluctantly, wanting to shout, *but I don't want to leave you.* 'As soon as we've managed to sort out an emergency passport and do all the police reports and hospital insurance admin. But please, I have to see you before I go.'

She paused, sighed. 'No. It will only make things worse.'

There was a long silence down the line, into which he had more of an urge to howl than he had ever felt before; even more than when he had discovered Rich's lifeless, bloated body hanging from that beam. 'Kat...'

'Don't,' she said sharply. 'Just don't.'

'But the baby...'

'We'll be fine.' Her voice still had that note of awful brisk detachment. He had never heard it before. But then, they had never encountered a crisis like this before.

'What will you do? Are you staying here or going back to London?'

'I'll go back to London. Too many bad memories here now.'

'Oh Kat. Please, let's meet later today. And anyway, I have all my stuff in the flat.'

'Your worldly possessions,' she said flatly and gave a bark of a laugh, without any amusement in it.

'I know. It's not much, but there are things I don't want to leave behind. Anything you've given me, for example.'

She exhaled impatiently. 'I'm sure your wife wouldn't be too happy with you staggering home with an armful of mementos of your infidelity. No, honestly, I think it's better this way. I hate goodbyes. And it's basically only a broken photo and a guitar anyway, apart from a few clothes.'

Liam was astonished by her coldness. This was not his emotional, passionate, warm Katya, the girl who'd been his whole world up until eighteen hours ago.

'I can't handle this,' he said, his voice cracking. 'How can you be so matter-of-fact about it? There's no way I can never see you again. I want to support you and the baby. And I owe you money, for everything you've paid for for me. I want you in my life. I'm coming over, in a taxi. I have to see you, Kat. What we have—'

'What we *had*,' she corrected. 'We always knew it was a gamble, and that this would probably happen one day. Now it has, we just need to get on with our lives. I don't want your money. If it had turned out that you were divorced, or even unhappily married, we might have had a chance. But you're neither.'

He felt angry now, the grief diverting itself along a different channel. 'You're pregnant with my child, Katya. I'm its father. I have rights too.'

'No. You really don't, Liam. Just think of it like a, I don't know, holiday romance.'

His real name sounded so bizarre coming from her lips.

'Please don't be like this. I know it's awful, and it might seem like I'm ending things but you have to see it's not like that. I'm not *choosing* to! Could we not at least see how things go?'

Even as he said the words, he realised immediately what a terrible, begging, bet-hedging cop-out this was. Katya actually snorted, which was no more than he deserved. 'OK... fair enough. I'm sorry, I shouldn't have said that. It's just an impossible situation. It's no-one's fault that we fell in love and I don't regret it. But please don't cut me off. I want to help you, I don't want you to go through this on your own. I want to know about the baby, I want to help with its upbringing, even if it's only financially. I don't know for sure, but I'm pretty certain I do have rights.'

He said this timidly, not wanting to start an argument with her. It would have been their first ever argument, if he had.

'Honestly, thanks, but I'd prefer to go through it on my own. And it will make things easier for you. I'm hanging up now, but just one thing before I do… Jack?'

Her voice softened when she called him Jack again.

'Yes?' he gulped.

'Thank you for an amazing few months. Thank you for supporting me when Otto died. Thank you for being such a wonderful friend, and lover. Thank you for loving me. And most of all – thank you for this baby.'

The line went dead and she was gone.

Gone, before he even had a chance to thank her for all the numerous things she had done for *him*, housing him, nursing him, literally getting him back on his feet.

He tried immediately to call her back, but she had already blocked his number from her phone.

Liam rolled over onto his side on the bed, which smelled of starch and Alanda. Then he curled up and sobbed like a child.

He didn't even have her address in London.

CHAPTER FORTY-ONE

Katya

Katya had been sitting in the lawn chair outside Otto's workshop when Jack rang, staring numbly at the serried rows of bright geraniums.

He had promised her he'd re-plant the garden with borders and shrubs and a riot of colourful flowers once his leg was better, but they'd never got around to going to the garden centre. Now Otto's lonely geraniums would have to stay there, standing sentry for ever – or at least until the apartment's new owner chose to get rid of them.

The apartment would be going on the market as soon as possible, she decided. She couldn't stay here any longer, not without Jack or Otto. There was no need. No point.

Her hands were shaking with the effort of holding it together, and when she had terminated the call, immediately blocking his number, she thought how strange it was that this grown man, 'Jack', had really only existed for four months. He was like a newborn baby coming into the world with no memories, accumulating a few while he was here – snow-capped mountains, soppy loved-up smiles, sunlight glittering on the lake, a tinny second-hand guitar – then vanishing again. He had been a construction, almost a figment of her imagination. If it hadn't been for the foetus inside her, she might even have been able to persuade herself that the whole thing had been a dream.

The morning sun was hot on her face, and every time she looked up at the kitchen window, she imagined him framed there as he had been the night before, crestfallen and beaten-looking with a glass of water tilting in his hand – and the guilty stab of hope it had given her.

That in itself could never be right, she thought. *My happiness, predicated on someone else's misery.* At that precise moment Jack could not have looked more miserable, and nor could he have sounded it, on the phone just now.

She had to do the right thing.

She had never felt so alone.

Would it ever have worked between them, long term? She wasn't sure she wanted to know the answer to that, or even if there was one. They had been in such a bubble: of fear, infatuation, passion, intense trepidation, a cauldron of volcanic emotions, flooding into the vacuum created by a unique set of very unusual circumstances. As she said to him on the phone, *if* his memory had returned and *if* he'd been divorced or single, or – less likely – *if* his memory had never come back then yes, perhaps they could have made a life together. But those were all very long odds.

She refused to allow herself to think about what he'd said about 'seeing how things went'. What did that even mean? That if it turned out his marriage wasn't as strong as it seemed, then he'd come back to her?

Screw that, she thought savagely. She could not, would not, wait around for him to choose, and even then, if he chose her, to have the unwelcome knowledge that she and their baby had been second-best. If there was one thing Otto had taught her, it was to forge her own path and never be dependent on anyone else's decisions. If it was meant to be, then Jack would find her, eventually, but in the meantime, she could not bear the thought of being on tenterhooks waiting to see if he would come back. She didn't want his money, or his long-distance pity. She did want his baby, though. The one positive thing to come out of all this.

Katya's face was starting to burn, so she moved her chair back a foot or so inside the garage, leaving her legs and feet in the baking sunshine. It was cool and dry in there, and she inhaled the sawdust-and-Otto scent deeply. The sight of Otto's hand planer left on the workbench, still with a curl of blond wood attached to it from the last time he'd been in there working, threatened to tip her over the edge.

She would never see Otto again, and, worse, now she would likely never see Jack again either. The two most important men in her life, gone, just like that. The impact of it hit her square in the solar plexus, like a cartoon cannonball ploughing straight through the middle of her, leaving a circle of negative space… but then, where would the baby be? She couldn't lose this one.

She started crying then, even though it had just been a stupid mental picture, because she couldn't shake the image of herself with this defined emptiness inside her. Her belly, as empty as Jack's memory had been, the baby having only existed for as long as Jack himself had. It was all she could do not to rush to the pharmacy and buy another pregnancy test, to make sure she hadn't imagined this either.

Was she making a huge mistake, by refusing to see him before he left? There would be no 'closure', that word so beloved of TV agony aunts and therapists. The last image she would have of him would forever be him leaving the apartment with his wife.

She wavered. It didn't seem fair to deprive him of his possessions, either, if he wanted them… but then she imagined saying goodbye and it was so painful a thought that she moaned out loud. No. It was for the best. He'd be out of her life as abruptly as he entered it. The baby would be the only – the best – reminder of him.

Katya was not a religious woman, but she prayed then that she wouldn't suffer a miscarriage – it was still only a few weeks and she knew how fragile the new life inside her would be, for at least another month. She couldn't bear to lose the baby too.

This stiffened her resolve about not seeing Jack before he went – too much emotion would definitely not be good for her. Wiping her eyes, she folded the garden chair back up and slammed the garage door closed.

Back in the apartment, she gathered all Jack's things, stuffing them into a black bin bag. There wasn't much, apart from the guitar: some sheet music, a few T-shirts, pairs of jockey shorts, shaving cream, a jumper he'd left in the laundry basket, a mug she'd bought for him that said 'I bloody love you' in cursive script on the inside bottom of it – let Alanda chuck it out if she wanted to – and a travel book on Les Portes du Soleil he'd bought before their night in the hotel.

Then she packed a book, her sunglasses and a water bottle into a small rucksack and briefly unblocked his number to text him, dry-eyed and resolute:

> *I'm going out for the day but I'll leave your things at the back, outside the workshop door – side gate is open. Please don't contact me. Good luck with it all.*

Then she hesitated, her resolve crumbling just for a moment, and added, *I'll love you always. K x*

She locked the apartment, taking the bag and guitar and propping them against the garage door, hoping that the sun wouldn't warp the guitar, and that one of the neighbours wouldn't spot it out the window and think it was rubbish up for grabs.

Not my problem, she thought. She put on her shades, straightened her shoulders and set off for a very long walk around the lake, determined to think of all the positives in her life. She hadn't lost anything she didn't already have before she'd met Jack. Financially, she would be in a much stronger position once she'd sold Otto's apartment. She could go home and see Nic now, and all her other friends. Perhaps she ought to look up Danny. Nic had heard on the grapevine that he was dating someone, but she owed it to him to tell him in person that she was pregnant. The thought of it made her feel strange, nervous and unsettled, so she stopped thinking about it and forced herself back to the positives – the biggest one undoubtedly being that Jack had left her with the best gift anyone could ever have given her.

'It's all good,' she said out loud, to convince herself of this fact, even while the tears were pouring down her cheeks.

CHAPTER FORTY-TWO

Alanda

Most of the terrace's residents had turned out into the street when Liam and Alanda returned from the airport, clapping and cheering as their taxi pulled into the drive.

Becky and Heather had strung a wonky 'Welcome Home' banner over the door, and strewn bunting along the edges of the front hedge. There was a camera crew from the local news channel, who Alanda later found out Jake had tipped off ('They'll come to the opening of a fridge door,' he said), and two local reporters. Louise next door had even brought her saxophone out and was inexpertly serenading them which, frankly, Alanda could have done without, but it was well-intentioned, she was sure.

All three kids swarmed around Liam as soon as he got out of the car, crying uncontrollably and hugging him, and Alanda stepped aside to let them welcome their father back, tears running down her own face.

Liam's old mate from the squash club, Colin, was there, lurking in an embarrassed way behind a parked car, trying to avoid the TV camera. Sadie and Jennie had both turned up too, flanking Alanda solidly, a small battalion of friendship to celebrate with her and wipe away her tears.

As Alanda suspected they would, Jennie and Sadie hit it off straight away when she'd introduced them. While Liam had been missing, she'd been a *de facto* single woman as well, and she felt that all three were bonded by loneliness. She was determined to grow the friendships, now that things would be getting back to normal for her, not let them slide. Women friends were everything, she thought, putting an arm around each of them. And, God knew, she'd need their counsel to help her unravel this latest crisis. She hadn't texted or called either of them to tell them about the bombshell of Liam's Other Woman. There had been too much else going on and, besides, it wasn't the sort of thing which could be adequately covered by a few lines of a text and a sad-face emoji.

'Are you going to bring Liam in to see his mum?' Jennie asked, as they observed the displays of affection, none of the kids making any effort to curtail them. Liam hadn't seen Becky's hair since she cut it really short and dyed it almost white, and he was rubbing the fuzzy nape of her neck with amusement and affection. Meanwhile Heather hung on to him with her arms round his waist and Jake repeatedly smacked kisses onto his cheek.

'Definitely,' Alanda replied. 'Do you think she'll remember him? She never talks about him anymore – apart from when she thinks he's very tiny and lives in the bottom of her wardrobe…'

Jennie smiled ruefully, squeezing Alanda's hand. 'Bless her. I have no idea – it's impossible to tell. She was a bit more away with the fairies than usual last week, with that urine infection, but now the antibiotics have kicked in she seems more settled.'

Finally, looking overcome and slightly mortified when he noticed all the mobile phones videoing their reunion as well as an actual camera crew, Liam managed to extricate himself from the kids' embraces. He caught Alanda's eye and made a pleading face, meaning '*get me inside*'.

Alanda stepped forward, cupping her hands around her mouth as a makeshift megaphone, and bellowed, 'Thank you so much, everyone! Isn't it lovely to have him home? We all really appreciate your support.'

All the neighbours clapped and cheered again and Liam turned and waved, as Heather and Becky ushered him back into his house. Jake stayed behind to speak to the news reporter on the family's behalf.

The rest of that first day back was a blur of chat and family, tears and laughter – and questions. So many questions, thought Alanda, many of which Liam was unable to answer. Where had his ID and phone gone? He had no idea – they must have been stolen at some point. Why had the police not realised he'd taken another flight, from Madrid? This one he thought he did know – he'd forgotten to tell Alanda before he went that he'd taken out a new credit card for his travel expenses, and paid for the second flight on it, hence it not showing up on his regular account statement.

Apart from the interrogation, it felt like Christmas. Heather remarked at one point, 'But without the turkey and the crackers and the board games.'

'Or the arguments,' agreed Becky. They'd just watched the local news report on his return, and all laughed at how camp Jake acted on camera, which made him slightly cross – but only slightly.

Alanda and Liam had decided not to tell the kids anything about what had gone on between him and Katya. There seemed, from Katya's reaction, little or no danger that she would at any point turn up and demand anything from him and, they decided, if she did, they would deal with it then. No point in borrowing trouble (one of Vi's old sayings) – although Liam told Alanda he felt deeply uncomfortable that Katya was refusing to let him support the child.

'It's wrong,' he'd said to her over the armrest on the plane home. 'I have an obligation to her.'

'It's her choice,' Alanda replied. 'If having nothing to do with you really makes it easier for her to cope, then you have to respect that. You said she's inherited that apartment so she's probably OK for money now anyway. I think I'd be the same. I wouldn't want the reminders. Easier to just start again.'

She had to turn and look out at the clouds, to avoid the expression of pain that flitted across her husband's face. She remembered thinking that she wished Liam's memory loss covered the period *after* his accident as well as before, so that he wouldn't be reminded either. It felt deeply uncomfortable, knowing that they must have been in love, albeit for such a short time.

Then she would feel freshly aggrieved that Katya would be so stupid as to embark on a relationship with a man who had no memory. *I mean*, she thought, *what did she expect?* If Katya had done any research at all on retrograde amnesia, she would have known that it rarely lasted as long as Liam's had, so of course it was all going to come out sooner or later.

She had more sympathy for Liam, though. Perhaps because it was easier to blame a woman who she would hopefully never need to clap eyes on again, but also because she couldn't imagine how terrifying it must be to find yourself in a world with no points of reference, no friends or family… it would be natural to cling on to the first person who showed you a bit of affection.

She couldn't wait to tell Jennie and Sadie, but not in a 'check out *this* as a juicy piece of gossip' sort of way. More because it was too heavy a burden to bear on her own shoulders. It was pretty clear that she and Liam were not likely to be discussing it further.

The two women came in, briefly, for a glass of fizz. Liam looked puzzled when he first saw Jennie, because of course he had only ever met her before in the home.

'Liam, do you remember Jennie?' Alanda said, rescuing him.

He was settling himself on the sofa in the front room and she could see his eyes alight with pleasure on all the things he hadn't seen for such a long time; furniture and pictures and the black and white photo-montage of the family on the wall. A new photograph had taken pride of place on the mantelpiece: Heather and Kevin on their wedding day, laughing in a snowstorm of rose-petal confetti on the steps of the church, and Liam kept staring hungrily at it – even though the real Heather and Kevin were in the room with him.

'I do recognise you,' he said to Jennie. 'I'm sorry… my memory is still a bit ropey.'

'She's the manager at Harcourt Grange, do you remember, she showed us round when we were first thinking of Vi going to live there?'

'Oh yes, of course, hi, Jennie,' Liam said, clearly thinking, *and what is she doing in my front room?*

Alanda laughed, seeing his confusion. 'We've become mates,' she explained. 'She and Sadie have both been brilliant to me ever since you went AWOL.'

'Ah. Well, that's excellent, I'm so pleased to hear it. Thank you for looking after both my wife *and* my mother. How is Vi?'

He raised his glass in Jennie's direction, and she leaned forward to clink hers against it.

'She's doing well. A bit of a UTI last week, but it's clearing up nicely.'

'I'm really looking forward to seeing her,' Liam said. 'Even if she probably won't recognise me.'

'She might,' said Alanda. 'She has her good days and bad.'

Jennie clapped her hands together in a decisive way. 'Right. I'm going to leave you all to it. You must have so much to catch up on. Alanda, how about lunch next Thursday? You, me and Sadie? It's my day off.'

Sadie was hovering in the doorway to the hall, putting on her trainers. 'Perfect,' she said, 'I'm on nights, starting that day. It can't be too boozy though.'

'Don't worry,' said Jennie. 'We can drink your share.'

CHAPTER FORTY-THREE

Alanda

September

'And this morning we're delighted to welcome to our sofa a very special guest, someone whose photograph you probably saw on social media earlier this year. This is Liam Lodge, here with his wife Alanda. Liam's spur-of-the-moment decision to change solo holiday plans from hiking in Spain to skiing in the Alps was to be the biggest mistake he ever made, when he lost his memory after an accident on the slopes... Welcome, both of you. Please, talk us through the story, guys.'

The very voluptuous blonde presenter smiled encouragingly at them, revealing a set of immaculate and dazzlingly white teeth, on which Alanda focussed to try to stop her concentration wavering. They were a proper set of gnashers, she thought.

This was the first of many interviews. All the requests had initially been made back in August on Liam's return, but he had flatly refused to do them so soon, and most of the producers and journalists had reluctantly agreed to a few weeks' wait. Even so, Liam was still in two minds about it. He was terrified, he said, at the prospect of forgetting what he was saying halfway through a sentence – or worse, forgetting the question he'd literally only just been asked. He had never been on television before and hated all forms of the limelight. Becky even teased him that his accident had been an extreme ploy to avoid giving a speech at Heather's wedding ('Too soon?' she'd asked, but they'd all laughed, even Heather).

But there was money in it: money that would help the kids and go towards Vi's astronomical care home fees. Liam hadn't worked for months, obviously, and couldn't again until his leg properly healed. Alanda barely made ends meet with the shop. They'd be mad to turn down the opportunities which had been flooding in since Liam's return.

Alanda hadn't been on TV before either. She was already finding it more exhilarating than petrifying – although she knew she would find the pre-recorded interviews that were lined up for next week less nerve-racking. She wished they could have started with one of those, to ease them both in gently. Live television was definitely the medium with the most potential for disaster. Liam still remained unconvinced that he wouldn't faint, fart – oh, how much Becky would enjoy that! – or puke on live TV, and in the cab on the way to the studios, Alanda had had to constantly reassure him of the unlikelihood of this happening.

The whole procedure was alien and, were it not for Liam's discomfort, would have been thrilling – from being picked up in a fancy car by the TV company at some unearthly hour, to getting her hair and make-up done by an earnest young woman who flicked her powder brush down Alanda's cheekbones whilst making small talk about Liam's experience and how traumatic it must have been.

Then there was an anxious wait in the Green Room, but there had been fresh pastries and nice coffee and other interesting guests to talk to. Alanda had even plucked up the courage to ask a young soap star, due in the slot before them, for a selfie. She'd had no idea who he was, but she was pretty sure the kids would be impressed when she showed them the photo.

Jake had been gutted that the production company hadn't wanted him on the sofa too. He'd been the one to push for Liam to do all these interviews in the first place when the press came calling, saying that it might help him – Jake – get a new job in PR, if Liam repeatedly raved about how Jake's skills had led to his identity being recovered.

Poor Jake had had a very tough time in the past few months, what with the fruitless job-hunting and the stress about his dad, on top of his recent break-up, so his plea had finally made Liam relent and do the interviews. Anything to help get his son back into employment again. That, and the money on the table.

Alanda couldn't help wondering how much bigger the sum would be if it came out that Liam had fallen in love and got a girl pregnant during his lost months. She could imagine the headlines: *Memory Loss Brit Skier Impregnates Girlfriend – Without Knowing He's Already Married!* Thank God they didn't know, she thought. She wondered if Katya would ever sell her story. If she needed the money, then maybe.

But if she needed the money, why had she not agreed to Liam's offer of support? The secret was probably safe, she thought, although she couldn't help but wonder if Katya had come back to the UK yet and if she was watching. Alanda didn't like the thought of Katya, greedily drinking in Liam's face on her television, perhaps prompting a change of mind about not wanting to stay in contact.

Would she ever feel secure in her marriage again?

Focus, Alanda, she told herself, trying to avoid looking into the screens of the swivelling robotic cameras moving around in her eyeline, controlled by invisible hands in another room somewhere.

'So,' Liam began, even though he and Alanda both cringed whenever they heard interviewees on the radio prefacing the answer to every question with 'so'. She noticed that he didn't dare glance across at her. 'I don't remember when or why I decided to change my plan and go skiing instead of hiking the Camino de Santiago – I suppose at some point between saying goodbye to my family at Gatwick and arriving in Madrid. I must have bought a flight straight to Geneva from Madrid, on the spur of the moment.'

The buxom presenter, whose name was Gabriella, turned to Alanda. 'And is Liam prone to spur-of-the-moment decisions?'

Alanda laughed, somewhat more heartily than was called for. 'Definitely not! The kids and I have always teased him for being so predictable. That's why we didn't think it was possible he could be anywhere other than where he was meant to be. It literally never occurred to us that he could have left Spain.'

Gabriella turned back to Liam, with an expression that was teetering on disapproval. 'Oh dear. Your poor family.'

'Yes,' he said. 'I know. I feel dreadful for what I put them through. It was compounded by me forgetting – or losing – my phone when I went out on the slopes, and having no ID on me.'

'But what about your luggage? Surely you could have been identified by that, when you failed to come back to your hotel? And surely there'd have been a record of your standby flight to Geneva?'

Alanda winced internally, aware that the tripartite question, the one with most potential for losing a thread on answering, was the one Liam had most dreaded.

But he handled it with aplomb, shrugging casually. 'You'd have thought. But apparently I paid for the flight on a new credit card for travel expenses I'd forgotten to mention to Alanda. If she'd known about it, the police would have been able to track me that way, and I'd have been found so much sooner… I don't know what happened to my luggage. I never found it and nobody ever came forward. I suspect that whichever hotel I'd booked, someone stole my backpack from the room, or Left Luggage, or somewhere. And the police have since admitted that it was an oversight that they failed to pick up on my ongoing flight on the system.'

'Those are terrible bits of bad luck,' Gabriella sympathised toothily. 'Alanda, when did you raise the alarm?'

Alanda smiled at Liam. She'd told the story enough times now over the past few months that she could just about do it without crying. 'He texted to say he'd landed safely but that was the last we heard from him, and there was nothing else after that. I was worried straight away – it was so out of character for him not to stay in touch. When he still wasn't answering our WhatsApps by the next morning, I was frantic – but I read somewhere that there's no point reporting an adult missing for at least forty-eight hours. So I made myself wait that long.'

'And what was going through your mind?'

Alanda gave a brief barking laugh. 'Everything. I've always had a tendency to catastrophise, so my brain was working overtime. I thought he'd had an accident or been mugged for his phone or something. Then as time went on, I thought it must be worse than that. That he was—'

She stopped and swallowed hard. 'Sorry.'

'It must have been terrible. And how many months did you have to wait before there was any news?'

'Almost four. Our son Jake arranged loads of social media campaigns to circulate Liam's photo and details – that's what Jake does, by the way, PR, and he's brilliant at it. He's on the lookout for a new position, so if anyone has an opening, please get in touch.'

She noticed Liam cringe slightly at the unsubtlety of her approach, but Gabriella didn't seem to mind. 'There you go, folks, snap him up! Jake Lodge! And that's how you found out that Liam had gone skiing?'

'Yes. A woman saw our Twitter appeal and remembered having a conversation with someone who answered his description, in a gondola in the French Alps, back in April. We didn't think it could be him at first, but when she said the date – April seventh, the date he went missing – and described what he'd said, and that he mentioned not having skied for many years – oh, and that he'd forgotten his phone – well, then we really started to think we might have found him. I started ringing round all the hospitals in the area, and eventually I reached the one which had treated Liam all those weeks for his broken thighbone, not knowing who he was. I flew out there as soon as I could and tracked him down via the hospital and the French police.'

'Gosh,' Gabriella said, taking a sip from a glass of water on the low coffee table in front of their sofa. Despite her bright red lipstick, her lips left no impression on the glass. 'That's very dramatic. How long were you in hospital, Liam, and where did you go when you got out?'

'It was a pretty bad break, so I was in traction for quite a while. And, of course, with the memory loss they were doing all sorts of other tests on me. But once my leg started to heal, I think they weren't sure what to do with me.'

This was the bit Alanda knew he would find hard to talk about.

'I'd have been really stuck if someone I met hadn't come to my rescue. There was this lady who was visiting her uncle on the same ward as me, and we became friends. I think she felt sorry for me. Her uncle died, and then there was a spare room in her flat, so she invited me to be her lodger for a few weeks until – hopefully – my memory came back.'

'Wow, how very kind of her,' Gabriella said, giving a fake little clap of her manicured fingers.

Liam nodded. 'I know. I was so fortunate. I don't know what I'd have done otherwise, with no money and no means of getting any.'

'And are you still in touch with your guardian angel?'

Alanda realised she was holding her breath.

'No. I'd like to be, though, to try and repay the money she spent looking after me, but she insisted that she didn't need me to and wants to remain anonymous.'

'Well, that's a wonderfully heart-warming story with *such* a happy ending!' Gabriella looked delighted and triumphant, as if she had personally engineered the outcome. 'Next up, I'll be talking to a man who breeds llamas and knits his own clothes from their wool. Is there anything final you'd like to say to our audience, Liam, before we leave you and Alanda?'

Liam cleared his throat. 'Just, well, that I'm so happy and relieved to be home with my family. And to give a huge thank you to the amazing staff at Thonon-les-Bains hospital, particularly Sister Celine and to… my kind benefactress who took me in and looked after me.' He rushed over these words, and Alanda knew that he would be horribly aware of the pain they could be causing both her and Katya, if she was watching.

They hadn't mentioned Katya's name since the conversation on the plane.

'Oh, and finally,' he ploughed on, as Jake had coached him, 'just to warn people: never do anything spontaneous that your family doesn't know about! I know I never will again. I should've just bought a Harley, like most normal men having a midlife crisis do.'

The interview finished with all of them fake-laughing heartily, as Liam leaned across and kissed Alanda on the cheek. The red ON AIR light went green and a floor manager rushed on to divest them of their microphone packs and accompany them out of the studio.

'Thanks, guys, that was really great,' Gabriella called, with a perfunctory wave to their retreating backs. 'All the best for the rest of your future together.'

Alanda changed her mind. She hoped Katya *had* watched it.

CHAPTER FORTY-FOUR

Alanda stood at the sandy lake edge, shivering. The sun had gone behind a cloud and the water no longer looked inviting without the sparkling ruffles on its surface. In fact, it looked positively murky and cold. Gooseflesh swept up and down over her body and she wondered if it was too late to back out.

'Whenever you're ready,' said the stocky young lifeguard, clipboard poised. 'I'll just give you the thumbs-up to carry on, assuming there are no problems. It's only fifteen metres, so I'm sure you won't have any, if you're a confident swimmer.'

Jennie was already in the water, sculling around the buoy to which Alanda was required to swim out, to prove she was an adequately strong swimmer before she was allowed to participate in the open-water swimming session.

Alanda picked her way into the shallows, adjusting her goggles. The sand became mud and her feet sucked through it. It was really chilly. But she couldn't leave Jennie in there to swim the route on her own. She felt self-conscious in her bikini when all the other women she'd seen, including Jennie, were in sensible one-pieces, but this was the only swimwear she had since her trusty old Speedo had gone all bobbly and transparent.

Trying not to think about pike lurking beneath the surface to snap at her toes, she got deep enough to throw herself in and began to swim front crawl towards the buoy, lifting her head every few strokes to make sure she wasn't veering off course. No white lines on a pool floor to guide her here.

She made it to the buoy, panting with the cold and the exertion, pulling off her goggles to look back to shore for the lifeguard's thumbs-up, which she responded to with one of her own.

'Isn't it lovely?' Jennie enthused, patting her on the shoulder with a wet splat.

'It's brilliant! The water feels so silky.'

'Doesn't it! I warn you, it's addictive.'

Alanda laughed. 'I think I'll have to buy a new swimming costume if I'm planning to come again.'

'Oh, you're fine. You look awesome in your bikini, by the way. Shall we do the long route or the short?' Each was marked out in a large circle by regular buoys, the shorter route hugging closer to the shore for the less confident swimmers.

'Let's go for it. The long.'

'Good woman,' said Jennie, putting her goggles back on and plunging off. Alanda followed, feeling utter exhilaration at the cool vastness of being in the lake and the novel soft caress of un-chlorinated water washing over her skin as she swam. Jennie was a slightly stronger swimmer than she was, and had pulled ahead by the time they reached the next buoy.

Alanda was puffing when she caught up with her, grabbing on to the buoy for support.

'Breaststroke for the next section?' she pleaded. 'I haven't swum for months.'

'Sure. We can chat then too,' Jennie said, moving to one side to allow two men to thrash past them around the buoy, the muscles rippling in their shoulders, buttocks tight in small tight trunks.

'I do like a swimmer's body,' Alanda mused as they set off at a more sedate pace. 'Nice big shoulders and a small waist.'

Jennie made a non-committal sound and Alanda continued, 'I mean, you wouldn't kick that first one out of bed for eating crisps, would you? He had a lovely physique.'

'I would,' Jennie said, not looking at her.

'Would what?'

'Kick him out of bed, and he wouldn't even need to be eating crisps.'

'Oh really? Doesn't do it for you? What sort of body do you like, then?'

Jennie was silent for a moment. 'One with breasts and a vagina,' she said eventually.

Alanda was so surprised she accidentally inhaled a mouthful of lake water and almost choked. Only through the sheer will of not wanting to act uncool in front of her new friend did she manage to stop herself. She felt like an idiot – all these weeks, and she'd had no idea.

'You're *gay*?'

'Is that a problem?' Jennie's voice sounded clipped.

'No! Absolutely not, not at all. I just feel awful for not asking about you enough to find out. All those times you talked about Alex I just assumed it was a boy Alex, not a girl Alex. I'm a bad friend, forgive me.'

Jennie laughed, and Alanda could tell she had relaxed again by the long, languorous strokes she made through the water. 'You're not at all. I didn't make it clear, and there were lots of times I could have done.'

'Why not, if you don't mind me asking? I wouldn't have minded at all. I don't mind at all. We're not in the 1950s.'

'Oh, I know, it's not that, so much. I suppose it was just… habit? I don't broadcast it at work. If Alex and I were still together I would have let people know we were a couple, but there didn't seem any point when I moved here on my own. Also, I guess… I didn't want you to assume I was hitting on you. I love your company, Alanda, and I'm so glad we've become friends. I wouldn't want anything to ruin that.'

'It won't,' Alanda said, stopping to tread water. Jennie did the same, and they were face to face. Alanda reached forward and gave her a quick hug. 'You've been such a good friend to me. In fact, I'm not sure if I'd have got through this year if it wasn't for you, and Sadie. I've always been rubbish at asking for help but you both have really been there for me. And I love that you've helped distract me by doing new things, like this.'

'Pushing you out of your comfort zone,' Jennie said, grinning. 'Come on, let's crack on otherwise we'll have the slowest lap time in history.'

'I didn't realise it was a competition,' Alanda said, mock-grumpily.

'Everything's a competition,' called Jennie over her shoulder, as she powered away, leaving Alanda to follow in her wake.

Well, well, she thought, getting back into her stride. *I can't believe I didn't realise; I really am slow on the uptake.* She was so glad Jennie had told her now, though. It wasn't right, not being able to be your true self with your friends.

They finished their 1.5km lap of the lake, alternating front crawl and breaststroke between the buoys, and Alanda staggered back up the sandy beach to where they'd left their towels, her legs like jelly and her heart thumping in her chest, but feeling utterly elated.

'That was amazing,' she said. 'I never want to swim in a pool again.'

'Told you you'd love it,' Jennie said, towelling herself briskly.

Alanda noticed how slim she was, how toned her legs and arms were, and instantly felt self-conscious, worried that in the light of the new knowledge that she was already looking at Jennie differently – but then dismissed the thought. Seeing your mates near-naked in swimwear for the first time was always somehow a key moment in a friendship, she mused, whatever their sexual orientation. There was something so intimate and revealing about it.

They changed in individual cubicles in the little changing hut on the banks, then spread out their wet towels on the grass to dry, sitting down next to them. Jennie had brought a flask of coffee and they passed the cup between them.

Jennie said, 'I saw you on TV the other week – you were great. You both were.'

'Thanks.' Alanda opened the KitKat she'd brought, passing Jennie half of it and biting into her half. 'It was a very surreal experience. Liam was petrified, but he hid it really well, I thought. Only a couple more local radio ones now, and I think we're done.'

'How is Liam?' Jennie asked. Then, more cautiously, 'How are things between you?'

Alanda sighed. 'OK, on the surface, but… I'm worried about him. I'm quite worried about *us*, if I'm honest. We've never been like this before. I thought it was going to be so amazing, having him back, but it's actually been stressful. We're sort of treading on eggshells around each other. Not arguing – we've never really argued – but he's so quiet and withdrawn. He's upstairs in the attic playing his guitar every night, I hardly see him. And he's started going out loads more, in the day and evenings, going for bike rides with his mate Colin and then to the pub. He and I can't go for long walks like we used to, because his leg starts to ache. Cycling isn't as bad, apparently.'

'It's a big adjustment, however you look at it,' Jennie said contemplatively. 'He's been pulled out of one life, a life that he thought he'd be in for ever, and however glad he is that he's back with you all, it must be weird for him.'

'It's weird for me too,' Alanda said, more vehemently than she meant to. 'He's moping around all the time, and I can't stop thinking it's because he misses that woman and wants to be with her.'

'I'm sure he does miss her,' Jennie agreed, and Alanda smiled ruefully. Neither Jennie nor Sadie ever minced their words. She had a sudden flash of wondering if those two would make a good couple. She and Liam had often speculated that the reason Sadie hadn't found a man was because she was in the closet…

'But he chose *you*,' continued Jennie. 'Just give him time to reacclimatise. I'm sure things will come back to normal soon.'

'I hope so,' said Alanda. 'I really hope so.'

CHAPTER FORTY-FIVE

Alanda was sitting at the dining table half-listening to a podcast about poltergeists on her phone whilst trying, for the third time, to get to grips with the principles of crochet. It was fine if she did it with the aid of an instruction video, but as soon as she attempted to follow a pattern, she got hopelessly lost. She was trying and failing to remind herself of the difference between the half-treble crochet and double-treble crochet stitches without having to resort to YouTube, when Liam clumped self-consciously through the room in brand new cycling kit, the hard plastic cleated soles of the clip-in shoes knocking hollowly on the tiled floor.

'Wow, you've gone the full MAMIL,' Alanda said, grinning at him. 'Love the padded butt. That lot must have cost a few quid.'

Liam frowned. 'I didn't buy it from the joint account. What do you mean, the full mammal?'

'Oh come on, you must have heard that acronym? MAMIL – Middle-Aged Man in Lycra.'

He managed a smile, but it was half-hearted. 'Good one,' he conceded. 'Anyway, Colin and I are heading out to the coast, via the New Forest and a lunchtime pint.'

'Again? You were out all day on Tuesday. I thought you were just showing me your new gear.'

Liam filled up his water bottle. 'The physio said it's good for my leg, as long as we don't do too many big hills. And the exercise helps me sleep.'

'As do the pints, I imagine.'

Liam had taken to going to the pub 'with the boys' after their rides as well as during. On Tuesday he hadn't rolled in until after nine p.m., having left before lunch.

'Not a problem, is it?'

Alanda put down the crochet hook and pressed Pause on the podcast. 'No, darling, of course I want you to enjoy exercising again, and spend time with your mates. It's just...'

Liam waited. His expression mingled impatience, guilt and concern, and Alanda thought what a rubbish poker player he would make. You could see the imprint of his every emotion so clearly.

'... you used to save your long bike rides for my days in the shop, when you weren't working, so we could do stuff together on my day off.'

He sighed, clumping over and sitting down at the table next to her.

'That's because we used to go for long walks, and that hurts my leg too much now.'

'I know, but we could still go for a drive and a long lunch somewhere, couldn't we? And short walks are OK, aren't they?'

She felt embarrassed, as if she was begging her own husband. It was an unfamiliar, unpleasant sensation, and she felt a flash of resentment towards him.

He squeezed her hand. 'Of course. Let's do that on your next day off – when is that? Saturday? But I mean, Al, it's not like I haven't spent hundreds of evenings over the years babysitting while you're out at choir, or swimming, or tennis, or whatever. I never moaned about that. I thought you'd be pleased that I was finally really getting into a hobby. And you can talk about being out for lunches – you're always out with Sadie and Jennie!'

'I'm not moaning,' Alanda said hotly. 'I'm just commenting. And a quick lunch in town is hardly the same as a whole day out on the bike.'

His words really rankled. Her own hobbies had always been her release from the frequent boredom and mundanity of being a mostly stay-at-home mum, and she only saw the girls once every couple of weeks or so.

'I didn't realise you resented it,' she added. 'For the record, it's not "babysitting" when they're your own kids.'

Liam stuck out his jaw and pressed his lips together, which made Alanda feel even more wound up.

'Honestly, Liam, all those years of us both busting a gut, you working full-time to keep a roof over our heads and me juggling the kids and the shop, and now that we're semi-retired and actually have the time to travel and do nice things – and suddenly I feel like I hardly ever see you.'

'I think that's an exaggeration,' he said, standing up again with a wince. He still had to push on the tabletop to help him up without exacerbating the ache in his leg, and Alanda wondered how on earth cycling fifty miles didn't manage to make it worse. 'Anyway, I've got to go now otherwise I'll be late meeting Col. Why don't you book us a nice country pub for Saturday? Forecast's looking good. Maybe the kids will come too.'

'Liam…' So many words crowded simultaneously into her brain that she suddenly couldn't speak any of them, lest they all splurged out at once and she might say something she regretted. Words of bitterness, loss, pain, loneliness, fear.

'What?'

What could she say? It would seem like an overreaction to kick off about him going for a simple bike ride – but of course it wasn't just that.

She swallowed hard, picking up her bit of botched crochet and ripping the wool out viciously, deriving a tiny amount of release from the action as the long strand puddled on the table in front of her. 'You'll think I'm exaggerating, but you know what us living like this feels like?'

Her voice cracked. 'I know it's been difficult for you. But it is for me too and, more and more, this is starting to feel almost as bad as it did when you were missing. It's like you're still not really here, even though you're back.'

He stood for a moment, stock still, frozen in his ridiculous Lycra, gaping at her in shock. She waited for him to rush over to her, wrap his arms around her, apologise, cancel the bike ride... but instead he gathered himself, walked briskly over and kissed the top of her head. Then he picked his helmet off the arm of the sofa where he'd left it and clicked out the back door without saying a word.

'Don't get lost or killed,' she whispered after his retreating back.

CHAPTER FORTY-SIX

Alanda

October

The young girl sidled up to their table in the restaurant and hovered by Alanda's seat as she finished the last forkful of her main course. Sadie, who'd been in the middle of relating an anecdote about the vagaries of the fire station's ancient plumbing, stopped speaking and they all looked curiously up at the interloper.

'Sorry to bother you,' the girl said shyly, her cheeks turning visibly pink in a wash like a sunrise. She was in her teens or twenties, skinny and quirky-looking, in knee socks, a short denim skirt and a seventies-inspired patchwork waistcoat. 'You're Liam Lodge's wife, aren't you?'

Alanda's heart sank. She'd had quite a bit of this since all the interviews, enough that she now had huge sympathy for anybody in the public eye.

'I saw you on *Gabriella* a few weeks back,' the girl rushed on. 'I just wanted to say, your story made me proper sob. I'd read all the appeals on Facebook and Twitter and I kept thinking I'd be so upset if my dad went missing like that, and I've got to say, I thought he was probably dead, so I was like, sooo happy when you found him! I didn't even know he'd been found till I saw you both on telly and I was just, like…'

She flapped her hand in front of her face, to indicate what she'd been like. Alanda smiled at her. 'Thank you so much,' she said. 'That's really sweet of you.'

The girl nodded and beamed and retreated back to her table, while Jennie and Sadie tried not to laugh.

'Oh good grief,' Sadie said. 'I thought she was going to ask for your autograph. You're, *like*, a real sleb now.'

'Jake did organise rather a lot of interviews,' Alanda said, refilling all their wineglasses. 'I wish he hadn't – well, no I don't, but I would, if it weren't for the money. We're giving most of it to the kids. Jake's been out of work for months so he needs it for rent and stuff. Heather can pay off some of their wedding expenses, and Becky wants to buy a car, so it'll come in really handy for all of them. If any more comes in we'll put it towards Vi's home fees. Everything's been quite tight since Liam's not been earning.'

'Did you like being on TV?' Jennie asked curiously, picking up the last piece of bread from the basket and using it to mop up the dressing from her salad.

'Well, yes and no,' Alanda admitted. 'I can't deny it's a buzz, although Liam found it a bit of an ordeal. But…'

She wasn't sure whether to say it or not. She had told them both about Katya a few weeks after Liam's return, so the initial shock and scandal of the revelation had died down enough that she tried not to monopolise their conversations with it.

The lunches with Jennie and Sadie had become a fortnightly event, something all three of them looked forward to more and more. 'Please tell me to stop banging on about it if it's getting boring,' she repeated, as she often did. The other two were either too nice to say that it was, or they were genuinely happy to help her by listening. Or perhaps they just thought, *and I thought* I *had problems?*

'Spit it out,' Sadie said. 'It's fine, that's what we're here for.'

Jennie nodded encouragingly.

Alanda sighed. 'I was just a bit worried, every time we did an interview, or there was an article about Liam in the paper, that *she'd* see it, and change her mind about not wanting to be in touch with him.'

They didn't need to be told who 'she' was.

'She hasn't yet, has she?' Jennie said.

'No, but I keep thinking, the more pregnant she gets, the more vulnerable and lonely she'll be feeling, and at any moment she's going to regret kicking him into touch, and decide she wants to get her claws into him again to play happy families.'

'It's a worry all right,' Sadie agreed. 'Anyone having pudding?'

Alanda felt a brief flash of irritation, and when she looked up, Jennie was giving her a look of empathy.

'No pud for me,' Jennie said. 'I think we should get another bottle of wine, though.'

Normally Alanda would have demurred, but she didn't have anything else to do that afternoon. Liam was going to Southampton at three p.m. to do a quote for someone's garden, and he was unlikely to be back before six, so she'd have plenty of time to sleep it off.

Not that Liam minded if she had the odd boozy lunch, but there had been quite a few recently…

'You two lushes go ahead,' Sadie said. 'I'm going to love you and leave you. I've got to do a big shop and then drop the dogs round to Doreen's before I go on shift, so I can't be on the lash all afternoon.'

'Who's Doreen?' Jennie asked, trying to attract the waitress's attention. The restaurant was one of those self-consciously kooky places, too many stuffed deer heads jostling for space on the walls, fake wood panelling and ostentatious glass chandeliers, the décor a mishmash of Victoriana, Georgiana and… whatever the Edwardian equivalent was. Surely not Edwardiana, thought Alanda.

The waiting staff were similarly quirky. Their waitress, frankly, looked like she was away with the fairies. *Must be why my fan likes it here so much*, she thought, glancing over to the girl's table, where she was sharing a pudding with an earnest-looking young man; her boyfriend, presumably. She caught Alanda's eye and raised her glass to her. Alanda smiled back.

'Neighbour and dog-sitter,' said Sadie, delving in her handbag for her wallet and leaving thirty quid cash on the table. 'Couldn't survive without her. Right, that should cover it, but let me know if it doesn't.'

Once she decided to go, she was gone, Alanda thought, amused. She didn't mess about, that woman.

'Sure you won't stay and help us drink it?' she said, but predictably, Sadie was already kissing their cheeks and waving goodbye.

The waitress, an unusually tall young woman in a hippie-type short dress with a frilly apron tied over the top, finally drifted over and took their order for another bottle of the Gavi di Gavi, whilst twiddling with a strand of her hair and looking into the middle distance.

'This is a bit naughty,' Alanda said to Jennie, who grinned at her.

'I know, right? I think we deserve it.'

'Just going to the loo,' Alanda said. 'Don't drink it all before I get back.'

The trip up the stairs to the Ladies' made her realise that she was already quite drunk, and she had to grab the banister to keep herself steady. The loos were miles away, along corridors, up more steps, round corners...

When she came out, she was just checking her phone to see if Jake had got the interview he was hoping for, and didn't notice the three small steps leading round the first corner back to the stairs. She missed the top one, falling heavily down the other two, twisting her ankle painfully and banging her knee hard on the wall.

'Bugger,' she moaned, lying in an undignified heap, panting with pain.

She dragged herself up to sitting and leaned against the wall, feeling her ankle and knee already beginning to swell. Tears of pain leaked from her eyes as she texted Jennie: *Have "had a fall"!* This was their little joke, about when you got to a certain age, you no longer fell over, you 'had a fall'. *Can you come and rescue me? Xx*

Within seconds she heard Jennie's footsteps pounding up the main staircase and running along the corridor.

'Oh Alanda! What hurts?' She crouched down next to her and put her arm around Alanda's shoulders, her other hand delving into her pocket for a tissue. 'Here, it's clean.'

Alanda took it, blowing her nose and wiping her eyes. 'So undignified,' she muttered. 'I think I've sprained my ankle, and bashed my knee.'

'Right. Let's get you somewhere we can have a better look. I'll get some ice from that ditsy waitress.'

Jennie helped her up and Alanda half-hopped, half-limped back along the corridor, leaning heavily on Jennie until they reached a small, empty upstairs dining room, with a sofa right in front of them. 'This'll do,' Jennie said, pulling out a chair to place in front of the sofa for Alanda to put her leg up on. 'More private too. Stay there and I'll go and get some ice. And the wine, obviously…'

Alanda sank back against the sofa, whimpering. She was pretty sure nothing was broken, but the pain was intense, especially in her knee, and she thought of poor Liam, how awful his pain must have been when he'd snapped his thighbone almost in half…

Then she thought of Katya comforting him and groaned again. It was torturing her. She pulled out her phone to text Liam, but thought better of it. She'd probably be OK in half an hour, with some ice on it. No point in making him cancel his appointment, when business had barely even begun to pick up for him. This would be a lucrative project, if he got it.

Jennie raced back, clutching a wine bucket and two glasses. 'They're bringing you an ice-pack,' she said. 'Let's have a look.'

It was an unseasonably warm early October day and Alanda hadn't bothered with tights that morning, so it was easy to see the large swelling already beginning to bloom on her knee, and a shiny puffiness begin to deform her ankle.

'Ooh,' Jennie said, pouring her a large glass of wine. 'You'll be needing this.'

Alanda accepted it gratefully. The waitress appeared with a Ziploc bag full of ice, and a clean tea-towel.

'Thank you,' Jennie said. 'Is it OK if we stay up here for a while, see if we can keep the swelling down?'

The waitress glanced at Alanda's knee and ankle, an expression of such horror on her face, anyone would think that Alanda had been involved in a chainsaw massacre rather than falling down a couple of stairs. 'Oh my God,' she breathed, looking as if she might pass out. 'Should I call an ambulance?'

'No, there's no need for that,' Alanda said. 'I'll just ice it for a while and see how it is. If it's bad later I'll take myself to A&E.'

'*I'll* take you to A&E,' Jennie corrected, and smiled at her.

The ice did help. So did the wine, thought Alanda. Somehow they polished off the second bottle and suddenly a third was in front of them.

'I don't remember you ordering that,' Alanda said, narrowing her eyes. 'I haven't partaken in a three-bottle session since I was in my thirties.' Her words sounded a bit slurred.

'Desperate times…' agreed Jennie.

'So, is this what you recommend when one of your old ladies has a fall?'

Jennie laughed. 'Of course! That's why they all love me so much.'

'Well, you *are* very loveable,' Alanda said, jokingly, leaning her head on Jennie's shoulder.

Jennie was still for a moment. 'That's the nicest thing anyone's ever said to me.' She sounded completely serious.

'Really?' Alanda drained her fourth – no, must be fifth, or even sixth? – glass of wine. 'Surely not.'

'I think so,' Jennie said. She turned her head and Alanda found that they were staring into each other's eyes. Jennie smelled gorgeous, and her eyes were huge, green and serious. Alanda remembered noticing them in the home that first time, when Vi had been claiming someone was slapping her.

She looked away, moving the ice-pack from her knee back down to her ankle. They had both begun to hurt a little less, as long as she didn't move.

'How's things with Liam?' Jennie asked, changing the subject briskly.

Or *was* she changing the subject? Alanda wondered. Maybe she was just fishing. She suddenly experienced a strange, unsettled feeling of the sort she hadn't had since she was at school, when you weren't sure whether a certain boy fancied you or if you were just imagining it.

She sighed. 'It's been different since he got back. Difficult and getting worse, frankly. I keep waiting for things to get back to how they were before his accident, but it's been two months now, and nothing seems to be changing.'

'Is it just because of the girl, or is he different in himself, like, the memory loss altered his personality somehow?'

Alanda considered, gazing at a series of oil portraits of top-hatted dignitaries on the panelled wall across the room.

'We never mention the girl. She's like the elephant in the room. But it's more him – well, us, if I'm honest. We're just not the same around each other. We've always been so relaxed together, and hardly ever got on each other's nerves, but now we're all kind of formal with each other. Not as tactile. Not as open. More grumpy.

He spends most of the day either in his shed, or upstairs playing his guitar. I miss him, Jen.'

It was definitely the wine, but Alanda found her eyes filling with tears again.

'Does he remember everything from your past together?'

She shook her head, then nodded. 'Most of it now, up to the point he said goodbye to us at the airport. He still can't remember getting to the resort, or anything about the accident, till he woke up in hospital with his leg in plaster.'

'So weird,' said Jennie. 'Must be very traumatic for him too.'

'For sure. Far worse for him. But he does remember everything after that, so I can't stop thinking that the reason he's so quiet is because he's constantly comparing me to what he had with the girl, and I'm falling short. I can't bear it!'

Emotion welled up in her and she made a noise in her throat that was half-sob, half-snort. 'God. This is why I shouldn't be allowed to drink more than two glasses of wine.'

Jennie laughed and handed her another tissue. 'Oh, I don't know. I think sometimes it's more important just to let it all out. At least we've got our own private room to drink and moan in.'

'True. I didn't even know this room was up here, you don't see it when you come past to the loos. It's nice. It would be a good room for a party...' Alanda petered out. She was trying hard to hold it together, but it wasn't working.

'I keep thinking – I fear my marriage may have run its course,' she blurted.

CHAPTER FORTY-SEVEN

Liam

It was another warm October morning. Liam was sitting in the doorway of his shed with a cup of tea, scrolling through Facebook trying to find evidence of Katya's whereabouts. Weather permitting, this had become a bit of a daily routine for him on the days when Alanda was in the shop. He would don his gardening overalls and work on the garden until his leg started to ache, have a rest, then potter round in the shed until it was time for lunch.

So this is what it's like, being an old man, he thought. Pottering. Strolling and scrolling. Regular naps, a spot of gardening. Myriad aches and pains. Almost no sex; Alanda was increasingly distant when she was home – she always seemed to be out at the moment – and he felt as if he had little energy to try and do anything about it. Ironic, since she'd complained so much about his days out over the summer.

He wasn't cycling as much as he had done back then either. Colin had a hamstring injury and after a near-collision with a car, Liam had lost his confidence a little bit. The potential of another crash had suddenly begun to play on his mind, to the point that he stopped going out for long rides altogether.

But, on the plus side, he was alive, almost completely recovered, and he still had his family. His memory had returned, apart from a chunk of the few days around his accident.

Alanda had let the garden get ridiculously overgrown while he'd been away. Not that he could blame her. She'd never been interested in gardening, and weeding gave her terrible backache. He'd restored it to its former glory within a few weeks of being home, and now winter was fast encroaching, he was employed in studding a whole new border with bulbs and edging it with a low fence; more to give him something to do than because the garden actually needed further improvement.

Enquiries for garden projects from new clients had dribbled in very gradually, but he had been surprised and shocked at how many of his old clients he'd lost in the past year. He and Alanda had assumed that his fifteen minutes of fame would be good for business, but it appeared to have had the opposite effect. People, it seemed, didn't want to entrust their garden design projects to a man with a famously dodgy memory. It was frustrating – although not, he thought, nearly as frustrating as Katya apparently having vanished into thin air.

Her bump must be starting to show now, at getting on for five months. The more time went on, the more he found it hard to believe that she hadn't been in touch to let him know how it was going, or if she'd discovered yet if it was a boy or a girl. Despite what she'd said, he really thought that she would come around and want him involved, however peripherally. She had been so over-the-moon happy when she fell pregnant and seemed so in love with him.

His thinking went around in endless circles on the subject, veering from incomprehension because of the love they'd shared, back to understanding that this must be the reason for her silence. One day he'd wake up absolutely yearning for Katya, the next, he'd look at Alanda and feel profound gratitude that he still had her and the kids in his life. It was exhausting and confusing. Then he'd decide he was being a stupid, insensitive male, making it all about *him*, when clearly for Katya, the pain of them not being able to be a family together was so great that it was easier, as she had clearly stated, to ghost him completely.

But then he would imagine next year, when it would be her time to give birth, and the wheel of his confusion would spin another revolution. Surely she'd want him with her then? He couldn't bear the thought of her having to go through that all on her own, without a partner or a mum or sister. Perhaps her friend – Nicola? Nicole? – would be her birthing partner. Hopefully.

Then, after that, what would happen? Would she contact him then, to let him know if the baby had his eyes, her skin colouring, if it was plump and healthy or, God forbid, jaundiced and sickly? When it started smiling, or said its first word?

The silence seemed uncharacteristically callous. In that final, awful phone call he'd made it crystal clear that he was desperate to know and be updated on the progress of the pregnancy. He had since written several letters to her, at Otto's address, but never heard a word back. She might well already have sold the apartment by now, but he'd figured it was worth a shot.

Liam wasn't on Facebook himself, never had been, but in the pub last week Colin had shown him how to look people up on the site. They'd done it first on Liam's phone, and then on Colin's, and Katya's name hadn't come up either time.

'Right, so it's not that she's blocked you,' Colin had said, scratching his arm, which had made Liam smile, reminding him of the first time Alanda had met him. Colin was a bit unfortunate-looking, poor bloke, in possession of a Mr. Potato-Head-esque bulbous nose and prominent ears, topped with wispy gingery hair. Alanda always tried to find something complimentary to say about someone on first meeting them, but Liam recalled how she'd really struggled with Col. Eventually she had stuck out her hand and said, 'Hi, it's so nice to meet you. Gosh, don't you have lovely hair on your arms?'

They'd laughed about it in bed afterwards.

'"Lovely hair on your arms" – really?'

'I know,' Alanda had said sheepishly. 'It was all I could come up with. And, in my defence, it *did* look nice with the sun on it, all kind of lit up and reddy-gold…'

Every time Liam had subsequently seen the hair on his friend's forearms, it reminded him of that moment, many years ago.

Back when he and Alanda had been happy. And now here he was, trying to stalk his ex-lover online… He could never have imagined it would come to this.

'She's not on there,' said Colin. 'Not under that name, anyway. And it's an unusual name, so there wouldn't be many of them. Who is she?'

Liam struggled to keep his voice casual. 'That's the woman who helped me out in France. She's changed her number and I can't get hold of her.'

'I've warned you about that stalking habit of yours,' Colin joked, and Liam had smiled weakly.

He had been trying to ring her, on and off, ever since he got back, but she never picked up. Eventually he realised she must have figured out it was him and blocked his new mobile number, or changed her own. They didn't have a landline so once, sneakily, he even risked trying from Alanda's mobile when she was asleep and had left her phone downstairs, but there was never any answer. He thought Katya had probably changed her number.

The realisation that she really, really did not want to speak to him made his heart hurt so badly that at times he feared he was having a cardiac arrest, necking precautionary aspirins at such a rate that he had to keep surreptitiously replacing the packet in the bathroom cabinet.

This particular morning, as he was tapping Katya's name into the Facebook search box yet again, his phone rang. Unknown number. His heart jumped.

'Liam Lodge,' he said.

'Hello Mr Lodge, this is PC Harding from Wiltshire Police. I've got some news from my colleagues in Thonon-les-Bains.'

Harding. Liam knew that name; it was the copper who'd been the family's liaison officer when he was missing, the person who had acted as an intermediary between the UK and French police. He almost blurted out: *Is it Katya? Has something happened to her?*

'Oh. OK… what is it?' he said instead, watching a robin hop around on the lawn a few feet from where he sat. The bird's tiny legs were so spindly, like pencil strokes, it seemed unbelievable that they could support its weight at all.

'Nothing bad,' said Harding, who must have heard the trepidation in his voice. 'Although I suppose it depends how you look at it.'

'Go on.'

'My French colleague, Officer Portas, rang me this morning. They made an arrest in Les Gets, a young man called Ferdy McNamara. Do you recognise that name?'

'Nope, sorry,' Liam said, wondering where this was going.

'He's an English kid who was on a gap year in the Alps. He was working at the place where you hired your skis and gear last year. Officer Portas said that he had already interviewed him after your accident, when he claimed that there had been nothing left in the lockers. Portas and his colleagues always thought that your possessions would either have been stolen from the ski-hire shop or from your hotel or chalet, but as you know, nobody ever came forward, and we couldn't find evidence of you having booked anywhere to stay. They looked at CCTV from the shop but there was nothing suspicious. It did seem odd that you didn't have your wallet or passport on you when you had your mishap—'

Mishap, thought Liam. That was putting it mildly. 'I'm pretty absent-minded,' he said. 'The woman who reported seeing me in a cable car said I told her I'd forgotten my phone – I must have left all my valuables in the side pocket of my rucksack. So, I'd left it all in the ski-hire shop, then. That's what I thought was the most likely scenario.'

He and Alanda had discussed this at length, and it did make sense. The presence of valuables provided a motive for someone to have stolen and then disposed of the rucksack.

'So this McNamara bloke stole it all then?'

The truth was, he didn't really care what had happened to his stuff. Although, he supposed, it would be good to be able to fill in a few gaps. He still had no memory of the accident, nor anything from the point that he'd said goodbye to his family at Gatwick.

'Yes. He recently had a row with his girlfriend who, unbeknownst to him, had found your wallet under their mattress some months before. She realised where he must have got it from, and when they split up, she reported him to the police, who arrested him. He confessed to stealing your backpack, taking some clothes, the phone and the money and disposing of everything else. They've charged him with theft.'

Liam sighed. 'So, if he hadn't done that, my family could've been informed of my accident straight away.'

He'd never have met Katya. None of this nightmare would have happened. He wouldn't have missed Heather's wedding, and he and Alanda would still be happy together.

'I hope they throw the book at him, the thieving little git,' he said, with more vehemence than he realised he possessed. The robin flew off in a flutter of panic.

'Quite,' said PC Harding, sounding a bit taken aback.

'Does he still have my passport?'

'Unfortunately not. He said he burned it.'

'Is he being charged with just theft, or obstructing the course of justice as well?'

'Just theft, I'm afraid.'

'What, even after he knew I'd lost my memory – which he presumably did, if the police interviewed him – and he was the only one who had the means to prove my identity? That's outrageous!'

Liam felt like a very grumpy old man. His leg ached and his heart ached and he wanted to hit something. Ideally Ferdy McNamara.

He was glad Alanda was in the shop that day, so he could attempt to get over his bad mood by the time she returned. He decided he'd make a curry, open a nice bottle of wine and tell her all about it over dinner. Make a bit of an effort, since she seemed to believe he'd given up trying.

CHAPTER FORTY-EIGHT

Alanda

November

'How's Sadie?' Jennie asked. 'Haven't seen her for a while.'

They were drinking mulled wine on Jennie's little patio, bundled up against a chilly bonfire night, the backdrop of everyone else's firework displays enlivening the clear blue-black sky. A fire crackled in the iron brazier, occasionally wreathing them in clouds of woodsmoke when the wind gusted in their direction.

'She's gone away for the weekend with that guy, the one she met on her dog walk in Lizzie Gardens. She seems very loved-up, so, fingers crossed.'

'Is that the one with the allotment and the motorbike?'

'No, that was the one before. This one has the two dachshunds and a property portfolio.'

'Pah!' Jennie inhaled a throatful of smoke, coughing it out. 'Nice! Well – the property portfolio's nice, anyway. I'm not keen on dachshunds. Give me Alfie any day.'

Alfie, who'd been huddled into Jennie's side on the outdoor sofa, lifted his head expectantly.

Jennie laughed. 'Yes, you're the man in my life,' she said, rubbing his ears. He looked pleased with himself, before sinking back to sleep. 'Have you met him?'

Alanda shook her head. 'No. We must get you guys over soon, and we'll get Sadie to unveil him then.'

'Just don't invite more couples, if you do; it's awful being the token single woman at a dinner party.'

'Shall we invite someone eligible for you?' Alanda asked teasingly.

'God, no, that's even worse!'

Alfie whimpered as a particularly loud rocket went off nearby, and Jennie cuddled him. 'Alf! Don't let yourself down. I'm planning to make our fortunes by touting you round chat shows as the only dog in the world who doesn't hate fireworks. Usually he doesn't mind them at all,' she said to Alanda. 'But that one was quite close.'

'So there's nobody you'd like to bring to this hypothetical couples' dinner party then?'

Alanda knew she was fishing, but Jennie was always really tight-lipped about her relationships, whether past or potential. She had gleaned that Jennie's last break-up, with Alex, had been a particularly bad one, prompting Jennie's move to the new job in Salisbury, but little more than that.

'I told you, I'm not dating at the moment. Can't be doing with all that internet stuff. I don't know how Sadie sticks it. I find it so tedious.'

'Yes, but,' persisted Alanda, 'is there no-one you've got your eye on?'

Jennie laughed. 'What, in the hip and happening Salisbury scene for ageing lesbians? All the gays I know down here are already hooked up with each other.'

'It's a shame. You're so lovely. I hate that you're on your own.'

'Oh, I don't mind, most of the time. And I'm not, anyway, I've got Alfie.'

Jennie filled up Alanda's empty glass from the flask on the table in front of them. There was another bang and a shower of crackling, popping stars descended in a waterfall of sparkles. They both tipped up their faces to watch.

'Did you know, those are called horsetail shells?' said Jennie contemplatively.

'No idea whatsoever. I could probably identify a sparkler and a Catherine wheel, but that's it. How do you even know this stuff?'

Jennie shrugged. 'My brain is full of useless random facts,' she said. 'I'm glad you think I'm lovely, though.'

Alanda smiled. Jennie was such a strong, capable woman, but every now and again she said something which made her sound vulnerable, and Alanda found it really sweet.

'You totally are,' she said, clinking her glass against Jennie's.

Jennie shuffled up a bit closer, and Alfie wriggled with her along the plastic sofa so he was still in close contact with her. 'It's getting chilly.' All three of them were now huddled up together.

'There is someone I like, though, since you're badgering me,' Jennie said, not meeting Alanda's eye.

'Ooh! Really? I knew I'd get it out of you eventually. Who?'

Jennie laughed. 'But I couldn't ever bring her to your dinner party.'

'Why not?'

'She's married. To a man.'

Not Sadie then, thought Alanda. Although Sadie was so smitten with this new bloke that her theory about the closet was probably unfounded.

'Oh. I'm sorry. Who is she, how did you meet her?'

Jennie hesitated. 'I haven't known her all that long, but we've got closer over the last few months… I don't think I really want to say, really.'

'Come on, Jen, I won't tell anybody.' Alanda wondered, slightly jealously, why she had never heard of this mystery woman.

'It's not that.'

'What, then?'

'I don't want to ruin our friendship.'

Alanda still didn't twig. 'Why would telling me ruin your friendship with her?'

Jennie reached out a finger and gently stroked Alanda's thumb. 'Because it's you, silly.'

Alanda thought she was joking at first. But then she realised that Jennie was touching her, squeezing her hand. That there was a subtle note of suppressed anxiety in her voice, even though she had spoken in a normal tone.

'Wait – what?' Shocked, she removed her hand, then put it straight back, not wanting to offend Jennie or make her think she was homophobic.

She turned sideways so she and Jennie were face to face.

'Are you serious?'

Jennie didn't meet her eyes, suddenly very interested in studying the dregs of her mulled wine. 'Yup. Hope that hasn't embarrassed you.'

Alanda paused. 'I'm really flattered.'

Jennie gently lifted her hand away, then bent forwards as if she had a stomach ache. 'Oh noooo. You're mortified. So am I.'

'I'm not! I'm not, honestly. I'm just surprised. I didn't realise. You know I adore our friendship. It's just – I'm just – taking it in.'

'Oh God. I shouldn't have said anything.'

They stared at each other then, and Alanda felt a rush of emotion at her friend's willingness to show vulnerability; the bravery her declaration must have taken. And, if she was honest, Jennie was gazing at her in a way that Liam hadn't done in months. Being desired like this was a heady, unfamiliar brew, she discovered.

She had missed Liam so much when he was lost, but even now that he was home, she was still missing him; missing the connection that seemed to have been severed the moment she'd waved him off at Gatwick all those months ago.

Perhaps it was that, or perhaps the three glasses of mulled wine she'd consumed on an empty stomach, but something prompted her to lean in close to Jennie and kiss her lips, softly but deliberately.

Fireworks exploded in a shower above them and they pulled away from each other, both hooting with laughter at the cliché of it.

Then, a moment; a beat, in which things could have gone either way. With the tension broken, Alanda knew they could have left it at that and never mentioned it again. Carried on with the friendship, carried on being stuck going round a grim hamster wheel of missing what she and Liam appeared to have lost without knowing how to get off; how to get it back.

Yet what was life, thought Alanda, if not a sequence of surprises and revelations? And here she was, suddenly being offered the opportunity to forge a new and totally unexpected path for herself… if she wanted it.

Funny, she thought later, that at that point it didn't cross her mind that she was being unfaithful to Liam. 'Unfaithful' would have been allowing herself to get picked up in a pub on a night out with the girls; a seedy affair with the handsome swimmer in the next lane to hers; a series of flirty WhatsApp messages with a supplier. Of course all these possibilities had crossed her mind and, of course, she had always dismissed them as impossible. Not to mention immoral. She would never betray Liam's trust like that.

This was different, she thought, as Jennie put her warm palm against the side of her cold cheek and kissed her again.

This was *Jennie*.

CHAPTER FORTY-NINE

Alanda

December

The two of them sat, exhausted and very full-bellied, in the evening wreckage of the post-Christmas destruction of their home. The kids and Kevin had all left, and Alanda was just back from driving Violet to Harcourt Grange.

It felt odd to be in an empty house on Christmas night, since at least one or other of the children usually stayed over in their old bedrooms, but this year they'd all wanted to go home; Heather and Kevin because they were newlywed homebodies, Jake to get back to Bowie, his recently acquired rescue cat, and Becky because she was driving up to Wrexham first thing on Boxing Day to visit her new boyfriend Olly, who was staying up there with his widowed mum.

The kids had cleared the dining table for the post-lunch board games but, on Alanda's insistence (not that it had taken much), left the dishes, so the kitchen looked as if a bomb had hit it. The counters to the left of the sink were completely covered with dirty glasses – G&T, wine, port, brandy, water – every glass in the house had been used. The ravaged carcass of the turkey sat in its carving dish, a congealing rim of fat puddled around it, and a bin bag full of used wrapping paper had spilled across the tiles. Crumpled party hats, mince pie crumbs, glitter and paper napkins littered the table.

'I suppose we should do the washing up,' Alanda said lazily, slumped back in her dining chair. 'I can't look at that lot anymore.'

'We ought to have let the kids help clear up while we had them.'

She sighed in response. 'Ah, I don't mind. They'd only have been bumping into each other and bickering and asking us every two minutes where everything goes. Besides, we wouldn't have had time to play Monopoly or that awful other game – what was it called?'

'Gutterhead,' Liam said, laughing. 'Mum's face, when Becky was drawing "blow-job"!'

Alanda laughed too. 'I didn't think she'd twig, but she obviously did.'

Violet had joined them for lunch and had fallen asleep in her chair immediately afterwards, so they had thought it safe to play a very tawdry game that Becky had brought along; a sort of filthy version of Pictionary. Unfortunately, Violet had woken up at a very inopportune moment and tried to join in.

Alanda had offered to stay sober enough to drive Vi back to the care home, an offer Liam had been happy to accept.

'You were gone ages,' he said now. 'I almost sent out a search party.'

'Oh for God's sake, Liam, I wasn't that long. Don't be such a drama queen.'

He stared at her. 'I was only joking,' he said, quietly.

He stood up, clasping Alanda's wrists. 'Come on, let's get it over with,' he said.

'I've only just sat down!' she grumbled, but allowed him to drag her up too.

'Nice day, though, wasn't it?' He reached out to tuck a strand of her hair behind her ear and she was horrified to find herself recoiling, yanking her head away from his hand so violently that she may as well have shouted, *get off me!*

Liam was even more horrified. 'Al! What the hell is the matter with you?'

He had never spoken to her that harshly before, but she could see how shocked and hurt he was, and that it spilled out of him as involuntarily as her own response had.

'I'm really sorry,' she said immediately. 'I'll wash, you dry?'

He followed her over to the sink and they set to, Liam scraping the plates and putting them in the dishwasher while Alanda donned yellow Marigolds and squirted washing-up liquid into hot water. Christmas carols played in the background on the radio, and she would forever more associate 'Silent Night' with the events of the next ten minutes.

'I'm sorry too, that I snapped at you. But I'm really worried. Something's up. Not just menopause stuff – is it?'

He dried the first glass and filled it with port. 'Want some?'

She nodded, so he handed it to her. The crimson liquid, next to the bright yellow of the rubber glove she was clasping the glass with, almost hurt her eyes.

'*All is calm, all is bright.*' The tones felt too measured, the voices impossibly young and innocent. Those choirboys had this ahead of them too, Alanda thought, all the myriad crises of adulthood. Money worries, failing relationships, accidents and illnesses, death and desolation.

Merry sodding Christmas.

She paused, staring straight ahead into the blackness out of the kitchen window. 'You know I will always love you, Liam,' she said, and he went very still next to her.

'Do I need to sit down?'

He sat anyway, on one of the kitchen stools. She stayed at the sink.

'You know things haven't been right since you got home. It's not your fault,' she hurriedly added. 'Just one of those things.'

'It's still fairly early days,' he said defensively. 'It's only been five months – I'm sure we'll settle eventually, get back to normal.'

She shook her head.

'It's been nine months since your accident.' Her voice was quiet but steady. 'When you were missing, after a couple of months I really assumed you must be dead – although I never admitted it to anyone. I suppose I started thinking about how I would go on without you. How life would be, what my priorities would be. I'd always thought I would die without you – but it made me realise that I wouldn't. I didn't. And then when I found out about you and that girl…'

Liam got up and stood back next to her at the sink. 'You know I've not heard anything from her since the night you came to her flat, and I'm sure I won't. She doesn't want anything to do with me.'

'I know. But it's not… it changed things… or maybe I've just moved on.'

Liam swallowed audibly. 'Moved on?'

Alanda turned to face him then, putting her hands on his hipbones, an old, familiar move of endearment, stroking their knobbles with her thumbs.

'Liam… I have to tell you something. I've fallen in love with someone else and – oh God, I'm so sorry to have to say this – but I'm going to move in with them. I'm leaving you, Liam. We had an amazing run, but it's over now.'

He tipped back his head and closed his eyes. 'Great. You're leaving me, on Christmas Day. Nice. Who's the lucky guy?'

'Not a guy, actually. It's Jennie, my friend. I wasn't going to tell you till tomorrow.'

'Nice,' he repeated. 'How long has it been going on?'

'Don't be like this,' she said softly. 'You know things haven't been right between us since you got back. It's only been about six weeks; we were just friends before then. But we didn't want to have an affair, so I thought it was better to come clean and be honest.'

He pulled away from her and raised his voice. 'Oh, very noble of you. Like I said, I've only been back five months! You're throwing away over thirty years of marriage for someone, a *woman*, you've been shagging for six *weeks*? You're not even gay, and now you're going to shack up with the manageress of a nursing home?'

'I didn't want to cheat on you. And – for what it's worth, I didn't think I was gay,' she said, almost contemplatively. 'But you were the only person I'd ever slept with. Perhaps if I'd experimented more when I was younger, had more partners before we met…'

'So you're saying our marriage was a mistake?'

'No, not for a second. Liam, I love – loved – you so much. I always will. But it just feels like we've run out of steam. We're only in our early fifties, we could have decades ahead of us. How's that going to go, if we're both in love with someone else?'

He opened his mouth as if to say he wasn't in love with someone else, then closed it again.

'You'd be free now, to be with her and the baby,' Alanda said gently. 'I know that's what you want. I can see it in your eyes, when you're thinking about her and missing her, and it's often. I'm not stupid.'

'She doesn't want me and I don't know where she is.'

'She only doesn't want you because *we* were together. This is your chance to find her, Liam.'

She saw the rage boil up in him, its flames stoked by too much wine and port, almost a year's worth of confusion and repression roaring into his head.

'Get you off the hook for cheating on me, you mean!'

Alanda recoiled again. 'I'm going to go now,' she said. 'I don't want to be here tonight. We can speak again when you're calmer and you've had time to think about it. I can't talk to you when you're like this.'

'What do you mean, *when I'm like this*? You've never even seen me like this before!'

'No, I haven't,' she conceded. 'I don't blame you for being upset, it's a lot to take in…'

She wanted to say more but couldn't think of anything that wasn't facile or patronising, so tailed off. Picking up her bag and coat from where she'd left them by the back door, she paused. 'I don't want to leave you with all these dishes,' she said. 'Shall we finish them first?'

Liam stared at her, unable to take it all in. Then he looked at the couple of dozen glasses waiting to be washed.

'I'll take care of it,' he said, raising his left arm and sweeping the entire lot onto the stone floor. Crystal wedding-gift port glasses, long-stemmed wine goblets, champagne flutes, tumblers – the sound of splintering and shattering was both shocking and deafening.

Alanda sobbed once, then fled out of the back door, leaving Liam stranded in a sea of broken glass. Her last view, as she glanced over her shoulder through the patio doors, was of him sinking into a crouch, wrapping his arms over his head.

'*Sleep in heaven-ly pe-eace*' the choristers on the radio were singing, so innocently, as she left, and she wondered how she would ever find the words to tell the kids.

CHAPTER FIFTY

Liam

Six Months Later

Life for Liam, in those first few months after Alanda moved in with Jennie, was actually less weird than he would have anticipated, had anyone forewarned him that his wife would ever leave him.

Less weird, perhaps – but not less horrible. It was astonishing to him, how quickly a new, grim, normal established itself.

He never had another meltdown after the fairly spectacular one on Christmas Day. After he swept up and binned all the shattered glass, he'd drunk a bottle of port out of a coffee mug and gone to bed, where he passed out and slept for sixteen hours.

He did not crumple into any more sobbing heaps, nor lock himself away and spend all his energies growing facial hair, nor did he start hoarding old newspapers and not washing. He just got on with things, trying to ignore, or at least work around, the deep, throbbing loneliness that accompanied him day and night.

It also helped that he still had his own bed to sleep in, with the garden, his shed, his attic full of guitars, the reclining sofa at just the right angle... He could just about convince himself that it felt more as if Alanda had just gone away for a few nights for a spa break, or to stay with one of the kids.

Although when he caught himself saying, 'Alexa, cheer me up,' just to hear another voice in the house, he had to have a word with himself.

The kids were all unusually attentive, to the point of initial shocked censure with Alanda for 'cheating on him after everything he's already been through' – Heather took it particularly badly – so he saw a lot of all of them. He suspected that they had drawn up a rota between them to make sure he wasn't feeling suicidal, and sometimes even thought that they were mystified that he wasn't outwardly more upset.

He missed Alanda terribly, of course, but if he was honest, he missed Katya just as much. He still saw Alanda, around town, or for the occasional coffee. Their communications tended to regard specific administrative or logistic tasks to do with the house or bills or whatever, but were always cordial, and they were on speaking terms, albeit slightly frosty ones. He was confident that they would even end up as friends one day, if his pride allowed it. He wasn't sure he was ready to see her and Jennie together though. Whenever he visited Violet in the home, he slunk past Jennie's office with his head down and took pains to veer down a different corridor if he saw her in the distance.

Life continued to tick along. Liam met up with Colin for a pint every Thursday night and the occasional bike ride, when the weather permitted. They mostly discussed the same topics on rotation; the criminal ineptitude of the prime minister and his cabinet, the risible inefficiency of the local council and the genius of Dave Gilmour. The rest of the time he played guitar in the attic, did a few small garden design jobs, worked on his cooking skills, saw the kids.

It was OK, bearable, although he couldn't help thinking what a tragedy it was that he and Katya had parted because of Alanda, and then Alanda had left him within six months.

He thought about this a lot, even going as far as to enquire about employing a private detective to find Katya, but it would have been so astronomically expensive as to be prohibitive. The windfall from his brother's will was long gone, as was the publicity money from the interviews, all either given to the kids, soaked up in the soup of recuperation and dwindling clientele of his gardening business, or paid towards Vi's home fees.

His hands were tied, and it frustrated him beyond measure. The frustration was, if he was honest, worse than the pain of the separation – although he was emotionally intelligent enough to realise that it could be merely a displacement focus from the grief of his losses.

Then one day, just as he was thinking he might re-mortgage the house to be able to free up some money, something happened that made him glad he hadn't parted with thousands of pounds on some gumshoe who probably wouldn't have had any more luck finding Katya than he had.

The message was in Liam's 'Other' folder on Facebook, a folder that, as a fairly recent Facebook joiner, he had not known existed and to which it took him a while to navigate – he could see that he had a new message, just not where it was. Eventually he figured it out. It was from a name he didn't recognise: Philip MacNeill. Curiously, he clicked on the icon to open it, assuming it was probably another, belated, publicity request.

Hi Liam, the message began, *You don't know me, but we have a mutual friend, Katya DeLorenzo. I believe she is the woman who helped you out after your accident in France. My wife is her best friend. So first off, PLEASE don't ever let on that I contacted you. They'd both kill me, particularly Nic. I do feel like a bit of a grass doing this, and I may well regret it in the morning (it's 11.30 p.m. and I'm halfway down a bottle of port) but it's been preying on my mind for months. I'd want to know, if it was me.*

Katya's had a baby and it is presumably yours, as she was pregnant when she returned from France last August. The baby was born in March. It's a boy and she's called him Charlie. Her life has moved on and she seems happy now, and I certainly wouldn't want anything to interfere with that, but you do have rights, as a father, and Charlie may well want to know his real dad when he grows up. But you have to respect her wishes, which are, I believe, that you aren't involved in the child's life.

Man to man, I don't think it's right that she's kept you out of the loop without any sort of choice. It happened to a mate of mine and he was really damaged by it, which is why I've taken this decision to tell you. I'm sorry if this has been a shock to you – you may well not even have known she was pregnant. But I thought you should know.

No need to reply.

Yours,
Phil

Phil, thought Liam, stunned. Not even adding his surname, as if he was a mate. He looked at Phil's profile photo, a picture of him and a glamorous blonde – so that's what Katya's friend Nicole looked like – each of them with an arm around a grinning small boy. Phil was a good-looking bloke, artfully stubbly, with a strong jaw and a head of thick dark hair.

That email would have come as a hell of a shock, Liam thought, if he hadn't known Kat was expecting his baby. But he had of course known. Little else had occupied his thoughts since his return to the UK.

Phil *was* a mate, as far as Liam was concerned, and this was like a gift from heaven. The only reason he had joined Facebook in the first place was so that Katya would be able to find him, if she was looking. This guy Phil must know where she lived and how to get hold of her.

After months of utter awfulness, there was a light at the end of the tunnel. Perhaps it was meant to be, that Alanda had run off with someone else, so that he really was now free to be with Katya… His heart swelled with excitement. Their story would, against all odds, have a happy ending after all. He could be a dad to Charlie – God, he thought, what would the older kids think of having an actual baby brother? And never mind them, could *he* cope with nappies, teething, tantrums, the noise, the stress…?

Yes, of course he could. It would be his second chance, now that Alanda didn't want him any longer.

The big kids probably wouldn't be all that bothered; they all had their own lives nowadays, and they were always saying they wanted him to be happy, weren't they?

Alanda was getting her new start with Jennie. She'd even broached the subject of divorce last time they'd met up, and they both agreed that they'd prefer to wait the requisite five years for a no-fault divorce rather than going through the courts. They'd have to put the house on the market but for the first time, Liam thought he could finally stomach the thought of moving somewhere else. He would always, always, love Alanda, but it wasn't fair to expect him to stick around in Salisbury, constantly worried that he would bump into them, avoiding the sympathetic looks on the neighbours' faces. Being that man whose wife left him for another woman.

He permitted himself the luxury of remembering Katya, a luxury he'd long shoved to the back of his mind out of sheer self-preservation, squashing it down whenever it popped into his head, as it often did at odd moments. Her tawny skin, big brown eyes – the baby would have inherited these, he was sure. Soft dark-brown curls, almost black. That particular bit of skin he used to love touching, even more than he loved touching the rest of her; that hollow just at the top of her inner thigh. The way she laughed, the way she stroked him, her long philosophical musings about nothing in particular, her wit and generosity.

He almost salivated with lust and longing at the thought of these no longer solely being blissful memories.

For the first time in months, he felt optimistic; properly optimistic and not merely hypothetically.

He wrote back straight away:

Dear Phil, Thank you so much for getting in touch. I really appreciate it and I won't say a word, I promise. I did know that Katya was pregnant but we did not part on the terms I'd have liked to – I really want to help support Charlie even if she doesn't want me in her life as a partner. I would just like the opportunity to offer again, now that she has had the baby. The trouble is that I don't have a means to contact her. If you could see your way to giving me a mobile number or an address for her, I would be eternally grateful. She won't know that my wife and I have now parted ways and I'm now in a position to offer her my support in a way that I was not last year.

I look forward to hearing from you, and thanks again. I'm so grateful to you.

Best,
Liam Lodge

CHAPTER FIFTY-ONE

Alanda

June wasn't quite warm enough in the year for them to want to resume open-water swimming again, so Jennie had chivvied Alanda into taking up running. She had duly completed the Couch to 5K app and started going out on regular jogs with Jennie, usually before work.

The trouble was, Jennie was just naturally more athletic, and she'd been a runner since her teenage years. Whilst Alanda's running stamina was undoubtedly improving, forty minutes of continuous jogging was still a struggle, and she worried about her knees.

'How is it,' she panted at Jennie's back, 'I can swim for an hour without stopping, but I feel like I'm going to die if I run for more than half an hour?'

Jennie jogged on the spot to allow Alanda to catch her up while Alfie, who Jennie took on a lead with them, stopped to sniff at the bushes. 'You'll get there. Just think, you couldn't run for ten minutes a few weeks ago.'

They were doing their usual route, which took in the magnificent cathedral and all the vast, beautiful houses within its Close gates. Alanda always distracted herself from the pain in her lungs and thighs by imagining all the houses' previous occupants over the centuries, poke bonnets and hooped skirts, top hats and glossy black carriages. None of *them* would be caught dead jogging, she thought crossly, as Jennie set off again.

'Can you slow down a bit?' she called, although she hated to have to do so. She was aware that Jennie already modified her pace to accommodate her, and even so, always crept ahead so effortlessly that Alanda felt plodding and inadequate behind her. She spent more time on their runs admiring Jennie's bottom and legs in their tight Lycra casing, the way she made it look so easy, than she did making conversation.

If she was honest, this summed up a lot about their relationship. Jennie was always in the lead. She made the decisions – as Becky once tactlessly pointed out, 'You can tell who wears the trousers out of you two.'

This had rankled with Alanda, who'd always prided herself on being a strong woman who knew her own mind and made her own decisions. She'd 'worn the trousers' in her marriage, and it was anathema now to see herself as the weaker partner. Perhaps because she was the newbie lesbian, Jennie felt like she had to metaphorically show her the ropes? You were always on the back foot when you found yourself in unfamiliar worlds – someone else's house, dog, hobbies, life… It took a lot of getting used to.

It was a minor gripe, though. Six months on and it *was* getting easier, she thought. She loved Jennie's company – loved Jennie – and the energy with which she powered through the days. Alanda had never thought of herself as a lazy person, but seeing how much Jennie crammed into twenty-four hours was both motivational and inspirational.

But, for all the new positives and invigorating experiences, she did miss Liam and their house. Her old house. Her old life. You couldn't just airbrush out of existence thirty years of marriage with someone you'd loved so much.

Sometimes Alanda thought that Jennie's enthusiasm was, in part, an attempt to do just that. Hopefully she would calm down and relax, eventually.

CHAPTER FIFTY-TWO

Liam

Phil MacNeill had grudgingly agreed to 'give him a few pointers' as to where Katya lived, but claimed he didn't know her email address or phone number, which Liam didn't believe for a second – the guy only needed to look in his wife's phone, obviously. But if Phil didn't feel it was appropriate to ask, or sneak a peek, then Liam wasn't in a position to object. He was just grateful for the information Phil did disclose:

> I don't know exactly what number it is, but it's a ground floor flat in a terraced house on Marchmont Road in Holloway, near the Coach and Horses, opposite a petrol station. That's all I remember, sorry, only been there once.

The Coach and Horses turned out to be in a grimy corner of North London, tacked on the end of a short row of Georgian townhouses. Each had four steps up to the front door and a basement room with a barred window; kitchens, by the looks of the ones Liam peered into.

The houses had doubtless been lovely when they were first built, but over the centuries the road had become a major artery into and out of town, with a bus lane, litter eddying around in the slipstream of the endless traffic thundering past and dark-grey grimy dust embedded into every surface.

Liam sat in his car on the forecourt of the petrol station across the road. He felt like some kind of criminal, lurking around waiting for his moment to strike; the notion intensified when an old lady walking past on the pavement, with a very arthritic-looking dog tottering along behind her, glared so hard at him through the windscreen that he literally shrank back in his seat.

He wondered if Katya would be happy to move to Wiltshire. Not Salisbury, they wouldn't want to be bumping into Alanda and Jennie every five minutes, but one of the outlying villages perhaps. Near the kids, but with the privacy to live their own lives. He couldn't imagine that she'd want to bring up their child in this grim environment if she had a choice, however nice the interior of the flat might be. And he wasn't sure if he could live here, away from his friends and the kids, in this murky corridor of North London.

The kids will take a bit of talking round, he thought. It would be a shock for them, not only to suddenly discover that he'd met someone else but also that they had a new little stepbrother. But at least it was Alanda who had, if anyone had, technically done the dirty. His own conscience was as clean as it could be – he had a pretty watertight excuse since he'd had no idea he was having an affair.

He and Alanda had still never told the kids about his relationship with Katya. He admired Alanda for that, actually. It would have been so easy for her to use it as an excuse for her own infidelity – after all, it had surely been a major factor in the collapse of their marriage.

He also had no idea which number Katya lived at – it could be any one of these fifteen or twenty houses. After about an hour he felt cold and stiff, so he climbed out of the car to stretch his aching leg. There had been no activity from any of the houses the whole time he'd been there and he began to wonder if Phil might have just fed him a line, to get him off his back.

He tried to imagine what Katya's flat looked like inside. Hopefully he'd get to find out shortly. She hadn't been in Otto's apartment for long enough to impose a sense of her own style on the décor; it had been enough work just to rid it of all the accoutrements of an old man living on his own and give it a lick of paint. He imagined this place to be bright and cheerful, like her clothes were. Then he wondered if she dressed Charlie in bold bright colours too.

He thought about knocking on a few doors to see if any of the neighbours knew who Katya was, but he didn't even have a photograph of her to show them. Although he supposed that saying, 'I'm looking for a drop-dead beautiful woman of mixed ethnicity who always wears bright colours, with a new baby' might be sufficient – there couldn't be too many people answering that description in the direct vicinity, could there? The row of houses wasn't very long, and Phil had said the flat was near the pub.

The Coach and Horses had definitely seen better days. It had a rusty hanging basket full of dead flowers outside and the windows were opaque with grime. In fact, it didn't look like it had been open for months, which was a shame, because Liam quite badly needed a pee, and there was an Out of Order sign on the door to the toilet round the side of the petrol station.

He wondered if Katya had been a regular. He imagined it in better days, her sitting at a table with a glass of wine and Charlie fast asleep in a Moses basket at her feet – although of course that was unlikely, as Charlie could only be a few weeks old, and the pub had the dead, abandoned look of a place that hadn't seen signs of life for months. In his little fantasy, though, she would be seated in an armchair next to a roaring fire, scrolling through her phone or reading a fat paperback, enjoying the change of scenery from her own four walls. He would walk in and see her face light up….

Working at home, as she did, must get lonely. He hoped she didn't need to resort to sitting in pubs by herself; that she had the company of other women. Perhaps an antenatal group, like Alanda had attended during both of her pregnancies.

Liam remembered those early days with a pang of longing. It seemed like a lifetime ago that he would occasionally come home from a job to find the living room packed full of shrieking women with enormous bellies, and then, a few months later, see the same women, much more subdued, their eyes dull with exhaustion as they hovered over the rows of changing mats on the carpet with a selection of newborns wriggling on them. It had reminded Liam of a Moroccan souk, where the wares laid out for sale weren't leather handbags or sandals, but babies.

His own babies always looked the most gorgeous – but then, didn't every parent think that? 'A face only a mother could love,' was something Violet used to say – not about him, he hoped. Did the mother of an objectively unattractive child still think it was beautiful? All three of his had been perfect, to the point that strangers would stop him and Alanda in the street to comment, especially on the twins.

He leaned against the side of the car and wished he smoked. What was he going to say when he saw Katya? *If* he saw her. He had already resolved that if she hadn't changed her mind, if there wasn't even a tiny chink of possibility that she had reconsidered wanting him in her life, he wasn't going to make a dick of himself or pester her in any way. He just wanted to tell her that he was now available and see if that altered her perspective at all. After all, they had been deeply in love. If his memory hadn't come back, or if he'd already been divorced, he had no doubt that they would still be together now.

He was very optimistic, he realised with a little jolt of anticipation. It was unlikely – although not impossible, he conceded – that she would have met someone new while she was pregnant and presumably mourning the loss of their own future. She really didn't strike him as the type who would just dust herself off immediately and think, 'Right – next!' Besides, he couldn't imagine any potential suitors being overjoyed at the thought of becoming a stepdad within six months of meeting a new girlfriend.

He couldn't wait to see her. It had been so long since he had felt excited by anything – probably not since he was reunited with the kids last summer – that the sensation felt almost overwhelming as it bubbled up inside him, giving him jitters that felt exhausting rather than energising.

Another hour crawled past. Liam's eyeballs ached from scanning the houses opposite, but apart from the angry woman with the old dog going into the one next to the pub, there was no movement from behind the dusty front doors, not even a shadow of anyone crossing a window. He supposed most people would be at work.

His bladder felt as if it was going to explode, so he got out of the car, intending to throw himself on the mercy of the petrol station employees. Surely they must have a staff toilet he could beg to use? He was loath to do it as, sod's law, Katya was bound to come out just then, and he'd miss her.

But as he began to walk across the forecourt, he finally saw something over the road: a flash of dazzling cobalt blue. It was Katya, in a bright blue jacket, emerging with difficulty from one of the houses mid-terrace, struggling to manoeuvre a buggy down the front steps. It really was her!

Liam made an involuntary noise in his throat, spun on his heel and dashed straight across the busy road, thankful that the lights at the junction had recently turned red and there was a brief break in the traffic. His legs were shaking so badly that he wasn't sure they'd hold him up, especially his bad one.

Katya had her back to the road so that she could guide the buggy down the steps backwards. Without thinking, Liam found himself saying, 'Can I help you with that?' and before she had the chance to reply, he had reached up the steps to grab the other side of the buggy's handle.

That was when she turned, alarmed, and said, 'No thanks, I can manage,' in such a strident tone that the subtext was clearly 'get lost,' and Liam immediately felt terrible. She was probably thinking he was trying to snatch her baby.

'Sorry,' he said, as she got the buggy down to pavement level. 'I didn't mean to scare you.'

That was when she turned, slowly, her gaze starting at his feet and running up to his face.

'Oh my God,' she said faintly. '*Jack*. It's you.'

'Hi,' he said quietly, worlds of emotion contained within that one word. He waited for her face to break open into a smile, for her to fling her arms around him as he wanted to do to her, but she just appeared utterly shell-shocked. For a long moment they stood staring at one another.

She looked stunning, he thought, drinking her in; it was the moment he had waited for ever since they were wrenched apart last year. Her hair was shorter, the curls tighter, and she had dark shadows under her eyes which he presumed were from broken sleep, but apart from the tiredness she was even more beautiful than he remembered.

A bleating sound came from the buggy and Liam tore his gaze away from Katya, peering in at his son.

'Oh... Kat... he's incredible,' he blurted, tears rushing to his eyes.

The child had the most perfect, regular little features he'd ever seen in a baby, his own children included: large, heavily fringed brown eyes, tiny little button nose and Cupid's bow lips. As Liam gazed down at him, Charlie kicked his legs, gurgled, then giggled.

Liam felt such an intense rush of love for them both that he worried he was going to explode, everything in him and of him simply bursting.

'He's called Charlie,' she said, smiling – although the smile was directed at the baby, not at him.

Just in time, Liam managed not to grass up Phil MacNeill by blurting, 'yes, I know.'

'Hi, Charlie,' he said instead, reaching into the buggy to touch the baby's tiny fingers, laughing as a squashy little hand stretched back and clasped his forefinger tightly. 'I'm your daddy.'

The smile fell from Katya's face. 'What are you doing here, Jack?'

He released his finger from the baby's clutches and turned to face her, searching every inch of the face that, a year ago, had been his entire world. He so wanted it to be again.

'I tracked you down—'

'How?' She seemed almost angry, in a contained way. But, he supposed, it was a hell of shock, him turning up unannounced. He replied as if she'd asked 'why?' instead.

'Because I needed to tell you something really important and I'm hoping it will change the decision you made when we last spoke. I'm sorry to spring myself on you unannounced, but I didn't have any way of getting hold of you.'

Then he worried she'd think he was criticising her for blocking him, or changing her number, or whatever she had done to ensure he couldn't contact her.

'But I'm here now. And – this is the thing, Kat – Alanda and I split up, a few months ago. Things just weren't the same between us and eventually she left me for someone else. So I had to see you, to see if there was any chance at all, because we don't need to worry any more about doing the wrong thing, or hurting anybody, or getting hurt…'

Katya was gaping like a goldfish. Liam wanted to hug her, smell her skin, lose himself in her, but there was something in the way she held herself that made it clear she wasn't ready for that kind of contact, not yet. There was a flash of movement at the nearest window, the edge of a blind being lifted and dropped.

'Did you realise,' Liam continued, having to speak up to be heard over the roar of a passing bus, 'that today is the first anniversary of when you told me you were pregnant? We were in that lovely hotel in the Alps. I was so happy.'

Her eyes filled with tears and Liam couldn't stop himself reaching out and grabbing her hand. As he caressed it – oh, the feel of her skin again! It was like sinking into a warm bath – a young bespectacled guy opened the front door and bounded down the steps to stand beside her.

'Hello?' The man looked between Liam and Katya. He was slender, but with plump, pink cheeks and a shock of sandy curly hair. His baby-faced looks reminded Liam of Doogie Howser, M.D., the main character in a TV show about a teenage doctor that had been all the rage shortly before he emigrated to England. 'Everything OK? Who's this, Kat?'

Liam dropped Katya's hand and turned to face him. A nosy, protective neighbour, he assumed, and only politeness prevented him saying, 'None of your business, mate.'

'This is Jack… Liam Lodge,' she muttered, and the man's cheeks immediately sagged, making him look ten years older.

Liam was initially confused. Why would this guy care if he came to visit? Did he know who he was?

He stuck out his hand anyway. 'Hi, yes, I'm Liam. Sorry, who are you?'

At this point it genuinely did not even cross his mind that this person could be romantically involved with Katya. *His* Katya. For some reason, whenever he tortured himself by imagining her with another man, he'd always thought she'd go for someone really edgy, a performance poet or a rapper or perhaps the owner of a wildly successful new internet start-up. Never anyone remotely like this baby-faced, square-looking guy.

So it came as a complete shock to Liam when the superannuated Doogie did not shake his proffered hand, regarding it instead with actual horror.

'I'm Danny. Katya's husband,' he said.

CHAPTER FIFTY-THREE

Katya tugged at the man's sleeve. 'Danny, it's OK. This is… you know… The guy I met in France.'

Danny, thought Liam. Without meaning to, he said it out loud, coughing out the name like a hairball. Would it have killed Phil MacNeill to give him the heads-up about this in his message?

'Danny? Your ex, Danny? You got – married?'

The ex with bad breath Katya had mentioned once or twice? It would have been almost funny, if he hadn't felt like the shock was going to topple him.

Katya looked shamefaced. 'We were on a break,' she said slowly. 'When Otto died.'

'A break? You never said it was just a break. You said you'd broken up.'

'Oh Ja – Liam, so what? Danny and I weren't together at the time I came over, that's all that matters. I wasn't sure if we were going to get back together or not.'

'Wasn't sure?' Liam parroted. His bladder was surely about to burst now. He could almost feel it pulsating, in time with the vein throbbing in his forehead.

Danny was glaring at him, but his features were incapable of delivering the menace he presumably intended, with the result that he more resembled a kitten batting around a ping-pong ball than any sort of actual threat.

Liam glanced down at Katya's left hand and saw the tiny diamond ring and matching wedding band. She must have been coerced into it, he thought, or felt it was her only option. It was the only explanation. Oh, why hadn't she just come to him?

It was like a Shakespearean tragedy. He had turned out not to be single and, after seeing him and Alanda together, Katya had assumed there was no hope for her and Liam. She probably saw some of the TV appearances too, he thought, and read the newspaper articles. All the presenters and interviewers had slanted it as a triumphant love story, a family's successful quest to get their beloved husband and father home again.

Liam sank back against the stone gatepost. Married. She was *married*.

'Katya... could we go somewhere to talk?'

'I'm not sure there's anything else to be said.'

She seemed different – harder, Liam thought. His resolve not to beg or plead seemed momentarily to have deserted him. 'Kat, please. I've come all this way. I've been sitting in my car for hours. Could you not just invite me in for a cup of tea and to use your loo?'

Katya and Danny exchanged looks. She put her hand on his forearm. 'Take Charlie to the park for me, just for half an hour, please?' she asked.

Danny did not seem at all happy about it, but he nodded, wheeling the buggy abruptly around. Liam wanted to run after him and snatch his son back; he wanted to shout, 'Can't *Danny* go to the park, on his own? I haven't even held my baby yet!'

Sighing, Katya trudged back up the steps and unlocked the door, ushering him into a narrow dark hallway with pizza leaflets and circulars piled messily up on a shelf by the door. It smelled of a sickly air-freshener, with a faint whiff of dirty nappies, Liam thought, following Katya down the hall to another door.

Inside, the flat was much nicer than the communal areas had suggested, and not unlike the one in his imagination – except the one in his imagination had not featured a husband living there with Katya and the baby.

The walls were a soft grey, not colourful as he'd visualised, but the furniture was very Katya: a sunshine-yellow tablecloth, turquoise velvet sofa, bright red scatter cushions and a multi-patterned rug. He thought of Otto's shabby old green sofa and felt another pang. Suddenly the months they spent together seemed like a lifetime ago.

She retreated into a small galley kitchen off the main room, stepping over a playmat with various textured objects hanging from a frame stretched across it.

'Bathroom's through there,' she said, gesturing to a doorway. 'I'll put the kettle on.'

Liam gratefully used the facilities, feeling a strange, disjointed sense of déjà vu about the situation – an echo of when Alanda had come to find him. It had all unravelled when she'd used the bathroom at Otto's, finding the photo of him and Katya, and the pregnancy test.

When he came out, feeling a stone lighter, he said, 'Do you still have that photo of us, the one that Alanda found?'

She had her back to him in the kitchen, frozen in the act of dumping teabags into mugs.

'I think it's somewhere,' she replied vaguely.

Liam sank down on the sofa, staring around at the photographs and baby paraphernalia everywhere. Taking pride of place on an otherwise blank wall opposite the sofa was a large colour shot of Danny and Katya on their wedding day, looking blissfully happy, feeding cake to each other and beaming.

Of course she doesn't still have the photo of us, he thought bitterly.

She emerged from the kitchen holding two mugs. 'This is like that scene at the end of *Castaway* when Tom Hanks gets home and finds out his fiancée's married to someone else,' she commented.

He wanted to burst into tears at the throwaway nature of the comment. This was real life, his life, not some stupid Hollywood film, darn it, he thought furiously.

It was interesting that, in the whole time he'd known Katya before, she had never once so much as mildly irritated him. Now he had an urge to shout at her, to yell '*how could you?*' – even to punch her. He'd never lifted a finger to anyone in his life.

Yet it wasn't her fault. Like Tom Hanks' character stuck on that island for years, he had to realise that life moved on, inexorably. You couldn't wait for ever.

But she hadn't waited at all!

Although, he reasoned, accepting the tea and blowing on its surface as a way of both cooling it, and himself, down, it would have been completely unreasonable of him to waltz off home with his wife and expect Katya just to wait around for the day he got divorced.

He wondered if Alanda would have waited, had his memory not returned. Probably not, in the light of recent events, he thought miserably.

'I totally understand why you needed to cut off all contact with me at the time,' he said. 'For your own sanity. I can see that we couldn't have kept in touch and got over each other at the same time. It would've just carried on between us, wouldn't it? Perhaps you were only doing it to protect me – in which case, thank you.'

He dipped his head briefly and she nodded, unsmiling. She was still standing.

'Can't you come over here and sit with me?'

There he was, begging again… She remained standing, although she did look more sympathetic than hostile.

He ploughed on. 'I agree, it would've been impossible. But things were different between me and Alanda, right from when we got home. I don't know how much of that was because I was still in love with you and really confused, or because she'd actually just got used to being independent, but whatever the reason, it's done now. Our marriage ran its course. It happens. As long as she's happy, then I'll live with it. I thought that now we'd have our chance to… I've missed you so much.'

His voice trembled and he had to stare very hard at a brightly coloured toy octopus on the floor to stop himself breaking down.

'We're not going to get that chance, are we?' he asked bleakly.

Finally she came and sat next to him, taking his hand and looking into his face. 'No. I'm so sorry, Jack. I swear I never meant to hurt you.'

He couldn't meet her eyes, his own now roaming the room, trying to snag on something that wouldn't cause him pain. The blank wall across from him seemed like the only option, but his attention kept being drawn back to the wedding portrait opposite. He realised something about it had bothered him from first glance, but until now he hadn't been able to pinpoint what.

Katya's stomach, in her fitted wedding dress, was completely flat. She looked younger.

'*When* exactly did you get married, Katya? You're not pregnant in that photo.'

There was a long, long pause, a black hole into which Liam was yelling, 'no, no, please don't tell me….'

When she eventually spoke, it was in a tiny, ashamed voice. 'Six years ago.'

It was like a punch in the solar plexus. He waited for her to say, 'but we got divorced, and we've only just re-married' – but of course, she didn't.

'Let me get this straight,' he said slowly. 'You were married when we met. You were married when you got pregnant. You went straight back to your marriage when my memory came back. So what was it to you, Katya? Just a bit of fun, something to pass the time while you were in France on your own? Because you were a bit bored and wanted company?' His voice cracked. 'I thought you loved me.'

She was crying now. 'I did love you. It wasn't like that. I thought we had a future together. Danny and I had separated.'

Liam was speechless. A sudden sound in the doorway made them both jump and turn.

Danny was standing there, holding Charlie under his arm as if the baby was an unexploded bomb. Liam hadn't heard him come in.

'She might have felt more than she expected to,' he said, bright pink, 'but she doesn't anymore. We're happy together.' Then he turned to Katya. 'Came back early – this one needs changing.'

Anger rose in Liam and he stood up. 'So it doesn't bother you that your wife shagged the first man she could find, behind your back? Doesn't say much about the strength of your marriage, does it?'

Danny looked mortified, but actually laughed. 'The opposite, in fact. It says everything; that I love her enough to let her do what she needed to do.'

Liam gawped at him. Was this how it worked with this generation then? Sanctioned infidelity? He suddenly felt very old.

'What possible reason could your wife have, to "need" an affair?'

Charlie began to cry and Liam thought that, in the twist of his baby lips and the tiny dimple in his quivering chin, he looked just like Jake had done as a baby. *I have two sons*, he thought, in despair and wonder.

Danny looked as if he was about to say something and then thought better of it, instead heading down the hallway, accompanied by a pungent waft of full nappy. He disappeared into the bathroom, Charlie's cries immediately muffled.

Katya stood up to face him, tears now streaming down her cheeks. 'You're such a lovely man, Jack, I swear I didn't mean to—'

'Yes, you said. You didn't mean to hurt me.'

'I didn't. It just happened. You'd lost your memory, but I knew it was likely to return and you'd go back to your old life, and I thought there was a chance that I could go back to mine. It was the hardest thing, letting you go – I didn't realise I'd feel that strongly for you. When the police told me they'd discovered your identity, I didn't tell you for a couple of days because I didn't want to lose you. I was about to tell you when your wife showed up.' She dropped her voice. 'I'd have started divorce proceedings. I wanted you.'

'But because you couldn't have me, you went straight back to your husband, even though you'd separated and now you were pregnant with another man's baby? And he just took you back?'

'Yes, but you don't know *why* Danny and I had been on a break,' said Katya, sobbing desperately.

'Go on.'

'Because it had all got too intense. We'd had so many disappointments. We lost all our savings. It put unbearable stress on our relationship. We didn't think we'd survive it.'

'Survive what? What got too intense? Why?' But Liam was beginning to think he had worked it out. Katya confirmed it:

'Not being able to have a baby. We'd been trying for years, IVF and everything. It was why we kept breaking up and getting back together – the stress of it was too much.'

CHAPTER FIFTY-FOUR

Alanda

'Where's Dad? Been trying to get hold of him but his phone's switched off.'

Jake sounded peeved. Alanda felt quite peeved herself – all the kids still behaved like she was Liam's keeper, months after they'd split up.

'I don't know, darling. Why, were you supposed to be meeting him?'

'No. Duh. Obviously, I'm at work.'

That was one good thing about this year so far, at least. Jake's publicity efforts in coordinating the 'Find Liam' campaign had borne more fruit than the success of its original intention and, as Alanda had hoped, led to a job offer from a social media marketing company based in Bournemouth. Jake had been there for four months and was, he said, 'having a blast.'

'No need to be sarcastic. You do work from home sometimes, it's not impossible that you'd invited Dad over for lunch.'

'Sorry, Mum.'

Jake didn't speak to her in that tone as often as he had done earlier in the year, when she and Liam had first announced their separation. Back then, none of the three kids could talk to her without sounding either faintly sulky, rude or sarcastic. It had been like a throwback to their teenage years and she'd wanted to yell at them that *Liam* had been the one to cheat first… although that would rightly have been perceived as a cheap shot, since he hadn't even known who he was at the time. She was glad she had resisted the temptation to try and defend herself that way.

Thankfully they didn't keep the worst of it up for more than a week or two. 'Mum, we're gutted,' Becky had said. 'But we know what you've been through. We want you to be happy. If this is really what you want, then we'll accept it… eventually. Just give us a bit of time.'

Alanda wished she *could* say it really was what she wanted, but it was too soon to tell, she decided.

Now she tried to placate Jake, who'd gone into protective overdrive.

'He's probably in the attic with his headphones on and can't hear his phone.'

'No, it's actually switched off. Do you think I should go over and check?'

'I thought you were working?'

'I am… and I'm really busy. I'm just worried, that's all. Could you maybe…?'

Alanda sighed. 'Jake, no. I'm in the shop on my own. Please don't worry. If you haven't got hold of him in a couple of hours, then you could go over after work.'

'Don't you care about him anymore?'

Alanda rolled her eyes. She could do without this. There were a couple of kids in the shop, boys of about twelve or thirteen who looked so furtive that they may as well have been wearing huge 'shoplifter in training' badges on their concave little chests. She kept an eagle eye on them as they traipsed past the shelves of mugs. They were now standing by the card racks, sniggering and nudging each other at the more risqué birthday cards.

'Of course I do. I just can't leave work at the moment.'

'Oh,' Jake said. 'I've just had a text from Heather. I asked her if she knew where Dad was, and she says she thought he'd gone to London. Why would he have gone to London?'

'Jake, you're doing it again – why would I know what your dad gets up to? He has his own life now.'

Although Alanda thought she could guess. Liam never went to London. He hated it. He hated the noise and the traffic and the general sprawl of it. There was only one likely reason he would have gone: Katya lived in London – or at least, she had done. And the baby must have been born fairly recently.

Her heart gave a lurch of pain, as if it had jumped sideways into the wrong place in her chest and was lodged there, unable to move. Liam would get back together with Katya. She knew it had always only been a matter of time.

'Look, I've got to go,' she concluded. 'Keep me posted, OK? Love you.'

Hanging up, she glared at the boys until, somewhat to her surprise, they timidly approached the counter and actually purchased a lurid *Happy Birthday Grandma!* card. They had just sloped out when her phone rang again.

'Hi gorgeous, how's your day?' Jennie chirped down the line.

Alanda smiled. 'It's all right, thanks. But I've just had Jake on the phone, in a bit of a state because he can't get hold of Liam.'

'Really?' Jennie sounded concerned, and Alanda thought again how lucky she was to have such a caring partner. Jennie was such a lovely person.

The first few months had been exhilarating. The newness of love, the naughtiness. The otherness of being with a woman. She and Jennie had been lost in each other, and Alanda had marvelled at the novelty of Jennie's soft skin and curves, so different to the coarse masculinity of Liam's wiry body. Why would anybody ever want to have sex with a man, she'd thought, when women were so much more sensitive and intuitive? It had been a revelation.

But these days she felt a bit more conflicted. She still loved Jennie, but now that the novelty had worn off and time went on, she was surprised to find that she felt less secure or confident about it all, instead of more. At the root, she thought, it was because it had all happened so fast. Suddenly she was no longer living in her beloved house with her beloved husband and all their years of togetherness, as if she'd been uprooted by a tornado and dumped into Jennie's life. It was a big adjustment to make.

Jennie's love for her was so all-encompassing, it was a little bit scary at times, Alanda thought, almost as if she was trying to ensure there was no way Alanda could ever hurt her, even if she'd wanted to – which of course, she didn't. Perhaps, though, they ought to have had an affair for longer than the few weeks they did, before she took such drastic action. It might have run its course in a way that wouldn't have blown both her and Liam's lives apart. But that would have been so unfair on Liam. She couldn't have lived with herself if she had joined the sordid ranks of those people who conducted lengthy ongoing secret affairs behind their spouse's back.

The trouble was, she couldn't shake the feeling that perhaps she had been a bit… hasty.

CHAPTER FIFTY-FIVE

Liam

Suddenly it all made sense. Katya's insatiable appetite for sex. Her utter joy at the positive pregnancy test, even though they had only been together a few weeks, and this was the sort of news that would usually be greeted with trepidation as well as pleasure, particularly given their own circumstances.

Liam stared at her. 'So you didn't want me. You just wanted a baby, and I happened to be there.'

'No!' she cried. 'I told you, I wanted you as well. I did. But after so long trying, I was just so happy when we found out I was pregnant.'

'It wasn't true, then, when you said you were on the pill?'

Katya hung her head. 'No,' she said. 'But I honestly didn't think I *could* get pregnant, and I didn't want to talk about it, so it was easier to pretend that I was. We'd had all the tests done, of course, and Danny's sperm count was only a little bit low, so they thought it must be my fault as well.'

'Why didn't you just adopt, instead of getting yourselves in debt and splitting up over it?' Liam was genuinely curious, although immediately worried that he sounded horribly judgemental.

'Danny would have. But I wanted to be pregnant and to give birth to my own child,' Katya said simply. 'Maybe I'd have agreed to go down that road eventually, if we'd got back together anyway.'

'Is my name on Charlie's birth certificate?'

Katya dropped her eyes and shook her head. Liam gritted his teeth. He'd suspected as much but it was exquisitely painful to have it confirmed. 'I've looked into it, of course, and I know that it's your decision. But for the record, I would like to be added, at some point, if you ever change your mind.'

She nodded, in a way that Liam knew was only to fob him off.

'And Danny didn't mind, that the baby wasn't his?'

Suddenly Danny was standing there.

'He's down for his nap,' he said to Katya, then calmly turned to Liam. 'No, I didn't mind. I don't mind at all. We have our family now, thanks to you, and that was what was missing for us. We'll tell him when he's old enough, and if he wants to be in touch with you, he can be. Then. And not till then.'

He crossed the room and put his arm around Katya. Liam thought the guy no longer looked baby-faced or square. Just a regular family man who loved his wife very much; enough to bring up another man's child as his own.

As much as he, Liam, had loved Alanda.

Everything shifted at that moment. What had been working itself up in his head for months, ever since his return from France, this tragic image of lost lovers, separated by the fates, waiting for their happy ending… it all shattered like a dropped vase. What he and Katya had together had been wonderful – but it really had been just a fantasy. What she had here, with Danny and Charlie, that was her real life.

His real life had been with Alanda, but he'd lost that now. He missed her then, more intensely than the ten million other times he had missed her since Christmas.

He'd lost everything.

'I'll go then,' he said in a choked voice.

The silence in the room was so painful and heavy Liam thought it would crush the air out of his lungs. Danny was staring at him expectantly – he may as well have had a speech bubble over his heading reading, 'Go on then' – and Katya's eyes were full of pity.

Liam took a business card out of his wallet and left it on the arm of the sofa. He took a deep breath and focussed all his efforts on keeping his voice steady. 'All I'm asking is that you keep hold of that, and when Charlie's old enough, or you change your minds about letting me be involved, you contact me. I would also appreciate it if you could email me your wish for me not to contribute to my son's upkeep in any way, so I've got it in writing. I don't want a call in five years' time with a backdated bill and a request for a paternity test.'

'You won't,' Danny said.

'I wasn't asking you,' Liam retorted. He wanted to cry. 'One more thing before I go… can I look at him, once more? Take a photo?'

Katya hesitated.

'Please?'

He thought if she refused him that, he really was going to lose the plot entirely, but she nodded and gestured down the hallway. Danny actually stood in front of the main flat door with his legs planted apart and his arms crossed, like a security guard. Liam rolled his eyes.

'Don't worry, I'm not going to snatch him, if that's what you're thinking.'

Danny blushed again, but didn't move.

Katya followed Liam into the box room nursery. Charlie was fast asleep on his back, his tiny fists raised by his ears, snoring lightly. He was surrounded by a small menagerie of home-made soft toys; a knitted rabbit, a fluffy penguin, an anthropomorphised felted strawberry, and Liam wondered who had made them. He wished he had thought to bring a gift of his own, so his son would at least have one thing from his birth father.

Liam gazed greedily at him, visualising in his mind's eye the way Charlie's baby face would grow and develop over the years ahead, a speeded-up montage of him slimming down, filling out, losing milk teeth, growing hair. All the milestones he would miss: first words, first steps, first solo bike ride, first day at school. Skinned knees, spitting out broccoli, facefuls of birthday cake.

'Can I kiss him?'

Katya silently lowered one side of the cot bars and Liam leaned over and touched his lips to his son's hot and soft forehead. Suddenly the prospect of losing Charlie felt worse than the prospect of not having Katya in his life.

He took his phone from his jeans pocket and switched it on, whereupon it immediately started pinging with a barrage of text messages and missed calls from Jake and Alanda. 'Oh, Jack,' Katya exclaimed in a cross whisper as the baby wailed and jumped, his little arms briefly flailing.

Liam thought something bad must have happened, but on scanning the messages, he saw they were all trying to find out where he was and why he wasn't answering his phone. He could deal with that later.

'Sorry,' Liam whispered back, although he wasn't. He wished Charlie could have woken up properly so that he could get Katya to take a photo of him holding him.

He made do with several close-ups of Charlie's sleeping face, and a short video of the small snuffling noises he was making in his sleep, then switched his phone back off again.

'Right,' he said, more briskly than he felt.

But he couldn't think of anything else to say. The word 'goodbye' refused to come. It was too final, too painful. Without a backwards glance at Charlie, he left Katya putting the side of the cot back up and walked out, not even deigning to make eye contact with Danny as he left.

Once he got outside, back into the noise and traffic fumes, all the emotion he'd suppressed inside Katya's flat came bubbling up to the surface. Rage and humiliation almost blinded him and, as he stood waiting for a break in the traffic to cross the road back to his car, he felt his body tip forwards off the kerb, teetering dangerously into the path of an oncoming bus. Only the thought of not succeeding, the risk of more long weeks of pain, disability and hospitals, as well as of the trauma of his kids, the bus driver and other passengers, pulled him back upright. As he stood there shaking, he saw a flash of the bus driver's angry, panicked face as the bus swished past.

It was a miracle that he made it home in one piece. He'd had an almost overwhelming urge to drive head-on into every concrete wall, veer across the central reservation of the motorway to greet the headlights of every HGV at eighty miles an hour, steer off every bridge into the welcome embrace of black water.

Each time, he forced himself to see the face of one of his children – one of the first three, at least. He was trying very hard to block out the mental image of his fourth.

You can't put them through this again, he repeated to himself like a mantra. *You can't.*

Yet what was there to stay for now? He'd lost Alanda, Katya *and* Charlie. The kids – the ones he was allowed to love – were grown up and had left home. They all had their own lives, while he had no-one and nothing.

Interesting, too, that once he had left Katya's flat, his mind's eye only saw her with Danny. The two of them, taking care of their baby together. Living their lives like any other young married couple. In an instant all the previous attraction he'd felt for her soaked away, and she became merely a pretty girl he'd once had a thing with.

He couldn't even allow himself to picture her as the mother of his child, because she'd made it quite clear that his role in their lives had been relegated solely to sperm donor.

He was wearily parking on the drive and trudging back into the house when he remembered all the frantic texts from Jake. Guiltily, he texted back, *Really sorry. Phone died. All fine. Went to visit a friend, home now. See you soon. Love you, Dad*

Such bland words, he thought. And only about half of them true.

CHAPTER FIFTY-SIX

Katya

Jack left so suddenly and shockingly, gone as quickly as he'd materialised on the front steps. His face had been a mask of grief in such a terrifying shade of grey that she actually feared for his survival; he'd appeared to blend in with the walls. The imprint of his body in the sofa cushions seemed to be the only evidence Katya had that his visit hadn't been some sort of unexpected and unwelcome hallucination.

'Are you OK, Kitty-Kat?'

She was sitting motionless at the table, her face in her hands. Danny pulled up a chair and sat very close to her, taking her in his arms. She leaned into him, inhaling his familiar scent, and it calmed her a little bit. Her heart was still pounding.

'He thinks I'm a terrible person who used him just to get a baby,' she whispered.

Danny hugged her. 'It was a lot for him to take in, that's all. I'm sure he'll come round. He'd probably been building it up in his mind for months, from the moment his wife left him, thinking that he could track you down and pick up where he left off with you.' He snorted faintly. 'Pretty shallow, if you ask me,' he said. 'How did he even find you? I thought you'd blocked him and that he didn't have our address.'

'I don't know. I did block him. I swear I've not had any contact with him at all since France.'

Then he paused. 'Kat – what was it like, seeing him again?'

Katya looked into his anxious face. She knew him so well, she knew exactly what he was saying and her heart went out to him. 'I feel lots of things – guilt, pity, a bit of anger, that he just assumed I'd be here waiting for him – but nothing that you need to worry about, I promise.'

They had split up so many times in the past, over the five years in which they'd dated before marrying, as well as the couple of IVF stress-induced separations after, that for a while they had both decided that they must just not be compatible. At first, it was silly things they argued about, like whose turn it was to take the bins out, and who had got snappy with whom, over what trivial thing. Apart from IVF, she couldn't even remember some of the reasons why they'd kept breaking up, both of them insecure about how the other felt. It was only when Danny proposed and she accepted, that things settled down more and the hiccups were less frequent.

The first three years of married life had been the happiest they'd ever spent together. They decided to try for a family – and that was when it all started to go wrong again. But they were married by then, and neither of them wanted to throw in the towel the way they used to at the first sign of stress.

The bottom line, Katya privately thought, was that she hadn't fancied him, not really. Not with that visceral, chemical attraction that made you yearn for your partner's body, to relish every inch of his skin, to bury your nose in his neck to breathe in his pheromones. Like she had done with Jack.

Meeting Jack was what had made her realise what she had been missing with Danny – but instead of thinking, 'I need Jack,' somewhat to her own surprise, she had instead re-thought the way that Danny and she interacted. Losing Jack, but Danny still taking her back, gave her a new and deep appreciation for what she'd had with her husband, and that once-fragile thread had gradually thickened and twisted into an unbreakable rope binding them together.

It felt good. It felt safe. She'd tested Danny to the limit and he had remained steadfast for her. Her attraction for him had blossomed, fertilised by deeper emotions of trust and appreciation, rather than the superficial fluff of appearance.

She never told Jack about any of this when they were together, not wanting to admit to him that she was still married. It had just been less complicated to take it all at face value. They had so much to deal with already, with Jack's memory loss and the past, which lurked unseen beneath the surface like a giant iceberg. She had decided that telling him she was still married would add another layer of stress that they could do without – for her, as well as for Jack. The miscarriages, recriminations and heartache she'd had with Danny were still so fresh in her mind that, when she arrived in France, it really helped that Jack knew none of it. In a 'fake it till you make it' kind of way, it had been healing for her to be seen as footloose and fancy-free. Falling in love with Jack had felt like the perfect antidote to her pain.

Taking the easy way out, as she had always done, when things got hard.

But now she knew she had been wrong. She had seen the hurt that running away and not being entirely truthful had caused to Liam and, previously, to Danny too.

'I'm sorry, Dan,' she said.

'What for?'

'Everything I've put you through. I love you.'

'I love you too.'

CHAPTER FIFTY-SEVEN

Liam

Eighteen Months Later

'What happened to whatshername, the hairdresser?' Becky asked. 'Olly and I saw you two last month in the market. You were holding hands. Don't tell me that's gone wrong too?'

'Shelley,' Liam said despondently. 'She turned out to be a bit of a nightmare. Started off by telling me what I should and shouldn't wear – after a month! – then bombarded me with abusive texts when I broke it off with her. Had to block her in the end.'

In the past, Liam would barely have known what an internet date even was, but over the last year the practice had occupied far more of his headspace than he would ever have thought possible. Bumble, Tinder, EHarmony, Elite – he thought he could probably have online dating as his chosen specialist subject on *Mastermind*. The relative merits and drawbacks of each site, the type of woman he tended to meet on each. Cost, length of time to set up profile, quality of date, likelihood of profile pic veracity… he must have had fifty or sixty dates. Apart from his weekly pint with Colin and meeting up with the kids, dating comprised his entire social life.

Colin had counselled him to have some time as a single man, that it wasn't so bad, and definitely better than 'rushing into something else new'. Liam supposed he was right and, in his own defence, he *had* tried. He didn't date anybody for the first six months of his new solo life, but the truth was, he couldn't cope with the emptiness. He had never lived alone, ever, in his whole life, and he hated it. He hated the stillness of the house in the evening, hated waking up alone, hated buying meals for one at the supermarket.

Most of all, he hated his life without Alanda in it.

When insomnia struck – most nights – he tried to get back to sleep by alphabetically listing the first name of every woman he'd met, and quite often got through the whole alphabet, bar the obviously tricky letters like X and Z. Now it had become habitual and he found himself doing it at odd times during the day too. Sometimes he'd mix it up, by using titles of pop singles from the seventies, or films instead, but for some reason he kept coming back to the women's names.

He didn't usually get far enough along in the actual dating process to sleep with the women, but he had slept with Shelley. Just once, right before she told him she 'insisted' that he threw out 'those horrible old jeans', in reference to his favourite pair of elderly and comfortable Levis. Both the jeans ban and the terrible sex had left him feeling empty and small. He'd ended it that day.

'Maybe I should set myself up as a consultant,' he said.

Becky was the most interested of the three children in his dating exploits, always badgering him for updates.

'Help them find the best match on the best site. I think there's a gap in the market.'

Abby, Belinda, Cally, Danielle…

Cally had been lovely. Knew her rock and soul music, had a great smile and was good fun. They'd had four or five dates until she had decided that she was still too hung up on her ex to be able to contemplate a new relationship. Why couldn't she have decided that *before* going on four or five dates with him, he wondered? Then he saw her back on the site two weeks later and wondered what he'd done wrong. It had been a bruising experience.

Erin, Fiona, Gemma, Hayley.

He'd liked Fiona too, but she got diagnosed with breast cancer after their first date, poor woman, and moved up north to live with her mother.

'Do it, Dad,' Becky said. 'Although it would be better if you could find a good one yourself first – you're not much of an advert for it at the moment, are you?'

She flicked through his list of potential matches on Bumble and dismissed them one by one. 'No – no way – ew, no – no – oh my God, she's seventy if she's a day! – maybe – no. Don't you find it exhausting?'

It was a Saturday in November and they were having a coffee in the cafe area of a local antiques warehouse, surrounded by quirky ceramic teapots shaped like cottages and display cases of tarnished brooches that nobody would ever wear again.

'Yes, I do,' Liam said, with feeling. 'I loathe it. But how else am I going to meet somebody?'

'Join a tennis club; they're full of ladies of a certain age and some of them are bound to be single.'

He shook his head ruefully. 'Can't. Leg won't let me.'

'Oh, yeah. Shame. Golf? Bridge?'

Liam rolled his eyes. 'I've considered my options, trust me. It's internet dating or nothing. It's a numbers game, I reckon – surely I'll find a good one eventually? I'm so glad you three are sorted. I would hate to think of you having to go through all this.'

The kids were all very settled, which was the only positive in Liam's life at that time. Heather and Kevin were expecting their first baby. Jake's job was still going well and he was seeing a new man, a reassuringly normal and kind school-teacher called Graham who they all really liked. Becky and Olly had recently got engaged and were planning a small wedding on a beach in Barbados next year.

Liam very much did not want to go to that wedding without a partner. Often, he found himself revisiting all the unsuccessful dates wondering where and with whom the fault lay.

Ingrid – pretty, but drank too much and only ever talked about her kids – Jacqui, Karen, Lisette…

Usually there was no specific fault from either side. Liam just came away from the dates feeling down and tired, inevitably missing Alanda horribly. He felt that he had known true love twice in his life, and the reality was that he was highly unlikely to be fortunate enough to make that a hat-trick. On the rare occasions he did feel a spark with someone, it always turned out to be short-lived. Within a date or two it became very obvious why that woman was single.

And yet he persisted. There must be one woman out there, surely, who would find him as attractive as he found her, and who didn't have any major character flaws, nor perceived him to have any?

He could not bear the thought of growing old alone, forever regretting that one hasty decision to go skiing.

He wanted to ask Becky how Alanda was. They hadn't seen each other for a few months now. But the kids had made no bones about how they absolutely did not want to be go-betweens, and Liam supposed it wouldn't be fair to expect them to. He knew they would tell him if there was anything important to know.

The last he'd heard was that she and Jennie were planning to buy a cottage together in the country. He was glad that she was more settled and happier. The thought of having gone through all this for *both* of them to end up unhappy was intolerable.

The trouble with it was that now she needed him to sell the family home, get legally divorced – they hadn't done the paperwork yet – and split the proceeds. Finalise it all. They had been assuming they'd just wait for the statutory five years to elapse before doing that.

But, God, he still missed her. He found he often missed her most when he was out on a date, with Marcia or Nicky or Olivia. At the end of the evening, more often than not, he would give them a polite peck on the cheek and head back to his empty house to send them the diplomatically worded text that was his go-to brush-off: *It was lovely to meet you. I had a nice time. But my heart didn't skip*

a beat and, I suspect, neither did yours. Good luck with the dating!
Take care, Liam x

He did not miss Katya, even though he had loved her with the whole of his damaged heart for the short time they were together. However intense it had been, it had never been real or permanent, he now realised. It wasn't a patch on what he and Alanda once had together.

All he wanted was to fill up the emptiness inside of him. Sometimes he felt so depressed that he wasn't sure how he could continue – but, somehow, he did. One foot in front of the other, one date in the diary for this week, one for next. Repeat ad infinitum.

Penny, Quinn, Rosie, Sue…

He'd get there. In the end. These things took time; that was all.

CHAPTER FIFTY-EIGHT

Alanda

Her breath surrounded her in harsh white clouds as she pounded along the deserted Town Path, counting three on each inhale and three on each exhale to keep her legs in rhythm. The cold had corralled indoors all but the most hardy, apart from a couple of chilly-looking dog-walkers she had run past in the park.

The Town Path was a narrow strip of tarmac alongside a stream, leading from the centre of Salisbury to the nearby village of Harnham. To the left of it, sheep and llamas grazed in open fields in the shadow of the imposing spire of the massive cathedral and, to the right, undulating water meadows stretched to the horizon.

Alanda loved running here when it wasn't crowded – apart from the fact that she had to run past the end of her old road to get to it. She always kept her eyes firmly ahead, refusing to let them wander down the terrace where she and Liam had brought up their family, and where he still was.

Much as she loathed the thought of him in there with another woman, pragmatically she knew it was inevitable and for the best. *You left him, remember?* She did not want him to be on his own.

The kids had filled her in on his latest girlfriend, Shelley the hairdresser. Alanda made sure she knew which salon Shelley owned so that she could avoid going there, and sincerely hoped that he had finally found someone who wouldn't take him for a ride like that Katya girl had.

When Alanda thought about Katya's behaviour, it made her want to track her down and punch her lights out. Poor Liam had almost had a nervous breakdown after that final rejection, coming mere months after her own rejection of him. Nothing made her more angry – besides, anger was an easier emotion to live with than the ever-present guilt. He'd stuck up for the girl, saying that the pregnancy had been an accident and that she'd been separated from her husband at the time they met, but Liam always had been naive.

She thought about it now, increasing her pace until she was almost sprinting along the path, causing a few sheep to panic and run away in the opposite direction, safe in their field but clearly not feeling it.

There was a huddled figure in a woolly hat sitting on a bench near the end of the path and Alanda instinctively began to veer to one side, to keep as much distance as possible between them. She thought it was a homeless person for a moment – nobody would voluntarily sit out in this weather, surely? – but he didn't have any possessions at his feet.

As she passed she thought, *Ha, it looks like Liam*, before coming to an abrupt halt.

It *was* Liam.

Panting, she paused her smartwatch and put her hands on her hips.

'Liam! What on earth are you doing out here? It's freezing!'

He looked up at her through watery eyes. Alanda couldn't tell if this was from the chill wind, or if he'd been crying. His expression was one of abject misery – he could barely raise a smile.

'Hi darling,' he said, and she didn't have the heart to ask him not to call her that; it was too painful. 'Fancy meeting you here. You kept up the running, then? Good for you. You look great.'

She sat down next to him, searching his face with her eyes.

'Thanks. Yeah, I'm actually almost enjoying it these days. Entered myself into a 10K in spring.'

'Brilliant,' he said listlessly.

'Are you OK?' Instinctively, she put her hand over his and gave it a brief squeeze. He wasn't wearing gloves and his fingers were red with cold. He looked older, more grizzled but, she reflected, still Liam. *Her* Liam, she could not help thinking.

He shrugged. 'Been indoors for two days so I decided I'd better get out and get a bit of fresh air. Then I thought I saw a kingfisher over there, up in that tree. Thought I'd wait a bit and see if came back. I've never seen one before.'

'Oh wow. I've never seen one before either.' She scanned the tree opposite but there was no splash of colour brightening its black broken spokes of branches. 'Can I sit with you for a bit?'

He was staring straight ahead, as if he literally couldn't face her. 'Sure. How's things with you?'

She opened her mouth to reply, to pick one from the usual stock responses – 'fine' or 'not bad' or even 'not great,' at a push. To her own surprise, none of the stock responses fell into her mouth. As if she was having some kind of out-of-body experience, she felt her shoulders begin to heave again, but this time from emotion, not exertion.

'Oh, Liam,' she blurted. 'I know I shouldn't say this, not after all this time and when you're with someone else, but I miss you so much.'

She didn't even realise she was crying until she felt the tears drip hot, almost burning, down her cold cheeks.

He laughed, not unkindly. 'Oh, I'm not with Shelley anymore. That finished a month ago. They never last.'

Then he turned and looked her in the face for the first time, wiping her tears off with icy fingers. 'It's because I miss you too, Al. Every day, every night.'

She was in danger of losing it altogether, so she stood up, putting first one leg then the other up on the bench to stretch her hamstrings, but it didn't help clear her head of all the erupting emotions. She sat back down again.

'How did this happen, Liam? How did we get to this place? I mean – I know what happened. I just don't know how we let things go this far.'

He put his hand on her knee and she gently crossed her legs so that his hand was trapped between them, in an attempt to warm it up. Then she leaned against him.

They had not sat this close together since the Christmas Day before last, the day she'd left him, and they both knew it was the unexpected nature of their meeting making them act with such spontaneity.

'I'm so sorry,' she said eventually, pulling out a tissue and blowing her nose. 'I'd do anything to change things.'

'How's the house-hunting going?' he asked, not looking at her but not pulling away from her either. 'I confess I haven't quite been able to face getting those valuations done on ours, but as soon as you find something you like, I will, I promise. It's just' – his voice broke – 'hard.'

Alanda sat up. 'About that…'

Liam cleared his throat. 'What?'

'I haven't told the kids yet, because I needed a bit of time to come to terms with it, but Jennie's been offered a job at a home up in Northamptonshire.'

'Oh,' Liam said, his shoulders slumping further. 'So you'll be moving up there. That's a shame, for Mum, I mean. She liked Jennie. And the kids, of course. I thought you wanted to be around for when Heather's baby comes? I hear you've been crocheting and everything.'

She reached out and took his free hand, trying to chafe some warmth back into it.

'I do. I will be. And I am crocheting, like a woman possessed, now I've finally got the hang of it. The thing is – Jennie's going without me. We're breaking up. It's just not working and she's decided she needs a new start. We moved into separate rooms weeks ago, but she said I could stay at her place until I find somewhere to rent.'

Liam was silent, then he said, stiffly, 'I'm so sorry to hear that.'
Alanda laughed. 'No you're not!'

He laughed too then, his face briefly transformed into the Liam from twenty years ago. 'OK, fair enough. I'm not sorry. Well – no, I really am. I'm sorry that you've been caused more pain. I'm sorry it didn't work out, if you wanted it to work out.'

'That's the thing,' she said slowly. 'What I know now is that I *didn't* want it to work out, not after the first six months or so. The more time went on, the more I realised I'd made a colossal mistake. I ran away from all the pain of… us, and I thought it was what I wanted; what I'd been missing. But it wasn't at all. Jennie is a lovely woman, and she felt so strongly about me that I got sort of swept up in it. I was confused about what I felt, but by the time I realised, it was too late. I thought you'd get back together with Katya. And I didn't want to hurt Jennie the way I'd hurt you.'

Liam pulled his hand out from its warm nest of Lycra legging and snaked his arm around her back the way he had, she reflected, on their first date. She was seventeen and he'd taken her to the cinema to see *Blue Velvet*. Before the opening credits had even rolled, she'd felt that arm sneak around behind her in exactly the same way as it was now, and within five minutes they had been kissing. She remembered nothing about that film except its title.

'Why didn't you tell me?'

'I thought you'd finally moved on. You were with Shelley and all I'd heard was that you seemed to be into her. I could hardly barge in and break that up, could I?'

He smiled. 'We're really not that great at communicating the important stuff, are we?' Then he stood up. 'I need to move. My leg is getting stiff and it's brass monkeys out here.'

Alanda felt dismissed. 'Sorry to have kept you.' Embarrassed, she fiddled with her smartwatch, ready to set it back to 'run'. 'It was good to bump—'

He grabbed her hands and pulled her into a hug. 'Don't be daft. I need to move, but I was hoping that it was in the direction of home, and that you'd come in for a cup of tea.'

'Oh!' she said. 'Yes. Yes please.' She laughed easily, all embarrassment forgotten.

They set off together, walking in step, Liam limping slightly, until a sudden flash of orange, cyan and emerald green stopped them both in their tracks. They watched the kingfisher swoop from branch to branch along the stream, until it alighted in a tree right in front of them, tipping its long beak to one side as it fluffed up its feathers.

'Would you look at that?' Liam mused.

'Beautiful,' agreed Alanda.

They continued walking, neither one of them able to say who had first reached out and taken the other's hand.

Both of them were smiling.

A LETTER FROM LOUISE

Dear reader,

I want to say a massive thank you for choosing to read *His Other Woman*. If you did enjoy it, and are interested in being kept up to date with all my latest releases, just sign up at the following link. Your email address will never be shared and you can unsubscribe at any time, I promise!

www.bookouture.com/louise-voss

His Other Woman is my first non-crime novel in over ten years, and I loved writing it. It felt good to get really stuck into an emotional dilemma of the magnitude that I hope none of you ever have to experience – what a nightmare it would be. I felt such deep sympathy for all three of my main characters, thrust into a situation that was nobody's fault, just one of those things. I was really rooting for all of them.

As with many novels, the idea came about through a 'what-if', after my husband Ade told me about an accident he had on a skiing holiday many years ago. He ended up in hospital, not able to remember anything at all from the last five or so years of his life. Very fortunately, his amnesia only lasted a day or so, but I thought, what if his memory hadn't come back, not for months? What if it had happened when we had been happily married for years, but he didn't remember and fell in love with someone else? As it did to Alanda, my world would have fallen apart.

One funny/odd thing, though, was that I didn't think to ask him *where* this accident had happened – I knew it was the Alps, but that was it. I spent days poring over Google Maps, figuring out a location for my story that would be a direct flight from Madrid (where Liam was meant to be), and eventually settled on Thonon-les-Bains in France. When I said to Ade, 'Can we go for a weekend once we're out of lockdown? I'm setting a lot of my book there and I've never been. Sounds lovely, on the banks of Lake Geneva…' he said, 'Oh, I've been there. That's where I was taken to hospital when I had my accident!' Of course, I then asked where exactly he'd been skiing when the accident happened – and it was Les Gets, the same resort I had randomly settled on. Spooky!

Anyway, I hope you really enjoyed *His Other Woman* and, if you did, I would be ridiculously grateful if you could write a review. I'd love to hear what you think, and it honestly makes such a difference, helping new readers to discover one of my books for the first time.

I love hearing from my readers – you can get in touch on my Facebook page, through Twitter, Instagram or my website.

Thank you,
Louise Voss

 Louise Voss Author

 @LouiseVoss1

 @Louisevoss

 louise-voss.com

ACKNOWLEDGEMENTS

Thank you to my agent, Phil Patterson of Marjacq, for your patience and humour. Really hope you get to make some money out of me soon!

Huge thanks to editor extraordinaire, Ruth Tross, whose skills I have long admired and in whose hands I feel very safe indeed, and to the whole team at Bookouture who have been so welcoming, particularly the most excellent Kim Nash and Noelle Holten.

I'm also so impressed with the brilliant and diligent copy-editing done by Jennie Ayres. Sorting out my very wobbly timeline was probably not that much fun. Thank you.

Thank you to Alanda Becker for giving me permission to use your name. I hope I've done it justice. And to Liz and Jonathan Lewis, for the cameo appearances of theirs.

Biggest thanks of all to my beloved Adrian Grieves. Not only because your tale of losing your memory on a ski slope was the inspiration for this book, but also for all the patient brainstorming you did with me with along the way, usually on long lockdown country walks.

Thank you, Ade and I love you more!